A HYMN OF THE DAWN

"House Remembered"   Tony May 1961

A Hymn of the Dawn

PADRAIC FALLON

THE LILLIPUT PRESS

DUBLIN

First published by
THE LILLIPUT PRESS LTD
62-63 Sitric Road, Arbour Hill,
Dublin 7, Ireland.

www.lilliputpress.ie

A CIP record for this title is available from
The British Library

ISBN 1 84351 036 7

FRONTISPIECE: *House Remembered*, mixed media on paper 1961,
by Tony O'Malley, © Jane O'Malley 2003
(AUTHOR'S NOTE: the artist omitted the upper middle window of the house)
MAPS ON PAGES 384-7: © Conor Fallon and Nancy Wynne-Jones 2003

Set in Sabon and designed by Stephen Raw
PRODUCTION: Jane Miller and Garrett Fallon
Printed by SRP Ltd

To those who have gone before

Preface

My brothers and I had an unusual boyhood in a corner of Ireland in the 1950s. It did not seem unusual to us at the time, as we had little to compare it with, but time and change have brought a different perspective.

As I grew older, I felt a need to capture part of the history of our youth and of the everyday life of a poet and his family before it was too late. To convey it in plain, bald facts would make it inaccurate, in much the same way that a photograph or a purely representational painting may convey a flat, misleading image, whereas an impressionist or an abstract work can transfer something more accurately, and still retain depth and mystery. The function of a poet, Graves wrote, is truth, whereas a scholar's is fact; and while fact is not truth, a poet who wilfully defies fact cannot achieve truth. I am not a poet, but I endeavoured to make that the guiding spirit of this work.

To paint that picture in words, cloaked as fiction, or near fiction, seemed to me to open many possibilities, except one, and that was that I must adhere throughout the work to the truth; not the literal truth, but to what my brother Conor calls the Organic Truth. I could dramatize, I could exaggerate, I could move events around in time – and I did all of these – but the resulting picture had to be true.

The device I used was to compress events that took place over several summers into one. Almost everything I have described happened in some form. The descriptions of the people and places are as accurate as I could make them.

The few events that I have invented are there to make the picture, as I see it, as truthful as possible.

I have thinly disguised many of the names of places and rivers and some of the names of the people who lived there, and live there still, because of the freedom it gave me to dramatize, to let the narrative run, and to show that I have taken liberties with facts.

I wrote this, my only book, very quickly and easily, the words flowing at a rate surprising to me whenever I snatched or stole the time. When it was finished, a void remained.

Acknowledgments

My three surviving brothers encouraged me strongly. Conor, the sculptor, saw immediately from the first draft what I was trying to achieve, and emails and phone calls full of suggestions arrived daily. Brian, in his quiet way, helped with the editing. Ivan provided his own memories.

My nephew David, Garry's eldest, was forced to act as head of research, as he lives in the area where the book is set, and, being a kind man, he cannot do enough for his uncles. For more than a year he sent me everything he could find that had been published on anything that might be useful or relevant, including the greatly valued *High Skies, Low Lands: An Anthology of the Wexford Slobs and Harbour* edited by David Rowe and Christopher Wilson, a mine of information that I ruthlessly plundered, particularly the chapters by Dr George Hadden/Owain T. Roberts on boats, and by David Rowe on punt-gunning and the harbour.

David went to local bookshops and museums and tramped across wet fields in winter to take photographs of spots on rivers that were dim memories to us. He persuaded Turlough Coffey to give me a Sunday morning tour of the North Slob. He sent me the volumes of Nicholas Furlong's and John Hayes' *County Wexford in the Rare Oul' Times*, almost certainly the most complete collection of captioned photographs in the history of the county; Billy Colfer's *The Promontory of Hook*, Richard Roche's and Oscar Merne's *Saltees: Islands of birds and legends*, Tadhg O'Sullivan's lovely book *Goodly Barrow* (now, thankfully, in print again), and a great number of others. He followed up with his father Garry's maps and charts, many of them stained with salt and covered in notes and compass bearings hastily scribbled at sea.

Conor found for me *Kilkenny: History and Society*, with an excellent chapter by Fidelma Maddock on the cot fishermen of the river Nore (the Owenore of this book) and on the plans of the Nore cot, a chapter that is remarkable for its accuracy and detail.

I went to see as much as I could for myself, and to meet and listen to the people who could tell their own histories. George Lett took up the old friendship between his family and mine, spending hours in his house above the Cot Safe talking of the tactics and mechanics of punt-gunning, a sport he defiantly carries on to this day in the tradition of his late father John.

John Dimond, champion of the inland waterways, gave up his weekend to take me from New Ross on his cruiser, on two successive days, up the Barrow to St Mullins, and up the Nore to Inistioge. Mary Cassin pointed me towards Michael Croke, kind man, one of the old school of countrymen, who took me to the site of the Big Net, explaining in detail how he, and his father before him, had worked it, then to his beautiful cottage above the Nore where he lives alone, and where his front door still shows the bullet holes from a night raid by the Black-and-Tans.

He showed me many photographs, and a piece of the Net itself that he had kept as a souvenir, then explained how a snap net worked, and told me tales of the river which I have worked into the story. I brought him a bottle of whiskey for his trouble, and I left with it, as he had no use for it.

Dr Austin Sullivan at the Irish Agricultural Museum at Johnstown Castle, once he discovered my eagerness to research the machinery of the time, dug into his archives and sent me everything he could find, including a parts list, printed in 1955, for Pierce's *Victor* mower. Similarly, Sue Fallon helped me with the frontispiece, for which I am grateful.

Tom Fort, Niall's good friend, read the first draft and introduced me to Caroline Dawnay, warm heart and top London literary agent who would not relent until she had found me the right publisher.

My assistant Jane Miller gave me every help, cheering me on, giving up her lunch hours to research this or that, and finding many of the illustrations used in the work.

I thank them all, as I thank my wife, who gave me unquestioning support in this, as she has in everything else.

The six sons of the poet

Garry, the eldest, full name Garrett.
Brian, second oldest, with the *i* pronounced as a *y*.
Conor, with each *o* short, as in *of*.
Niall, with the *i* pronounced as a *y*.
Ivan, with the *I* pronounced as *eye* rather than *ee*.
Padraic, the youngest. The first *a* is pronounced as in *awe*. The third letter, *d*, is silent. The emphasis is placed on the first syllable.

Chapter One

Rain swept the country, sheets of grey over darkened land. It was the beginning of June and it had rained for a month, on and off, but that morning the wireless weatherman had forecast a change. The wind would swing to the south, and a high would follow.

The people of the town huddled in shop and church doorways as the rain drummed on the narrow streets and passed slowly over the trawlers at the quays.

The poet saw the wet shroud cover harbour and foreshore. He stood, cigarette in hand, at the window of his office over an archway overlooking the quays, watching a flatbed lorry loaded with sacks of coal splash through the downpour, the townspeople on the street below scurrying to avoid a wetting, probably grumbling at the weather as they did so.

These townspeople of Eskerford were a mixture of Old Irish, Danes, and Normans. The Danes had founded the town. They left a legacy of Viking names, seamanship, and the local accent, which was broader and more guttural than the rest of Ireland. The Normans took town and country from them and left a series of keeps, castles and abbeys, model farming, and an intense respect for money. The Irish probably left a strong inclination to rebel, for which the town had paid with blood.

Cromwell called the port a nest of pirates, slaughtered many of its people, and sent others to the West Indies as slaves. At the end of the next century, the rebels of

Eskerford lifted their pikes for the Rising of the Moon and sent a rude message to the Crown:

> *Look out for hirelings, King George of*
> *England;*
> *Search every kingdom where breathes a slave.*

Eskerford people, freemen at last, still sang of these events and of many others. They loved a ballad and were not particular about its scansion. The poet, who moved to live there with his young family soon after Hitler had invaded Poland, took to the people at once and to the country around them, perhaps because of its novelty to him and perhaps because he, too, liked a ballad.

Eskerford town lay on the shallow east coast, close to the corner of the island. The county was bordered on the west by a great estuary that carried three handsome rivers to the south coast. The southern border was a rocky coast, feared for its wicked tides and submerged reefs. The Bluestairs Mountains lay to the north-west, looming over several counties.

A river entered the town's harbour from the north. It rose in the hilly glens of the adjoining county, meandered into another county and back again, cut its way through handsome farming valleys where salmon spawned in great numbers and flowed south into a wide rocky gorge, joining the harbour between the reed-beds of a muddy, shallow estuary. It ran at high summer levels in these early June days while the rain forced the cot fishermen to huddle in crude wooden shelters.

In the meadowlands a mile to the west of the town stood the old Georgian house that was home to the poet, his wife, and their six sons. Prospect House was big, cheerful, squat, with walls of three feet in thickness, handsome rather than elegant, early eighteenth century, whitewashed; with a grove of high evergreens to one side, a farmyard, byre and haybarn to the other, and a paddock at the rear. The area at the front was gravelled. Beyond the gravel, opposite the hall door, ran a thin strip of lawn, with a palm tree and a flower rockery. Between rockery and grove lay the avenue, lined with young poplars.

The house faced down a slope of farmland towards the town, a slope steep enough to conceal the town itself, but not the steeples of its twin churches. At night, the light from the Fascar lighthouse swept from its rock at sea across the front of the house, flashing its beam twice in rapid succession every seven and a half seconds. Prospect's eyes were nine big windows with twelve panes in each, its mouth a big blue door with a Georgian fanlight. In fine weather the door lay open, even at night. There was little crime in Eskerford, still less in the country around.

Inside, the house was shabby, though much less so than when the poet had brought his family to live there a few years before. They had had to wait a year or two for electricity, but when it arrived modern sanitation immediately followed, and they began to make the house comfortable and pleasant. Most of the big, high-ceilinged rooms had been refloored and decorated. The rear wall of the flagged kitchen had been demolished and replaced by a conservatory, built out into the yard to give more room and light. One of the big bedrooms had been turned into a bathroom.

It was a cold, draughty house for much of the year, but it had space, three storeys of glorious space which the poet and his family craved after spending the later War years in a house in the town. Labour was reasonably plentiful: a ploughman called Benny; a maid called Martha who came from the town several mornings a week; a well-digger called John who did other odd jobs and played the fiddle to the boys in the evening; and the sons of the poet, who read or went about their chores in the rain on this, the third day of their long summer holiday.

Prospect was a tiny working farm as well as a home, as the poet had bought the twenty acres of rather wet land that ran with the house. There were six fields, not counting the Paddock, or the Orchard with its apple and fruit trees and vegetable drills. The poet and his family made good use of them. The Front Field grew wheat or hay; the Well Field, from where the household's water was carried in buckets until electricity arrived, was used for pasture; the Pond Field for pasture or hay, although it also grew prolific amounts of rushes; the Wheat Field for hay, pasture or wheat; the Rush Field for root vegetables, potatoes, sprouts and cabbages for the house, and turnips for both house and cattle; while the Flat Field grew wheat, rotating with hay and pasture.

Throughout the year, the boys milked the cows, and from October to April fed them twice a day in the long byre, pulping turnips, bringing hay; weeding and thinning the long drills in late spring and summer by hand. They cleaned the byre, put the cows out to graze in summer, helped to rebuild the sheds in the long farmyard, wallpapered the stately but damp drawing room, and assisted John and the local handyman to build the big greenhouse and the new sun room. They made hay with Benny, following him with pitchforks as the horses pulled the iron mowing machine around the meadows, and, later, trampled the hay into layers in the barn, packing it down to make space for the next. At harvest time, when the reaper-and-binder arrived, they set to once more.

When work was done, they were free to do as they wished, within reason. They read: books were everywhere in the house, not only on shelves and big oaken bookcases, but on window-sills, tables, bedside tables, beds, and bedroom floors. They fished, they sailed, biked the countryside, played cricket and listened to the Test match commentaries, fiddled and sawed in Garry's fake family orchestra; listened to Schubert, Beethoven, Haydn and Sibelius from their beds in the darkness as Garry rewound the crackling gramophone and music filled the house, played soldiers in the whin bushes in the corner of the Well Field known as the Rocks, fought and argued among themselves, and looked to each other rather than to the outside world.

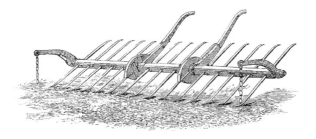

Chapter Two

It was still raining but the sky was lightening in the south-west when Padraic, the youngest, bounced into Niall's room. Niall, fourth in age, sat at his desk, staring gloomily at an old split-cane fishing rod with a splintered top.

The Straw in the Hair, its cover a curious mixture of beige and black since some boy had spilled Bitumastic on it, several Zane Greys, a Maurice Walsh or two, a copy of Corbett's *Man Eaters of Kumaon* and the last three issues of *Stream & Field* lay scattered on his bed. An old wicker trout creel and a brass reel lay at his feet. Fishing rods hung on the walls.

Padraic started when he saw the smashed rod, as well he might. He had broken it. He had stood on it when he and Ivan, the second youngest, had wrestled the night before. Ivan, after much pleading from Padraic, promised to be silent. Padraic, inspired and crafty, had placed the rod under the desk leg, broken pieces on either side. It would appear an accident, Niall's fault.

"Go away," said Niall.

Padraic ignored this and advanced further into the room. "If you're going to the Carrick tonight, can I come with you?" he asked.

"No," said Niall. "Hey, you don't know how this rod was broken by any chance, do you?" He looked suspiciously at the youngest. Padraic had a big mop of curly brown – almost black – hair and wore a pair of green shorts and a cotton shirt that had been white that morning. "Hey!" said Niall, "What the hell have you got in your pocket?" The gruffness was mixed with a little fear. He stood up quickly: "Bloody hell! It's squirming! You haven't got a mouse there, have you?"

Padraic backed away. "No, no – it's only a baby one. But listen, listen, *listen*! I don't see why I can't come fishing with you tonight. I'm old enough now. If Ivan can go, I want to go too."

Niall stared at the squirming pocket. "Well, you can't, and that's that – don't let that bloody thing out in here. Get out," he said, backing away until the desk tilted, "and take the mouse with you. You're not supposed to bring them into the house. Daddy'll break your neck if he finds out. I've got a good mind to tell him. Go on – get out."

The smaller boy knew when to retreat. He turned to leave and began to yell, rather than sing:

> *What's the news, what's the news,*
> *O my bold Shelmalier*
> *With your long-barrelled gun of the sea?*

All at Prospect were used to hearing the youngest burst into song. "Take your bloody long-barrelled gun and get out," said Niall, grinning in spite of himself.

Padraic fled to the top of the steps that led down to the landing on the main staircase and jumped. Niall heard a scream as he tripped on the bottom step, a scrabble of feet as he recovered, then another outburst as he ran down the stairs to the hall:

> *Say what wind from the south blows his*
> *messenger here*
> *With a hymn of the dawn for the free?*

Niall began to whip the ends of the rod together. He looked out at the weather and began to hum a song of his own. It was clearing.

—◆—

It had stopped raining when Padraic reached the farmyard. He ran into one of the outhouses, glancing warily about him. Satisfied that he was alone, he put his hand in his pocket and withdrew a fully-grown mouse, holding it so it could not bite. He placed it in a manger half-full of last year's hay. It gave him a puzzled look and vanished.

He looked about the outhouse and saw, in the straw beneath the manger, a pair of hen's eggs. He picked them up and gingerly lowered them into a water trough. The eggs floated. They were rotten. His face lit up. Rotten eggs were the farmyard equivalent of a hand-grenade. When broken, they released poisonous smells of sulphur and stale gas. He slipped one into each pocket.

He ran back to the house and into the drawing room where he found Brian hunched on the worn ottoman sofa, parting his hair, reading.

"Buzz off," said Brian absent mindedly

"What are you reading?"

"Nothing that would interest you."

"What is it?"

Brian turned to stare at him. He was the second eldest, read Classics at Trinity, and would soon begin in journalism. Generally, he was the quietest of the six brothers, sometimes preferring to listen rather than join in the shouted conversations at the kitchen table; a big intellect that the poet had recognized early. Brian consumed books of verse, and read everything he could find on seventeenth- and eighteenth-century European history. The poet frequently showed him a work fresh from the typewriter.

"But you can't read yet."

"I know, but would I like it?"

"No."

"What's it about?"

"Poetry."

"Like Daddy writes?"

"No. These are in Latin. Now buzz off."

Padraic had already lost interest. He left the room and found Garry, the eldest, a veterinary student in Dublin, at the kitchen table, rubbing his hands, a sure sign that he was excited. On the table were plans of a boat, beyond them the thick volumes of Dixon Kemp. To one side were notes in one hand, on the other side, notes in another. Garry was ambidextrous. He was slight and neat, with straight hair, while that of his brothers was wavy and curling. He picked up a pen.

"Go away," he said. "I'm busy."

Usually he indulged the youngest boys and caught their imagination with the creativity of his own, which he appeared to enjoy as much as they did. He had taken Ivan and Padraic a few weeks before to a tree at the corner of the Paddock and shown them the trunk where the fairies planned a feast. Miniature pieces of chopped apples, nuts, and so on were served daintily on plates of leaves. Acorn cups were filled with water. The fairies lived in the distant Bluestairs Mountains, as in:

> *Up the airy mountain,*
> *Down the rushy glen;*
> *We daren't go a-hunting*
> *For fear of little men.*

Ivan had looked sceptical. He had seen Garry making several trips across the Paddock. Padraic had been totally taken in, and shuddered when he imagined the fairies' watch-dogs. He was afraid of frogs.

"Are you going to build a boat?" he asked.

"No," said Garry. "But we might buy it." He regretted his indiscretion at once, and quickly added: "We can't afford it. It would cost too much to rebuild."

"Where is it now?"

"In the Cot Safe. It's been lying there for two years. It's in bad shape. Most of the timbers are rotten."

"How big is it? Could we all fit?"

"She's only seventeen feet." There was a pause, then Garry said: "She's a beauty."

"What would you do with her?"

"Sail her," said Garry. He began to rub his hands and whistle soundlessly as he looked at his plans.

"What's her name?"

"*Snipe*."

"Would she go up the river?"

"She would for most of the way. Now flip off."

"Could we camp in her?"

"Go away, or a small boy will be hit."

"Do you think Niall is going fishing tonight? All right, don't hit me, I'm going. Wait till I'm bigger."

He moved very quickly despite his bluster. That was just as well. Garry's hand had shot out. Padraic just made it to the door.

He found the dogs following Conor up the farmyard on his way to the Well Field. "HEY! CONOR!"

Bruno turned and ran back, jumping at Padraic to lick his face. "Get off!" Then: "HEY! CONOR!"

"What's up?" asked Conor, the third eldest. He was the handsomest of the brothers; tallish, lithe and fast; a good wing three-quarter; high in his classes at school.

Padraic paused, then he said: "I've got some news you don't know about."

"What?" Conor was growing impatient. He had to bring Hawthorn, Blossom and Slaney into the byre to be milked. Niall, who should have been helping, had still to appear.

"We're buying a boat," said Padraic importantly, waiting for the reaction.

"Who told you that?"

"I'm not telling you."

"You're a little twerp," said Conor, grinning in spite of his irritation.

"No, I'm not. Garry told me."

"Well, Daddy said the planks are rotten." Conor turned away.

Padraic ran after him, his feet splashing in a puddle. "There's something else I want to know."

"What?" asked Conor, walking on.

"Is Niall going fishing tonight?"

"Probably. Why?"

Padraic ran again to catch up. "Get off, Bruno! Get down! Conor…"

"What is it now?"

"Is he taking Ivan?"

"I haven't the faintest idea. Probably."

As Conor strode away and turned into the Hen-Run, Padraic lost his temper. "If Ivan's going, I'm going!"

"I bet you don't."

"But why can't *I* go?"

"Because Sport's a dog."

The small boy grew wild with frustration. "I'm going!"

Conor laughed, and shouted back from the Well Field gate: "But you're scared of the dark."

Padraic shrieked: "I'm NOT!"

"Yes, you are," came a faint shout from the Well Field. "And you're too small. You wouldn't even make it to the Tortoise Rock, and that's only halfway.

———◆◆———

On his way back down the farmyard Padraic heard the rattle of Benny's cart and the ring of a horse's shoes on stone. The ploughman was middle-aged, with a flat cap and a black pipe with a windshield over the bowl. He wore a collarless shirt and shaved only on Saturday evenings, as most local men did. He was a bachelor, and lived with his two sisters several miles across country.

Benny had clear views, most of them negative, on small boys, but Padraic ignored them. When the horse and cart drew up outside the kitchen, the boy raced up, placed a foot on the hub of the wheel, and leaped into the cart. It shook violently. Peggy, the horse, took fright. Padraic felt something crunch and break in each pocket of his shorts. "WHOA!" shouted Benny and looked back to see what had landed in his cart. "Begob a man!" – his favourite expression. "You gave me a fright!" He looked at the stricken face of the imp. Then the smell reached him.

Chapter Three

The Angelus tolled from Eskerford's churches when the family car came up the drive. The poet drove, his wife sitting in the front on the bench seat, Ivan in the back.

The boys' father was of medium height, thickset (stout, said the locals), with a big, squarish face, a strong pronounced chin, round spectacles, and a mop of grey-white hair. It was an imposing head, arresting and pleasing. He wore an old tweed coat with leather elbows and cuffs, and tweed trousers that did not match the coat. He was shod in brown brogues, old but highly polished – a job delegated to the son that was nearest at the time – and he wore a bow-tie. When he smiled, which he did much of the time, the beam seemed to extend from ear to ear.

He was from the West, from an old Gaelic sept that had been pushed, first by Cromwell, then by the ebb and flow of history, further west, until his family had settled in Athenry, a mediaeval walled town set in the rainy landscape and stone walls of the county Galway, where his family jobbed in cattle and sheep and owned a hotel and a butcher's shop. He was sent to a bleak boarding school in Roscrea during the Great War. There he began to write, drawing on the mythology of Greece and Rome as well as his native country. While his younger brother prepared to go to university in Dublin, he took the Civil Service exams, passed, and became a Customs & Excise officer. He also became a champion sprinter, and won medals for handball and hurling, as his father had. He married the daughter of a successful, autocratic Dublin builder and was posted to a town on the Cavan border where the two eldest boys, Garry and Brian, were born, then returned to Dublin, where Conor arrived.

Before the outbreak of the Second World War he applied for a transfer to Eskerford, a part of the country that was as different from his own as it was possible to find in a small country. He developed an instant affection for the town and its people, a strong interest in the folklore and ballads of the sea, and soon grew to know the old schooner captains and fishermen. This region was as different from his Gaelic, unchanging landscape as it was possible to find. From here, with a release of fresh energy, he wrote his poetry and his verse plays for radio. With his salary from the civil service and the income in kind from the tiny farm, plus his plays, a column in the *Irish Press*, and his contributions to the radio programme *Balladmaker's Saturday Night* that went out on the airwaves of the country's only broadcasting station, the family lived well: spartanly, in the sense that money was scarce, but well, and certainly better than most.

His wife had been a near-beauty, and still retained most of her looks. She was tall like her brothers, who were, in the main, lanky, awkward, witty Dublin men who had been appalled when their sister vanished into the countryside. She dressed well in the fashions of the time. She had inherited a mathematical brain from her father and a sense of compassion from her mother, a strong-minded, eccentric woman whose great-uncle, a medical pioneer, had been knighted by Queen Victoria and who had reared his great-niece to become a nurse, an unusual profession for a woman at the time. The boys' maternal grandmother did not believe that Hell existed, and told everyone so, in very certain terms, to the embarrassment of their grandfather, who supported the Knights of Columbanus as a counter against the Freemason builders of Dublin. He was tall, Kildare-born, moustached, Victorian, a self-made man, upright in a three-piece suit with silver watch-and-chain, who gave each grandson a half-crown when they met.

This daughter of the Victorian master builder and the eccentric nurse was an excellent cook of plain food, a wonderful provider to her family, and a strict mother when it came to table manners, but she had two significant weaknesses: she was a pushover for a hard luck story, and she was addicted to crossword puzzles, the more difficult the better.

The family had continued to expand after they had arrived at Eskerford. Three more sons arrived: Niall, Ivan, and Padraic. The last was proclaimed the baby of the family, at which stage the poet gave up his quest for a daughter.

The boys' mother had been shopping that afternoon. Her husband had been working; that is to say, he had been in his office for a few hours. The post at Eskerford was undemanding. Years before, the harbour had silted up, the bar across its mouth frequently dredged to keep the port open. Shipping switched to other harbours, but news of this had evidently not reached Civil Service headquarters. A kindly government still provided him with a uniformed assistant, a keen young Munsterman called Horgan who did most of the work. This suited very well. Like most people of West of Ireland blood the poet did not relish early mornings, and on Mondays he rarely went to his handsome office before he had lunched with his family. The greater part of his energy flowed into his writing, which he did mostly at night, frequently working into the small hours, the sound of his old Remington typewriter on his rolltop desk in the dining room carrying up the broad stairs, the brown bakelite ashtray overflowing with cigarette butts on the following morning.

Ivan, the fifth son, had been taken to town as a treat. He was very handsome, with big eyes and stocky limbs. He had been christened after the Soviet Union had won Stalingrad and the Kursk Salient. Padraic had nearly been named Joseph Stalin for the same reason, until his mother had intervened and insisted that he be named after his father.

The arrival of the three in the car was a signal that the working day had ended. Life converged on the big kitchen. John Roche, a strong, short man in his late twenties whom the boys admired for his stories of the mysteries of the river country, finished edging a ditch between the Paddock and the Hen-Run and came to say goodnight. Benny greeted the returning three and climbed back onto his cart, called, "Hubbawf!" to his horse and moved off, the wheels scrunching the gravel. Conor appeared from the byre, the milking done. Niall arrived from his room, holding a repaired rod. Brian sauntered in, Ovid in one hand. Garry was there already, rubbing his hands. Padraic, who had changed his clothes and washed himself sketchily, jumped from one foot to the other, shouting: "Did you bring me anything?"

The noise was deafening. The three dogs – Sport, Bruno and Colleen – barked madly, particularly Sport, who was Ivan's dog. The boys' mother was trying to persuade someone – anyone – to bring the food parcels and the rest of the groceries from the car. The poet, cigarette in hand, had walked out to the yard to talk to John. Niall grabbed the roll from the newsagent to find the *Eagle* and settled into the corner armchair to discover how Dan Dare was getting on with the Mekon. Phoebus, his enormous yellow cat, jumped onto his shoulders in an easy leap. Greedy,

Ivan's cat, rubbed her tail against Conor, scenting fresh milk from the byre.

Gradually, the chaos subsided. Ivan and Padraic were sent to the car. John was leaving for the day, wheeling his bike from the Dairy. The poet sat at the table with Garry, looking at the plans for the boat. The boys' mother began to prepare supper.

Outside, the sun was beginning to push through the clouds. The wind had swung into the south-west. In the Paddock, a song-thrush stamped its feet on a worm-cast, snatching its prey the instant it appeared, and began to sing. Swallows flitted across the yard, a little higher than before. The wind was bringing warmth, the beginning of summer.

Chapter Four

The noise level rose again when the family of eight sat down to supper. The poet talked to Garry on one side (about boats) and to Brian on the other (about George Moore, or the poet Paddy McDonagh, or Æ). Conor talked cricket to Ivan. Padraic, wedged between his mother and Niall, harassed his brother. He tried persuasion first. When that did not work, he switched to threats: "If you don't take me, I won't let you play with my cricket ball," and so on until his brothers rounded on him and told him to be quiet, while his mother threatened to send him to bed at once. That silenced him, but only for half an hour, until the table was cleared and Chinese chequers began while their mother washed up.

Garry had made the chequers board, decorating it with coloured-ink drawings of pagodas and dragons, carving the men from lengths of wooden dowelling and painting them. The game was taken seriously, particularly by their father, who frequently made his moves after puffing a haze of cigarette smoke over the board. The boys saw his hand move into the fog and one of the little men in conical hats reappear in the far den. He shook with laughter until the objections subsided. Niall generally played from the opposite den, planning the complex moves that he called "lulus". The move frequently disappeared before his turn arrived when one of the others unintentionally blocked it by moving a man into his intended route. "I had a bloody lulu!" Niall yelled when this happened. "You spoiled it!"

Ivan brought a jug of pure water from the pump in the Well Field for their father's nightly glass of whiskey. The poet said that the gunmetal pipes that ran from the well to the house left a taste.

Padraic was sent to bed when the game ended. The kitchen grew quieter. Their father drank his whiskey, chatting quietly to the three eldest and his wife. Ivan buried himself in Zane Grey's *Forlorn River*, and Niall went to his room to prepare his fishing gear.

Strictly speaking, he was not fishing that night, but poaching. The Carrick, a little stream that ran into the Eskerford River, lay three or four miles across country from the house. To reach it, he had to cross the neighbouring land, intersected by lonely lanes, climb a hill with a big rock shaped like a tortoise below its summit, descend the rough ground on the other side to a crossroads, pass an old building called Malone's Forge, then ascend a steep hill past a big house called Belmont, before reaching the spot that scared them all: the Haunted House and its neighbouring graveyard by the Carrick. Behind the graveyard was the place where he intended to lay night-lines baited with worms.

It was common knowledge locally that at the old iron gates of the graveyard, under a big oak, the ghost of a man, seven feet tall, stood waiting at certain times. Midnight was said to be one of these, but some had reported seeing him at sunset, others at dawn. It was not known for what or whom he waited, and no one had stepped close enough to find out. It was believed that he had been buried in the graveyard years before – some said fifty, some seventy-five, others a hundred – and it was agreed that he wore a very long topcoat and a hat.

Opposite the graveyard, a narrow lane that ran past a crumbling stone wall covered in ivy led to a largish white house that had been deserted for some time. This was the Haunted House. It had no other name as far as anyone knew, and, remarkably, since the few people who lived nearby liked to speculate on such subjects when they were safely around their hearths, there did not exist a theory of why it was haunted, or who haunted it, or even whether there was a connection between it and the graveyard a few hundred yards away. It was known to be haunted, and that was enough.

The combination of the house and the graveyard, particularly when a full moon cast a wide shadow below the ghost's sheltering oak and a yellow light on the whitewashed walls of the house, was enough to make sensible people avoid the place at night.

Niall and his brothers wished to avoid it too, but the only access to the pool on the Carrick that he planned to poach was from the little road that led down the steep Carrick Hill to the Eskerford river, half a mile away. On the other three sides of the graveyard was an area of shockingly thick briars, thorns that would rip clothes and skin until even the stubbornest boy would retreat in a bad temper. Niall had learned the hard way, but was brave enough to dash like a mad sprinter past the oak, through the open gates, and then skirt the old stone graveyard wall until he came to a gap in it where the stones had fallen over the years, and climb down a steep bank to the pool that held the biggest trout in the river.

He had seen the fish in daylight when the boys had explored the area. Conor had seen the pool first. He had walked into the graveyard in broad daylight, noticed the gap in the wall, had climbed through it and found the river below him. He called to his brothers, and it was Niall who noticed the big brown trout lying to one side of the pool, swallowing nymphs as the gentle flow in the little channel carried his food to him.

Niall had tried to tempt the fish to the spinner twice before, casting awkwardly upstream to avoid the overhanging bush in the darkness. He had lost a devon, a serious dent in his pocket money, and had decided that foul means were the only means and that, whatever happened, he would have the fish. Tonight, the time had come.

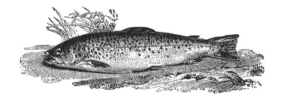

Chapter Five

The vixen had left her young in heavy cover under the whin bushes in the far corner of the Well Field. She was scouting carefully along the edges of the Rocks, stopping every few yards to scent the night air when she heard the murmurs of young voices. She scented them before she saw them against the night sky a few moments later: two figures, one taller and broader than the other, the taller carrying a fishing bag.

She crouched until she saw them climb the thorny bank, white with elder, on the Prospect boundary, waited a minute or two, then resumed her hunt on the other side of the patch of rocks and whin the boys had named the Rocks. She settled down to wait; then, to her alarm and annoyance, she heard another human approach from the direction of the house. This time the figure was running, his breath coming in little gasps as he followed the route the first two had taken before he, too, climbed through the briars on the bank into the neighbouring farm, yelping slightly as he grazed his knees. All grew quiet again.

Padraic had waited in the big bedroom he shared with Ivan until he heard his brothers leave the house by the kitchen door. He watched the flash of the lighthouse until he estimated they would have reached the Hen-Run, before stealing downstairs, shoes in hand, then tiptoeing through the front hall and out the open front door. He made little noise as he edged his way into the Grove. Once under the full darkness of the big *macracarpas*, he stopped to put his shoes on, took his short-cut across the Paddock, avoiding the Hen-Run, climbed the fence at the corner and jumped down into the Well Field. He set out to follow the poachers.

He knew the route, which was fortunate as the only light that night came from the stars. Earlier, when he had begun to plan his expedition, he had decided to allow them to get well ahead of him. He would follow at leisure which, given his short legs, showed that even he could be wise on occasion.

Ahead, the boys made good progress. They started when they heard a snort a few feet away, but Niall whispered: "Cow". They moved on, the beast making off quickly when it sensed them. Early summer night smells and sounds drifted towards them on the light breeze: woodbine, wet grass, bracken and the sweet scent of flowering whin. Soon Niall stopped suddenly and sniffed the air: "Do you smell that?" he asked Ivan quietly. "No – what is it?" asked Ivan uneasily, squinting back along the path they had come. "Fox," said Niall. "We must have walked right past it."

When they reached the lane at Boycotts, they moved very quietly past Whitty's cottage, as the Whittys kept a dog, and the dog barked at every noise. They had another reason to be stealthy: the Whittys were said to have a son who was not quite right.

Once past the cottage they followed the lane for another three hundred yards before Niall, pausing for a moment to check his directions, hissed: "Here!" and climbed over a narrow gap in the hedge.

Padraic also passed the cottage without causing an alarm, but missed the gap in the hedge. He walked up the lane until he came to an unfamiliar gate, realized his mistake and retraced his steps, his shoes pattering loudly, until he found the gap and climbed over it. Once in the field, he froze when he heard the dog bark.

In front, the two boys also froze. "Why is that dog barking?" hissed Niall in Ivan's ear. "We're well beyond Whitty's." They waited, but heard nothing, as Padraic was standing three fields back in petrified silence. Satisfied it was not a threat, they moved on, seeing the slight loom of the next hedge and judging their directions by it. After a further ten minutes, the ground began to rise and they knew they were not far from the point where the fields ended, and the scrubby heath, ferns and whin of the hill with the Tortoise Rock began.

Padraic was also moving on, the scare over Whitty's mongrel forgotten as he realized he must hurry. He began to run, and was still running when he reached the end of the meadows and saw, against the skyline, the dark shapes of his brothers climbing the bank before the beginning of the open ground. He stopped, shocked by his own impetuosity, and waited to discover if they had heard him.

They had not, because they had been making enough noise of their own. Their path was strewn with bracken and broken whin branches, the ground rough with rabbit burrows and other natural hazards, and they knew they were well beyond dog and man. When they saw the outline of the rock above them, they rested for a moment, then moved on, swinging to the left, down the hill towards the crossroads and Malone's Forge. Behind them, a few minutes later, a little figure did the same.

The two reached the stone wall that bordered the road, climbed over it, walked quietly past Malone's Forge, where lights were showing; up the hill, past Belmont House with its rusting gates lying agape, and towards the spot they dreaded: the top of Carrick Hill. They were very tense. When they were within a hundred yards of the oak, they began to run, Niall clumsily, as he carried the fishing gear, and the bag swung dangerously as he ran. Ivan, who had won two cups for running, quickly outstripped him. "Hang on!" Niall called in a rasping whisper as the oak and the graveyard gates approached in the darkness: "Not so fast!" Ivan slowed a little, and they dashed in tandem past the oak, looking wildly about them as they ran. When they reached the gates they ran through like greyhounds, the bag bumping Niall painfully, past the gravestones on their left, staying close to the old graveyard wall on the right. When they reached the corner, they turned left sharply, Ivan almost bumping into the wall, and ran down the wall until they reached the gap, slowing as the danger receded behind them. Once through the gap, they stopped, their breath coming in great panting gasps. Ivan waited while Niall lifted the bag from his shoulder, laid it between them, and sat gratefully on a rock. They had made it.

Padraic had not. He had crossed the hill around the Tortoise Rock safely, but his feet were beginning to hurt. In spite of that he carried on, his ambition to surprise his brothers at the graveyard beginning to dim. What would happen, he wondered, if his parents found his bed empty? He thought he knew the answer to that, and hurriedly thought of different questions: would he have the nerve to run into the graveyard? What would he do if he saw the ghost? He knew that he was close to the point of no return. He hesitated, decided to turn back, changed his mind and turned again, changed his mind again several times, and finally set off past Belmont, up the hill to the Carrick.

Chapter Six

Niall and Ivan had rested for long enough. Niall opened his bag, removing a jar of worms, two stakes he had whittled, two fishing lines (one for him, one for Ivan), hooks from a brown paper bag; an electric torch; and a small wooden mallet he had borrowed from John's toolbox. He switched on the torch, hissing at Ivan to be silent. There was no need. Ivan was looking back into the blackness of the graveyard, worried that a tall shape, ringed in a white light, would appear from behind a gravestone. Niall slid down the steep bank towards the head of the little pool, Ivan close behind him, then swept the area briefly with his torch. He placed a small stone on each point where he would insert his pegs, switched off the torch, reached for the mallet, took one of the pegs, found the first stone, pushed it to one side and, as quietly as he could, thumped the peg into the ground. He did the same with the other, leaving a space of three feet or so between them. Ivan shone the torch while Niall opened the jar of worms and began to bait the hooks, running two big worms up each until shank and eye were covered. He tied the other ends of the lines to each peg in turn, and, unrolling the line from its loop, crouched at the water's edge. By his estimate, the trout, if it was still there, should be about fifteen feet downstream.

Niall lowered one of the baited hooks into the water, waited until the current began to carry it downstream into the pool, and paid out a length he estimated at fifteen feet. He waited for a pull, but the trout would probably not begin to feed before first light. He did the same with the other hook, adding another foot of line.

"We're done," he grunted to Ivan.

"Good," said Ivan, beginning to recover his nerve.

Niall rose, switched the torch on for a second, switched it off again, tapped Ivan on the shoulder, and murmured: "Let's get out of here." At that moment, they heard the scream.

◆ ◆

It sounded as they imagined a banshee would – a high-pitched shriek, again and again – but it also sounded disturbingly familiar. It seemed to be moving, as they could hear crashing noises and running feet.

Ivan yelled: "Niall! It's coming towards us."

They were beginning to run when Padraic came through the gap, screaming, and, twisting his ankle, fell in the river.

"Bloody hell!" yelled Niall when he heard another scream followed by a splash. "What the hell is that?" and switched on the torch. They ran towards the pool, and in the torchlight saw a white face below a mop of curly hair break the surface, scream, and sink again in a froth of bubbles. "It's Padraic!" Niall yelled. He dropped his bag and launched himself into the pool which was too deep for Padraic but not for Niall. He waded and kicked himself across the pool to his brother, grabbed him by his collar and, shouting to Ivan: "Come on!" began to drag him to the riverbank. Ivan waded in, grabbed a fistful of collar, and pulled hard. Soon, Padraic lay on the bank, crying, but safe.

When Padraic had reached the top of Carrick Hill, he had summoned up the courage to run past the oak. He had begun his dash when he saw the ghost.

Afterwards, he could recall only a dark shape moving towards him in the starlight from beneath the oak. It seemed to breathe heavily. He yelled and ran through the gates towards his brothers. When he reached the gap in the graveyard wall, he ran through it, tripped over the root of an old yew tree, and fell in the pool.

———◆◆———

Niall felt Padraic's ankle carefully. "It's just twisted," he grunted.

"We'll have to carry him home," said Ivan. Padraic was quiet, from pain, exhaustion, or both. All three were very wet and very cold.

Niall handed the bag to Ivan with a brief: "Carry that. I'll take him. We can find out what happened later." He lifted Padraic easily over his shoulder in a fireman's lift and they set off along the graveyard wall. When they reached the gate, they heard a noise from beneath the tree.

Niall could be stubborn, and perhaps he did not relish the prospect of running while carrying his brother. He switched on the torch, Ivan shivering behind him, and shone it at the base of the oak.

Two piebald ponies gazed at them curiously, rope halters tied to a branch of the tree. Itinerants had left them to graze the long acre in a place few would disturb.

———◆◆———

The journey home was weary but uneventful. They stopped to rest under the Tortoise Rock, then resumed, with Ivan attempting to carry Padraic, but after a few minutes Niall saw Ivan was struggling. "Give him to me," he said. Padraic went back on Niall's shoulder and they set off once more. They rested again before reaching Whitty's cottage, passed it without alarm, and, fifteeen minutes later, climbed wearily into the Well Field. They walked past the Hen-Run into the farmyard. The dogs began to bark.

Niall rose at dawn and walked up to the landing at the front of the house. On the right was his parents' bedroom, on the left that shared by Ivan and Padraic. He looked in. Padraic was asleep. Niall went downstairs, wheeled his old-fashioned bicycle from the Dairy and cycled to the Carrick in the early morning sun. The ponies had gone. When he reached his night lines he tested the first: nothing. The second held the big trout. He drew it in and killed the fish quickly. Then he wrapped it in grass, placed it in the bag on his bicycle carrier, and cycled home for breakfast.

Chapter Seven

Snipe was due to arrive. The poet had bought her for a few
pounds when Garry had convinced his father that he
could rebuild the little boat. They had looked at expensive
new planks at the timber company in Eskerford, but it was in
a boatyard on the Uisceford Estuary, more than twenty miles
away, that the poet had found the second-hand planks. After
a little resistance, the yard threw in pitch and putty and
caulking oakum. The poet had a genius for deals.

The fishermen at the Cot Safe at Eskerford would
transport *Snipe* to Prospect in return for a bottle of whiskey,
of which the poet had plenty. His official duties included the
inspection of Eskerford's bonded liquor warehouses. He
tested the contents of the casks with a hydrometer and kept
what he freely interpreted as the ullage, unaware that, when
his back was turned, his wife, on health grounds, drew off a
fifth and diluted the rest with water, creating a store of her
own that she hid behind a press in the kitchen until she
brought it to her father at Christmas.

The four youngest found it difficult to wait for *Snipe* to
appear. They went to the spinney below the drive, Padraic
still hobbling a little, and climbed the ash they had named the
Scout Tree, close to the rambling house of their nearest
neighbours, the kindly Finucanes.

The only vehicle they saw for some time was Willie Clane's
horse and trap. Willie was drunk as usual, lying in the trap
with his back to his horse, the faithful animal drawing him

home. Then came Madge of the wild hair, who had been their maid at Bayview, the house the family had rented close to Prospect in the early War years. She had doted on Niall, who greeted her as she cycled past. Then Nicky Fortune came down the hill on his bike and the boys called to him. Nicky believed he could sing like Mario Lanza, and insisted on sharing his gift with the countryside, particularly at night under a full moon.

The four boys had waited for almost an hour and were cutting their initials into the bark when they saw the old van appear with its trailer. They shinned down the ash and ran through the field to the house.

"It's here, Garry!" shouted Conor.

"*Snipe's* coming up the road!" roared Niall in his baggy shorts.

"Your boat is here," yelled Ivan.

"It's behind a van," shouted Padraic, who was thirty yards behind the nearest brother.

Garry ran around to the front of the house and stood on the gravel, outwardly calm as the van turned in through the gates and came slowly up the drive. It was followed by their father's car.

The van followed Garry around the side of the house, and up the farmyard where *Snipe* would be housed. The trailer was unhooked and pushed into the shed where *Snipe*, amid grunts and instructions, was lifted onto the concrete floor, where she sat at an angle, since *Snipe*, American-designed and Eskerford-built, was hard-chined, and had a centreboard instead of a keel. The fishermen were taken to the kitchen for a cup of tea.

Garry rubbed his hands and whistled soundlessly as he looked at the boat; last of the class that had been popular in Eskerford before the War. The poet stood beside his eldest. The younger boys looked inside the hull, at the rotten planks, at the disintegrating rudder that hung drunkenly from its pintle, then left. Garry took a measuring tape in a leather case from his pocket.

Chapter Eight

Garry's rifle was a Winchester .22 with a pump action and a magazine that held fourteen bullets, Brian's a Remington single-shot of the same calibre, but with a longer barrel. Garry could kill three rabbits to Brian's one at a reasonable range. Brian could kill rabbits that Garry could scarcely see. Brian could not ride a bike, and the donkey drops he bowled at cricket were a family joke, but he was immensely strong and energetic, did prodigious amounts of work on the small farm, rowed and boxed at university, and would probably have won his boxing pink had not the poet, fearing brain damage, persuaded him to concentrate on rowing.

As the cows were milked each morning, the two walked up the farmyard, down the lane past the Orchard, through the gate into the Pond Field, and up the path towards Prospect's boundary. The early morning mist was lifting as they climbed a stile into the next field, hid in the hedge thirty yards apart and waited. The main burrows were forty yards away, towards the other side of the field, on the edge of an area of whin and rock. This was their first stopping point, as the grass the lazier rabbits ate was short in the adjoining area, giving them a clear shot.

Rabbits began to drift out of their burrows to feed on this sunny June morning, but the two waited. When the numbers grew to thirty or forty, Garry selected a big buck and shot it in the head. Brian immediately killed another on the far edge of the feeding ground. The remaining rabbits ran for their burrows, but Garry swiftly shot a further two. Brian killed another at long range. They had killed five. Their mother wanted more.

They collected their kill and pondered the next step. Garry was anxious to return to his boat, but reluctant to burden Brian who sensed this and said: "You go back. I'll go on to Boycotts." Garry accepted this and took Brian's rabbits from him. Brian set off towards the townland of Boycotts. He checked his rifle was unloaded and climbed the first hedge, then walked along the headland of the next field. He reached a gate at the corner, climbed it to avoid the noise from rusting hinges, and moved into the field.

This was unusually long, and the feeding ground was at the far end. To stalk the rabbits, Brian would have to either push through the meadow itself, or shoot the rabbits at long distance from the headland. He chose the headland, pushed a bullet into the breech of his rifle and moved quietly until he came to a bend. From there, he could see the feeding ground nearly a hundred yards away. It swarmed with rabbits. To achieve a clearer shot, he retreated to a stunted old blackthorn tree and climbed to the top of the bank, clutching the branches for leverage. He settled himself, using a branch as a rest for his rifle, and looked down the long barrel.

His keen eyes spotted rabbits in all corners of the feeding ground. He decided that there must be many more around the corner, concealed by the waving meadow grass. He looked carefully for a suitable target and settled for one in the furthest corner. As the shot rang out the rabbit jumped vertically, dropped back to earth, and lay still. Brian quickly pushed another bullet into the breech and shot the rabbit next to the first. The rabbits began to run. Brian shot another that was slow to move, then another that ran towards him.

The remaining rabbits disappeared.

He collected his kill, houghed them with his sheath knife and tied them with binder twine, hung them from his belt and walked to the far corner where there was a gate into the lane. He planned to cross the lane, then a further two fields beyond that, and reconnoitre. If the rabbits were not feeding in that area, he would swing left across the open fields in a big circle and re-enter Prospect land from the west, crossing the path that his brothers had taken on their way to the Tortoise Rock a few nights before. There should be rabbits still feeding along his route. He walked down Boycotts lane for a hundred yards, slipped though a gap in the bank, and entered the next field. He stopped. At the far edge of the field a man was running hard in the opposite direction. Brian almost dropped the rifle. The man was naked.

◆━◆

He watched the man vault the gate into the next field and disappear. He listened. A minute or so later he heard the sound of bare feet running up the lane. Then he heard a dog bark, and the sound of a door slamming at Whitty's cottage.

◆━◆

Brian walked back to the lane, shaken. He decided to avoid the cottage by walking back towards Prospect, then to swing west again to pick up his planned route. He set out once more, the rabbits swinging from his belt as he strode. When he was a safe distance from the cottage, he relaxed. It was a beautiful morning. Blackbirds and thrushes sang in the hedges, and a lark called in the blue air above him. Wild flowers had flourished after the rain, and buttercups formed a yellow mist along the headlands. In the distance, the Bluestairs were a haze of blue and purple.

Four fields further on, he slowed and walked cautiously to

the next hedge. It was as well that he did, since an angry-looking shorthorn bull glared at him from the other side. Brian stepped back. The bull pawed the ground, then ran straight at him, crashing its horns on the fence between them. The beast shook his head angrily, turned away and ran down the side of the field, clearly seeking a gap. Brian clutched his rifle and ran, halting only when he had run through the gate into the next field and closed it. Then he began to breathe freely.

He decided to shorten his route. He would still circle around to the Well Field, but the circle would not be as large as he had planned. A cuckoo called as he went on, passing field after field, seeing nothing but cattle and the occasional donkey until he reached the gap in the hedge to the Well Field. From habit, he surveyed the field before entering it, looking last of all at the Rocks. A dozen rabbits grazed in the grass next to the yellow whin. He shot four of them before he turned for home.

When he reached the house he laid the rabbits out on the table in the Dairy and deftly skinned and cleaned them, using one of Garry's scalpels to make a long incision from neck to groin, then neatly peeling the skin from the bodies in one action. He waited until his father arrived for lunch and told him about the madman in the field. His father listened attentively, frowning, questioning his son about the man's appearance – short, light-coloured hair, ungainly, almost like an ape – then shook his head and went in to eat.

Chapter Nine

Both rifles, safely emptied of bullets, were paraded next morning when the Clonard Flying Column met for its first drilling session after breakfast. Garry, the captain, wore a smart military cap with a leather band, for which he had fashioned a brass badge, and a khaki shirt with epaulettes. He carried a short swagger-stick, neatly varnished, which he used to demonstrate the objective on the map he had pinned to the hen-house wall.

The hen-house, made from the finest timbers, was a present to their mother from the master carpenters at their grandfather's yard and was ruled to be too good for the Prospect hens by Garry, who decided to make it the flying column's headquarters. Inside were a deal table and chairs and an easel to which maps were pinned. The units designed to house the hens had been redesignated as lockers to hold each soldier's kit. It was comfortable, said Brian, as long as you did not expect to stand up straight.

Garry lived a great deal of his life through his brothers, planning diversions of all kinds that he thought they would enjoy. He had been planning the establishment of the flying column for several months, and had accumulated war surplus items such as canvas haversacks; an air raid warden's helmet; gas masks that gave off a disgusting rubbery smell if the wearer breathed through his nose; a commando dagger; metal water-bottles with canvas holdalls that were attached to webbing straps and belts; surplus army pay-books in which he had written the name of each officer and NCO; and a brass hand-compass and direction finder. These were displayed around the hen-house as his men arrived.

Garry told them the mission was of the highest importance, then began to allocate a rank to each.

Trouble began at once. Brian was happy enough with his position of lieutenant. Conor was happy to be a sergeant provided there was someone else to take his orders. Niall, however, was indignant at being a mere corporal.

"Why can't I be an officer," he demanded, "and have a real rifle?" He glanced with contempt at the wooden replica that Garry had given him.

"You *are* an officer," said Garry. "You're a non-commissioned officer. So is Conor. An army can only have a small number of real officers."

"Then why is Brian a real officer? And why is Conor higher than me?"

He still grumbled as the parade began. Then the next problem arrived.

Ivan and Padraic ran into the Hen-Run, furious at their exclusion. They stopped when they saw the file marching towards the farmyard, Garry drilling his men to chant in unison:

> *I had a good job and I LEFT.*
> *YOU'RE RIGHT!*
> *LEFT, RIGHT. LEFT, RIGHT.*
> *Sound off, one, two.*
> *Sound off, three, four.*
> *Let's go back and count some more.*
> *HUP! TWO, THREE, FOUR!*

Ivan, very muddy, planted himself in front of Garry. The file halted. "Why are we not in the army, too?" Ivan demanded.

"It's not fair," Padraic added.

"You're not old enough," said Garry firmly. "You have to be able to march long distances, climb over ditches and cross streams, without making a noise. You'll only complain all the way." He added, thinking quickly: "And this is a serious march. Even Niall will find it hard to keep up." He turned to his men: "Parade, 'SHUN! About face! Quick march!" He marched to the head of the column, swagger-stick held neatly under his right arm, and, left arm swinging, led the flying column back to its headquarters fifty yards away.

Ivan and Padraic ran alongside Garry, skirmishing and harassing, annoying the column. A constant medley of complaints, threats and pleadings came from the two youngest. It was not their fault that they were small. They could walk the pants off any of them. Hard as nails they were. It was not fair, it was just not fair and, please, Garry, let us in, we want to be soldiers too.

The captain of the flying column desperately sought an escape route. A test! That was it.

"To become a soldier, you have to pass a test," he said, standing in front of the HQ, improvising as he spoke. "You have to understand weapons. You have to be able to take the Winchester apart and assemble it again."

"Oh!" said Ivan, springing forward and taking the rifle from Garry. He sat on the steps of the HQ, undid cocking lever and magazine in a few moments, waved the parts at Garry, then quickly slid them back into place again. Garry watched, eyes widening. Padraic grabbed the rifle from Ivan, nimble fingers pulling the rifle apart, then put it together again, faster even than Ivan, then looked up:

"Shall I do the Remington too?" he asked.

Garry's eyes widened further. "When did you two learn to do that?"

Ivan looked up at him innocently. "Well, you do spend a lot of time away at Vet College, you know," he said finally.

Garry tried to be angry, failed, then realized that Niall would be happier as a corporal if there were two private soldiers in the column. Perhaps it was for the best. Garry, a soft heart, could refuse his brothers little.

"OK," he said, "you're a private in the army. Which would you rather be: a private first class, or a private second class?"

Ivan suspected a trick. He considered the offer. First was better than second, but at school second class was above first class. "Second class," he said.

"Right," said Garry. "You're a private second class. Actually, second class is below first class, but if you drill and march well, you might be promoted." He took Ivan into the hen-house, sat him at the table, took an army pay-book and wrote Ivan's name in it, adding, "Private, Second Class" below; handed it to Ivan. He did the same for Padraic, who was hopping anxiously from one foot to another beside the table.

The column, its numbers increased to five, stood at ease in front of the hen-house as their captain briefed them on their mission. "I have orders here," said Garry, waving a piece of paper which he had typed on his father's machine earlier, "from the commander of the region to occupy the highest point in the area. That's the top of the Mountain." He gestured with his swagger-stick at the map pinned to the hen-house wall: "We have orders that no one must see us, or report us. That means a forced march across country. No roads. I will navigate with this compass and map. Troops! Dismiss! We meet again at eleven hundred hours."

That was only ten minutes away. Niall dashed back to the house to collect the rations for the day, placed the sandwiches in his canvas haversack, filled five bottles of water, including Garry's army canteen, and ran back.

They were ready. Garry called them to attention, then barked: "Clonard Flying Column – quick march! Left, right, left, right, left!"

They marched in descending order of age past the Orchard, Padraic taking three steps for each two of his brothers', earning constant reprimands for stepping out of line and chattering to Ivan and Niall. Garry looked at his compass every few minutes, his map flapping in the breeze.

He had already decided that it would be unsoldierly to march the column through gates, particularly if that involved a detour from the compass bearing. They would march in straight lines, he decided, no gates, so the column marched straight over ditches and banks, regardless of briars and blackthorn bushes. Tempers were scratchy when they reached the Prospect boundary. Garry ordered them to advance at a crouch. "We're in enemy territory," he told them. "Oh yeah?" whispered Niall to Conor, looking at the fields they knew so well.

They came to the road that led downhill to the Eskerford river. From here they would cross through the fields that led to the Birdless Woods.

◆—◆

Garry and Brian had first entered the woods on a fine day in spring in the early years of the War, when the family lived at Bayview, and had discovered the small stream behind the handball alley. In one of the pools they saw a small trout, which darted downstream when it caught their shadows. The wood became denser as they went on, the sunlight barely reaching the ferny bottom. They knew that the wood belonged to Colonel George, whose father had founded the Royal Canadian Mounted Police, the Mounties. The colonel, popular man, owned the estate whose farm bell, from its perch over the handsome walled farmyard, tolled the labourers to work in the fields in the morning and from the fields at noon to eat. The bell could be heard clearly at Prospect, nearly a mile away. They would not be in trouble if found trespassing here.

The two had walked through the woods in a wide circle and re-emerged on the road to the Mountain when Brian had said: "Did you notice anything peculiar about those woods?"

Garry had thought for a moment. "I felt they were a bit sinister," he said after a pause.

"Did you hear a single bird while we were in there?" Brian asked, looking across at the waving tree tops.

"No, I don't think I did," said Garry.

"Not a magpie, or a jay," said Brian. "Not even a hawk to frighten them. There's not a bird in those woods." From then on, they were known as the Birdless Woods.

The column commander checked the road was empty, then signalled his men across, one at a time. Enjoying themselves thoroughly by then, they threw themselves into the spirit of the outing and crossed the road like commandos. Then they were in the wood; a strangely quiet wood of beech, elm and oak, with a scattering of hazelnut trees along its perimeter. A small, clear stream ran through the dip in the middle. Niall had attempted to tickle trout here, inspired by the poet's stories about his own father, but without success.

They stopped to refill their water-bottles while Garry considered his map and compass bearings, then set off again, on a line that would allow them to avoid the handball alley in case anyone played there, although it was rarely used, and then only in the evenings or on Sunday afternoons. He intended to cross two estates, each belonging to retired colonels, and he was determined to avoid the estate offices. They walked, still crouched, at a safe distance from both big houses, through grounds densely covered in rhododendrons, escallonia, azaleas, flags and rows of laurel bushes. They avoided the walks that ran before them; the gardens a blaze of colour; butterflies fluttering past; the hum of bees in their ears as they waited, crouched, before the commander waved them on.

The ground grew less cultivated as it rose and they passed through the fields of the second estate. Then they emerged cautiously onto scrubby ground thicketed with ferns and mountain ash, with scattered outcrops of stone. They were on the Mountain. The Pinnacle, Garry's strategic objective, was in sight.

◆—◆

To call it a mountain was an exaggeration, but it was the highest point for some distance, and commanded good views over Eskerford itself. Garry and Brian had pictured the Norman invaders arriving here, fresh from their landings on the other side of the county, lifting their helmets with their nasal visors to wipe the sweat from their foreheads, squat, stocky horses cropping the grass as the riders looked down on the Viking town, mentally preparing for the next battle. As it turned out, the Normans need not have worried, as the Danes ceded the town without a struggle.

The flying column advanced, still crouched, then Garry waved at them to crawl, to use the ferns as cover. Tired, backs aching, and a little hot from the midday sun, they obeyed, with a subdued level of grumbling from the lower ranks.

They were within thirty yards of the Pinnacle, which was little more than a small, stony hillock with a monument at its peak, when Garry stopped, turned to his men, and asked in a low voice: "Clonard Flying Column! Are you ready to charge, to fight to the last man?"

"You betcha!" said Niall, clutching his wooden rifle.

"To the last man!" said Ivan.

"OK," said Garry. "I will lead the attack from the left, taking Conor and Ivan with me. Brian will take the other flank, with Niall and Padraic. Remember to throw hand-grenades."

"Where are they?" asked Brian. Garry opened his haversack and removed several oval-shaped wooden balls, cross-hatched with a chisel, and handed them to him to distribute.

They broke cover and ran for the Pinnacle, lobbing the grenades at the base of the hill, yelling like Indians until they gained the top, out of breath, pointing their rifles at imaginary enemies, giving no quarter.

When the battle was won, they sat on the ground, resting, emptying their water-bottles and eating their rations. The commander used his commando dagger to scoop a little hole in the ground. He planted a brass military button in the hole.

"What's that for?" asked Conor.

"To prove we've taken the objective," said the commander.

They were tired as they set out on the return journey, so Garry decided to risk taking the road for part of the way. They hid when they saw a Franciscan friar, tonsured head shining in the sun, walking up the hill; brown cassock, crucifix dangling from a rope belt, and open sandals leaving little doubt of his calling. They waited until he was past, hearing him mutter to himself as he walked, whether a prayer or a private conversation they could not discern. Otherwise the road was empty.

A stone water trough with an iron pump above it lay up the hill from the ball alley. They stopped to refill their water-bottles and saw a big goldfish gazing at them from its depths, reflecting red and gold in the sun, an exotic sight.

The boys looked at each other. "How did that get there?" Garry asked.

Chapter Ten

Benny's face under a stained cap was weathered: skin like leather, crows' feet around the eyes, days of stubble, strong, yellowing teeth. He had gone barefoot until his teens. He could not read, but had a vocabulary of his own. The boys seized on his words and phrases, remembered them, and repeated them. When he was tired he said: "I'm teetotally charoosed." When he felt sorry for himself he said: "I wisht I'd a-died when I was a yearlint." When his cart bounced on a rut it was: "Oh me narse." Best of all, he called a pretty woman "a fine hoult".

His two spinster sisters fed and laundered him. On Saturday night he shaved, oiled his hair, combed it flat, and put on a clean shirt and collar, a tie, his best brown serge suit, and a pair of heavily polished brown ankle boots known locally as Yalla Boots. Then he cycled into Eskerford to the cinema. He met other bachelors like Nicky Fortune on the road, all with a common purpose. When they entered the town, he was part of a procession of men in serge suits on bicycles. The single women, headscarves fluttering, skirts held demurely by one hand placed over their knees if there was a breeze, formed a separate, more sedate procession. In the South Main Street he bought a bag of sweets and went to the Cinema Palace, bicycle-pump upright in his coat pocket, clips still holding his trouser bottoms in place. He and the other countrymen sat quietly at the back, smiling as the rowdies in the front rows hooted the villain and shouted "COME ON THE CHAP!" to the hero.

When the picture ended he stood with the others on the street for an hour or so, talking in quiet, well-mannered country voices, watching the passers-by, remarking now and then: "That's a fine hoult." Then they would mount their bikes and ride home in the darkness.

Sometimes it was rumoured that Benny was courting. He was said to like Mary Anne Broaders, but to be frightened of her brother. He had been seen with a stout, youngish woman called Thrush Goggin, who lived on the road to the Mountain, but had misunderstood her name and called her Push, so Push Goggin she was from there on ("A fine hoult", said Brian); and he had been spotted with the sister of Chris Pope, whose brother was a fierce little man with very tall boots, who had helped at haymaking at Prospect and whom the boys had named Chris-in-Boots. Chris also was said to frighten the ploughman.

On Sunday mornings, the bachelors and spinsters cycled into town to hear Mass, part of a much larger convoy as the immediate countryside flocked to Eskerford. Many travelled by pony-and-trap, the beautiful conveyances of which Eskerford people were so proud. There were tub traps with high, iron wheels shod in solid rubber; with bodies of shining, varnished wood, a padded railing on top at the sides, a door at the rear, carrying four passengers in comfort, two on each side facing, plus the driver. In the rarer back-to-back traps the passengers faced forwards and rearwards. Whatever the trap, the harness was carefully polished and the brass shone. The less proud or less fortunate travelled in carts pulled by horse or jennet or donkey, passengers sitting loosely on the side-lace seats that were peculiar to the county. The more fortunate drove motor cars. Some walked, hoping – usually correctly – that a neighbour would offer a lift. All dressed in their best, whatever their circumstances. The road past the Grove of Prospect on Sunday mornings rang with the sounds of horseshoes on the metalled surface, jingling brass, creaking harness, calls and greetings. The single women generally sat with families at the front of the church. The bachelors sat or stood at the back. At the more popular Masses – the shortest ones where the priest would say Mass in a jumble of Latin, taking a quarter of an hour or less – the bachelors crowded the doorway and the yard outside. They preferred the earlier Masses. The last at noon was High and very long, with much incense and singing, including the hymn that was sung most often in Eskerford's churches:

Faith of our fathers living still,
In spite of dungeon, fire, and sword.

Eskerford was very fond of its religious processions which were held on Sundays and holy days like Corpus Christi and the Feast of the Ascension, the mayor always near the front in his chain of office. Town dignitaries, clergy, various confraternities and sodalities, boy scouts, and children dressed in first communion suits and white dresses marched through the streets, the band playing:

In comes the captain's daughter,
The captain of the Yeos;
Saying: "Brave United Irishmen,
We'll ne'er again be foes…

The ploughman braved the confessional each Easter, sweating a little, waiting outside the box with his friend Blackbird Murphy, who had earned his nickname by whistling all day before spending his evenings in the pub, where he whistled at the bar until it closed. The previous Easter they had singled out the box of a genial, forgiving friar, and waited. Their courage almost failed them as the door of the confessional opened to bring a patch of light in the gloom and they saw that they had drawn the wrong friar, that they had a martinet instead. Blackbird went in first, mumble, mumble, mumble; emerged looking relieved, penance three Our Fathers, three Hail Marys.

Benny asked quickly, hand on the door: "What did he say about the drink?"

"He didn't mention it," whispered Blackbird, "so I didn't either."

Benny usually halted at Prospect on the journey home from Mass for a cup of tea, as did Mrs Fielding, who did odd clothing and curtain repairs, and two or three others. The conversation ranged from the weather, to sport, to the crops, to the few wild men in the local IRA, which the ploughman called the Rah-Rah-Rah, and back to the weather again. The weather, of course, was of great importance to Benny, and he was convinced that nuclear tests were deranging it. "It's the bum," he proclaimed, blowing noisily on the tea in his saucer. "The atomic bum. The weather's never been the same since the Yanks and the bum." "Yes," said the youngest boys, delighted with the excuse, "the bum, the bum, yes, it's the bum."

On one of these Sunday mornings in early summer, when the countryside around began to spring colour and fresh growth after the rain, Padraic, whose favourite position in the kitchen was to lie in front of the Aga, at full stretch and in everyone's way, discovered that Benny wore long-johns.

He had been gazing at the turn-ups on Benny's trousers. For once, Benny had removed his bicycle clips, giving a good view of his magnificent white, long underwear to the incredulous boy. Padraic shouted: "Look what Benny's got on his legs!", sprang to his feet and pulled up the ploughman's trouser leg.

Benny was deeply embarrassed. "Begob! Get off! Get off, cain't ye!" he shouted in the uproar. Padraic was smacked by his mother. He hung on until he was smacked again. He backed off. Ivan was smacked for joining in. Order returned. Benny hung there, deeply embarrassed, a very modest man who would not have allowed even his sisters to see him in his underwear. The boys' mother, ashamed, apologized, but Benny left abruptly, mounting his bike and pedalling away quickly.

◆━◆

Strictly speaking, he was not an employee. He was contracted by the week from Nellie Fortune who owned the horses, ploughs and carts. He worked around two-thirds of his time at Prospect, doing the autumn ploughing in the equinoctial gales, walking behind the heavy iron plough as it made long furrows in the dry ground before leaving the field for the winter frosts to break up, careful not to leave a trace of grass showing if he was ploughing pasture, as this betrayed a bad ploughman.

His bitter enemies were the worms local people called *thraens*, the pests that wormed their way up into the drills to eat everything that grew on them before the crows arrived in turn to eat them and to become worse pests. His cure was *thraen wather*, holy water blessed each Easter by the Franciscan friars and dispensed to the faithful, to be scattered across the fields. His belief in this was so strong that the poet secretly came to believe in it too, became convinced that the cure predated Christianity, and surreptitiously asked his wife each Easter to bring back a bottle of it.

Benny had once told the family of when, as a barefoot ploughboy, he had been given his first wage, a penny coin, and how he had walked into Eskerford, excited, to spend it. He had looked in every shop window in north and south main streets and had come to a halt at a greengrocer's, eyes fixed on a very red apple. He had bought it, carrying it outside the town on the road home, resisting the temptation to sink his teeth into it until he was alone. Then he had sat on a stile and taken the first bite, to find he had bought a tomato, the first he had ever seen. He had cried for hours, he told the family at Prospect.

Benny's horses – everyone, including Nellie, regarded them as his – needed little guidance. He had cared for them since they had been born, and Peggy, the older one, had been born eighteen years before. They stood patiently as he harnessed them each morning, placing saddle-pads on their broad backs and belly bands below, lifting the great collars and attaching the chains that transferred the horses' pulling power, the collars smelling of decades of sweat, the metal hames holding the collars in place. They were the traditional Irish draught-horses, the most adaptable breed in the world. Marengo, Napoleon's favourite, whose bones were now in a British museum, had been bred in the county. These plough-horse strains pulled the plough patiently, turning at the headland when Benny lifted the double-share from the furrow and called, "Hubbawf!" as they swung to restart on the next, beginning down an invisible line towards the far end of the field, steadfast in blustering wind, trailed by clouds of seagulls and rooks.

In spring, he harrowed the furrows, then took the moulding plough to make drills for potatoes and turnips, opening a drill on one side and neatly covering whatever he had planted on the other. In the other fields grass and wheat went in simultaneously from the iron sower, wheat to be harvested that autumn, then the field to be closed off from the cattle, and the grass to be cut in the summer of the following year. The first cut made the best hay.

Demand for his skills dwindled each year. Most of the county, which saw itself as a model of modern agriculture, had turned to the tractor. The poet, however, preferred to plough with horses, not from sentimentality but because he believed the tractor was unsuitable for Prospect, that its weight packed the clay to a dead pan, leaving rainwater trapped in the topsoil.

The ploughman ate his midday meal with the family in the big kitchen but was absolved from eating what everyone else ate. Benny demanded nothing but fried rashers of bacon and eggs, with thick slices of bread and butter, which he ate with his mouth open, and tea that he poured into his saucer to cool, blowing on it noisily before taking the first draught from the saucer. One of his habits posed a problem: Benny would lick his knife clear – or almost clear – of egg before plunging it into the butter. The boys' mother created the solution: Benny would have his own butter. This was taken from the fridge before each meal, on its own dish, and laid in front of Benny's place. Afterwards it was segregated in the fridge. It was known, unoriginally, as Benny's Butter and was usually left severely alone, even by the hungriest of boys.

The hungriest of the boys was Ivan, so hungry that his mother called him The Gannet. Family legend said that Brian had eaten twenty-seven helpings of turkey and ham one Christmas, a claim Brian denied, saying that he had eaten three or four at most, with perhaps an additional helping of stuffing. This was paltry, he said, in comparison to Niall's achievement of eating eleven rounds of sandwiches at one sitting, but both agreed that they lacked Ivan's consistency. Ivan ate enormous amounts of food every day, with a quiet intensity that his family admired. While the others were relatively content to leave a gap between meals, he was not. One afternoon he dashed into the kitchen, found a loaf of bread and a tin of corned beef, threw open the fridge, snatched up a dish of butter and made a pile of sandwiches which he ate quickly. Niall watched him admiringly, and waited until he had finished before saying quietly: "You've just eaten Benny's Butter." The others were still laughing when Ivan ran from the room. "He's teetotally charoosed," said Conor.

Chapter Eleven

A sea breeze blew gently from the south when the poet drove his old black car, exhaust booming, down the steep hill into Ballykeep, a little fishing village on the broad estuary of Uisceford Harbour, where the three rivers that drained the southern midlands of the country flowed past to the sea.

The open sea was only a mile away, and the poet could see the squat lighthouse that the Normans had built on the edge of the promontory of Crook to the south. Two villages on the Eskerford side of the estuary lay between the poet and the promontory, the furthest with a fort on its headland commanding the entrance to the estuary proper, the nearest where the estuary curved to the left. Opposite the nearest village was a great mudbank marked by the Spiderman, an automatic light on stilted metal legs, warning shipping to keep to the fairway.

It was a beautiful day, the light breeze flirting with the ebbing tide. He was still in the same county as Prospect, but only just. The next county began on the other side of the estuary, half a mile away. To reach it, he merely had to hoist the flag on the pole below the quay and the little foot-passenger ferry would set off across the tide to fetch him.

All water-borne traffic for the city of Uisceford on the river Saor, and for the town of Rosspoint on the Bree, passed this way, along the deep channel on the far side, until it reached Creek Point, around a bend in the river above Ballykeep. There the ships bound for Uisceford turned to port, and there the Saor entered the main estuary.

On the far side of the estuary the country was a yellowy green, with darker patches in the haze where high, tree-covered bluffs swept down to the riverbanks. Below Creek Point the banks of the estuary on the Eskerford side rose sharply into high, rocky bluffs – almost small cliffs – while on the Uisceford side it was nearly as steep. Opposite Ballykeep was the little grey village of Departure West. It nestled below and slightly to the right of a partly wooded hill shaped like an elephant's head, the trunk dwindling down to the water to the south. Below it was a long, low headland, grey-green in the sunlight, rising gently until it became a cliff that faced the open sea. Departure had been a calling point for the ships that sailed to America, often carrying the emigrants from the hungry island to a new world. The lighthouse on the peninsula below was, for many, their final sight of home.

Ballykeep was sheltered by its stone quays and by the high rocky ground behind it that was a vulgar yellow with flowering whin. The harbour contained a dozen or so salmon boats: the stubby, half-decked Uisceford Harbour yawls that ran out into the tide, shot their nets, and swept the estuary for fish as they ran up to the spawning redds in the headwaters of the three rivers. All of them were engined but they retained both masts, the after one usually carrying a small sail on a gaff-rig, mounted on iron bitts near the transom, allowing the yawls to hold their positions against a violent tide race. They were handsome in their fashion: short foredecks, tallish wheel-houses positioned well forward, stubby foremast forward of that again, no afterdeck or even a hint of one, broad beam, and deep keels to hold them in the tide.

A dozen skiffs and praams and one or two pleasure boats, chained to ring-bolts on the harbour wall, bobbed alongside them. Jackdaws squabbled on the roof of the Norman bailey above the harbour.

He heard a voice from the boatyard behind him. "How are you today?" asked the boatyard owner, who knew him well. "I'm grand, thanks, Paddy," said the poet. "Did they get any salmon on the tide last night?" "They did," said the owner. "There was a fair run of fish." He looked at the salmon boats with affection, even though his boatyard built only larger, sea-going trawlers. "It's good to see them make a few shillings. Too many of 'em have had to go to England for work." That was a common story. Much of the country had been drained of people because of the postwar economic stagnation that gripped the young republic. Both men were silent for a moment.

The poet looked beyond the owner, at the harbour and at the hard above it. He could see nothing there that would suit his quest. "I'm looking for something that the boys could take right up the Bree, or the Owenore. They want to camp, and fish, and the divil knows what," he said.

"Everything here has got a fairly deep keel," the yard owner replied. "You need it, like, with the rise an' fall we get. That wouldn't do atall up above."

"Something like a big cot," the poet mused.

The owner looked at him strangely. "A cot! We never see a cot here. You get them up above," gesturing up the estuary, "and you get them down below, but the yawl's our boat. You need a good keel on her here, or you'd be swep' up and down the estuary like a paper boat. But there must be plenty of oul' cots in Eskerford."

"Surely," said the poet. "I'll ask around."

◆━◆

Before he left he walked into the shop next to the harbour. The premises seemed empty. He rapped on the counter. "Are you there, Watty?" he called. The shop smelled of fish, mingled with soap powder and stout. It combined pub and shop and fishmonger.

A door opened and a man emerged, face cheering when he saw the poet. "What way air ye? Are y'after a peal?" – meaning a grilse, or young salmon.

"I am," said the poet. "D'you have any?"

"Pick one yerself there," said Watty, motioning the poet past the counter flap, pointing at several boxes loosely filled with ice on the floor. Silver gleamed through the ice. The poet bent to pick a four-pound grilse. Watty wrapped it in brown paper. The poet fished out two half-crowns, they chatted for a while, and the poet left.

◆ ◆

He was not in a hurry that morning so he drove slowly back, choosing a roundabout route across the south of the county towards Eskerford, stopping at Kylemore Quay, a busy fishing harbour, ambling along the harbour dock past heaps of discarded crabs, listening to the screech of the gulls, ignoring the smell of rotting fish, greeting the hands working on the nets, and the skippers of the big trawlers, buying a basket of prawns, a rare treat for his family. He climbed the steps to the harbour wall and looked across at the two Sáile islands, one much larger than the other, the land-bridge to one exposed at low tide.

He restarted his car and blew smoke through the open window as he jaunted along the back roads, the sea in sight for much of the journey, stopping to look at a neat thatched cottage with a single gable window peeping through the thatch. A stone-lined well stood in the front garden; above it a big spindle suspended on iron stanchions with a handle on one side to wind rope and bucket. Every wall in the place was whitewashed to a startling brilliance; the garden a blaze of flowers because of the sandy, friable soil.

He drove on to Eskerford town, to the Cot Safe. This was a sea shelter with a wall of rocks on the harbour side to shield it from the gales to which Eskerford Harbour was most vulnerable. It was mainly used by fishermen. It lay on the south side of the main harbour, beyond the White Boy, the light that marked the end of the breakwater wall.

The Cot Safe looked more like a mud trap than a harbour, since it flooded only at high tide. Behind it were the fishermen's warehouses, and around this Batt Street area were rows of fishermen's houses. In summer evenings, retired fishermen and blue-water sailors sat on the bench above the Cot Safe smoking, shouting at the children playing in the mud below: "Get out o' that boat! D'ye hear me? GET OUTTA THAT BO-AT!"

Two fishing families, intermarried, shared the big warehouse above the Cot Safe. The poet was popular with them. A fussy Customs official could make life difficult for the owners of the fishing boats, but the two families realized that this would not be the case soon after the poet's arrival. He, in turn, had taken to these people at once, and listened for hours at a time to their stories of seamanship, of the great storms that had robbed them of many of their relatives; of tides and races and rocks and sandbars; of lightships and lighthouses; of the mariners and old schooner captains to whom they introduced him. They told him stories of the sailing cots and of the Eskerford wind-jammers and schooners that had once thronged the quays; many stories in particular of the *Antelope*, last of the Eskerford schooners, built in the yard above the Cot Safe, her launch signalling the end of a shipbuilding era that had lasted for centuries.

He bought fish from them at wholesale prices, and sometimes an additional plaice or haddock was placed in the parcel as a present. He spent many hours at the warehouse, mostly listening, collecting ballads for his programme from the sailors and fishermen, some of them recorded in this warehouse on the big tape machine the station loaned him.

A little later, accompanied by one of the fishermen, he knocked at the door of a small house in a terrace fifty yards away. It was opened by an elderly man in a cap. They talked for a while. The old man listened, then nodded, and, soon after, all three men climbed into the car.

The poet drove across town, past the north station, taking the road by the river, past the bridge, and on again for a few hundred yards past the boat club, and finally parked. The three descended a path under the railway and reached the river. A few yards out from them, lying in the mud, moored by a rusty chain to a big ring-bolt on the bank, was an ageing herring cot, along with other vessels, skiffs and cots, some looking as if they would not float again.

The three studied the cot from the bank, the poet jingling the change in his trouser pockets, a habit of his. The fisherman donned thigh boots and waded through the mud to look closely at the cot.

It was built to the traditional Eskerford design and had probably spent thirty years out in the bay fishing for herring. It was flat-bottomed, which meant it would not lie close to the wind, but was easy to launch. It was double-ended, like a canoe, with stem and stern posts of solid oak. The Eskerford cot typically lacked any decking, and was clinker-built above the waterline, smooth carvel below, planks of Irish red larch overlapping, elm frames. It was ballasted with heavy stones, had a centreboard, no keel, and therefore was not a boat, but a cot, an important distinction. Its overall length, the poet discovered subsequently, was twenty-six feet, roughly four times its beam. The largest of the Eskerford cots was slightly larger, thirty feet or so, some with a third mast stepped far aft.

Boatbuilders in this area had been constructing cots for centuries, a tradition that probably went back to the Celts, great sailors and under-rated boatbuilders, a world beyond the Fir Bolgs, little bag-men, coracle-builders.

The flat bottoms of these cots made them ideal for estuaries and shallow coasts. The smaller ones were the traditional cots of the estuary fishermen. Larger cots like this often carried sail, and had additional freeboard aft to launch them safely, stern first, into surf. They were sturdy and safe if the crew were used to their ways, and they were particularly popular with herring fishermen. Almost certainly, this cot had been used for that purpose, and had probably been double-masted, with a sprit rather than a gaff-rig: a spar connecting the mast to the after top corner of the sail, booming it out, simple but effective. Each cot would have had a simple foresail, and a crew of four to handle oars and sails and net. The largest cots had oars of sixteen feet.

The poet felt the call of the sail suddenly as he stood there, the first time he had felt this for several years, smelling the ooze and salt and rotting seaweed, looking at the workman-like lines of the big cot, remembering *Barnstormer*. He had rebuilt the sailing cot during the War, fitting her with a gunter rig that hauled up tight to the mast, to hold such a press of sail that the bitts cracked alarmingly in a stiff breeze. He had over-rigged her so much that he had had to ballast her with pigs of iron instead of stones, but it had been worth it.

He remembered the pride Eskerford people had taken in

the heavy racing cots, particularly in the *Fair Do*, the fastest of them all, and how competitive the races in Eskerford Harbour had been, so competitive that some owners blackleaded the hulls to reduce water friction. Later the Mermaid class became the rage and sent the cot as a yacht into decline. Perhaps, he thought, that also signified a social change in the town, perhaps in the country as a whole. The Mermaid was the favourite of the professional classes, while the sailing cots were adaptations of working boats, the serious playthings of those, apart from a few amateur enthusiasts like himself, who made their livings from the sea.

He had crewed during the War for a fellow enthusiast, Tom the auctioneer, the kindest and most loyal of friends, who owned a Galway hooker, the loveliest working boat ever built, but an Atlantic boat, not designed for the shallow harbour and coasts of Eskerford. They had planned a day's sailing in it with Paddy, the retired master-pilot, and the poet had pressed his two eldest sons to crew. He had visited the warehouse first and drawn off a little whiskey to toast Tom, and as he walked with his older sons to the quays he saw a fogbank creeping in from the west. The captain, pilot and crew decided that they would sail through the fog into the open harbour, but they failed to tack the hooker in time and grounded her keel on a sandbank a hundred yards out from the poet's office, and sat, ashamed, until the tide lifted them off, vainly hoping that the old master-pilot's presence on board would not be noticed. When they sought warmth in the poet's bottle he discovered, to *his* shame, that he had mistaken the casks in his hurry and drawn off sherry instead. They drank it anyway.

He had grown bored of sailing an open boat around the same harbour and had sold *Barnstormer* to two brothers who lived by the great shallow bay on the south coast. The brothers had fallen out soon afterwards and had resolved the ownership of the cot by sawing her in half, turning the halves into small cots. A strange death, he thought, or perhaps two beginnings, twin berths for twin births.

Coincidentally, John Walsh's *Fair Do* had been cut in two as well, also as a result of the row between her owners. The area above the Cot Safe was filled with spectators as the nineteen-foot cot was dragged up on the grassy area to the right of the little haven, a tragic Gemini, a legend cut into halves by a cross-saw; survived by the inevitable ballad:

> *When we got to the windward, oh boys, it*
> *was grand*
> *To see the* Fair Do *beating in to the strand.*

Some time before he had wandered through a house auction and picked up the two thick volumes of Dixon Kemp, one of Queen Victoria's naval architects, for half a crown. He had found a sketch of the standard Eskerford cot inside and had read Dixon Kemp's words: "The fishermen hereabouts are a bold and hardy race, and they need to be, for herring fishing on a December night is desperately cold work..." Kemp had gone on: "It is a pretty sight to see forty or fifty boats out of a night; but it is very cold work, and only one but brought up to it could stand it."

He found a treasury of boat designs in Dixon Kemp that kept the Aladdin lamp burning late while he examined them. He moved on to Uffa Fox, whom he considered a genius, the greatest small boat designer. Sometimes, as he listened to the German bombers over the Fascar, he would dream of building a little cruiser with a proper cabin and a fin keel; nothing grand, of course, but a boat he could sail off this coast without shipping a small sea down the back of his neck.

He emerged from his reverie as the fisherman, standing in the mud on the river side of the boat, called: "She's sound enough below the waterline; and so she should be as she's been in the water every tide. But she'll need a bit of caulking above the waterline." He bent down again, peering at the planking. "I can see daylight here and there," he laughed. "She needs a bit of caulking, all right, so she do. So she do. But she'll be fine once you do that. Fine," he repeated, wading back through the mud.

———◆◆———

He told them the news over the kitchen table that evening. "I have the loan of an old herring cot for you for a couple of weeks later in the summer," he said. "I thought the oldest four of you might like to explore the Bree."

He had anticipated the uproar and excitement that would follow and had his replies ready.

To the youngest: no, they would stay at home. They were too young.

To Garry: a bit of caulking above the waterline. That was all.

To Conor: the boat would hold four, five at a stretch, plus gear.

To the youngest again: they would go to bed at once if they complained once more.

To his wife: yes, the boat was safe.

To his wife again: it was a seaboat, of course it was safe.

To Garry: she's big enough.

To Conor: they could probably manage two of the rivers in the space of two or three weeks. Not three. Too much.

To Padraic: bed at once, or he would get a clout on the ear.

To Niall: that spot above the boat club. Lying there for years.

To his wife: in a tent. Yes, he had already found one.

To his wife once more: bully-beef. They could buy bread and other perishables in the towns they would pass through. Milk and eggs they could buy at farms.

To Garry: he would borrow a lorry. They would take her to Ballykeep and put her in the water there. He could caulk her by the slip.

To Brian: bring your books. And your bushman. Your axe, too. No, no rifles.

To Padraic: haven't *you* gone to bed yet?

It grew calmer when he had chased Padraic up the stairs. Brian sat back in his chair, parting his hair; Garry hunched forward, his charts in front of him, excitement bringing on his stammer. Conor and Niall borrowed Garry's map. "I wish we were going tomorrow," said Niall, stroking the great yellow cat.

That night, as a young moon threw a yellow light over the meadows and woods around Prospect, the house began to fill with anticipation. As he drifted off to sleep, Conor thought he heard the call of a barn owl, a rare sound. He rose to look out the window, but the bird did not call again. He heard only the sound of Niall breathing in the next bed, and the sound of the typewriter from the dining room.

Chapter Twelve

The boys' mother had never wished for a daughter, even if her husband had. She was in her prime, happy with the role she had evolved over the years. Running the house was her self-allotted task: cooking, washing up, shopping, cleaning, doing the perpetual Prospect laundry. She had also made herself responsible for the garden, which consisted of the rockery on the thin strip of lawn at the front of Prospect, and the rose- and flower-beds that struggled in the poor soil around the house, and she had quickly added the harvesting of eggs and fruit and vegetables from the Hen-Run, Orchard and fields.

She guarded that domain fiercely, refusing to allow anyone other than Martha to help with cooking, washing up or laundry. This was women's work, she intimated strongly. If Martha was not there, she did it herself. Hoeing the gravel to keep it clear of weeds, keeping bedrooms tidy, hoovering daily, and bedmaking were jobs for the boys, under her supervision, and she made very sure that the boys knew it, using sharp words and a smack on the ear for the younger ones if they ducked the work.

She had gladly shouldered the burden of running the larger house when they moved to Prospect, regarding the long hours of work a small price to pay for living in a home where her work was, in her eyes, rewarded many times over. She had developed a great love of the countryside and had never regretted for a moment leaving the city and its fashions.

Her favourite time was early morning, when the house was still quiet, before the farm animals needed attention, and before the hungry calls from male voices for breakfast. On cold winter mornings, when the draughty old house called for extra woollen jumpers, she opened the kitchen door to admit three dogs and a dozen cats, fed them, then sat to eat her toast and drink her tea, slippers on the floor, stockinged feet warm in the open bottom oven of the Aga, reading a book or finishing her crossword from the previous day, immensely grateful for the peace. In summer she walked to the Hen-Run in the early light, singing one of Moore's melodies, collecting the eggs, a file of dogs and cats trailing her; talking to the cows who ambled to the Well Field gate when they heard her footfall. Sometimes she wandered on to the Orchard to pick the new potatoes, her spirits singing as she lifted each clamp to see the annual miracle of growth renew itself. In autumn she collected mushrooms and blackberries; in spring, the wild flowers from the hedgerows.

When she had finished washing up after lunch, she stopped work, energy abruptly spent. She sat at the kitchen table for an hour and did her crossword, upset at any interruption. This was her own time, and her family respected it. Three or four afternoons a week her husband drove her to Eskerford, where she shopped and met her friends for coffee. Each Sunday afternoon she went to bed for two or three hours, drawing the curtains, recharging her energy for the week to come.

She had strong views on what was good for her sons. Each week she lined all six up in the kitchen, handed each a cup of tea with senna to dose them against worms, and stood there until each drained the cup. Some of them developed a lifelong hatred of tea as a result. Toothache, a hatefully frequent visitor, was dosed with a teaspoonful of whiskey poured into the tooth to anaesthetize the nerve, producing a lifelong association of whiskey with pain. Any boy with wet feet was told to dry them immediately and stay by the Aga or the fire in the dining room until they were warm, because wet feet led to colds and fevers, as did wet heads, whatever Pax the doctor said. Boys sent to bed with colds or flu were given fresh oranges, Jacobs' cream crackers, and a hot lemon drink several times a day.

Her Dubliner's sense of sentimentality was at its strongest when she saw a woman struggling to raise a family. She lavished help on a traveller – called tinkers then – a red-haired, freckled mother of twelve wild, red-haired, freckled children, who walked from wherever her clann had pitched their camp of brightly painted caravans and piebald horses to receive bundles of clothes, milk, butter and bread, probably meat, too. The family watched the hoard of food build up, listened as their father pulled her leg, and heard their mother reply: "It's for my tinker woman."

Sometimes the woman would appear at the kitchen door several times in a week, sometimes not for a month. Benny and the poet suspected that her clann drove their horses into the Front Field to graze after dark, but the boys' mother insisted they did not. Many times the boys awoke to hear the shout: "Get up! The tinkers' horses are in the Front Field!" Many times they drove the horses through the gates, out to the road. Within minutes short, red-haired men, bane of every farmer, emerged furtively from nowhere, like another people from a mist, and led them away to graze illegally elsewhere. Not her tinker woman's clann, said the boys' mother.

Her husband believed that the whole of anything would be improved if every man improved his own part, however small. His wife would not have put it in that way, but she shared his view in practice, helping those she knew or knew of, without charity committees or coffee mornings or any form of affectation, shunning the abstract, embracing the tangible, her creed that of Yeats' airman:

> My country is Kiltartan Cross,
> My countrymen Kiltartan's poor.

Every Saturday afternoon three or four children came to collect the scraps of bread, potatoes and other leftovers to feed their family's hens. They lived in a tiny cottage that housed a drunken father, a desperately brave mother, and thirteen children. The boys' mother ran out quickly each time with a sack of food, even though the poet did not object; he positively approved. The boys had been in that cottage on one errand or another and had seen the children fed, when school finished, from a big iron cauldron that held only potatoes, with not a sign of meat or fish.

On one of these beautiful June evenings after supper, her husband took her with Ivan and Padraic up the river as the setting sun cast long shadows on woods and fields. At a little crossroads they turned down a steep lane, wildly overgrown and smelling of fresh grass and wild garlic. They drove down it gingerly, opening and closing several gates on the way until they arrived at a small, whitewashed house at the end, a tiny stream running past it. The river was directly below them, partly shielded by a belt of poplars. Above it were terraces of strawberry, gooseberry and blackcurrant plants, laden with fruit. Above that again, uphill from the house, were rows of beehives sheltered by a wood. The air droned with the sound of the apiary. It was classically sylvan, said Brian after a visit, a scene from Virgil's *Eclogues*.

Sitting on one of the terraces was a man who looked like Saturn: big head, white hair, magnetic grey eyes under shaggy eyebrows, naked to the waist, chest and shoulders of bronze, a pagan sun-worshipper. The boys stared, astonished. The man seemed to be covered with bees. Some sat on his shoulders, some crawled on his neck, others swarmed about his head, yet none appeared to sting him. He stood, the bees leaving him in an angry flight on a line to the hives.

"What way air ye, Mam?" he asked hesitantly, towering over the boys' mother, shaking her hand, turning then to the poet, who was looking hungrily at the strawberry beds: "And how's the bossman?"

His conversation at first was stilted and polite, with long pauses before he would say: "Yes, Mister. Yes, Mister." Some time before, Garry and Brian had named him Yes-Yes, and Old Yes-Yes he had become to the family at Prospect.

They talked for a few minutes, then the mother gave two punnets to each of the boys and led them up to the terraces. For the next hour they picked strawberries, big strawberries, firm and juicy, gorging themselves while their mother scolded them to fill the punnets instead. She scolded their father too, who was doing the same, while Joe looked the other way, politely studying the shadows on the river.

—◆—

The poet's nickname at school had been Plum; not because of his shape – he had been a whippet then – but because of his love of fresh fruit. He was very happy to discover that the mild climate and soil of Eskerford combined, so this model county claimed, to produce the best strawberries and raspberries in the two islands. When they arrived at Prospect he sought the likeliest soil and had the Orchard drills planted with strawberries, raspberries and blackcurrants as well as peas and potatoes, but he was disappointed with some of the results. Blackcurrants and gooseberries flourished, as did peas and potatoes, but strawberries and raspberries seemed small, lacked flavour; were thin, poor things. Then he discovered Ballydicken.

He had sought a well-digger; had asked this person and that if they knew of one. Someone said, "Try Joe Kirwan at Ballydicken." Where was that? inquired the poet. Oh, 'twas way up the river in the back of beyant; down a steep lane, mind yourself going down; 'twas right on the river itself; great for strawberries, and the honey! The taste of his honey! Himself and the bees were like brothers; a lonely place, a lonely place; beautiful, mind you, but lonely.

That awoke a fairly distant memory for the poet. He remembered, soon after he had come to Eskerford when they had rented for a few months a modernish, characterless house half a mile down the road from Prospect, meeting a quiet giant sinking a well in a field nearby, striking up a mild acquaintance at the time.

He found the place after a few wrong turnings, ambling along in his old bus, as he called the big noisy car, smoking a cigarette; stopping to look at a horse and rider practising jumps in a lonely field, reminded of a Jack Yeats' painting; gazing at the bluffs across the river, the sun beaming a few shafts between the April rainclouds to cast a thin, watery light on the growth of the river valley. He went down the lane in bottom gear, springs squeaking their complaints, worn brake pads grumbling, splashing in rain puddles, the car rattling like a cart, and drew up at the house.

Out came Joe and his two brothers, bachelors too,

saluting in the manner of courteous, country people, Joe the head of the family. He was a water-diviner, and brought his hazel forks to wherever someone wanted a well sunk. When the fork swung to the downward vertical, he marked the spot with a stone or wooden peg, then approached it once more from a different direction, triangulating with simple Euclid, then feeling the strength of the pull to guess how deep the well must be sunk. He found other objects, too, as the boys had discovered when they had hidden a half-crown in the Grove and asked him to search for it.

He earned his living from divining, from casting well cylinders in concrete, and from his fruit and lettuces, but his bees, the poet discovered, were his love. He had been seen to stop his old lorry as he glimpsed a swarm of bees on a branch of a roadside tree, to snap off the branch and thrust branch and swarm into the cab, arriving home with a few stings; spending the next hours coaxing the angry arrivals into their new home.

It was he who recommended John, another diviner from the riverbank. A wristwatch worked for neither man. The poet believed that the natural electricity of a diviner stopped the works.

When they had filled the punnets, the poet picked a rough honeycomb of honey and paid, they talked for a while longer, then the poet took his single-barrelled shotgun from the car boot, and motioned his sons to come with him. Ballydicken was overrun with rabbits. The boys' mother waited peacefully in the front passenger seat, talking to Joe and his brothers who had ventured shyly from the house.

They walked to a field above the lane. As he closed the

gate behind him the poet saw a rabbit, fired at it, wounded it in the hindquarters and finished it off by hitting it on the head with the shotgun butt. Shooting was not his skill.

━━◆━◆━━

When Niall milked Hawthorn the next morning, Phoebus, the tomcat who killed rabbits as casually as another cat would kill a mouse, pestered him, hungry for breakfast. He jumped on Niall's knee. Niall pushed him off. On impulse, the boy shot the stream of milk at his cat. Phoebus, fur wet, upset, ran to the end of the byre. Then he returned. Niall did the same again. Phoebus backed away once more, licked the warm milk on the byre floor, then approached again. This time, as Niall squeezed milk in his direction he opened his mouth and kept it open. "Watch this," Niall said to Ivan as his brother arrived to milk Slaney. Phoebus performed, eyes firmly fixed on the white stream, pink tongue struggling to lap the flow.

Ivan's big tabby, Greedy, had followed him to the byre. Ivan put his bucket under the cow's udder and began to milk. When the bottom of the pail began to ring, he squirted milk at Greedy, who took to the trick immediately, mouth wide, tail working in pleasure.

There were usually a dozen other cats at Prospect, most of them descended from Padraic's cat, Mutt, who was a week older than Padraic. Soon after the family arrived at Prospect, the McCanns, owners of the little sweetshop up the road, gave them two kittens from the same litter, brother and sister. Jeff was the brother, Ivan's cat. He was run over by a car when he was two. Mutt lived, and became inseparable from Padraic, particularly at night, when the no-cats-in-the-house-at-night rule was broken. Mutt hid until bedtime beneath the blankets on Padraic's bed. On winter nights, when the insides of the front windows of Prospect were opaque with ice, the boy would plunge his feet down the bed to find a ball of warm fur. Mutt, knowing she was safe from eviction by then, would make her way to his pillow, settle there, purring, and the boy would sink into the peculiarly innocent sleep of childhood. His parents at first separated them, then gave up.

Mutt had the respect of the other cats, even Phoebus, who cowered from the matriarch. The others made way for her when feeding, or on the armchair at the corner of the kitchen, their usual sleeping place during the day. At night all cats, Mutt excepted, were shooed outside with a sweeping brush to keep the farmyard free of rats and mice, although Phoebus took the occasional night off from hunting, and sought Niall's bed.

Bluebell was the odd cat out: beautiful, fluffy, half-Persian, a present to the boys' mother from a friend. She had arrived at Prospect when the beech wood beside the Paddock was carpeted in a blue mist; her eyes, the same colour as the flowers, shining from her dark head and coat. The boys' mother named her immediately, even though she would not consider allowing a bluebell into her house because of the bad luck it would bring.

They soon discovered that Bluebell's treat was to eat the Marrowfat peas that were steeped in water to soften them in a crock on the window sill of the larder each Saturday night, ready for lunch on all except summer Sundays. The bowl had to be covered with a cloth, as Bluebell, gentle blue eyes following the boys' mother as she opened the packets of dried peas before going to bed, was to be found each Sunday before Mass, delicately scooping out the softened peas, one at a time, licking her lips after eating each pea. When the protective cloth was placed over the bowl and weighted down all round, the cat gave the boys' mother an imploring look, and miaowed twice in rapid succession, a call her owner immediately interpreted as: "Peas, please!" So began the post-Mass ritual each Sunday, when the boys' mother removed hat and coat and hurried to the larder where Bluebell sat on the windowsill, fluffy tail writhing in excitement, calling for her peas. Each Sunday she was rewarded with half a dozen Marrowfats except in summer when garden peas came in from the Orchard, wonderfully fresh sweet peas that Bluebell turned her nose away from, calling "Peas, please!" piteously until she was shooed from the kitchen.

John drowned Prospect's kittens to control the cat numbers, a task the boys had united to reject. The poet, resigned to this, told John to put each newborn litter in a sack and sink it in a water trough. The boys accepted that this was part of life and death on a working farm, but they noticed that John did not relish the job, and that when the time came for execution the poet had left for his office.

The three dogs occupied an equally important place in the family affections, although Sport, the irritable Irish red setter, was viewed as the leader. He was Ivan's dog, and had been given to him on his third birthday. Sport was the self-appointed sentry at Prospect, barking at anything. In summer, when swallows swooped over the yard and Paddock the dog would chase them madly, furious at the intrusion. He hated thunder, once trying to enter the house at night in a storm by chewing a hole in the kitchen door.

It was Sport's third life at Prospect. Garry and Brian had taken him for a long walk as a young dog. Sport had rushed in front of an oil lorry and had been thrown into a ditch, his back broken. Garry felt the broken back, said there was little hope but that Sport must be left where he was. He would return later. The two walked home slowly, despondent. Sport waited for them in the yard. Amazed, they carried him to a shed, laid him on blankets and fed him. The dog recovered, but his temper grew short. The previous year, when Padraic had been playing in the yard, the dog had bitten his face, leaving a tiny scar for life on the boy's upper lip. No one blamed the dog, nor the boy, but when a local said he would like him as a gun dog Sport was given away; with many misgivings, but given away.

He turned out to be gun shy and ran when a shot was fired. The man brought him back and this time he stayed, because the family decided he was fated to stay.

Sport was important for another reason. Brian had invented an answer to the annoying questions that small boys ask, repetitious, irritating, unanswerable questions. In the folklore of Prospect, the sentence: "Because Sport's a dog," became the standard reply, as effective as it was frustrating.

Bruno was seen as the poet's dog, running to greet him when he returned from Eskerford, sitting at his feet at mealtimes. He was a Cairn terrier; the other dog, Colleen, a purebred Welsh collie. Both were sunny, good natured animals who played with the boys, but Sport had more character and was respected for it.

Cows, of course, are cleverer than dogs or cats. If anyone but Conor milked Blossom, her yield fell by a third. No message could have been clearer. Blossom, a big, affectionate, strawberry roan shorthorn with long eyelashes, was the daughter of the gentle Hawthorn.

Eight cattle made up the total herd at Prospect. They stood chained in their stalls to be fed on a winter evening in the cheerful byre, always in the same order from right to left: Bambi, a big-boned red cow, daughter of the fabled Mary Ann; Blossom; Bunty, a Hereford cross bullock; Black Bobo, who gave little milk but ran like the wind and jumped a ditch like a steeplechaser; Hawthorn; Bantry, a part-white Jersey, mad, always spancelled – hind legs hobbled with rope – and tricky to milk; then Slaney, a red shorthorn who yielded next to nothing and whom Niall referred to as Big Fat Slane; and, finally, Trailer, a roany shorthorn who was probably kept in the bottom stall because the boys thought her boring.

Four or five cows in milk at any one time presented a great deal of milking by hand, and eight cattle in total presented a great deal of work throughout the year, particularly as the wetness of the Prospect land meant that they had to be fed indoors for six months or more. The boys grumbled at the work, of course, but enjoyed the companionship and friendliness of the cattle who chewed the cud as they were milked, and the atmosphere of a byre full of warmth on a black winter evening; the heart of a working farm. There was also a by-product: milking strengthened their arms and hands greatly, giving them milkman's muscle – a ridge of added muscle in the area above thumb and index finger – of which they became inordinately proud, constantly flexing them and boasting to each other. Padraic, in particular, was intrigued, often asking Brian, Conor and Niall to circle thumb and forefinger while he declared himself to be the judge of whose milkman's muscle was most impressive, Niall usually ending the judging session with the rhetorical question: "Did you know that Robespierre could peel an orange with one hand?"

Hawthorn was so named by the poet because the hedges were white with blossom when she arrived. The farmer who sold her to him gave him three half-crowns as luck-penny and the luck stayed with the new owner. Hawthorn was queen of the little herd, succeeding Mary Ann, a cow the boys had believed would never be replaced in their affections when she died, probably as a result of an eye infection that they believed had been caused by a lout with an air rifle. They buried Mary Ann in a headland in the Flat Field, grieving for a wise and very generous cow. Then Hawthorn came, and they regained their enthusiasm. Hawthorn now walked with a limp, having knocked her hip out of joint on a gate. Hip or not, she had delivered a beautiful calf which was called Blossom, probably in her honour. Conor was placed in charge. When Blossom had her first offspring, Conor was first to milk her. The empathy between them grew until Blossom greeted a different pair of hands on her udder by swishing her tail, coated in dung, in the milker's face. When she came round – when the cow was ready for the bull – it should have been Conor who led her, but Conor happened to be out that day with Garry, who was gaining experience with Barty the vet.

Conor was probably the most academically clever of the brothers – although Garry had won a prize at university, and Brian could quote Horace from memory – and he was probably the most versatile. He was good at all sports: rugby, cricket, hurling, handball. He was also very strong, with a nervous, explosive strength. During the previous school term Ivan had been cycling up the steep slope of Summerhill from school on a grey, wet day. Three youths from the town idled in the other direction. When they saw the schoolboy they spread across the road to stop him, to taunt him as a privileged College boy. Ivan dismounted and wheeled his bike to put it between him and the youths, the oldest of whom was six or seven years older. One snatched Ivan's bike and threw it on the road. Another pushed him. Soon he was surrounded. He looked desperately down the hill and saw Conor cycling up.

When Conor saw his brother in trouble he stood on the pedals. In a few moments, he arrived to stand beside Ivan. "Leave my brother alone," he said flatly. The youths jeered.

One of them pushed Ivan, who fell backwards to land on the road.

Conor threw his bike at the largest youth and hit the next on the nose, breaking it. The third tried to kick him. Conor grabbed the youth's leg and threw him on the footpath. The lout he had thrown the bike at was scrambling to his feet. Conor hit him twice, once in the solar plexus and then, as the youth's head fell forward, full in the mouth. The boy turned and ran. Conor ran after him like a stag and, overhauling him, kicked him in the backside. The boy screamed: "Oah, you bully!" and ran on. Conor let him go.

He helped Ivan to his feet, then picked up his bike. The youths had vanished. The two brothers set off again for Prospect, walking their bikes until their breathing recovered. As they cycled past the Scout Tree and saw the lights of Prospect, Conor spoke: "Say nothing at home." Ivan, still in shock at his brother's anger, obeyed.

◆—◆

Niall led Blossom to the bull when she came around. The poet told his fourth son: "You'd better take her this afternoon. Conor could be very late. I called in there earlier. They're expecting her. Ivan and Padraic can go with you."

Blossom would go to the bull that had charged Brian. The boys would lead her by the road. The summer breeze had virtually died when they set out, Blossom with a rope halter, although she scarcely needed it; Niall, at her head, Ivan and Padraic alongside their brother.

After twenty minutes, they turned off into the lane to Boycotts. They passed Whitty's cottage and reached the farmyard where the bull was penned. The boys watched it nervously as it pawed the ground and glared at them. A metal ring was set in its nose, halter attached. The owner clutched the halter tightly, dragging the great head around as he led the bull down the yard.

The events that followed bewildered Padraic, who knew nothing of the facts of life and vaguely supposed that he had been deposited on earth on the day of his birth through some opaque arrangement between his parents and the county hospital. After a conversation between Niall and the bull's owner, Blossom was led into the pen. The bull snorted and shuffled quickly to the cow's rear, which he sniffed loudly. Then he suddenly reared on his hind legs, revealing an enormous, dripping organ before his forelegs slammed on the cow's hindquarters.

"No!" shouted Padraic, "He'll kill Blossom."

"Keep back," said Niall impatiently as the bull began to rock back and forward violently on Blossom's hindquarters. The boys watched, fascinated and a little frightened. The cow was obviously not enjoying the assault, but endured it with dignity.

It was over quickly, so quickly that Padraic still did not know why the gentle cow should be punished. Blossom, sensing that nature had taken its course, moved forward. The bull, feeling the issue was in doubt, slid back to earth, clearly unhappy, pawing the ground. His owner grasped the halter and dragged him away. Blossom was led through the gate and the gate closed. The bull charged, his owner desperately dragging on the rope. "Go quickly!" he shouted.

They did not need the warning. Niall hurriedly led Blossom through the farmyard towards the lane. The two youngest fled. They were a hundred yards down the lane when Niall appeared with Blossom. All heard a crash from the direction of the bullpen, a curse and a yell: "He's out! Hide yourselves!"

Niall, determined that his little brothers' safety came first, shouted to them to climb one of the high banks at the side of the road and shin up one of the trees overhanging the lane if they could. He opened the gate of the next field and led Blossom inside, then stepped back into the lane to intercept the bull before it could reach his brothers. He called and heard an answering shout from Ivan to say they had climbed a ditch, that they were safe. He rejoined Blossom.

All seemed quiet. Niall opened the gate again and stepped into the lane, looked up and down it, saw nothing. Then there was a thundering of hooves around the corner. A moment later an enormous, snorting animal was charging straight at him.

Ivan and Padraic had jumped onto a high ditch further down the lane and had scrambled to its summit, Ivan catching his shorts in the barbed wire. When he had freed himself, the two had a full view of what followed.

Niall whizzed down the lane, big knees pumping. He had flashed past, still in the open, when the bull appeared. It was within twenty yards of him when the boy looked over his shoulder, saw the animal closing the gap, yelled, and plunged into a high bank of nettles. He scrambled over the fence and reached safety as the bull slammed to a halt, bawling. The younger boys, ungrateful brats, began to laugh.

Chapter Thirteen

That evening, as they played chequers and Niall rubbed his stings, they listened to the weather forecast on the wireless in the kitchen. Sunny, with a light breeze, perhaps a shower in the West later, said the weatherman.

It was still light when Padraic went to bed. One of the two big Georgian sash windows in the bedroom was open at the bottom, propped by a book. The sash cord had broken years before. A breeze from the meadows ruffled the worn curtain.

If he sat up in bed, he could see the sea, a distant line on the horizon. As the sun set, the moon came up and the lighthouse began to sweep the corner of the island.

He had seen, from close up, the great light and its apparatus of mirrors and lenses during the previous summer. His father had persuaded one of the fishermen at Ballygeary, the deep water port around the sandy point from Eskerford, to take the family to the lighthouse. The skipper held the contract to use his boat as lighthouse tender, running coal and food and changes of crew. The boat smelt of rotting fish, diesel fumes, and tobacco. Raymy the skipper and the poet smoked in the wheel-house throughout the voyage. Padraic and Ivan were sick. The others, to judge by their colour, were close to it. That was forgotten as they steamed closer, and the lighthouse, an upright white speck when they embarked, loomed tall above them. The rock on which it stood seemed awesome and threatening. The swell, even in this calm, carried the waves high onto the outcrops, where they broke in lazy fingers of foam.

Raymy, member of a heroic lifeboatman family, pointed to another rock, almost submerged in the swell, a hundred yards or so away, north-north-west of the lighthouse. "That's the Gypsy," he shouted above the noise of the engine. "Ninety-nine ships have struck there." They stared at the rock, part of the same reef as the Fascar, as it disappeared and reappeared above the swell. As they watched the waves break over it, they thought of the wrecks lying almost directly beneath them. They could see great lengths of kelp on the edges of the rock, rolling to and fro in the swell, like the beard of a drowned man, and wished they were at home.

They looked up at the towering white lighthouse before they slid over the side of the trawler into the rowing-boat and, hearts in mouths, were rowed across in relays to the jetty on the lighthouse rock, the long, slow swell carrying them up to where the rock was visible, then down into the troughs from where all they could see was the white tower of the lighthouse itself. They landed on the west side, then clambered up half a dozen steps to a platform, past a water tank, then up a slope to the accommodation building, treading the steps cut by some brave spirits in the year that Napoleon had retreated from Moscow. The swell boomed in the blowholes on either side of the path. During the War a drifting mine had washed into one of these and exploded. It did not kill or injure, but the blowhole was enlarged.

The lighthouse-keeper and his mate met them. While their father sat on a rock and smoked – he had been here many times – the keeper led them into the building that buttressed the lighthouse, showed them the cosy space that was their living room, and their spotless sleeping quarters down a passage from it; then into the lighthouse itself, up the narrow circular stone stairs to the light. The stairs seemed to go on for ever and Padraic, with his short legs, gasped for breath when they reached the top. The keeper asked with a smile: "Did you count them?" "Count what?" asked Ivan, as Padraic could not speak. "The steps," said the keeper. "No, we didn't," said Ivan shortly. "There's one fewer step on the way down than there is on the way up," said the keeper. "What d'ye make of that?"

"That can't be right," said Padraic, who had recovered. The keeper was offended for a moment. "Go and count them then," he responded. Padraic and Ivan looked at each other, and shied at making the journey a further three times. Ivan was smart. "We believe you," he said with his winning smile. The keeper relented. "Not a soul (not a *sowl*) has ever got the right answer," he said proudly. "Do *you* know?" asked Ivan. "I might," said the keeper.

To the south-south-west, they could see the point that was the corner of Ireland, six and a quarter miles away. On the opposite side was the entrance to the channel and to the Irish Sea itself with a ship here and there trailing tiny plumes of smoke. The keeper opened a stained chart to show them where the reefs, rocks and lightships were marked, then pointed due east to where, on a day even clearer than today, he sometimes saw very distant peaks, the mountains of Wales, another country. From here to the Smalls, one of the most dangerous stretches of water in the world, was only a little over thirty miles. The narrow channel acted like a great funnel, producing a tidal race of five or even six knots, strong enough to sweep many ships to the rocks, said the keeper. Further down the coast, near the point, the tide rip was even greater, with waves of up to thirty feet in a gale.

He told them how the building of the lighthouse had cost many lives, and how the sea had done its utmost to prevent its construction, sending storm after storm that swept the labourers from the rock. Many had chained themselves to the great blocks of stone that had been hoisted onto the rock to build the structure, and had lain there night after night while the seas broke over them. That had not saved them, said the keeper to the boys, as the blocks had been swept away too, taking the workers with them. Nature finally relented, and the light shone for the first time in the year of Waterloo.

They could hear the boom of the seas on the rock below. "You can feel it shake in a storm," said the keeper. They looked at the great light and its reflectors that shone the beam that swept into their bedroom, then down once more to the Gypsy rock, almost directly below them, which seemed as menacing as before. "Ninety-nine ships sank there," said Padraic wonderingly. "Yes, so 'tis said," said the keeper. "They're still waiting for the hundredth."

He led them down again. Padraic counted the steps carefully. When they reached the bottom of the tortuous stairs, the keeper asked for the count. Ivan said one number, Padraic another. The keeper smiled: "You're both wrong," he said.

When they emerged through the metal lighthouse door they saw the fishing boat standing off, waiting. The tender was ferrying two of the older brothers back and had nearly reached the fishing boat. They walked to where their father was still sitting, reading a pocket-sized hardbound copy of Propertius. "Well," he said, "did you get the number of steps right?" "No," said Ivan. "I think it was a trick." Their father smiled. "If it is, no one has solved it," he said.

They set off on the path to the jetty. A wind was getting up, and the swell was more noticeable. "How long do the keeper and his mate stay on the lighthouse at a time?" asked Ivan suddenly. "Six weeks," said their father, and then: "The German bombers used the light to navigate by during the War. We could hear them from Bayview."

On a wall beside the path lay a big fish. It was a pollack, landed by one of the lighthouse men a few minutes before. Padraic reached up to touch it. The fish, still alive, jerked. Padraic jumped.

They were sick again on the return voyage to Ballygeary in a freshening breeze, but recovered when they stepped ashore. Once on the quay, they looked to see where they had been. The lighthouse was a distant speck. When they reached Prospect, the night was drawing in and the light swept the coast again.

Chapter Fourteen

The sun lit the farm when their mother roused the household, calling impatiently up the stairs to her sons to get out of bed. Benny had already arrived. The smell of frying bacon floated from the kitchen. The horses stood in the yard, hitched to the iron hay machine, mowing bar folded up in its safety position like a bird with a broken wing.

The machine had left the ironworks in Eskerford fifty years before. It was nearly obsolete, but it would do another fifty if called upon. Seventy years before the *Victor* horse-drawn, open-gear mowing machine had been the wonder of its time, exported to all places of the world where grass was cut for hay. It was simple, very reliable, tough as iron, and it was a marvel to the boys who ignored the ploughman's threats and scrambled over it when it arrived.

It had high travelling wheels of iron, six heavy spokes to a wheel, without tyres but with ridges to give grip on slippery ground. A pierced iron seat on a reclining bar was perched behind oilbath and wheels, relieving the horses of the driver's weight. To one side was the mowing or finger bar with its sixteen steel teeth that was lowered to cut. A heavy curved plank at the end of the mowing bar, the swathe board, guided the cut grass into windrows.

When the tractor had arrived, the Eskerford company had tried to meet the challenge and had adapted the same machine, but it looked clumsy and out of place, a duck masquerading as a swan. It did not take, and the firm went into a slow decline, although its iron bicycles, indestructible but too heavy to be ridden up a steepish hill, were still to be seen in the remoter parts of the county.

They trooped through the farmyard after breakfast and down the lane behind Benny. The younger boys carried brimming buckets of water. The horses pulled the hay machine into the Pond Field, iron wheels clicking.

With a quick glance at the sun, Benny took an oilcan from the iron toolbox on the shaft, brushing away the hayseeds as he sought the oiling points, lifting each metal cap on its spring; inserted the nozzle into each, squeezing his thumb on the oilcan's pump action. He undid the catches to the mowing bar, lowering it gently to rest on the ground of the headland, then climbed into the iron seat and gathered his reins. He leaned forward, seat swaying, pulled a long lever to engage the gear, called, "Hubbawf!" to the horses, and the wheels began to click once more, but this time there was the sound of the knife whizzing from side to side inside the bar. When Benny drove it into the edge of the meadow the grass collapsed, felled by an invisible reaper. Hayseeds flew from the mowing bar. Butterflies and other insects rose in alarm. Benny squinted at the line of cut, pulling his horses slightly to the right to adjust his path, and urged them to a faster pace. Soon he had settled into a rhythm, the horses jerking their heads as they grew used to the strain on their collars.

The boys lazed in the sun for a while. At this stage their job was to scatter, with pitchfork or pike, clogged overlays of hay, particularly at the corners of the field, to prevent the mowing bar from jamming. The younger ones ran the occasional errand and brought buckets of water for the horses, the latest score in the Lord's Test match, and a bottle of stout for Benny before lunch. The boys watched it as he pulled the cork, put the bottle to his mouth and drained it, froth dripping from one stubble to another.

Padraic ran behind Benny, well clear of the vibrating teeth of the mowing bar, looking for field mice. The smell of new-mown grass drifted back to him in the bright sunshine. A cuckoo called repeatedly from the Front Field. Haze hung over the distant Bluestairs. The county revelled in a heat wave.

By lunchtime even the cuckoo was quiet. Benny still sat in his swaying seat, guiding the horses in a decreasing parallelogram around the field. His cap was stained with fresh perspiration and he stopped occasionally to wipe his forehead and relight his pipe, squinting into the sun until his crows' feet disappeared for a moment. They broke for lunch, tired but in high spirits, when a third of the field was cut.

The work continued, Benny moving the machine to the next field when he had finished cutting the last, anxious to achieve as much as possible while the weather held. His life at this time of year was an uneasy balance between cutting too soon, before the seed head emerged, and too late, when the seed head hung and the grass became indigestible, turning to cellulose which passed through cattle and left little nourishment behind.

Weather was the constant worry. If rain was in prospect, he would not cut, since his objective was to retain as much nourishment in the hay as the grass contained when it was in flower. Very hot sun also removed part of the nutriment from mown grass, but that was a lesser risk. If there were light rain showers the mown grass would have to be turned with a pitchfork and stood until the wind dried it again, the hay made only when it turned from green grass to a dry brown.

When Benny had finished cutting the two fields he rehitched the horses to the hay gatherer, a tumbling rake whose tines were curved towards the end. It ran along the ground on two curved wooden boards, without wheels, clearing enough ground for the tines to gather the mown grass. When the rake had gathered as much as it could hold, the ploughman lifted the wooden handle, the rake tipped, caught and dumped the grass in a heap, and the next row of tines came into play. In some wet years the mown grass, having been turned by pitchfork to allow the air access, was gathered into small grasscocks and left to dry further, but in this dry summer the grass was left on the ground to dry until it was made directly into haycocks, seven or eight feet tall and equally wide at the bottom.

The poet appeared occasionally, bow-tie undone. He walked across the field to Benny, spoke to him, chatted to his sons, then disappeared up the lane. A few minutes later, they heard the boom of his car as it went down the drive.

Tired though they were, they were in high spirits at lunchtime one day when their father arrived with a welcome visitor off the Dublin train that morning: the musician Séamus Ennis, native Irish speaker, master uilleann piper, singer and tin whistle player, producer of the folk programme *As I Roved Out*, broadcast as a series by the BBC on Sunday mornings.

Visitors to Prospect were relatively rare and were particularly welcome to the boys as a result. During the autumn music festival that brought many great musicians and performers to the town from other parts of the world, the house was full, as the poet had many friends in the musical world, and numerous writers and literary critics from Dublin and from overseas travelled to the town. Other visitors would appear occasionally, generally from Dublin, like the wandering, white-bearded Pope

O'Mahony, who was as happy in summertime under a hedge as he was in a bed. They enjoyed the visits from London of Bill and Sandra Crossley-Taylor, Bill a former Coldstream Guards officer whose shoes carried a guardsman's deep polish that the poet envied. At first the youngest boys found one or two of their visitors a little serious, particularly the older poet with the long face and black hat who came each year with his wife, but they were impressed by the regard that their father had for him, grew to like him, and were sorry when he left.

They liked Maurice Fridberg's visits very much, as the friendly Dubliner knew their appetite for books and arrived with a car load of them without warning, but the visitor who fascinated them most was Ernie O'Malley, art critic and revolutionary. The boys' mother warned them not to stare at the visitor's gloved hand, explaining in a whisper that his fingernails had been torn out when he was tortured by the Black-and-Tans, but it was the fact that three bullets from the Civil War were still lodged in his body, like Buck Duane in one of their favourite Zane Greys, that held them spellbound. They tried not to stare at his hand, but the friendly gaze of the man with the wounds showed that he was used to it.

Sometimes they could not resist adding a little extra to the excitement that arose when a visitor came to stay. On the kitchen dresser stood the Staffordshire pottery bust of a heavily rouged and formidable Victorian or Edwardian lady. It had been left at Prospect by the previous owners, who had probably grown tired of the enigmatic half smile of the creature and decided that the bust was at home in Prospect, in the same spirit as they had left a sizeable plaster statue of St Francis which had been broken during a particularly rowdy fight between the boys. The pieces still lay in a corner of the attic.

The family's initial instinct was to throw out the lady, or to use her for rifle practice, but the boys' mother had decided to keep her, a strange household goddess, and had named her Liz.

During the music festival of the previous year, Prospect had entertained one of the boys' favourite visitors, the composer Freddie May, who sang for them and drank whiskey with their father late into the night. Before they went to bed Garry and Conor had taken Liz and placed her in Freddie's bed, face sideways on the pillow, with the sheet pulled up to her chin. They waited until Freddie went to bed, listened expectantly outside his door, and ran when they heard the yell.

Back on this hot haymaking day, when lunch was over, the musician called to them: "*Éist! Éist!* Listen to me," then sang, not an Irish song as they had expected, but a folk song in a Wiltshire burr:

> *The vly, the vly,*
> *The vly be on the turmut.*
> *'Tis all me eye*
> *Fer I to try*
> *To keep vly off the turmut.*

A fly was a *fry* in Benny's vocabulary. As the boys crowded back into his cart and it rattled down the lane towards the Pond Field, the ploughman sang:

> *The fry, the fry,*
> *The fry be on the turnip...*

◆◆

They were very tired at the end of that day and could

scarcely eat at first, but the recovery powers of youth soon made the kitchen ring again. Chinese chequers were set aside as the musician played his tin whistle and sang.

Padraic was sent to bed before dark. His window was wedged open. From the Front Field came the rasp of a corncrake as it walked hesitantly along the headland beyond the palm tree. It called until the moon came up and the palm leaves began to rustle in the evening breeze. The local people called it the bane crake or, occasionally, the meadow crake. To the poet, who had heard it called the *traonach* in his native West, the bird was the symbol of early summer.

The music was still drifting up the broad stairs of Prospect when Padraic drifted off to sleep. His father was singing of a Galway hooker:

> *Oh! She's neat,*
> *And she's sweet,*
> *She's a beauty in every line.*
> *The Queen of Connemara...*

Next morning the haymaking began again and continued without a break until the final haycock stood. Prospect's green, waving meadows became fields with light brown haycocks dotted about them. The haymakers worked on Sunday, since the church gave dispensation when hay had to be saved. The poet politely ignored the church, and refused to allow it to interfere with his life. Sermons from the pulpits of the churches of Eskerford passed him by because he was not present, but he did not attempt to persuade his wife and sons to follow his example. Garry had driven his mother and brothers to Mass as usual, Benny had ridden in on his bike, and afterwards the work had begun again.

The haycocks would lie in the sun for six or seven weeks until they were ready to be moved to the barn, timing that would be decided by Benny who would reach his hand deep inside, pull out a wisp of hay and sniff it, testing it for heat, a guide to fermentation or mustiness. The younger boys looked forward to the joys of jumping in fresh hay, of building little tunnels as it was packed into a barn, and to the sweet smell that clung to everything.

They would use the barn as an outdoor reading room in daylight throughout the year, settling companionably into the hay with their books, pockets full of apples, Beauty of Bath and Cox's Orange Pippins, while rain drummed on the galvanized iron roof. In that barn they voyaged with Slocum, searched for King Solomon's mines, fought with Hornblower, escaped with Edmond Dantès, spied from *Dulcibella*, stalked the temple leopard with Corbett, and were chased by Mormons across the sage of Utah. It was a well-travelled barn.

Chapter Fifteen

Niall was taking Padraic to fish for bass on the Eskerford river. Conor and Ivan prepared to cycle to the Edenbeg, a little river on the other side of Eskerford, to fish for trout. Garry planked *Snipe*. He had built his own steam-box to mould the planks, some of which, with a slight feeling of guilt, he had stripped from the headquarters of his flying column. Brian was in Dublin for a few days, preparing for a permanent job in journalism in the autumn. The boys' mother was hanging her washing on the clothes-line that stretched across a corner of the Paddock. Their father worked in the sun, glossy white head bent over his typewriter laid on the seat of a kitchen chair.

Niall had to dig his bait, which entailed a bicycle ride into Eskerford, over the bridge on the other side of the town, to the rough shingled ground at the water's edge at low tide. Padraic would travel sideways on the crossbar. The bike was loaded with a spade; a bucket; two short rods with light red whippings – for which Niall had used his mother's nail varnish; a bag with reels, nylon fishing line, weights, scissors, hooks and other paraphernalia; a bottle of diluted orange juice; and a stack of corned-beef-mixed-with-onion sandwiches. The salt air gave the boys a keen hunger.

They rode the three bikes down the drive to the road where they kept in single file, into the town, past rows of low, shabby houses, to the square by the north railway station; turning left towards the bridge. They crossed the estuary here, riding around the tar barrels placed to slow motor and horse traffic; the bridge was old, and could take little stress. The boat club lay upstream. Above them, they could see the estuary with its reeded banks; below, the harbour.

When they crossed the bridge they parted. Conor and Ivan would keep to the main road for a while, while Niall, his little brother on the crossbar, turned right towards the harbour, near the strand named after the Dutch skipper of the ship that had transported Cromwell's slaves to the West Indies, or, for those who preferred the alternative explanation, the Dutch shipbuilder whose yard was here three centuries before. Niall stopped, Padraic hopped off the crossbar, and Niall laid his bike on the ground. Seagulls were everywhere, circling and swooping overhead, cries filling the skies. Twenty yards along the strand lay the wreck of a wooden ship, blackened ribs protruding from the sand like a bison's skeleton. They took spade and bucket and they set off across the shingle until they arrived at the sandy foreshore, where Niall sought the tell-tale deposits the lugworm left after the tide receded. A warm, salty breeze came from the harbour, mixed with the smell of coal tar. The town gasworks was to windward on the other side.

He found the tiny sandhills topped with coiled trails and began to dig. Padraic watched as Niall turned over the first spadeful of sand and grit. Nothing. The next produced two or three big, wriggling worms. "Good," Niall said. "Put those in the bucket. Put some sand in first." Padraic did so in time to see the next spadeful yield the same again. Niall tried the next miniature sandheap; more lugworms. The bucket began to fill.

When Niall decided they had enough, they set off back across the shingle towards the bike. Niall placed the handle of the bucket over the handlebars, then held the bike upright. Padraic hopped on the bar, Niall mounted and, wobbling slightly, they set off towards the road. Once there, Niall began to pedal harder, big knees pumping. They had about two miles to cycle, or Niall did while Padraic talked.

They travelled back across the bridge and turned right, parallel to the river, on the main road to Inish Gortaídh. Edwardian villas with gardens rolling down to the road lay on their left, the river on their right. The occasional car or lorry overtook them, swinging to avoid the laden bike. Niall's strong legs were beginning to ache when they reached the bridge at Carrig and stopped to rest.

The river entered a wide gorge here. On the opposite bank, on a high rock, a ruined Norman castle, built soon after the waves of invasions down the coast in 1169, its walls covered in ivy, guarded the crossing. A steep hill soared on the left on their side of the river, a tall monument to the soldiers of the Crimean War at its summit. On the bank beside the bridge was a tavern, the Bridge Inn, with a dubious reputation. It was well situated, with a pretty but neglected garden creeping down to the river. The opposite bank was visible for a quarter of a mile or so upriver, giving a view of parkland above the steep, heavily wooded slopes that plunged down to the water. A light cross-breeze brought the estuarine smells of ooze, mud, decaying vegetation and salt from a tide that was just past the ebb.

They were not in a hurry, as it would be half an hour before the tide began to turn. They sat on the low wall overlooking the river, watching the salmon fishermen begin to stir. Downstream, the river curved gently to the left. Above the curve, on the right bank, they could see the boreen that led up to the steep hill, down which flowed the Carrick. Above it were the graveyard and the Haunted House. Above that again, to the left, the ground sloped up to a hill, a strange rock just below its summit, probably an erratic from a glacier. This was their old friend, the Tortoise Rock.

It was very still. The boys could clearly hear the voices of the cot fishermen shouting that it was time to man the boat, or *bo-at*, and would so-and-so hurry up mendin' the feckin' net or they would miss the tide altogether.

It was time for the boys to move on. Padraic vaulted backwards onto the crossbar, Niall stood on the pedals, then settled in his saddle. They continued upriver, past the bridge and its tavern, passing under the Crimea monument, hidden from sight by the steep outcrop above, and on past a long hedge of escallonia. Concealed in this hedge were secret steps that led to the gardens of the big house above, steps that Garry had discovered when he had visited the gardens.

The railway line ran behind the hedge. The passing trains were invisible, but their steam was not. At night the sparks could be seen against the dark bluff. The trains whistled before they entered a short tunnel under the bluff; a sound that they could hear clearly in the kitchen at Prospect on anything save the foulest night; the magical sound of the Dublin train, the sound that carried the mysteries of the city.

Niall halted less than a mile from the bridge. The road ran alongside the river without walls or other obstructions. On the right, a grassy clearing lined with a rough bank of rocks lay next to the river. This was where they would fish.

Niall took each rod in turn and assembled it. He clamped the fixed-spool reels to the butts, paid out the nylon through the rings, tied a dropper two feet from the end and a one-inch hook to the dropper. He took two one-ounce lead weights and tied them to the ends of the lines. He had cast them in his own sand mould, melting the lead from a piece of old drainpipe in a pot on the Aga.

He took a lugworm from the bait bucket and threaded it up the hook, ignoring the sandy ooze and blood; then another. He lifted the first rod and went to the edge of the river.

"Stand back," he instructed his brother. He pulled back the bail-arm of the reel and swung the rod over his shoulder, casting the bait seventy-five yards into the river; held the line for a minute, paying it out until he was satisfied that the weight had settled on the sandy bottom, then wound the handle until the bail-arm clicked over. He checked the tension on the reel, gave several turns to the wing-nut at the top of the spool to loosen it, then placed the butt of the rod between two rocks, checking the tension again; then picked up the other rod and did the same. Upriver, they could see a heron stepping cautiously into the water, a comical figure, one long leg cocked as it considered the next step.

The boys settled to wait, lying with their backs to the warm rocks in the sun, gazing at the river which was around a quarter of a mile wide at this point. There was a disused quarry on the other side, a few hundred yards upstream. In the woods above it, rooks circled.

Every few moments Niall's eye would check the rods, watching for the tell-tale jerk, followed by another, that would signal a bass fresh from the sea coming up to feed on the tide. The river was noticeably higher, lapping the edge of the rocky wall a few feet below.

They heard the sounds of oars and the echoes through the hulls as the cot fishermen appeared, rowing upstream. Niall squinted at them. "I think they've seen a salmon," he said suddenly. There were two cots in view, one practically opposite, the other still a hundred yards downstream, the oarsman in each rowing hard but steadily.

Niall shouted: "Salmon!" and Padraic glimpsed a silvery object breaking the surface. The fishermen had seen it too, as a shout went up at the same time. They were rowing more quickly, shooting past the spot where the salmon had risen, towards the boys' side of the river. The first cot was making rapidly for the shore, while the other stood off, apparently under orders not to interfere.

When it reached the shore a man jumped from the boat and reached back over the transom, pulling the end of the net with him. Two men remained in the boat. One rowed; the other paid out the net, leaving a line of bobbing corks on the water to buoy it. The boat described a wide half-circle in the river, turning back towards the shore, most of the net trailing in the tide.

When the boat reached the shore again the remaining two men jumped out and splashed in their black thigh waders to the shore, pulling the other end of the net with them. While the first man stood, the other two hauled the net.

At first Niall and Padraic thought it was empty, but as the bag of the draft came closer they saw a silvery splash; then another, behind it. "They've caught two salmon!" Niall exclaimed, glancing quickly at their own rods.

He was nearly right. The fishermen had caught three, all grilse, fresh-run fish, pure silver, that had spent their first winter at sea, having left the river as smolts a year or more before. They had probably re-entered the river of their birth that very day. The boys watched the fishermen knock them on the head in succession with a wooden club – the handle of an old cot oar – then re-embark. Throughout this a conversation took place with the men in the other cot who were clearly being told, with many jeers, that they could feck off and fish somewhere else.

The boys settled down again as the sounds of the cots rowing downstream receded. The river rose steadily. Insects droned as noon approached. Both boys began thinking of the sandwiches in Niall's bag, but if they ate them they would be hungry again in the early afternoon.

Hunger still gnawed at them when Padraic saw Niall's rod jerk once, then bend wildly as the strain came on the line. "Fish!" he shouted. Niall rose but walked, rather than ran, to his rod.

"It's a bloody eel," he said grouchily.

"How do you know?" asked Padraic. Niall picked up his rod, which was bending steadily, and began to reel. "By the way it pulled the rod," he said, plainly in a bad temper. He hated eels. They stole his bait and twisted the dropper terribly around the line so that weight, hook, and line had to be patiently disentangled; sometimes even had to be cut and everything retied and rebaited.

Hook and bait inched up onto the mud. Something brown and long writhed horribly at the end, twisting itself into knots as it wrapped its flattish tail around the line. "I told you," said Niall disgustedly. "Just my luck." He lifted the rod quickly as the writhing mass came up over the rocks towards him. Then he put his boot firmly on the eel to prevent it from turning its body, slippery and glistening, around the line again. "Pass me the sheath knife," he called to Padraic. He reached down to the wriggling eel and cut off its head. Then he kicked the writhing body into the grass. He pushed the head off the hook with the blunt side of the knife and kicked the head after the body. "That'll serve *you* right," he said, his first note of satisfaction since he had seen the rod bend.

He was rebaiting his hook when Padraic called again, as his rod had jerked twice and then again, "that's a bass!"

Niall shouted, "That's no bloody eel," excitement mixing with certainty. "What do I do?" yelled Padraic. "Pick up the rod and reel steadily," said Niall. "Don't jerk it!"

Padraic did as he was told, lifting the rod shakily and beginning to reel. He felt the pull of the fish as it tried to run. "Keep reeling!" said Niall, since bass are not salmon and do not need to be allowed to run far. "Here, let me feel it," he said, taking the rod from his brother and lifting the point. He could feel a strong pull. "That's a lulu!" he said. "A bloody good fish. Keep reeling."

Padraic kept reeling. The nylon line, under tension, began to whine. The rod bent further. "Ease off a little," Niall said, standing at his side. Padraic did so, reeling slowly. The fish was not far from the shore.

Its head broke water, a large bass, around four or five pounds. They both shouted. A second or two later the fish's head disappeared as the hook jerked from his jaw.

It happened too abruptly for Padraic to understand immediately what had happened. One moment he had been reeling in the first fish he had caught – they did not count sticklebacks, or the little fish trapped in rock pools when the tide left the beach – but in the next he held a rod that had straightened mysteriously, pressure gone.

When he did understand, he was close to tears. Niall tried to comfort him. "There'll be more, don't worry. Here, let's get a fresh lugworm on and start again quickly. There's probably a great run of bass coming up on the tide."

Padraic, bitterly disappointed, obeyed. Niall threaded fresh worms onto the hook and the bait went whirling out into the river again. They settled back on the rock, Padraic still deeply downcast. "It was just bad luck. You didn't do anything wrong," Niall assured him gruffly.

Within half an hour, as the fish that Niall had hoped for failed to take their baits, hunger began to torture them again. "I'm starving," Padraic complained. He seemed to have forgotten his lost fish. The sun had passed the zenith. Niall deliberated. "We'll wait another twenty minutes," he announced finally. They waited. Niall pointed to the heron that was still patiently waiting at its spot in the water by a broken bough covered in weed and told Padraic stories about Quosk, improvising as he went and conscious throughout of the sandwiches within his reach.

At length, Niall announced: "OK, let's eat." Padraic jumped to his feet as Niall lifted the bag and took out the sandwiches in the paper wrapping. Padraic saw the big crusty doorsteps, grabbed the top sandwich and began to eat wildly. Niall admonished him for his poor manners, but was soon doing the same. They drank from the old tin mugs that Niall had brought for the orange squash. There were still three or four sandwiches left and Padraic was beginning to bulge when Niall's rod jerked twice.

Niall still had a sandwich in his mouth when he ran to the rod and lifted it. "Another lulu!" he shouted while Padraic jumped up and down – although he was a little sad that it was not *his* rod that had bent. Niall began to reel steadily, rod tip high. When the fish pulled hard, line slid out from the spool through the bail-arm, but Niall left the tension as it was. He would be patient, particularly in view of the loss of Padraic's fish.

The bass began to tire. When they saw its head break the water Padraic shouted: "It's as big as mine – no, bigger!" Niall drew the fish slowly on the shore. Then he ran to his bag, took out his home-made priest and hit the fish on the back of the neck. He put the priest back in his bag and took out a weighing scales. The fish was five and a half pounds, Niall's heaviest to date.

They admired it after Niall had rebaited his hook and sent the bait out into the river again; a beautiful fish, with a dark area down its back to its broad tail that nature had given it to conceal it from herons and gulls.

The afternoon wore on. They saw another chase by the cotsmen, this time on the other side of the river. Again, this seemed to be successful, judging by the tiny splashes in the net as they hauled it, but they could not see how many salmon had been netted.

The tide was turning. Niall began to think of packing up because of the uphill journey home. Padraic's rod jerked again – twice – and began to bend. "Bass!" Niall shouted, as Padraic eagerly picked up the rod and began to reel. The fish came in easily. It was not a monster, but it weighed three and a half pounds, and it was the first fish that Padraic had landed. He danced around the bass, watched by his grinning brother, until Niall said it was time to go.

Niall had already cut lengths of binder twine, slipped them through the gills of both fish, and tied them to his handlebars. He stripped the reels from the rods, threw his lugworms into the river since they would not keep, packed the rods and the rest of the gear, and put his fishing bag on the carrier over the back wheel. They set off, past the bridge and the tavern. On their right was a series of ponds and marshes. Through these, the little Carrick entered the main river. Beside it was a boreen – scarcely more than a dusty track – running at right angles to the main river. This was the shortest way home. Retracing their path into Eskerford would mean they would have to ride two sides of the triangle. The drawback was that the hill was so steep that the cyclist was forced to choose either to ride at walking pace, or to walk the bike up the hill.

Either way, they had to pass the old graveyard at the Carrick and its spreading oak, but this time they would pass it in daylight. They walked quickly by, with darting glances at the oak and the cemetery's iron gates, then past

Belmont where they remounted and freewheeled down to Malone's Forge. Then it was a walk again, up the steep hill with the Tortoise Rock on their left. When they reached the top they had an easy run home, passing Parle's farm, then the Birdless Woods below them on their right, before reaching the crossroads, turning left and freewheeling downhill, full of high spirits, past McCann's shop and the Grove of Prospect until they reached the front gates.

An old black car boomed up the road from Eskerford. It turned into the gates behind them and stopped. "Aren't you great boys!" their father shouted from the driver's window. "Who caught that big bass?"

When they reached the house, they found Conor and Ivan ahead of them. Conor showed them a creel filled with seven trout, the largest more than a pound.

They ate the fish that evening. Conor gutted and cleaned the trout, Niall the bass. The fish were fried quickly and eaten with new potatoes dug hours earlier from the Orchard. That night Padraic dreamt of eels.

Chapter Sixteen

Next morning the poet walked down the wooden quays of Eskerford in the sunshine. A light south-westerly breeze blew across the harbour towards the Crow, the northerly point of the harbour's entrance. He stopped to talk with his friend Seumas Galvin, a man of sixteen stone who sailed every hour he could spare from his tree and plant nursery. A train puffed past them towards the south station, the boards grumbling under its weight.

They looked out at the harbour as the steam blew in wisps about them. It was almost flat calm, empty of shipping; nothing but small trawlers and a few pleasure craft.

For a moment, the poet saw a different picture as they looked, vividly recalling the storm of the previous winter, a hurricane that had split a great tanker in two, thirty miles or so from where they stood.

He had written about it in his newspaper column; had described in detail how the Eskerford lifeboat had answered the distress call, and he had been greatly moved by the heroism of the Doogans, Walshes and Wickhams who manned her; men, he wrote, born with a silver spume (the poet loved a pun) in their mouths at the Battery across the harbour before the sea engulfed it.

The lifeboat, steaming past the light from Fascar Rock through a storm that hit Force Twelve at times, in conditions that every seaman dreaded, had found the forepart of the tanker with the help of a Royal Navy aircraft-carrier, which stood off, arc lights shining on the wreck. Because of the flying scud and spray, the coxswain had seen the wreck only at the last moment, and had put his helm down instantly and cleared the jagged edges of steel with only feet to spare. Seven men were aboard the wreck, including the master and the mate.

To approach by the book, from the lee of the wreck would have been suicidal. The broken steel tail would have sunk the lifeboat as she manoeuvred alongside, so the cox'n stood off, circling, satisfied that the wreck would float for some time, that the men on board were more comfortable than he; waiting for daylight, shutting down one of the engines to save fuel when he could, he and his mates vomiting copiously for the first time since childhood, sick as drunks, their boat thrown in every direction, yet keeping station, eyes fixed on the wreck in the lights from the carrier, signal lamps flashing through the storm.

When grey dawn came they made their run, ignoring the book and approaching from windward, laying her alongside the towering hull, engines churning, ready to run if there was a sudden change of wind; took off all seven as they scrambled down a rope ladder, and made for home, the carrier flashing its congratulations.

The poet had followed all this on the night as best he could, one ear to the wireless, the other to his office telephone as he listened to the latest news from his friend Eugene, owner of Black's Hotel and secretary of the lifeboat association. When the news arrived, he breathed a great sigh of relief, then grinned at the thought of the celebrations that would follow as Eskerford, old sea town, honoured its heroes. He would help that celebration, he thought as he lit a cigarette, and would expand it through his column to include the whole country if he could. And he had.

◆━━◆

A ship was berthed this summer morning at the quays:
the *Farlogue*, for which the poet had a particular affection.
In the early part of the war, with a large *ÉIRE* painted on her
side to proclaim her nationality, she had saved an
abandoned British ship bombed by the Germans off Fascar
Rock and beached her near Eskerford. Later, in a storm in
the Bay of Biscay she had rescued a number of German
sailors whose ships had been sunk by the British; had
ignored calls from both nations and brought the sailors
back to be interned in Ireland. A few months before this she
had been accidentally strafed by the RAF. Three of the crew,
including the captain – a man the poet knew well – had been
badly injured. She had been halted several times at night by
menacing U-boat captains who had interrogated her by
megaphone (a frightening experience, her crew had told the
poet on their return) and allowed her to steam away.

The poet remembered other wartime incidents. German
bombers had mistaken a village a few miles away for a
Welsh railway terminus and bombed it. Three people had
died. On another occasion he saw a German Heinkel
bomber falling in flames after an attack by RAF fighters,
and drove towards the cloud of smoke near the beach. The
locals reached it before him and pulled the dead Germans
from the cockpit and fuselage. When the poet arrived he
saw, to his shock and disgust, that the German pilot's ring
finger was missing.

In a different era, a young man had sailed, probably from
near the very spot where the poet now stood, to found what
would become the greatest navy in the world. There were
plans, the poet knew, to erect a bronze statue to him on the

Crescent Quay, close to the poet's office.

He strolled past the *Farlogue* without stopping, but with an affectionate glance. She would have to be cleared before she could discharge her cargo, but Horgan would take care of that; would enjoy doing so. He turned up towards the North Main Street, called in to his friend May at the newsagent, bought *The Irish Times, The Listener, New Statesman, Horse & Hound* (he was a keen racegoer) and, for Brian and Garry, both boxing fans, *The Ring*. He left and walked to the general provision merchants near the opposite end of the town. He met many people he knew as he went, but greeted those he did not if they looked in his direction. Not to do so would be impolite, just as it was rude not to salute anyone he saw from his car.

At the shop he bought a carton of Churchman cigarettes and talked to the owner. "Do you remember that war surplus stuff you bought?" he asked. The owner looked dark. "I do," he said. "I still have a lot of it." The poet asked: "Wasn't there a lot of bully-beef?" The owner replied: "There was, and I've still got that too."

"I might buy a few cans of that from you," said the poet. "The boys are going on a river trip for a few weeks. Can I have a look?"

"You can," said the owner and led him into a store-room at the back of the shop. The poet inspected the stack of cans on a shelf in a corner. There were several dozen large rectangular cans, each containing around half a stone of bully-beef, rations for the soldiers in the desert or for the invasion of Normandy. None was rusty. Although it was more than ten years old it would not have spoiled. They agreed a price. He bought a dozen or so cans and agreed to pick it up a few weeks later. The boys might grow tired of bully-beef, but they would not starve. He left and walked to the Cot Safe.

During one hard winter of the War, everything scarce or rationed, one of the fishermen from this little sea shelter had taken him punt-gunning.

The north and south sides of the harbour were tidal marshes. Beyond them lay polders of reclaimed land below low-water level. Long walls, built in the previous century, walls high enough to contain spring tides, dammed sea from polders. Canals and great ditches, cut in the reclaimed land, drained surface fresh water into an open tank. On the north side a great centrifugal pump, miracle of Victorian engineering with factory chimney and engine house, emptied the fresh water into the harbour. The open, low land of the polders, known as the Slobs, was remarkably fertile.

Nature was defied; nature flourished. More than two hundred different species of wildfowl and waders, many of them winter visitors, found the habitat perfect. Eskerford harbour, its entrance only half a mile wide, was protected by the lines of sand dunes running north and south that faced the sea. Inside was shallow water, with mud banks exposed at low tide. Food was plentiful in the shallows, on mud banks and on the sea-grass that grew there; food in freshwater cuts, on reclaimed land, and in the reedbeds of the estuary. These were winter quarters to migrants or native birds on a scale that made international ornithologists twitch.

Late autumn to spring, thousands of birds arrived to winter here, the warmest part of the island. For the Greenland white-fronted geese, greylags, shovellers, whooper swans, snow-geese, brent-geese, teal, widgeon and pochards the harbour was a haven.

Sea-grass, otherwise known as widgeon- or eel-grass, grew in spring and summer on the flats of ooze, the flats known locally as *slimes*, on the edges of the harbour. At the height of summer the grass was two to three feet high, and the wildfowl fed on the tiny snails or periwinkles that clung to the grass, running their beaks up and down it before moving on to the next clump. The sea-grass died each winter, to be washed ashore as *woar*.

Wildfowlers from the area and from other countries pursued the birds from the beginning of September until the end of January. For many, it was their living; for others, sport. Over the years the wildfowlers developed equipment and skills to reap the harvest that nature flighted to them.

They developed a punt, known as a float, a cousin of their own cot, which carried a long gun – a cannon, with modern grapeshot – in which they stealthily approached the birds after the ebb, by day or night. It was in one of these floats that the poet punted on a cold winter's day, regretting his weakness in accepting the fisherman's invitation.

He had cycled, as the shortage of petrol and tyres cut car use to a minimum, to the Cot Safe before dawn one windy morning in early December. The wind gusted from the north-west across the harbour when he arrived, but he kept the rendezvous; only the east wind kept the fishermen at home. He was cold when he reached the Cot Safe and was relieved to see a black kettle hissing on a stove that glowed red when he wheeled his bike into the warehouse. His friend greeted him. The poet smoked his first cigarette of the day as he drank a tin mug of tea and looked about him.

He had seen the floats, puny things, outside in the Cot Safe, quailing when he gauged their size and closeness to the waterline. He studied the harbour in what little light there was. At least he could not see breaking waves.

Inside the warehouse it was sheltered, nothing like as cold as it was outside. It smelled of paint, tar, oil, old nets, and stale fish. The walls were hidden by nets, cork buoys, ropes, and great trawl boards. There were aisles of trawler gear on the floor, gathered over several generations; skiffs and praams scattered about; rudders and centreboards; nets everywhere. The poet found it homely, comforting. Whatever the weather, there was continuing life inside this big shed.

"It's not a bad morning, but a bit too windy," said the fisherman, bringing him back to this cold dawn as he led him outside to the Cot Safe. The poet, shivering, summoned up what enthusiasm he could, then examined the punts. They looked tiny, far too fragile to take to the water on a day like this. Each was around fifteen feet long, flat-bottomed, decked, with a coaming running along the ends of the cockpit. Bow and stern ends were curved, like canoes. The sides were straight, like walls, with no sign of flare. Each, at its broadest, was little more than two feet in beam, and the poet guessed that its height above the waterline could not be more than nine or ten inches. On the water, with the weight of its single crew member sinking it lower, it would present the slightest of profiles to the feeding birds.

The poet had heard that this was a common design. Similar floats, with their long guns, were to be seen in the shallow waters of East Anglia in Britain, floats owned by rough North Sea men who defied challengers from the foreshore with the retort:

> *This is the law I quotes*
> *For the flats where the sea-grass roots:*
> *Where the tide flows, I floats.*
> *And where I floats, I shoots.*

The fisherman returned to the big shed and staggered out with something that looked like a cross between a cannon and a drainpipe. It appeared to be around nine or ten feet long and it narrowed towards the muzzle. It was painted grey and it had a set of trunnions towards the breech-end. They splashed across the mud of the Cot Safe together, the poet thankful that he had managed to borrow thigh waders the night before. The fisherman laid the gun on a narrow thwart at the after end from where it ran forward through the prow, where a gap was shaped to hold it in place. The trunnions slotted into position on a wooden support shaped to accommodate the broader barrel. From behind the support ran two thick ropes which were stretched over the bow, then knotted under the tiny prow. The boat itself would take the recoil, the poet guessed, the float shooting backwards as the gun kicked. It did not appear possible to change the direction of the shot by swinging the gun from side to side. The poet guessed that the float would swing instead, and the fisherman confirmed it. "You point the float to point the gun," he said.

"John, how d'you raise or lower it to change the distance of the shot?" asked the poet, cupping his hands in the wind to light his second cigarette.

"Wait and I'll show you," said the fisherman. He splashed across the mud of the Cot Safe, the poet behind him.

Inside the warehouse, the fisherman picked up a wooden implement that looked like the bridge of a giant's violin, clearly home-made, painted the same colour as the float. From one end of the bridge ran part of the handle of a sweeping brush. "This is the elevator," the fisherman explained. "Put it under the gun, and use the handle to push it backward or forward. Pull it back towards you, and the gun fires lower, and so on. I've a notch cut in the gun itself for a shot of fifty yards. All I have to do is match the elevator to the notch. It's a simple yoke, but it does the job. There's others that use their weight."

"What d'you mean?" the poet asked, handing back the elevator.

"If you want to raise the shot, you just sit further back in the stern, get your weight there, like," said the fisherman. "And if you want to lower it, sit as far for'ard as you can behind the gun. But we like the elevator better." The poet was thankful that he would man the float that would not carry a gun. He began to relax. These floats had been developed over many decades – over centuries – and the only casualty had been at night, seventy or eighty years before, when one float had fired on another in the darkness, mistaking the other for a flock of birds. One man had died.

The poet had heard many stories about the wildfowlers of the east coast since he had arrived at Eskerford. The fishermen had told him of one who had lived alone on the Crow – a lonely, desolate spot, even in summer – who was known as Robinson Crusoe, and of another, a woman with one arm who had become a legend because of the enormous bags she shot.

There was a rich market for wildfowl during the hungry War years, with a brace of mallard fetching up to sixteen shillings, more than half a week's wages for many. Some of the cheapest eating places in the town served something they claimed to be wildfowl, under the umbrella name of *gráinneog*, Irish for a hedgehog. It was almost certainly seagull.

The fisherman returned from the shed, loaded with wooden items. One was a pole ten or eleven feet long, with a fork on the end, the other a shorter version. There were three paddles. One was of a standard length, the others – a pair – short and stubby. "This is the setting pole," said the fisherman, gesturing at the longer tool, a pole with two prongs of darker wood – probably oak for toughness, the poet guessed – screwed on opposite sides into the bottom of the shaft. "We use that for poling in the deeper water. The prongs stop it getting stuck in the mud. Otherwise we use the big paddle. When we're close to the birds we use the little ones. They're called the creeping paddles. D'you know Chummy Byrne?"

"I do," said the poet.

"He uses an Indian paddle – big hickory job they use in canoes in Canada." He hurried off, since it was full dawn, the ebb with only a short while to run. He returned with poles and paddles for the poet's punt. Across the harbour, in the grey light, the poet could see flocks of wildfowl flighting in on the wind.

When the fisherman returned again, he carried the breech end of the punt gun, an old canvas bag, and a shotgun that showed signs of wear.

The breech end of the punt gun was a stubby piece of wood, hollowed to hold the steel breech into which the cartridge would be inserted before they set off. Heavy threads indicated that the breech end would be then screwed into the barrel, completing the gun, a Holland and Holland, the world's finest gunmakers.

A steel ring protruded from the back end of the breech. The fisherman explained that this was the cocking mechanism, the gun's hammer in effect: pull the ring back, and a spring cocked the gun. A wire ran from the cocking ring through a hole in the wooden cover, to hang below the breech end, clearly the lanyard that was pulled to fire the gun.

He opened the bag to show the cartridges. The poet had seen them made; had seen the fisherman's cheerful little sons, George and Laurence – clearly future punt-gunning addicts – rolling shot on a surface covered in black lead, smoothing them into perfect spheres. The shot was made by boiling a lump of lead, then pouring it down a long, hollowed stick into a bucket of cold water where it cooled in little, spherical drops, after which it was riddled in a sieve, the smallest shot falling through to be smoothed by the boys.

Each cartridge was almost a foot long; the brass base, made to order in an engineering shop, one and five-eighth inches in diameter. It held four and a half ounces of black gunpowder and twenty-three ounces of single BB shot, wrapped into a greased brown paper cylinder, gummed at the join and taped at the top. The primer went in first, nestling in the brass base, then the powder, followed by a wad of oakum, greased to increase compression, a cardboard cylinder on top; then the shot, topped by a little paper; crude but deadly.

They put their sandwiches and thermos flasks in the sterns of the floats. The poet carefully stepped onto the central line of the float and sat on the thwart. The punt sank alarmingly in the water, leaving only a few inches of freeboard. "Don't worry," the fisherman said, eyeing the poet. "You're safe enough. We're very sheltered here." He took the breech end, selected one of the cartridges, inserted it into the breech, screwed the breech to the barrel, then tied a piece of sacking loosely over the barrel to protect it from spray.

They set off. Their objective was the slimes on the south side of the harbour, but, the fisherman explained as they left the Cot Safe, the wind direction would force them to pole the floats to the north-east at first, to keep them far to windward of the birds. Once well past that line they would pole inshore, then double back, allowing the turning tide to carry them up to the slimes. He would have liked a brighter day as the ideal approach was with the sun behind them. The birds might be nervous, he said, as they did not feed well in a gale. This was not a gale, but there was enough wind to prevent the birds from settling as well as he would wish. Duck scented humans quickly. Geese were not as sensitive, but all wildfowl constantly looked for movement in the vicinity, even when feeding from the sea-grass.

The fisherman paddled past the half-horseshoe of the Cot Safe wall until they reached deeper water. Then he stood, knees bent, and switched to the long setting pole, using an action that the poet found intriguing. He swung the pole without turning his body, bringing it forward for its entire length, placing it on the muddy bottom, then lifting it out once more, again without turning his body. The poet did his best to do the same. He had punted in Cootehill twenty years before, and enough of the action returned to him to enable him to avoid making a fool of himself, but he envied his friend's smooth, unhurried movements.

They poled on, the wind driving the clouds across the harbour but scarcely ruffling the surface of the brown water.

As they pushed through the shallow harbour past the mudbanks, the day grew brighter and the wind keener. The poet was grateful for the two heavy woollen jerseys he wore beneath his oilskins. He could hear the distant whistling of the birds, and watched the view broaden as they entered the more open space of the harbour.

The fisherman had explained earlier that the safety rules adopted since the accident meant that, at night, the floats could only approach the birds from the leeward side. During the day the rules did not apply, which was just as well as an approach from leeward would not have been possible that morning.

After half an hour they were abeam of the birds. They went on for another twenty minutes until the wind was safely behind them, then turned inshore, swinging around until the floats pointed towards the sea-grass where the birds fed, entering the little channels between the mudbanks, channels the locals called *pills*. The fisherman switched to the bigger paddle as the pills grew shallower. After passing another series of cold, dripping mudbanks, through short-cuts the fisherman knew as well as he knew his back yard, they saw the birds clearly.

There appeared to be about half an acre or more of birds feeding on the slimes. Even from a distance of more than two hundred yards, he could hear them. They seemed to be mostly duck: teal, widgeon, and mallard, according to the fisherman who had placed his paddle back in the punt, and was studying the wildfowl carefully through an old pair of binoculars. "We'll have to wait a while," he said finally, as the poet brought his float alongside.

"Why?" asked the poet.

"We'll wait until the tide turns. They're still coming in. We won't get close enough until they start feeding properly. You need to see the whites of their arses."

They paddled to a mudbank, where they waited, well hidden. The keen wind cut into them. The poet began to realize that punt-gunning involved more waiting than action.

They talked in low murmurs as the fisherman explained that they would try to get within sixty or seventy yards of the birds, and that they would be lucky to get so close in this wind. After nearly an hour of waiting the poet saw that fewer birds were flighting in from the harbour, and he could see an increasing number of white tails as the birds up-ended to feed in the shallows. He was very cold.

They moved away from the shelter into the open at last, paddling hard but quietly. The sky was beginning to darken, which augured rain, sleet or snow. The wind was rising. Here in the sheltered water it was calm enough; just a slight swell, and the little craft were surprisingly stable. They glided through the water with scarcely a bow wave, the poet glad to be on the move again.

The fisherman shipped his paddle as they drew closer. "Lie

flat now," he called very quietly, "face down." The poet obeyed. The fisherman removed the sacking from the gun, took the creeping paddles, stretched his body flat, and putting his arms out on either side of the punt, began to paddle. The poet did the same. The pace was slower, and the fisherman took advantage of the banks along the route to conceal their approach, choosing the pills that gave them maximum cover. The poet heard a click as the fisherman cocked the punt gun.

They were less than a hundred yards from the birds, and the fisherman was still paddling slowly and very quietly. The poet, kneeling on the bottom of the punt, both paddles moving through the water as quietly as possible, was beginning to wonder if he could hold his body in such a strange position for long. He dared to lift his head on only a few occasions to look at the birds. The noise grew louder, a din of bickering, excited waders and wildfowl, diving, splashing in the shallows, clustered around the sea-grass. There seemed to be hundreds of white tails there, perched on little muddy islets exposed by low tide.

Eighty yards, the fisherman judged, and stopped paddling, letting the momentum of the floats carry them towards the birds as he released the short creeping paddles that were attached with string to the thwarts.

At the last moment he motioned the poet to stay where he was and altered his float's course slightly to port to aim at the densest gathering of birds. He was about to fire the great gun when the nearest birds saw them and rose in a noisy, frantic wave of jerking wings and shrill calls.

They had seen the punts too late. There was a sharp crack as the fisherman jerked the lanyard and the powder ignited, sending the wave of shot into them. The poet raised his head in time to see the wind whip away a puff of acrid black smoke.

The shot had cut a corridor through the wildfowl. Above them, a cloud of squawking birds took flight.

The poet's ears rang from the explosion. The air above them was full of circling ducks and geese, gaining height on each circuit as they fled. The mudbank in front of them was empty except for the dead and wounded birds.

A mallard with a broken wing was trying to take to the air, feet splashing on the slimes, then on the water, as it headed for the harbour. The fisherman lifted the shotgun, eased off the safety catch, swung the gun to his shoulder and shot the bird dead.

The poet looked at the bodies in the water and on the bank itself. "How many did we get?" he asked.

The fisherman grinned. "Ten or twelve anyhow," he said and reached for the short setting pole.

They brought the floats to the edge of the slimes. Around them were dead mallard, widgeon, golden plover, teal, and at least one goose. Some lay in shallow water, some on the slimes. The fisherman hopped out of the float in an easy motion and splashed around in his black thigh waders, wringing the necks of the crippled birds. The poet gathered the kill, counting as he went. In all, they had killed fourteen head, including a goose that the fisherman termed a *Bernicle*.

They turned for home as the weather came in. A shower of sleet swept across the harbour. The poet stopped poling for a moment to pull down his hood, looking across at the harbour through rain-spattered spectacles. Above it, the town looked grey and uninviting. The wind blew in their faces, and it blew that way for much of their journey home, but in less than an hour they were back at the Cot Safe, where they pulled the floats up onto the mud and tied the painters to a rock on the wall.

The fisherman's father, a bearded patriarch, greeted them

with mugs of tea. While the poet warmed his bones by the stove, teeth still chattering, the fisherman returned to his punt, undid the frappings of the gun to the prow and, with a grunt and a heave, lifted the gun out and carried it inside the shed, where he laid it gently upright against the wall. He unscrewed the breach end, cleaned it thoroughly with an oily rag, then regreased it. He wiped the salt from the long barrel with a greasy cloth and ran a short pole, oiled rags wrapped at the end, down the barrel to remove the spent powder that would eat into the metal if not removed. When he had cleaned it thoroughly he wrapped the gun in a fresh roll of sacking and laid it in a corner, out of sight. At the end of the season he would give it its annual cleaning, with hot water and washing powder, before oiling it and putting it away until the following September.

He turned towards the old stove, taking a mug of tea from his father. He accepted a cigarette from the poet and inhaled. "That was a grand morning's work," he said, "though not as good as some. My best shot was out on the back of the Crow – forty duck and eleven curlew. But we're happy enough as it is."

On this sunny morning, a decade later, the poet was welcomed at the fishermen's headquarters. He bought his fish, fresh from the trawler that had docked at the quay near his office, and chatted for a few minutes. Then he left, rambling down to the other end of the town, past the ivied walls of Esker Abbey, where a king in sack cloth had scourged himself for assassinating his head priest at a great cathedral in Kent, and continued until he entered Black's Hotel. Eugene greeted him, imposing in a dark three-piece suit; an active promoter of the annual music festival that was bringing international recognition to the town. The poet had helped as a volunteer press officer for the festival, once collecting a famous tenor from the airport at Collinstown, an oiled Mediterranean man with a wonderful voice, whose fragrance lingered in the car. He told his wife he had collected a prima donna with an ample chest. When she looked mystified or suspicious he chuckled. The two friends talked of this, and of the glorious summer in an easy manner, then the poet set off again to the quays.

In his office he checked his books, made a few entries with his old Parker pen, gazed out the window at the harbour where a heat haze was gathering, and left without bothering to lock up.

Chapter Seventeen

It was late evening, with a half-moon. Conor and Niall lay hidden beneath a blackthorn tree on the Prospect boundary. They had been there since before dusk, and Niall was suffering from cramp. An old pair of binoculars lay between them. The elder was in full blossom, ghostly white. It gave them almost perfect cover, as the headland up to the hedge was overgrown with cow-parsley, wild grasses and dog-roses. As long as they remained silent, they had a good chance of seeing a badger. The night breeze came from the south-west, the same direction as the sett, which was in the whin bushes at right angles to them.

Garry and Brian had seen the badger's boundary road the day before during their morning rabbit stalk. They had been seeking a fox's earth.

They had spotted the fox's droppings, a common sight. Foxes warn other foxes off their territory by leaving their faeces in full view. Only a blind fox without a sense of smell would fail to spot them. The faeces resembled those of a common dog, however, and the brothers could have concluded that was what they were, and moved on, but Garry, who combined veterinary knowledge with a strong interest in nature, had sniffed the smell of foxy urine and the scents which foxes produce from the glands in their tails as a warning to other foxes. He inspected the droppings further; poked them with a stick while Brian's nose wrinkled. In the droppings were pieces of bone and hair, and of a partially digested apple. Foxes like fruit with their meat.

When they moved on a few yards, they found pawprints in the still-soft earth. "Forepaw," said Garry, motioning with the barrel of his rifle at one print. It showed four toes. A fox's forepaw has five, but only four show unless the ground is muddy. Garry rested his rifle against the whin bush and peered underneath.

On the other side of the bush he could see freshly dug soil, and concluded that this was the fox's earth. The bush had traces of hair hanging from its spiky branches, fluffy hair that was red at the base from a fox in its summer moult. Brian went with him to the other side of the whin bushes, which entailed climbing over a bank covered in briars and blackthorn bushes. They did so, checking their rifles. The poet lectured them endlessly on safety.

They approached the line of whin bushes slowly. Garry scanned the ground for traces of fox. Instead, he found another set of prints. These were of forepaws with five toes showing, and they were much broader than those of a fox. The toes were parallel. They had to be those of a badger.

They found evidence that this family of badgers shared part of their sett with foxes, although foxes, when summer arrives and their cubs are half-grown, rarely use their earths.

The boys had heard how the fox, seeking a ready-built earth, would sometimes lay its faeces at the mouth of the badger sett. The badger, a clean animal, would leave in disgust. Garry knew this was nonsense. Each mammal – one a mustelid, the other a dog – tolerated the other. It was not common for them to share the same piece of ground, but it was not unknown. There was no evidence that they fought. Lore also held that the badger was solely a herbivore, while a fox ate nothing but meat. Garry knew that to be nonsense also. Badgers ate rats, small rabbits, hedgehogs, frogs and several dozen worms a day when they could find them.

Garry stood, seeking the path a badger makes when it travels from its sett to its natural boundary. Brock the boar badger usually leaves his sett each night and travels along a path he has worn, sniffing as he goes, until he reaches his boundary, a rough circle of latrines. He deposits enough scent in each to warn badgers from a different family to stay away. The patrol finished, he then hunts.

If the boys could find his path it would lead them to the sett and, they hoped, the entrance the badger then used most frequently. They set off in a wide circle, Garry going clockwise, Brian the opposite. When Brian had travelled for less than fifty yards, scanning the ground like an Indian scout, he saw a tiny path with signs of recent use. He signalled to Garry, whose head he could see across the top of the whin bushes.

They followed the badger's line to the sett for thirty yards. It led them back to the area where they had found the badger's pawprint and, seemingly, directly into a large whin bush, but their eyes were skinned and they found the line deviated around the whin. They pushed between the bush and its neighbours, Brian swearing softly as the spikes tore at his hands. They found an entrance to the sett, near the summit of a little hill of freshly piled-up earth.

In front of the entrance were small piles of old leaves and dried grass – used bedding, as badgers regularly like to change their sheets, as it were, being fussy mammals. They venture out frequently to uproot fresh grass, tucking it between their forepaws and chin before backing into the sett, looking solemnly comic as they do so.

The two stood for a moment, seeing fresh pawprints around the sett entrance. "I reckon this is it," said Garry thoughtfully, leaning his rifle against the gorse bush. "This is the entrance they use most. We'll tell Conor and Niall. They're always saying they want to see a badger."

When they reached Prospect they found the two middle brothers in their room, Niall reading the *Angling Times*, Conor deep in *Riders of the Purple Sage*. Garry told them what they had seen. The two decided to lie in wait on the following evening.

◆ ◆

They grew more uncomfortable as darkness fell and a yellowy light enveloped the meadows. Conor whispered to Niall a tale he had heard from John about a weasel, the local term for a stoat, as Ireland does not have weasels. Its young had been exposed when a meadow was cut. The mother weasel had watched from a bank, eyes filled with hate, as the haymakers had gathered up her young and taken them from view. Then it had found the jug of buttermilk the men had left on the bank, and had spat in it. The saliva of a weasel was said to be poisonous.

A few moments later, he said, the men returned and released the young weasels into the undergrowth. The mother weasel was conscience-stricken. She ran to the jug and pushed it over with her muzzle, deliberately spilling the contents before running through the undergrowth to gather her young. The men were safe again.

The story finished, the boys looked about them. The light breeze brought an occasional small cloud that obscured the moon for a time, but the night was clear and quiet. The cattle were at the bottom of the field, close to the entrance into the Pond Field. They could hear them grazing and an occasional snort as they moved on to fresh grass. The scents of whin blossom and honeysuckle drifted on the night air.

The evening before, Brian, who had been re-reading James Stephens' *The Crock of Gold*, had told them the story of the Philosopher who had married the Thin Woman of Inishmagrath, the woman of the terrible temper, a dreadful housekeeper, who had finally flown into such a rage that she had spun in a circle so quickly that she had disappeared. One morning the Philosopher awoke, depressed, and grew more depressed as he lay in bed, listening to the sounds of his wife making the breakfast porridge in the kitchen below. There will be lumps in the stirabout, the Philosopher thought, and grew even more depressed, but then, Brian told them, he had thought: If there were no lumps it would be perfect. Perfection is finality, and finality is death. The Philosopher grew cheerful again, and rose from his bed.

They considered this as another small cloud covered the moon. The story had deeply impressed Niall, and Conor could see how it had appealed to his younger brother's temperament. He remembered how, during the previous winter, an outbreak of feline enteritis had swept away half of the family cats. Niall had buried them in the Grove, under the *macracarpas*. Conor counted nine little graves, three of them open. "How many cats have died?" he asked Niall, who was packing the loose soil on one of the graves with a garden trowel. "Six," grunted Niall, straightening up from his work.

"What the hell did you dig so many graves for then?" Conor asked.

"In case more die," said Niall, as if it were perfectly obvious.

Back in the present, they heard a rustling on the edge of the bank. They stiffened, all attention. Conor picked up the binoculars. "I can't see anything," he whispered. "I'll have to move forward." He did so gingerly, binoculars in one hand, his coat rustling against the blackthorn bush. When he had gone about five yards he sat up and brought the binoculars to his eyes, sweeping the area until he stopped abruptly, focusing on an area of whin bushes to his left. He watched for a minute or so, then motioned to Niall to move forward. When Niall had inched his way until he was beside his brother, Conor handed him the binoculars. "Look there," he whispered, pointing.

Niall looked. At first, he could see only darkness. Then, as the objects came into his focus, he saw an animal with a long bushy tail, surrounded by four smaller, playful animals.

It was not the badger. It was a vixen with four young foxes. She had taken them on an outing.

They watched, taking it in turns to use the binoculars. Even without, they could see the foxes clearly.

At first, the vixen allowed the little foxes to play, rolling on her back as the young swarmed over her, nipping at her ears and licking her face. Then it grew more serious. This was evidently a training session, as the vixen then singled out each of her young in turn, hunting it away from the others, forcing it to walk alongside her in a manner that suggested a rabbit hunt. Occasionally, the vixen would sniff the night air, and wait for the young fox to do likewise. She did this in turn with each of the young. Sometimes they would follow her, sometimes she would follow them. A low growl greeted any playfulness.

This lasted for a few minutes before the vixen led her family away into the darkness of the whin. As they left, the boys noticed that the last little fox limped.

They lingered as they talked about what they had seen. They talked of how a fox would entice a hen, a rabbit, or a pheasant to its death by walking past it, for days, even weeks, keeping its distance, endlessly patient, doing so until the target lost its fear of the predator and relaxed. Then the fox pounced.

They waited, growing colder, but did not see a badger. When hunger began to gnaw, they gave up and walked back into the Well Field, the old iron pump from the well on their right silhouetted against the light from Duggan's farmhouse; the light from an Aladdin lamp, since the Duggans had not yet switched to electricity. They walked, talking as they went, around the far edge of the Orchard, through the Hen-Run, down the farmyard where the dogs began to bark, and into the kitchen, where a cloud of cigarette smoke hung over the Chinese chequers board and their father beamed at them.

Chapter Eighteen

A small black car turned into Prospect on the following afternoon. A tall man in his middle years, clean-shaven, hair thinning, with a wonderfully melodious voice, a man stooping a little from the tuberculosis that had cost him a lung, stepped out to greet the family. The artist, close friend and frequent visitor, had come to stay for a few days.

The youngest boys rushed to the car. Their mother smiled when she saw the visitor and went to meet him. "Hello, Tony," she said. He kissed her and said: "It's lovely to see you, Don." He turned to the two boys. Ivan was very muddy, and both boys' legs were covered in scratches and streaks of green from dock leaves.

"Ivan and Padraic," the artist said solemnly to the two urchins, "how would you like to build a hot-air balloon?"

"Honest?" they asked at once.

"We will if you'd like to. We'll build it together tomorrow."

Their mother asked: "Can you stay, Tony?"

"I'd love to, Don, just for a couple of days," said the artist gratefully. She looked pleased. The artist was a bachelor who rarely ate properly. They had met when he worked in the branch of the bank at Eskerford where the poet kept his overdraft. He had been transferred to a branch in Rosspoint, twenty miles away, a few years before. He lived and painted in a set of shabby rooms near the bridge at

Rosspoint, the smell of damp mixed with that of linseed oil; finished works leaning against peeling wallpaper, canvases scattered on the floor, his bed covered in drawings.

He had been born in the neighbouring county, a county renowned for the elegance of its hurling, but, like the poet, he was of Western stock. His father and forefathers had been Atlantic islanders. One of his family, a fierce, piratical creature, had led a sea-borne rebellion three hundred years or so before against the conquerors of the mainland and had become a legend, not because the rebellion had been startlingly successful for a time, but because she was a woman.

While the boys' mother made him tea, he wandered down the farmyard, Ivan and Padraic at his heels. He stopped suddenly. Around the corner, from behind the barn, came Conor and Niall, each of them riding an enormous pig. As the squealing animals approached, Niall fell off, but jumped on again immediately, clutching the sow's ears. The boys dismounted when they saw the artist. The pigs ran away.

"Well, boys," said the artist, "are you training them for the Grand National?"

Conor grinned. "Niall swears that Porky is faster than Gert."

"Who won?"

"I did," they said simultaneously.

"You fell off," said Conor.

"But I'd won by then," said Niall, doggedly, who had fallen on the muddy side of the yard and looked it.

As the brothers argued, the artist went to find Garry and discovered him bent over the thwart of a small sailing boat that shone with a new coat of green paint. "God, Garry," said the artist admiringly, "have you done all that to that old boat your father showed me in the Cot Safe?"

Garry greeted him and said deprecatingly: "Oh, she wasn't that bad. What do you think of her, Tony?"

The artist walked around *Snipe*, giving the rudder a little push. It swung easily on its new pintles.

"She's a beauty, all right, Garry," said the artist. "Will you race her?"

"No, she'd be too slow. I thought for the first summer I'd do a little cruising, and then use her in the estuary."

Padraic had followed the artist into the shed, cupped hand outstretched. "Look what I've got, Tony," he said.

"Watch it," said Garry, looking narrowly at the hand. "It's another mouse."

"No, it's not!" said Padraic angrily. "It's a shrew."

◆ ◆

Garry shuddered at the sudden recall of an incident a few months before when his little brother's passion for catching mice in his bare hands had nearly led to his death. He had taken Conor and Padraic to see Barty's racehorse, blind Interlace, that had lashed out at a stable lad who had approached him from the wrong direction. The lad had been killed.

As Garry opened the stable-door, Padraic saw a mouse run inside, under the big stallion's hooves, and pursued it. The blind horse took fright and lashed out wildly. The two brothers watched the small boy in an agony of indecision, fearing that to alert him to the danger would paralyse him with fear. Padraic darted from beneath the horse a moment later, clutching the mouse and looking up at his brothers proudly, puzzled when he saw their expressions of relief.

◆ ◆

The artist watched as Garry chased Padraic from the shed. The dogs were barking. A car, exhaust muffler missing, drew up on the gravel. They emerged to see Bruno racing towards the kitchen, newspaper in mouth. He was followed by the poet, face all smiles.

"Is that you, Tony?" he asked.

"How are you, Pack?" said the artist, gripping his hand warmly.

"Can you stay?" asked the poet eagerly.

"I can, if that's all right," said the artist. "I have a couple of days owing."

"You should quit that bloody bank and paint full-time," said the poet earnestly.

"I'm thinking of it," said the artist. "I'm going over to St Ives in Cornwall for a week in October, when the tourists have left. There's an interesting school of painters there."

The poet nodded. "Once you go, you'll probably stay," he said as they entered the kitchen. The artist looked doubtful. He drank his tea, chatted, and, lighting a tiny pipe, wandered up the farmyard to the byre where Niall and Ivan were milking. He saw an ugly tabby cat on its haunches, mouth open, a stream of milk hitting its pink tongue. In the next stall a yellow cat, as big as a small dog, did the same.

After supper, he wandered with the boys' parents past the Hen-Run and into the Well Field. The boys played cricket near the Rocks. Conor was on-driving Brian's donkey-drops into the Orchard ditch, or hooking them into the Rocks. When the bowling changed, a fast ball from Ivan took his off stump. Padraic insisted on batting next, and was out first ball. "I wasn't ready," he shouted. They allowed him to stay at the wicket. The next ball was caught behind by Niall, the family wicket-keeper. "I didn't touch it," protested Padraic. "You did," they said in unison. "It's my ball," said Padraic. "I'll take it if you don't let me have another go. That wasn't fair." He was allowed to stay on, hit a lucky single, swiped at a further two balls, and was stumped by Niall. He left the wicket with bad grace, flinging the bat on the ground in front of Ivan, who batted next.

The three strolled back to the house at dusk. The sky was a darker blue, the sun a declining red star. Bats flew past. They entered the farmyard, the air filled with swifts, smudgy pencilled lines against the white house. "Listen," said the poet, his cigarette glowing. A rasping noise came from the Front Field. "The corncrake."

◆

The men sat with their whiskeys, the boys' mother with a brandy-and-ginger-ale. She rarely drank. Family and a few friends provided their social life. They generally evaded invitations. They drove to Dublin several times a year and stayed with his parents. In the week before Christmas they took the two youngest boys as well, a visit Ivan and Padraic looked forward to so much they ached. Their mother took them shopping in Grafton Street and O'Connell Street, and to the stallholders in Henry Street and Moore Street, the accents of the real Dubliners music to her ears after the voices of the country. She saw her own family. The poet drank with his friend, the editor of *The Irish Times*, and went to the Back Bar at Jammets and to Neary's, where writers and critics gathered, returning only in time for his supper; sometimes very late, his voice a little slurred. She did not grudge him this. He saw few other writers, theatre or radio people in Eskerford unless they visited.

When money was relatively plentiful the two caught mail-boat and train to London, to see Brian George and his other friends at the BBC, and to watch the latest plays on the London stage. During the day, while his wife shopped for presents for their sons, he rambled around London, to the bookshops of Charing Cross Road and Coptic Street; to Hampstead to see Keats' Cottage; to The Grove to see Coleridge's house; to the mean streets of the East End, hoping to catch a glimpse of a gangster; and, with a friend, to the Press Gallery of the House of Commons from where he saw Churchill with his feet up.

The poet had discovered a fellow spirit in the artist who, in turn, was deeply interested in his friend's work. When the artist grew depressed or ill the poet urged him to keep painting, persuading him that painting was his life.

The artist frequently brought a painting or a drawing as a gift to the family when he came to Prospect. He had brought one on this visit, and went to fetch it from his car. The family crowded around to look at it, an oil of the artist's old home, a view from the back of the house, in the centre a black cat on an upturned bucket.

The poet held it in both hands, boys behind him looking over his shoulders. "That's a grand work, Tony." He looked at it again and passed it to his wife. "Thanks. Ivan," he said when he saw the water jug was empty, "could you go to the well?"

The artist looked at the boys standing around the table; at their mother, who had lost a little of her freshness, and said: "Don, I'll take them all to Farracloe tomorrow if you like." This was a beach, seven miles of rolling dunes, that ran north from the Crow on the other side of Eskerford. It was the best beach in the world if one ignored the sea temperature. "We might make a start on the balloon in the morning, then go to the beach."

"I'll come as well if you're going in the afternoon," said the poet. His wife looked pleased. She would have the house to herself and have a nice *quiet* cup of tea.

The artist took a sheet of paper from a pocket. "I saw this the other day in the library and copied it. It's a public notice after the '98 Rising. It says: It has Come to the Authorities' Attention that the Roads and Woods in the Area outside the Town are infested with Rapparees, Tories, Wood-kerns and other Disaffected Folk, and that they will be Pursued and have the King's Justice Ministered to Them. I've heard of rapparees and tories, but have you ever heard of a wood-kern?"

They pictured the wood-kern: bearded, unkempt, a thinner Ben Gunn from *Treasure Island*, hiding from the redcoats behind every tree, living off frost-bitten potatoes, the odd snared rabbit; probably a dispossessed smallholder, a half-acre man, revisiting his old home at night, watching its new owner with hatred, pondering revenge. He had staring eyes, a straggling beard, was in rags, starving, ribs showing. The descriptions grew wilder as the table competed.

The artist moved on and told of how his father, the islandman, had confronted a platoon of British soldiers after the election of 1918 had returned an overwhelming majority of Sinn Féin MPs. "We're under martial law, I see," his father had said to the British captain marching his soldiers into the town. "How so?" the officer asked politely. "You no longer have a democratic mandate to rule," said the islandman. "Leave us. You have no right to be here."

The boys' mother stirred, uneasy. The period seemed recent to her. She had been a young girl on the edge of a crowd at Findlaters Church in Dublin when the occupying forces had opened fire. She remembered the Crossley tenders racing at night through the streets of Dublin, the screech of brakes, the bang of the tailgate on cobbles as the soldiers raided the houses, hunting for rebels; her eldest brother, an aviator and aero-engineer, on the run; and the terrible silence in the city on the morning after Collins' men shot dead three army intelligence officers in a house on the North Circular Road near the Phoenix Park.

Brian asked the artist to retell his story of the drunk in his home town who threw the family crockery over the half-door into the street each Saturday night, then beat his wife. The artist told them of how the reprobate's sons would take him by his head and feet, carry him to the rear of the bacon factory, and throw him in the little river. An old woman in ankle-laced boots, who detested the drunk, would halt them, and say to the sons: "Stand back there, till I take a fop at him!" As she kicked him, the drunk would shout: "I'm ready to meet my God, Maggie. I'm ready to meet my God!" His sons threw him into the river, in which slush and offal floated, discharged by the factory. He emerged half-drowned, an hour or two later, and the cycle recurred. The poet listened intently, wheezing with laughter as the artist mimicked first the old woman, then the man; caught up in the descriptions of ordinary people in small Irish towns. He had included in a poem one of the artist's characters, Old Madge, who threw off her clothes and danced in the street when the pub closed.

Ivan returned from the pump with a jug of clear water, and asked: "How big will the balloon be, Tony? Will it fly?"

"It should, but it's a funny thing. Some fly for miles. Others burn up on the spot," said the artist. "I built one that flew across several fields and set fire to a haycock." He took a fountain pen from his pocket and drew, in the jet-black ink he used, a design for the balloon.

It would be around three feet high, two feet in diameter: a light wire structure, pasted with crêpe paper. At the bottom would be a little cross-strut with a circle of wire in the middle, in the circle some burning rags.

The boys sang. The artist, in a good baritone, joined in:

> *At Boolavogue, as the sun was setting*
> *O'er the bright May meadows of Shelmalier,*
> *A rebel hand set the heather blazing,*
> *And brought the neighbours from far and near.*

Brian sang 'The ballad of Brian O'Linn', Niall following with 'Molly Bawn'. As the boys went to bed they could hear the rumble of talk from the kitchen. The conversation had changed to Arthur, the Grail, Tristan and Iseult; how their romantic tone was more European than the Irish myths; and on to the *Mabinogion*; the poet, knowing that he would have been lynched at the Eisteddfod, airing the theory that the Cymic legends, although much later than the Irish cycles, were a joint inheritance, possibly named after Mac an Óc, love-god of the Gael, a Celtic Apollo and patron of poets, known also as Aongus of the Birds, the Wandering Aengus of Yeats.

Chapter Nineteen

The sun cast shadows across the shorn meadows around Prospect the next morning. The artist had risen early to find the boys' mother already up, filling a hand-churn to make butter. "Morning, Don," said the artist. "I'm just going to look around for a bit of wire."

"You look rested," she said. "Try the Dairy, or one of the sheds."

He went out to the yard. Jim crowed from the Hen-Run. The air was full of bird song. Jackdaws, rooks, wood pigeons, swifts, swallows, sparrows, and house-martins saluted the hottest day of the summer, the summer sounds a sweeping contrast to the artist's damp lodgings, or the bar of the commercial travellers' hotel.

He stood in the yard, watching the martins flit to their little clay dwellings in the eaves of the house; a shorter tail than the swallow, legs and underparts of white, a bird sacred since religion began, dweller in holy places. He watched an indignant martin eject a sparrow that had taken over its nest in its absence.

He looked in the Dairy, but did not find what he sought. He sauntered around the back of the barn and looked in over the wall of the sty at the two pigs and their young. Porky and Gert heaved themselves to their feet slowly and nuzzled his hands. Enormous, greedy animals, they were surprisingly gentle and affectionate. On a visit during the previous autumn he had seen the boys' mother picking blackberries in the Front Field, a dog following her. When he walked into the field to join her he saw it was not a dog, but Porky, who was very fond of blackberries. As the boys' mother picked the fruit, she popped a small handful into Porky's open mouth, the pig blinking gratefully.

He went into each of the sheds in turn. In the second he found a coil of thin wire. He took it and went out into the sunshine again, past the ruined coach house to the byre, a cats' chorus greeting him. A dozen of them clustered at the door, mewing, waiting for morning milk. He went inside.

In the cool half-light, Niall and Conor milked Blossom and Hawthorn. Niall, overnight, had become a hunchback. When the artist's vision adjusted to the light he saw that Phoebus had had breakfast and was asleep on the boy's shoulders.

The artist walked back down the farmyard. He chose Garry's workshop, where *Snipe* lay. He borrowed Garry's pliers and began to fashion the balloon skeleton, taking lengths of wire, measuring them, snipping, bending each length into a rough ellipse, doing the same with the cross wires, the equivalent of lines of latitude on a globe. By the time the call to breakfast came he had almost completed the skeleton.

From the farmyard he saw John arrive on his bike. The artist had seen John's uncle fight: Boxer Jem, idol of the county, the greatest world heavyweight champion that never was; body like a barrel, huge shoulders; too gentle a nature to win. John, though smaller and slighter, was very like him, particularly in the face. Artist and well-digger chatted in the sunshine of the yard until breakfast.

The table was subdued by a grumpy poet who was feeling the effects of the late night. He cheered visibly when he saw the artist and motioned him to sit beside him, Garry moving down a place. The artist tucked into a Prospect breakfast.

He had the good sense to decline a second helping, walking out with the poet who was leaving for Eskerford. They stood on the gravel near the palm tree which rustled gently. "The poplars are coming on, Pack," he said. He knew that the poet was fond of his trees, planted soon after the family had arrived at Prospect.

They looked at the waving trees in full leaf. "Sometimes I lie in bed and just listen to them," said the poet reflectively. "They seem to talk to me." He climbed into his car and started the engine, relieved that it fired first time, as well he might, since as often as not – particularly in winter – one of his sons would have to swing the starting handle for ten or fifteen minutes before the motor started. When that did not work, the entire family were called out to push the car down the drive – sometimes out onto the road – before the motor fired.

The artist returned to his work. Two excited boys ran in, shouting: "Is it ready, Tony?"

"No, it's not," he said kindly, studying the two. They were almost clean. "I have to finish the body, then go into town to buy the paper which will be the skin. I hope to finish it before lunch, leave the glue to dry, then we'll go to the beach. We'll launch when we come back from Farracloe."

He was fitting the inner latitudinal rings when the boys left, running hard for the Grove where they shot up the tall evergreens to swing from the top branches, switching effortlessly into the next tree in dizzying leaps. Their mother watched them as she and Martha hung out the family washing on the line in the Paddock. They heard Ivan shout when he reached the top of the tree: "One more step, Mr Hands, and I'll blow your brains out!" It was followed by a rebel yell from his younger brother.

The artist soon completed the body of the balloon and

decided it was time to go to Eskerford. On the way to his car he shouted at the trees: "Ivan, Padraic: would you like a trip to town?"

They shot down at a speed that made the artist wince. "You'd better have a quick wash," he said as they ran up to him. They altered course without stopping and ran into the house. As he started his car they clambered in, fighting for the front seat. Ivan won. They drove into town, windows open, the artist humming a *Lied* of Schubert's. They waved to Nicky Fortune, and to Sonny Sutton, forever walking his greyhounds, and to Madge, once the family's maid. They saw Matt Lacey, a bent beanpole in blue overalls and wide hat who had shouted at their mother: "Listen here, woman! Listen here!" Then they saw a neighbouring widow, in her pony-and-trap. Padraic, who had been leaning against the front seats, shrank into the back. He saw her as a witch, and was even more terrified of the vicious little terrier that ran alongside her pony-and-trap. It snapped at his ankles if he was on foot when they met. She grimaced at him as they overtook her.

They turned left at the crossroads, passing the Convent of Mercy where Padraic went to school, past the small furniture factory, the John of God convent, and down the hill into the town. The artist turned right into the Main Street, brisk with delivery vans, a few cars, horse-drawn vans, carts and traps. They parked in the Bull Ring beside the monument to the Pikeman of '98. Below this were the bodies of the rebels who had been executed and buried on this spot.

They walked up the Main Street past the Medical Hall and Woolheads' toy shop to Bucklands, which sold books, newspapers and wrapping paper. May greeted him: "How are you, Tony? I see you have trouble with you," smiling at the boys. The artist selected several rolls of crêpe paper. "I think we'll have red," he said. He paid; stayed to chat for a while. On the busy footpath outside the shop he asked the boys: "What about going to Fran Moran's for an ice cream?"

As the two boys ate their cones, he said: "Will you be all right here for half an hour? I want to see Michael. If you get bored, have a walk around the town. I'll see you back at the car."

He could see they were happy, left them and walked to the bank where he had worked. At the mahogany counter he asked for the manager. An insolent clerk looked at his shabby tweeds and asked him his business. The artist said simply: "I'm a friend." The clerk looked suspicious, hesitated, stepped from his stool, walked to a frosted glass door, knocked, opened it, spoke a few words and barely had time to open the door wide as the manager rushed out, hand outstretched. He was a portly man, bald, with a reddish, good-humoured face that lit up with pleasure when he saw his friend. "Tony! How are you?"

The artist had been very ill at one stage, but he did not say so. "Come and have a quick drink at Katty Roche's," he said. They left the bank – the manager giving the clerk a scowl – and walked to the pub where the artist had spent many evenings when he had worked in Eskerford. They talked, had one drink, then left, the artist heading first to Fran Moran's. When he saw the boys were not there he went back to his car and found them watching the traffic and townspeople. As the artist rejoined them, they spotted another familiar figure walking towards them with a rolled-up newspaper in his hand. It was the boys' father.

"You're spoiling those boys, Tony," he said, smiling at them.

"It's great to have the opportunity, Pack," said the artist.

"Are you going back to the house?" asked the poet, waving to a bent man in a bowler hat and a blue suit, an old schooner captain.

The two cars took different routes out of the town, met at the crossroads of Clonard and travelled in convoy to Prospect. It was very hot.

Benny and John were at the kitchen table when they arrived. The wireless was playing Joseph Locke:

> *And so I go*
> *To fight the savage foe.*

"How are you Benny?" asked the artist, warmly.

"Hot," said Benny, lifting his cap and scratching his head. "The fries'ud atecha."

Brian appeared. He had been out at dawn shooting rabbits, had then spent a hot two hours cutting *buachalán buídhe* – yellow ragwort – on the headlands of the Wheat Field with Abdul, an old hooked sword with a black handle studded with silvery stars. He had taken his book to the cool of the Grove to recover.

They were about to eat when Garry appeared.

"She's finished," he said, with a mixture of weariness and triumph.

"Well done," said the poet, looking hungrily towards the Aga where his wife was heaping food on plates. "We'll go and see her when we've eaten."

Four or five conversations took place at the same time. The poet talked to his eldest son about the newly completed boat, speculating on whether she might need a bit of weather helm; the artist talked to Benny; Padraic interrupted; John talked to Niall about the river. Ivan and Conor talked of bass fishing from the rocks at Crook Head. Brian took surreptitious glances at his book, open beside his plate. The boys' mother asked the entire table if they were ready for more.

Much of the food on the table came from Prospect: rabbit stew; boiled, floury potatoes – so floury the skins had burst;

turnips and other vegetables; soda bread piled high in the middle of the table; butter; gallons of milk – Padraic, in particular, had a prodigious liking for milk; cream ladled over the apple pie; jam and crab-apple jelly; and the fresh eggs they had eaten for breakfast. All had come from the little farm.

Sundays were more formal. The poet bought a single bottle of wine each week, choosing a Graves or a St Emilion for some reason known only to him, which they drank with lunch. The youngest boys were given a little to cover the bottom of a glass; told to put their noses in and sniff the bouquet. When his wife questioned this the poet told her that a supercilious wine waiter would never humiliate one of their sons.

A jackdaw flew into the kitchen and settled at the top of the dresser, looking haughtily at the cats.

"Alphonsus!" said the boys' mother. "Where have you been?"

"Tschack!" said the jackdaw in a horrible, grating voice.

"Say hello to Tony," coaxed the boys' mother.

The bird shook his head. "Tschack!" he said again, to her disappointment.

She had spent many hours trying to teach him to speak, but Alphonsus had managed only a few sounds. When the fledgling had fallen down the chimney in a pile of soot on a wet morning in spring, the boys' mother had nursed the miserable little creature, kept him warm beside the Aga, forced warmed milk down his beak, kept the cats from him, and willed him to live. By the time she took him up the farmyard for his first flight he was rudely healthy and very spoiled.

When she lofted him into the wind Alphonsus dropped like a stone, flapped his wings in panic, gaining a foot or two before dropping again, this time to the ground. She waited, then did the same again. Alphonsus flew for a few yards before landing on the gate to the Hen-Run. He clung there unsteadily, the wind lifting his tail, eyeing his mistress.

He took off on the third day when his instinct told him that he was designed to fly. He flew up and up until he reached the roof of Prospect above Garry and Brian's bedroom where he landed, looking uncertainly about him.

Most of the family gathered in the Paddock to watch, wondering whether his family in the chimneys of Prospect would recognize him. He sat there while the other jackdaws went about their business, but the family could not see any sign of kinship.

He was an orphan as a jackdaw, and so became a member of the human family. He perched on the top of the dresser for hours at a time, occasionally defecating, to the disgust of the boys. They thought nothing of cowdung, but drew the line at this.

As the weeks drew on, Alphonsus learned to control his bowels. He spent more of his time in the air above the house and Paddock and began to partially feed himself on grubs and beetles, his natural diet. He generally came when he was called but heeded only the call of his mistress, ignoring the boys. When she walked to the washing-line or to the Hen-Run the jackdaw usually appeared from the air to land on her shoulders.

He developed into a fine, adult jackdaw without the help of his relatives in the chimneys. His lavatorial habits improved further, with only the occasional accident. As spring waxed and the days grew warmer he spent more nights in the open, generally appearing at lunch time. The family were disappointed that he was a bird of few words, but when someone told the boys' mother that jackdaws would only speak if their tongues were slit she replied that she would rather leave him as he was.

Chapter Twenty

"Pack," said the artist to the poet as they bowled along in the artist's car on the road to Farracloe. "How did you get about in the War years?"

The poet flicked his cigarette end out of the open window as the artist swerved to avoid a stream of cyclists on their way to the beach. "Arrah, the same as them," he replied. "By bike."

"What about when you had to go to Dublin?"

"Train. You could use a car in the first year or two of the War, but petrol and tyres became very scarce. I once cycled all the way to Dublin when the train wasn't running."

"Did you get there?"

"In a manner of speaking. I set off from Rowe Street on a nice morning, and I was puffed by the time I got to Unyoke. I got to Inver Dee which, as you know (the artist had lived there for a time) is halfway, when I had an idea."

"What was that?" asked the artist, looking across at his friend's face, reflecting that it was a difficult one to draw.

"I was cycling through the main street and wondered if there was a schooner taking on cargo for Dublin," said the poet. "Sure enough, there was, with a captain I knew. He said he would sail in two hours for Dublin when the tide turned. He was delighted with the company. He asked me if I was hungry, and I told him I was starving. So I was. I'd ridden over forty miles.

"He cooked me the biggest T-bone steak I'd ever seen in my life, let alone eaten. I ate every bit of it, and I've never enjoyed a steak as much. Soon after, we slipped out from the harbour wall on the tide. We docked at Ringsend before dark. One other thing I remember: when we were docking at Ringsend, the fella who tied us onto the bollard there was the ugliest man I'd ever seen in my life. I've never forgotten how ugly he was. I dreamt about him for days.

"There I was in Dublin, fresh as a daisy and fed like a fighting cock. I cycled to my people's house in Baggot Street. They couldn't understand why I wasn't jaded. My mother kept looking at me closely in that way she had. Mary and Ellie (the poet's sister and cousin) kept asking me if I was exhausted. I told them I was so fit I'd ridden all the way without a bother. I kept that up for hours until I told them the truth."

The artist leaned his elbow through the open window. He was in shirtsleeves, without a tie, smoking his pipe. The roadsides were overgrown with cow parsley, the banks heavy with briars and dog-roses.

"Your column in the *Press* is a great read," the artist remarked. "It brightens up the paper. I enjoy the others too."

The other two columnists on the *Irish Press* were Lennox Robinson and Brendan Behan. Much to his amusement, the poet's column appeared on the agricultural page of the newspaper, wedged between articles on potato blight and poultry, advertisements for fertilizer and the latest diesel tractors.

The scent of wild flowers and salt air greeted them as they turned off for the beach, Garry following in their father's car with the rest of the family. A procession of cyclists, swimming costumes dangling from saddles, preceded them. The townspeople were making the most of the fine weather.

They parked to the right of a line of holiday railway carriages. Beside the car park was a tiny shop with a large banner saying HB, the sign of good ice cream.

They found a deserted hollow among the dunes and waving sand reeds. The boys changed while the poet and the artist lay on the sand to talk, watch, and smoke. They would not swim.

Conor and Niall ran across the beach into the water, followed, more soberly, by Garry and Brian. Ivan and Padraic were racing as fast as they could across the beach behind Garry and Brian when they heard Niall yell. "IT'S COLD!" Mother of God, it's FREEZING!" He was up to his middle by this stage, the moment that every swimmer is reminded of the true temperature of the water.

"It's not that cold!" snapped Conor, who knew how cold it was, but would not admit it. He plunged in, strangling a yell. Niall gritted his teeth and dived.

Garry, Brian and Ivan reluctantly followed, but Padraic was in a funk. He stood on the edge, waves lapping at his toes.

"Come on in, Padraic!" Niall shouted. He was beginning to enjoy himself.

Padraic sensed that he was being watched by his father and the artist. He did not want to appear to be a coward, but he could not face the agony that his brothers had just undergone.

"Come in!" shouted Garry, splashing about. Garry maintained that he had negative buoyancy and therefore could not float, but he could swim, after a fashion. "It's fine once you're in." Brian had waded in gingerly and then plunged, ducking his head.

Padraic hesitated, then walked in to the sea.

When it reached his ankles, he turned and ran back to where his father and the artist relaxed.

"Why didn't you go in?" his father asked.

"It's too cold!" said Padraic. He slumped down on the sand between the two men.

"God, Padraic," said the artist with a smile, "that was the quickest dip I've ever seen. Did you get your ankles wet?"

The poet lit a cigarette by holding his spectacles to the sun, directing the beam onto the end of the cigarette until it began to smoulder. "If he did, that's as far as he went," he said. "Aren't you ashamed of yourself? Look at your brothers. They're all in the sea."

Padraic kneaded the warm sand with his toes. "I don't care!" he said defiantly. "That water's freezing. I'm not going in!"

The poet and the artist resumed their conversation. A light breeze from the sea cooled them.

The view was a wide one. To the south the beach stretched almost to the Crow, the northerly outer point of Eskerford Harbour. To the north, it gradually disappeared into a heat haze, merging with the sea. The sea bottom was a continuation of these sand dunes, shoaling dangerously to the north-east.

The sounds of the people playing on the beach and the swimmers reached them. Gulls wheeled overhead, seeking the remains of picnics. Padraic could see his brothers skylarking in the water. Brian was chasing Ivan who had surfaced behind his brother and pushed him over. Garry was making his way back to the beach, wading in water up to his knees.

The poet walked along the dunes, a book in his hand, illustrations of wild flowers on each page. It was called *Familiar Wild Flowers*, and he had bought the set of six at auction on impulse. He compared a flower he had picked with the illustrations in the book. When he was satisfied that he had matched them, he placed the flower in the page and pressed the book closed. The artist joined him and talked as the poet bent to pick the different species. This was not an interest the artist or the poet's family had seen before. Nor would they see it again. It was a passing fancy, passed to him by the artist Estella Solomons, wife of his friend, the poet Seumas O'Sullivan.

Padraic ran to the beach to rejoin his brothers who had come ashore. They took turns to hit a tennis ball with the warped racquets that Niall had brought. Conor, Niall and Ivan ran a race, the poet umpiring. The artist, Garry, and Brian had gone for a long walk down the beach. When they returned they brought eight sixpenny wafers of ice cream, courtesy of the artist.

They sat in a circle on the dunes as they ate, talking, listening to the sounds of the sea and beach.

Conor, Niall and Ivan swam again before the family packed up and walked to the car. Padraic, goaded by his brothers, made one more attempt to enter the water but retreated when the cold water reached his ankles. The poet began to think of the next subject for his newspaper column.

It was late afternoon when they arrived back at Prospect. After supper, the artist went to inspect the balloon. He had cut the red crêpe paper into strips and glued it to the frame. The glue had been wet when they had left for the beach. It had dried since. He cut lengths of rag with big scissors, soaking it in a mixture of oil and paraffin he had mixed in an old paint can. He inserted them in the wire circle at the base of the balloon.

It was time to prepare the launch-pad, near the sun-dial on the edge of the Grove. The artist gathered armfuls of bricks, built them into two little facing walls with gaps to allow the air to circulate, and laid two billets of wood cross-wise on top of the walls.

He went back to the farmyard, Ivan and Padraic at his

heels, lifted the balloon, and carried it back towards the Grove. He laid it carefully on the platform.

The family came to watch. The artist rummaged in his coat for his matches, then lit the rags. They smouldered slowly at first, then burst into flame. The hot air from the fire rose into the balloon.

The balloon started to shake slightly, trembling. It began to sway gently in the breeze. The family watched.

The balloon lifted slightly. Then, to cheers and shouts, it rose several inches from its launch pad.

It lifted a foot, then tilted. Smoke poured from the oily rags.

The side of the balloon caught fire, flame flickering through the red crêpe paper. The cheering died.

The side became a mass of flames which spread instantly to the rest of the balloon. Within seconds the skin had burnt, leaving only the skeleton. Smoke continued to pour from the rags. The skeleton toppled on its side.

The family looked at the artist, who smiled. "It was aerodynamically unsound," he said.

Chapter Twenty-One

Padraic was on his way to McCann's to buy a tin of baking powder. He cut through the Grove past banks of nettles taller than he, along a path that was almost invisible and which was kept open only by frequent use. The area between Grove and road was ground for a civil war that began each spring and ended in winter. Briars strangled nettles, and nettles poisoned briars, a terrible strife that, in spring and summer, ceased only when the two united to present a common front to anything else that tried to grow there.

The path ended at a small gap in the blackthorn hedge that was Prospect's roadside boundary. A big elm spread its branches over the corner of the boundary with the road and with McCann's property. Under the elm was the gap known as the Stile. It was not a genuine stile, simply a hole in the hedge on the other side of an earthen bank, almost invisible from the road, but the boys had called it the Stile when they had arrived at Prospect and the name had stuck.

Padraic climbed through it and saw Nicky Fortune cycle past, his round face red from pedalling up the hill. "Hello Nicky!" the boy shouted. The shock of hearing his name called from a thorn bush almost caused the man to lose his balance. The bike wobbled as he turned to see a grinning boy step onto the road.

The boys heard Nicky Fortune more often than they saw him. He lived with mother and elder brother in a house at the bottom of the lane near Bayview and sang the songs of Mario Lanza on his way home from the Cinema Palace on Saturday nights. Sometimes, at full moon, the boys woke as he leant his bike against a wall, lifted his head to the goddess and sang:

> *Overhead the moon is beam-ing,*
> *Bright as blossom on a bough.*
> *Nothing is heard but the song of a bird*
> *Filling all the air with* DREAM-*ing.*

His voice absorbed the strain of most of the song until he reached the highest notes, when it cracked and the neighbouring farm dogs howled. Once, on an errand to Mrs Fortune, Niall had surprised Nicky miming, arms clasped to his breast, like a tenor at an opera house, while Caruso sang from the gramophone behind the lace curtain.

◆—◆

Padraic entered the shop and knocked on the counter. Nicky Kelly appeared, blue beret perched on his round head. Braces held up his trousers. A leather belt held in the lower part of his stomach. The upper part, uninhibited, sagged generously over the belt.

"Who wouldn't get his feet wet, begob!" said Nicky.

Padraic felt a shiver in his spine. "What's that? What do you mean?"

Nicky grinned. "You're in the paper today. Did y'not know?"

"What paper? What do you mean I'm in the paper?" Padraic recalled that at lunchtime his brothers had exchanged knowing nods and laughs without sharing the joke.

"The *Press*," said Nicky. "Hould on while I get it." He went back into the family's living quarters and re-emerged with the newspaper and his wife Annie. She smiled at the boy.

"It's something your father wrote," said Nicky, looking through his half-moon spectacles, pursing his lips as he searched for the right page. "There y'are," and he folded the paper. "Can ye read yet?"

Padraic felt ashamed, but saw no point in lying. "Not yet."

"Well," said Nicky, holding the newspaper close, "it says that in a lovely day at the seaside, his youngest son would do no more than get his ankles wet. That's you," he said triumphantly. "Now don't that beat Banagher?"

"Does it say anything else about me?" asked Padraic anxiously.

Nicky scanned the page, still holding the newspaper close. "No. It don't."

"Oh," said Padraic, relieved. "Can I have a tin of baking powder?"

He handed over the coins and raced out of the shop, running down the road to the Stile, clutching the tin, along the path, ignoring the nettles, into the backyard and through the kitchen door.

"Why are you in such a hurry?" his mother demanded.

"Is it true that Daddy has written an article about me, saying I wouldn't go in the water because I was afraid?" asked Padraic in a rush.

She smiled. "He mentioned it, but only as a joke. Don't take it seriously."

"But everyone knows," said Padraic angrily. "Nicky Kelly read about it in the paper."

"Everyone knows that a lot of people don't like cold water, particularly small boys," she said. "Everyone also knows that some grown men don't like it either. Did your father or Tony go in the water?"

"No," said Padraic.

"You bet your boots they didn't," said his mother.

Chapter Twenty-Two

Snipe sailed close-hauled, centreboard down, down the estuary towards Eskerford Harbour in a light breeze, Garry at the helm, his father sitting to one side of the forward thwart, smoking.

They had launched the boat from the slipway at the boat club, borrowing trailer and van again. *Snipe* looked well as she left Prospect, green paint shining in the morning sun; rudder newly varnished, as were upper woodwork and thwarts, and her mast, unstepped for the journey.

She floated gently off the trailer as the helpers at the boat club lowered it down the slipway. Garry held her anxiously while the two helpers paid out the rope. The trailer was pulled back and the little boat rode proudly in the estuary current.

They lifted the mast and placed it in the step, then fussed over the rigging, tightening either forestay or shrouds to give her the rake they thought would suit.

Out on the water the poet lifted *Snipe*'s little anchor, ebb and river current drifted them and they hoisted jib and mainsail, sheeting them home. *Snipe* began to sail, picking up pace, the waves bumping against her bows. The wind freshened. *Snipe*'s progress quickened perceptibly, the sound of the waves against the bow more urgent.

"How's the helm?" the poet called.

"Fine," said Garry, beginning to relax. "She's a beauty."

The poet was superstitious. "Don't speak too soon," he growled. "Let's bring her nearer the wind again."

Garry luffed the helm, sheeted in the sail and they leant outwards to sit her up. Spray began to come inboard, *Snipe* bouncing along on the strong ebb. They tacked back and forth, with many calls of "Ready about!" and "Lee-oh!" down to the White Boy, where they would bear off into the harbour. They sailed past the quays a few minutes later, the poet's office a few hundred yards away. *Snipe* was in the open harbour, bows pointing towards the two white marks on the wall on the north side, painted for vessels to steer a line from the White Boy.

The poet gazed across the harbour towards the mouth. A fishing boat was crossing the bar on its way in past the sunken Battery, followed by a flight of gulls.

They gybed frequently as they crossed the harbour, then tested her on a beam reach which both expected would suit *Snipe* best. It did. Satisfied, they resumed their course, sailing to within a few yards of the slob wall, their sails a strange sight to anyone standing below sea level on the other side. The engine-house chimney towered over them as they gybed again.

To the north, beyond the wall, lay a tiny island where the town's patron saint had settled after a bad-tempered argument with St Patrick, refusing to accept the rules and edicts of the country's patron saint. St Patrick insisted that his rule covered the entire island and expelled him from the religious community of all Ireland. The rebel, according to the account the poet had read in the *Book of the Dun Cow*, answered that he would always belong to the church in Ireland and that the place where he resided would always be called Ireland. He moved to the north side of Eskerford Harbour, and lived as a hermit on a tiny island which he named Beag Érin, or Little Ireland, and had the last laugh;

as cute as a Christian, thought the poet.

He looked past his eldest son at the receding outline of the town. A heat haze drifted in from the south, but he could see his office and several fishing boats at the quay. Above the town was the loom of the Bluestairs; almost directly to the north a conical shape, the other hill of Tara, in the next county.

The other sailing boats in the harbour were evidently preparing for the summer regattas, one of which he had won in the old *Barnstormer*, crewing for his friend the fisherman. He remembered how the judges had ruled that *Barnstormer* could not enter because she was marginally too long, and how he had cheated officiousness by sawing a couple of inches from the prow.

One of the Mermaids, two sailors aboard, had left the boat club behind them. It was coming up and would soon overtake. It altered course to run parallel, throwing a fine bow wave. One of the sailors called: "*Snipe* ahoy!"

"How are you, Dick?" called the poet.

"Grand," said the man at the helm. "Isn't it great to be out? Garry, you've done a great job on that old boat."

"Thanks, Dick," said Garry gratefully

The man at the jib of the Mermaid laughed: "Has your little boy got his feet wet yet?"

"He will," said the poet, regretting what he had written, and changed the subject. "Where are you going?"

"Just round the bay and back," said Dick. "We're in training now." He put the tiller over and the Mermaid surged ahead; slightly, the poet saw, to Garry's chagrin.

If Garry was upset, it did not last. He was sailing his own boat, fulfilling a dream.

He had been very ill a few years before with acute peritonitis. Only when the crisis had passed, when Pax the doctor, a close family friend, had told the poet and his wife, who had been sick with worry, that their eldest had been close to death but was no longer, did Garry learn how ill he had been. The family then lived in the town, having moved from Bayview, a house they loved. Garry, during his long recuperation, had fretted at being confined. As he recovered he went for long walks with Brian up the river, but the dreadful winters after the War – when deep snow covered all, the roads were impassable, and blizzards kept everyone indoors – made his confinement tiresome and frustrating.

During his recuperation he had dreamt of two things: to have his own boat, and to move back to the country, to a large house. He hated being in the town. He dreamt of the big, decaying houses of the area, those owned by what had been called the Ascendancy class, turning them in his imagination into rich manors full of gentlefolk with elaborate manners. He asked for and received permission to visit some of them.

As he walked in the grounds on cold, dreary days, he imagined life in the big houses at the peak of their owners' wealth and power, and visualized a lifestyle that was more romance than reality. He studied the owners' coats of arms and drew them. He scanned the local newspapers and seized on the advertisements for the occasional sale of a big house, looking at them longingly. His father, to calm him, told him quietly that his own family was a great deal older than many of the owners of the big houses, that some of these people were relatively recent blow-ins, that his family had had their big houses too. Garry, who had never considered this before, seized on the idea of researching his own family's genealogy, and set about it with feverish enthusiasm, writing away for information on births and deaths and marriages. When he arrived at an impasse, he badgered his father for more information, but his father, who had already told his son about his cousins the

Nettervilles, had no wish to live in the past, and said only: "If you want to find the missing link, look for a member of the family whose first names were Anthony Fox."

He set out to find traces of Anthony Fox, drawing numerous family trees and puzzling over them, boring the pants off Brian who humoured his older brother but secretly did not have a strong interest in family trees; writing away to so-and-so, and becoming frustrated once more until his father bought *Snipe*. Anthony Fox waited, but Garry would find him in the end.

He was a young man of enthusiasms, many of which did not last. He had become obsessively interested in the Soviet Union a few years before, had begun to learn Russian, had read every book he could find on Soviet history and had listened eagerly to the English language transmissions from Radio Moscow, cocking his ear closely to the wireless because the strength of the signal varied greatly. Exasperated, he had written to Radio Moscow, asking if they could do better. A month later, the family were startled to hear his name being called by the announcer. "Garry," said the voice over the ether, "we did not know our programme was so popular in Ireland. We are very pleased to hear from you."

"Oh Jaysus!" said the poet. "They'll think we're spies."

He had lost interest soon afterwards in the Soviet Union and had decided that he would learn to fly instead. That did not last long, either, but he was consistent in his love of boats; consistent in that he would always love them, but inconsistent in that he would never love the same one for long before he longed for the next.

He had chosen a profession that would allow him to live away from town or city, but he could have chosen almost any profession he wished. He was an excellent draughtsman, so his grandfather the master builder urged him to become an architect, an urban life. He was good with his hands, but he had no wish to become a builder. Science in the abstract bored him. He decided to become a vet, to practise near the sea where he would spend every spare moment in a boat.

◆━◆

A few months before, in the Easter holidays, gaining practical experience with Barty the vet, he had probably saved a man's life.

He had played it down, embarrassed. He did not wish to appear a hero.

He was driving Barty's second car, a rickety Morris, dropping medicines in at one of the vet's clients – a farmer at the far end of Barty's practice – and was approaching a bridge, a dangerous bridge, S-shaped, when he saw a small crowd leaning over, looking at something in the water. He stopped when a Guard waved; saw a woman who recognized him. "Here's the young *vit*," shouted the woman as Garry opened the car door. "He can swim."

Garry ignored this, looked over the bridge at the river in full spate, the tops of the bankside rushes showing above the flood. "What's going on?" he asked the spectators. One, a woman, told him it was Paddy so-and-so, she thought he had gone under the bridge, the lord have mercy on him, the poor cratur. Another, a man, said: poor fellah, he wasn't much good, God help him. How long was it since he had disappeared? A few minutes, they said. Garry, angry, took the calving rope from Barty's car, tied it around his waist, shouted at the others to follow, and ran to where he thought the riverbank was in the flooded field. He was knee deep in brown water, looking up and down the river, preparing to jump in, a panicky voice inside reminding him that he had negative buoyancy, another that he wore his best shoes. He told the men to hold the rope and was stepping off the bank when he saw, a few yards upriver, a patch of pink mackintosh. He stopped, still on the bank, saw an arm slowly raised, like Excalibur from the lake, clothed not in white samite but in pink mackintosh, and grabbed it. He pulled hard, almost falling forward into the river until the men behind tugged on the calving rope. A man's face appeared, purple, covered in mucus. They brought him to the bank.

The man coughed and began to breathe. Garry was very pleased that he lived, but he was even more pleased that he did not have to give him the kiss of life.

When they brought him up to the bridge and a Guard took over, Garry learned that the man lived on the other side of the bridge with his wife, their ten children, and his mother. He had never held a job. The night before, in a rainstorm, the driver of a car had failed to see the bend, had assumed the road was straight, and had driven off the bridge into the river. The car submerged; the driver escaped.

The local, a father of ten, filled with curiosity or scenting a reward, had carried a wooden pig trough and a long pole to the site next day, climbed in the trough, pushed it out into the river, and began to feel for the car using the pole.

Came the inevitable: the trough capsized and the man sank like a stone, so quickly that his head stuck in the mud on the bottom, so fast that his nostrils were clogged with mud. That, said Garry afterwards, was almost certainly what saved him.

The family at Prospect heard little of this at the time, but a week later a shaken man appeared on a bicycle and asked for Garry. He shook the veterinary student's hand, and said: "Me mother says I'm to thank you for savin' me life. And I do thank you." Shyness overcoming him, he cycled away, the family staring at the departing figure, then at Garry, who ducked quickly back into the house.

◆ ◆

They had passed the Old Battery to starboard, and to port the long line of trees that ran out to the Crow. They could see the beach at Farracloe to the north-west. To the south was the familiar white guardian, the Fascar Rock lighthouse. The sea here and to the north passed over great shoals with exotic names: Dogger Bank, Moneyweights. Towards the end of the War, sailing far to seaward of these, the poet had seen a great fleet on the eastern horizon, steering south, part of the invasion force steaming from Britain's Atlantic ports for the beaches of Normandy.

The poet took his binoculars and scanned the sea about them. A fishing boat steamed from the harbour, heading east for the fishing grounds. Other sailing boats dotted the harbour. Gulls cried overhead, and constant flights of resident duck, gannets and cormorants flew from their feeding grounds. The tide had turned.

They had a quicker voyage home, tacking back and forth to aim at the harbour mouth, the tide well on the flood, carrying them home. The breeze was dying as they entered the estuary, but it was enough to bring them to their temporary mooring. An hour later, after mooring and rolling up mainsail and jib, stowing everything away and making all snug, they were rowed back to the slipway in a borrowed praam and were soon back at Prospect.

◆ ◆

They went out again several times that week, becoming more adventurous as they grew to know their boat, one day leaving at dawn on a mighty sail that took them down past the south-east point of the island. From there, on a day of unequalled visibility, they could see the Casks light; due west beyond that lay the two islands, Sáile Mór and Sáile Beg, and they could picture but not see the waves breaking against the steep walls of the larger, outer island; the saint's bridge from the smaller island a long black line at low tide, at its edge the rock called St Patrick's Boat that the saint had cursed to stone when it sank beneath him. They talked of the modern-day eccentric who proclaimed the sovereignty of the islands, styled himself prince, built a cement throne, and flew in a plane-load of cats to kill the rabbits after similar experiments with ferrets, then foxes, had failed.

They took *Snipe* close to the south-east point of the country, close to the iron teeth of the rocks that stretched to catch an unwary vessel, and turned on a close reach for home with the wind brisker, seeing a big basking shark cruise past them, the air filled with the cries of kittiwakes and herring gulls, the smell of the sea cleansing their senses.

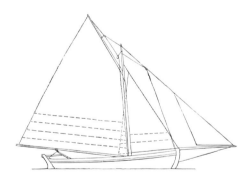

Chapter Twenty-Three

One morning the poet opened a buff envelope to find a contract for one of his rare plays for the stage. He looked at the fee. It was not generous, but it was enough to finance the beginning of the next project at Prospect.

The poet planned to convert a long room at the back of the house that had been used as a tool-shed into a breakfast room. That would lead into a big greenhouse he would build at the back of the house, and into a new sun room on the side facing the Grove.

When he could afford it, and sometimes when he could not, he had improved Prospect. The bathroom, the kitchen with its Aga, the conservatory at the end of the kitchen which had turned the most heavily used room in the house from darkness to light, and the reflooring of the big attic rooms had all been financed by the additional literary income. A stream of other projects, including the redecoration of the entire house, outside and inside, had been partially completed, mainly by the older boys.

He would not involve himself directly in the new works, of course. His family had not seen him take any form of exercise, or perform any act of manual labour since the War, when he had worked on his boat. Nor did they resent this.

The poet knew he could settle for the main part of the big project, and hopefully finish the other parts later, but he wanted strongly to go for the whole. To do that, he would need help. He would need at least one extra skilled man, and most of the materials to be free. The cheque in front of him would not pay for all of it.

He meditated on this for a while amid the chatter of the breakfast table and the background noise of the wireless. The sound of cartwheels in the back yard signalled the arrival of Benny, to be followed, a minute or two later, by John on his bike. He continued to think while his wife gave each of the men a cup of tea.

He rose from the table, pushed back his chair, and tied his bow-tie before picking up the envelope with its cheque. He walked out into the hall, his wife following, through the open front door to the gravelled front and his car. Before starting the car, he said: "I think I'll give Jim a call this morning." She nodded. Her youngest brother Jim, her favourite, was increasingly taking over the running of the family building business in the capital. "Ask him if he'd like to come and have a little holiday with us," she said. The poet visibly brightened. "So I will," he said, and drove down the drive.

He hesitated when he reached the front gates. He had intended to go to his office in Eskerford. Instead, he turned right, up the hill, past McCann's shop and up to the hillier country around Clonard Cross. At the crossroads he turned left onto an unmetalled road, down the hill past Mahony's thatched, whitewashed cottage until he arrived at the crossroads at a long, straight undulating road. The poet turned right.

When he saw a row of three cottages on the left, he stopped at the first, climbed out of the car and knocked, ignoring the mongrel that strained at its rope to attack him. A handsome woman came to the open door.

"Good morning, Mam," said the poet. "Is Pat in?"

"He is," said the woman. "I'll get him for you now."

The poet waited. The dog quietened for a moment, then threw itself forward again when a small, slight, wizened man with a sharp chin and a perpetually good-humoured look appeared. He wore a flat cap and a set of blue overalls.

"How are you, Pat?" asked the poet, beaming.

"Oh! Still alive," said Pat Fitz. He wrinkled his eyes in the bright sun as he spoke. Every word seemed to come through his nose. These emerged as *Snillalive*. "Still alive," he repeated. "Cuttin' along fine, you know. Cuttin' along fine."

"Have you got the time for a job?"

The handyman considered. The poet had learned quickly that the men of this county did not like to be rushed, just as they did not like to be rushed in his own part of the country.

"I suppose I could be free in a week or so," he said, after a pause. "When would you want me?"

"That would be about right," said the poet. "It would be about six weeks' work. Is that all right?"

"Oh! 'Tis all right with me. 'Tis all right with me, I suppose," said Pat. "Will you let me know?"

"I will," the poet promised. "I've got a bit of building to do on the house. I'll know tonight whether I can go ahead. Either way," he said as he prepared to leave, "I'll drop in tonight and let you know."

"Good enough," said Pat. "Good luck to you now," and he waited politely until the poet drove away.

Horgan was waiting at the office.

"The *Farlogue* is in," he said, nodding at the window. The poet had already seen the ship. "I know," he said.

"I thought so," said Horgan in his musical Munster accent; *I tawtso*, his favourite expression.

"Would you look after her?" asked the poet, lighting a

cigarette. "I have a call to make." He picked up the telephone and cranked the handle. When the operator responded: "Number please?" he replied: "I want a call to Dublin."

The four youngest boys thinned turnips, a job they hated. After breakfast Benny had shepherded them to the Flat Field. They looked in dismay at the long lines of drills and little plants. Niall groaned: "Mother of God, look at those drills!"

Benny grinned. "*Noill*, you were born tired."

Niall looked at the blazing sun. Although it was still early, it was hot. "I wish I had been," he said with feeling. "If I had, I wouldn't have to do this bloody awful job."

"Come on," said Conor, who hated it as much as anyone, but knew there was little point arguing. "At least we're paid for it."

"Thruppence a drill!" said Niall, hitching up his baggy shorts. "It's slave labour." He tried to calculate how many drills he would have to thin before he could buy a new reel, and grimaced when he reached the answer.

To thin each drill, they had to uproot four out of every five young turnip plants, and pile them in heaps. It was back-straining work. They were perpetually bent until they stopped and stood straight. Fingernails broke in the thick soil. They grew hot and thirsty. Crisis point came when they stopped to look at how much had been achieved, and how much remained, but they kept at it. It was slow, tedious work, but they knew that the turnips would not grow large if other turnips crowded them, and that the cattle could not feed themselves during the winter. By lunchtime, they had completed less than half of the field, and their young backs ached. It was Padraic's first taste of real work. He did not enjoy it.

Brian was also very hot, slaughtering *buachalán buídhe* in the Well Field, smiting left and right like a Saracen with Abdul, muttering under his breath. He did not hear the lark overhead, or stop to consider what a beautiful morning it was. He was fixed on his task. Halts came only when he threw Abdul on the ground and walked to the well, put his head under the pump and worked the handle until he had cooled. Then he began again.

◆━◆

Garry was building a hot press, or linen cupboard, in the bathroom. It would cover an entire wall. The bathroom was large, and the ceiling high, so the press would be big, as it needed to be for a family that used so many sheets and towels. He would leave a significant space between press and wall, large enough to conceal the hot water cylinder and the electric pump that drew in the water from the Well Field. It would almost be a room in itself, with a door opening from the bathroom at the end near the short flight of stairs up from the landing.

He had spent part of the morning measuring and re-measuring, jotting notes and measurements and drawing lines in thick pencil on the walls. He would begin with a simple, heavy frame: a rectangular shape that would run along floor and ceiling and both walls. The companion frame would be set three feet further back. The shelves would rest between them, as would the supports that would separate each shelf. Two large sliding doors would run along the front, and give access to the shelves. He would place another door on the right to give access to the pump at the back of the press. He began to saw as the swallows darted outside the open windows.

John was laying a drain along the edge of the Paddock. He had cleaned the open ditches with his spade and was lowering a line of concrete cylinders to the bottom. The ditches were unsightly things, with frequent pools of stagnant water that seeped from the edge of the Well Field. They were covered in briars and undergrowth until John cleared them.

When the drain was complete he would cover it with earth and build a mud trap – an open, concrete tank – on the edge of the yard. The drain would run into the mud trap. Every few months the mud would be removed and carted away. Grass would replace the open ditches and an eyesore would vanish.

━◆◆━

Alphonsus, in contrast to the family, had been having an idle, pleasant morning. He had had nothing to do except fly to the roof, hop to the chimney nearest the Grove and argue with the other jackdaws. Eventually, they had driven him off. He had settled on the eaves above Conor and Niall's bedroom to find beetles and earwigs. When he heard a sudden chattering from the other jackdaws and an outburst of cooing from the wood pigeons in the Grove, he looked up and saw a sparrowhawk darting over the beech wood at the edge of the Paddock.

The female sparrowhawk would rarely attack so close to the house, preferring an ambush in thick woods, but the jackdaw did not know that. "Tschack!" he cackled, and flew for the safety of the kitchen. The sparrowhawk circled for a while as John watched, then darted across the Grove towards the road.

━◆◆━

When the jackdaw entered the kitchen he made straight for the top of the dresser, to perch there, flustered, cackling loudly.

The boys' mother and Martha were folding sheets after a morning's ironing. The boys' mother was listening to *Mrs Dale's Diary* and talking to Martha at the same time. Steam puffed from a pressure cooker on the hob. Loaves of freshly-baked soda bread, white and brown, lay on the cupboard top to the side of the cooker, the scent of baking bread wafting to the jackdaw. From the bathroom above came the sound of sawing. Alphonsus rested his head on his breast and dozed.

———◆◆———

The two pigs dozed in the sun, their young scattered around the floor of the sty. Occasionally one of the bonhams, or piglets, squealed with rage when its sibling sat on it.

———◆◆———

The sparrowhawk cruised back and forth over the big elm at the Stile. She had had a good morning, killing a baby rabbit soon after dawn and carrying it back to her young in the nest. Soon after, she had set out again. The lark over the Well Field saw her and climbed, knowing the hawk could not reach her at such a height. The sparrowhawk settled at the top of the elm above the Stile, twisting her head to watch the road and the edge of the Grove.

Soon she saw, on a rattling cart, a woman with an incipient moustache and a face like a witch. A vicious little terrier ran beside the jennet. Fifty yards behind her, on an old black bike, rode a very thin man in blue overalls, with a long, crooked body and a wide hat, who overtook her, raising his hand in salute as he passed. "Mornin'," he said.

"And a good morning to you, Matt Lacey!" said the crone. "You're back. And have you had your hat straightened again, is it?"

"Oho," said the man hurriedly, "that's the way of it, is it?" and began to pedal faster. When he had ridden a safe distance in front, he muttered: "Bad cess to you, you ould bitch! And your feckin' dog!"

The road grew quiet. The sparrowhawk perched in the tree for much of the time, flying over the Grove occasionally. When she drifted back over the road again, a thermal carrying the scents of resin from the Grove and melting tar from the road up to her, she saw two people emerge from McCann's shop, a man and a woman.

The man was old, the woman middle-aged. She wore a floral print overall and her hair in a neat bun. He wore a cap and a brown serge suit, with big, flappy trousers. They were joined by a very round, middle-aged man, with a rolling gait like a sailor. He wore a blue beret and an old and very shiny blue suit, a belt holding in his big stomach. "Yais," the old man said repeatedly, "yais," while the younger woman – his daughter, Annie Kelly, née McCann – was plainly giving him instructions. "Yais," said the old man again, and set off down the road towards the town. Annie and her husband Nicky stood for a few minutes, gazing up and down the road, then went back inside.

The sparrowhawk watched the old man walk almost directly below her. Insects hummed in the thick undergrowth between the Stile and the Grove. Shortly after, she turned and quickly flew back towards her nest. In the Well Field, Brian lifted his head and watched as she stooped on a tree-sparrow and killed it, bearing it off in a great soaring glide.

Tempers were still short in the Flat Field but the piles of

uprooted young turnip plants grew steadily and lunchtime approached. Niall brightened as he suggested to Conor: "We might go over to the Edenbeg when we've finished this evening. What do you think?"

"*Ex*-cellent idea," said Conor, in an exaggerated drawl. "It won't be dark before ten."

"Does anyone want me to bring anything from the house?" asked Padraic hopefully. With luck, someone would say yes, and he could dawdle through until lunch. He was tired and very bored. He thought the job pointless, best left to other people.

"No," said Conor forcefully. Benny grinned sardonically and lit his pipe, replacing its metal windshield and puffing blue clouds of smoke into the summer air, saying nothing. Work began again.

◆◆

The poet had made his phone call. He had also completed his office chores, nodding gratefully to Horgan who had brought him a carton of Camels from the captain of the *Farlogue*. He retied his bow-tie, left his office after a few words with Old Jack McGrath, the caretaker, and walked up to the main street where he bought his newspapers.

One of his official posts was Receiver of Wrecks, a job he exploited shamelessly to help the deserving. When he had to auction a salvaged vessel, such as a lifeboat without an identifiable owner, he would ensure it was sold to someone who needed it most, avoiding the petty bureaucracy that the necessity of a public auction would otherwise impose, appearing to go through the full process; the opposite of petty officialdom. During the War he had overheard a passer-by – a fisherman, or sailor, he did not know which, but plainly a beneficiary of his peculiar system – say: "That fellah is the cleverest man in the county." He had been embarrassed, but ridiculously pleased.

He heard his name called and turned. A big, bent man with iron-grey hair and an old blue serge suit had come out of a side street. The poet beamed. "Hello, Paddy." This man was one of the first to welcome him to Eskerford, pilot-master of the harbour until he had retired a few years before, and it was he who had taught the poet to sail. He had been born in the old Battery, the harbour defence on a sandy spit that marked the entrance to Eskerford Harbour, the fort that had surrendered to Cromwell without firing a shot, and he had seen his old home sink after the sea breached the dunes. The pilot had been bosun on the last of the Eskerford-owned cargo schooners before taking the pilot-master's job, and bore the scar of a blow from a marline-spike on his neck from a drunken, mutinous Cape Horner.

The older boys liked him very much, and hung on his words during the War when he called at the rented house in Eskerford, sitting around a smoking fire while he told them sea stories, and of his mother's clock at his old home in the Battery, which stopped for years at a time and began to tick again only when a member of his family was about to die, then stopped again.

The Battery had been a village as well as a fort, with a church and school of its own. It had sheltered the biggest fleet of fishing cots in the county, the pilot cutters, and its own lifeboat. It was home to the pilots who guided the incoming shipping over the bar of Eskerford Harbour, sometimes as many as twenty ships towed by the same tug in a single haul. The sea had finally cut through the sands almost thirty years before, leaving two great breaches that cut off the Battery, drove the villagers from their homes and finished the community. The tops of the walls were now barely visible above the harbour's surface.

The poet chatted to the pilot and walked back to his car on the quay. The sea as far as the Crow was light green, lighter again when it crossed the shallow of the harbour bar, and suddenly darker beyond. The light breeze was from the south. The fine weather appeared to be as fixed as the weather in this part of the world could be.

He started the car and drove slowly home. Those outdoors at Prospect heard the boom of the exhaust as the car neared the gates. For those in the Flat Field it was the most welcome sound in the world.

───◆───

Bruno ran to meet the poet as the car halted on the gravel. The poet followed him and the newspaper into the front hall. It smelled of the palm flowers placed in the old white china stand with a leg missing.

He greeted his wife: "Jim is sending a lorry down the day after tomorrow. We're in luck. He's building a new branch for the bank in Phibsboro. They're throwing out the entire floor of tiles, lots of timber as well, and he's going to have a look in the yard to see if he can throw in anything else."

Her face lit up. "And can he come down as well?"

"He'll be here on Friday, and will stay until Monday or Tuesday," said the poet, knowing how pleased she would be.

"That's wonderful," she said.

Garry grinned when he heard the news. During the War and his illness that followed, a visit from his bachelor uncle – his very generous bachelor uncle – filled him with such anticipation that he counted the days until he arrived. When Uncle Jim left, Garry's depression was profound.

Brian was next in, mopping his brow, followed by John. Then came the slaves of the field, weary, thirsty and very hungry, especially Ivan, who darted towards the cooker and lifted the lid of the steaming pot.

The poet told them of his plans as they ate. Building would go ahead. There would be weeks of work, digging foundations, mixing cement, making concrete blocks, chipping grout off used tiles, laying the screed, tiling a vast area, building walls, cutting glass, glazing the great greenhouse which would run along half the back wall of Prospect, building the sun room out from the breakfast room, painting and whitewashing. All of the boys would have to help, or it would not be finished before winter, leaving the house open and exposed, an unthinkable prospect. It would be completed if they gave it their all, completed in time for their expedition up the inland waterways from which they must be back in time to work on the harvest. It was tight, but certainly possible, weather favouring.

There was nothing formal in the manner in which he told them this. It came in bits and parts, answers to questions, asides, interruptions; but when he finished the poet looked around the table and saw only enthusiasm, expressed and demonstrated in different ways, but enthusiasm, creative enthusiasm.

The mood changed abruptly when he enquired about progress with turnip-thinning. He had touched a nerve. "Why don't you work until four and we'll go to the beach?" he said, patting Bruno's head. Conor and Niall looked at one another and decided the Edenbeg would wait.

Chapter Twenty-Four

Padraic had won a postponement of a return to the turnip thinning, to the irritation of his brothers, by offering to run an errand to McCann's for his mother. He tried to whistle as he walked the path between nettles and briars, produced only a splutter, remembered that Ivan could not whistle either, and grinned to himself.

He leaped lightly over the Stile to an empty road. He was not in a hurry to return. If late, he would blame Nicky.

He liked the shopkeeper's tales; listened, open-mouthed, looking up over the counter at the big round face; missing lower front teeth; greasy, dark beret; days of stubble; squashed nose; small eyes; collarless shirt open at the neck. He heard of voyages in this-or-that barquentine, clipper, or schooner. Most were to America, to New York in particular, which was as far as the moon to the boy. Arguments with the shop's few customers usually ended abruptly when Nicky played his trump: "Have you ever been to Fifth Avenue?" He said this with an air of triumph, knowing it clinched all; his emphasis on the vocative: *Have* YOU *ever been t'Fifth Avenyah?*

Padraic was shocked when his family dismissed Nicky's tales. "Sailor!" scoffed Niall. "He wasn't a bloody sailor. Not a real sailor, anyway. He was a ship's cook!" Benny chimed in: "The furthest that fecker has been to is Liverpool. And they say he was sick on the v'yage!" John, a rare critic, added quietly: "He has himself a nice number now, anyhow," a clear inference that Nicky had married the shopkeeper's daughter and a comfortable existence on the same morning.

The boy decided this was unfair, sour grapes. If it was true that Nicky had married solely for comfort, why did his wife Annie look at him adoringly when the voyages to Fifth Avenue were told and retold? The family were wrong, and he was right, Padraic decided, not for the first or last time.

He continued to listen, spending increasing time, to his mother's annoyance, at the counter. He liked the stories and liked even more the wry, cryptic comments about the locals. On winter nights, sent to buy paraffin, he gladly walked the dark path to the Stile as a gale swept through the trees, sometimes in the pitch dark, totally sure of his way, to listen to Nicky while the draughts in the shop caused the oil-lamp on the counter to gutter, throwing dancing shadows on the opposite wall of the shop. On that wall hung an advertisement for pipe tobacco, painted enamelled tin, of a laughing man with a face like a leprechaun. The face grimaced and contorted in the uneven light, the eyes blinking repeatedly. Padraic, staring, half expected the man, like Pinocchio, to speak.

A similar advertisement for cigarettes hung on the drab, brown wall to the left of the counter; a bearded man in the uniform of a sailor of the Royal Navy; cap with the word *Hero*, a tribute, it was said, from the matelots to Charles Stuart Parnell, nationalist hero, who was said to have abolished hanging at the yardarm.

There were other attractions that appealed more to a greedy boy. Glass jars of boiled sweets, bullseyes and so on; below them shelves of Fry's Turkish delight, Kit Kat, Aero, Fry's Cream bars, Rolos, Cadbury's fruit-and-nut; below that again, opened brown cardboard boxes of Cleeve's toffee, a ha'penny a square. The lowest shelves held no interest, just baking powder, flour and so on; same with the shelves to the right, by the window, smokers' corner: Sweet Afton, Gold Flake, Woodbines, Players Number One, black plug like Benny smoked, Mick McQuaid. Below were the lemonades and orange squashes. In the opposite corner of the shop, below the leprechaun selling pipe tobacco, was the paraffin pump. It was not much of a shop, but it was a magical place to a small boy.

Every Saturday afternoon when pocket money was paid, the younger boys blew it all in a single spree: Cousins' lemonade, either chocolate or Cleeves' toffee, a difficult decision; chocolate was better, toffee lasted longer. There were periods of self-denial, not for Lent, but to save up for a fishing rod or reel. Ivan and Padraic ignored this, but Conor and Niall suffered Saturday afternoons in torment, sometimes for months at a time.

Padraic entered the shop on this hot afternoon to find his friend leaning on the counter, looking through the shop window at Matt Lacey cycling slowly home.

Nicky said, in a voice that could not be heard outside the shop: "And was you there Lacey sez she!"

"What?" asked Padraic. "What do you mean, Nicky?"

Nicky turned to look at the boy, who clearly needed a bath. His face and hands were covered in earth from the turnip field, mother's orders flouted.

"He's after having his hat straightened," Nicky said.

Padraic was slow to understand. "Who? Who're you talking about?"

Nicky nodded at the road, even though Matt had passed by now. "Yer man," he said.

"Matt! Matt Lacey! Why would he want his hat straightened out? What's wrong with his hat? Is it crooked, or something?"

Nicky smiled, exposing the gap in his teeth. "He's in *a hape o'form* like Sonny Sutton's greyhound, now he's back."

"Back!" said Padraic. "Back from where? Where's he been?"

"Where's he been?" repeated Nicky. "Why, everyone knows he's been in Inish Gortaídh. Shur everyone knows that."

"But what was he doing there? Was he working?" asked Padraic.

Nicky smiled triumphantly. "He was having his hat straightened. Didn't I tell you that before?" He started to hum a come-all-ye, stopped and said again: "And was you there Lacey sez she."

Padraic was bored with the riddle. "What's New York like?" he asked.

That set Nicky off again on some long voyage or other that had taken forever. They were joined by Annie, from the living quarters behind the shop, who listened, smiling. When the story ended, she asked the boy: "What was it you came for?"

"Oh, God," said Padraic, turning pale. "I've forgotten."

Annie patiently reeled off a list of items. None registered.

"How much did your mother give you?" asked Annie.

Padraic fumbled in his pocket; found a florin. "Two shillings," he said.

"That could mean anything," Annie sighed. "You'd better go home and ask."

"I suppose so," said Padraic. "They'll be very angry. You see, I'm supposed to be thinning turnips."

"'Tis safer to ask," said Annie wisely.

Padraic turned to leave, apprehensive. Nicky called after him: "And WAS you there Lacey sez she!"

◆

When he reached home, his mother waited at the kitchen door. "What kept you – and where's the salt?"

Padraic started. Salt! That was it. How could he have forgotten?

"Nicky kept me. I couldn't get him to stop talking," he said, moving from one foot to another. "By the time he'd finished, I'd forgotten what you asked me to buy." He looked at her hopefully.

"Go back and get it. And come straight back with it!"

He shot off, relieved; ran to the shop, blurted his order, paid, put the change in his pocket and ran back. When he handed the box of Saxa salt and the change to his mother, he asked: "Why would Matt Lacey need to go away to have his hat straightened?"

She stared at him. She had settled with the crossword after lunch. "What are you talking about?"

"It was something Nicky said. Matt had to go to get his hat straightened. But he rode past the shop, and his hat looked the same as usual."

"Oh, Nicky is always talking in riddles," said his mother, turning to her crossword again. "Just go and help your brothers."

They bounced along the road to Farracloe two hours later, Padraic perched on Garry's knee in the front, Ivan on the bench seat between them and their father. Padraic kept his head out the window. He felt sick. The poet was smoking, the breeze drifting the smoke into Padraic's face. The other three were in the back, Brian deep in a book.

Conor and Niall, a duet, sang:

O Doctor, O Doctor, O Dear Doctor John,
Your codliver oil is so pure and so strong,
I'm afraid of me life I'll go down in the soil
If me wife don't stop drinkin' your codliver oil.

As they neared the beach Padraic asked his father: "What does it mean when someone has been away to get his hat straightened?"

The poet swung the wheel slightly to avoid a cyclist. "Where did you hear that?"

"From Nicky?"

"Nicky who?"

"Nicky Kelly."

"Oh! That old blathermouth," said the poet, displeased. "You spend too much time in that shop listening to his old stories."

"I like Nicky," said Padraic, "but what did he mean?"

"What or who was he talking about?" asked the poet, lighting a cigarette from the butt of its predecessor.

"He said Matt Lacey had been away to have his hat straightened."

The poet glanced across at Garry, who shook his head slightly. Each knew how indiscreet Padraic could be.

"I don't know what he meant, but he talks in riddles anyway," said the poet, with another sideways glance at Garry, who nodded. Padraic missed this and turned to Garry, who said immediately: "I don't know either."

The poet changed the subject as he turned off to the beach without bothering to signal. "When are you going to give us another performance of your orchestra, Gar?"

This caused near uproar. Conor and Niall broke off from their song, shouted unintelligible remarks, interrupting each other; so that only partial phrases, such as "burn the poor man's favourite coat," and "that bloody mouse" were distinguishable. Brian lifted his head and smiled. Garry and Padraic looked embarrassed.

◆—◆

Soon after the family had arrived at Prospect, Garry, always driven towards perfection, had built a series of fake musical instruments from wood and cardboard; had built them so finely that, from a distance, they appeared genuine. He had built a cello (Ivan); a violin (Conor); an oboe (Brian); a French horn (Niall); and a second violin (Padraic). The stringed instruments shone with varnish. He conducted in the white-tie-and-tails that his paternal grandmother, intensely anxious that he should look his best, had given him for his first hunt ball.

The music came from the wind-up gramophone, hidden behind the curtains of the dining room. The big mahogany dining table was pushed to the side. The boys sat on a row of dining chairs, Garry waved his baton, disappeared behind the curtains, placed the steel needle of the gramophone on the record, the tin loudspeaker hissed and crackled and Garry reappeared to tap on his painting easel. As the opening bars sounded he waved his arms, straight hair flopping, turning the score of Beethoven's Fifth Symphony, the orchestra's favourite. The players sawed at the strings or puffed their cheeks. Garry pointed the baton at the players, beating time with his other hand. The boys, particularly the younger ones, thought this fun, great gas. They fiddled and blew with enthusiasm.

The son of one of the greatest British conductors was an amateur composer and was an old friend of the poet. Adrian and Joyce, son Robert, and daughter Jane, a beautiful, willowy English rose, were regular guests at Prospect; neither pompous nor formal and therefore very welcome. Adrian was an amiable baronet who dressed in shabby tweeds, Joyce an aristocrat of good manners, a favourite with the boys' mother. They had come for the annual music festival in Eskerford and had, as usual, stayed with the family.

It was the poet's doing. "It would be a howl, a bit of jizz," he said, if Garry showed off the family orchestra to the son of the conductor. Garry, easily influenced by his father, seized on the suggestion, gave the stringed instruments an extra coat of varnish and put his players into rehearsal. The guests would arrive before dinner. The six boys and the gramophone would perform when they had eaten.

The guests arrived, wet through. They had been caught walking on the beach when the Irish weather surprised them. They were ushered in to the drawing room. The poet, amiable host, poured a big whiskey for Adrian who accepted it gratefully, then he insisted on taking Adrian's favourite tweed coat, to hang it to dry on the Aga. He bore it into the kitchen, lifted the lid of the simmer hob, and placed the coat over it carefully. Then he returned with more whiskey to the drawing room where a big fire warmed the visitors.

The party began to hum. The guests recovered from their soaking and were warm again. Whiskey and gin flowed liberally. Outside, the gale whipped the rose trees against the windows; inside, it was warm and hospitable.

The boys' mother went through to the kitchen to see to dinner. The acrid smell of burning cloth greeted her. The kitchen was full of smoke. She rushed to the Aga and saw the coat had a perfectly circular hole between the shoulder blades, smouldering and smoking at the edges. She stared, horrified. Then she quickly threw it on the kitchen table and doused the fire with a wet cloth from the sink.

She walked quickly back to the drawing room, outwardly calm, and tried to summon her husband who was deep in conversation with Adrian and Joyce. "Pack," she said, but he took no notice. She walked over, took his arm; interrupted: "Pack, can you give me a hand with something?"

He looked puzzled, but obeyed. When they walked through to the kitchen she picked up the coat and said: "Look what you've done to Adrian's coat! And it's his favourite! He didn't even want you to take it!"

The poet stared. "Oh, Jaysuschrist!" he muttered. "He'll never forgive me."

She was the first to recover. "You'd better tell him at once."

He did. Adrian rushed through the hall to the kitchen and picked up his coat in dismay. "Oh! I say! My poor old coat," he said.

His lady intervened. "Don't worry," she said to the poet. "I've been longing for this to happen for years. I'm fed up with that wretched, shabby old thing!"

Her husband looked at her sorrowfully. "Joyce! It was my favourite. I had it during the War."

"I'm so sorry, Adrian," said the boys' mother. "I can't think what came over Pack." She glared at her husband.

Adrian soon recovered, helped by another glass or two of special proof whiskey on which duty had not and would not be paid. By the end of supper he was his old self, talking of literary movements in Britain in the Thirties, the War, postwar music, painting. The dining table buzzed.

Garry, in contrast, grew nervous. How pitiful his silly, sham orchestra would look in front of the son of one of the most famous conductors in Europe! The whole thing would be a disaster. He was sure of it. He would look and feel ridiculous, particularly in white-tie-and-tails.

Padraic also felt uncomfortable. He had decided before supper that the show should include more than the orchestra and that he would add to the fun by loosing a mouse when attention was elsewhere. He had one in his pocket and was trying to eat with one utensil, using his other hand to prevent the mouse escaping. His mother looked at him suspiciously from time to time, and said sharply: "Use your knife and fork properly."

When they had finished, the poet, his wife and guests moved across the front hall into the drawing room. Led by Conor, the boys cleared the table, then pushed it into the corner of the room. They put the chairs in place. Garry reappeared in white-tie-and-tails, head bowed, and checked that the gramophone was working. The others collected the bogus instruments from their bedrooms. They sat, feeling the first tingles of stage fright.

The mouse grew restive, trying to bite Padraic's fingers as he pushed it down into the bottom of his trouser pocket. The boy could not see a way to keep it there with both hands occupied. He looked desperately about him. The only convenient parking place was Niall's French horn, leaning against his chair.

He took the mouse from his pocket in his cupped hand and dropped it into the bell-shaped mouth. There was a scrabbling noise as the mouse broke its fall.

Ivan went to summon the audience. He opened the drawing room door and shouted: "Ready!"

The audience took their places. Garry vanished behind the curtains. The gramophone screeched, crackled; was silent again. Garry hastily re-emerged, bowed to the audience who applauded with cheers and catcalls, shot back behind the curtains again, placed the needle on the record, waited until the speaker began to hiss, came back through the curtains, tapped his baton, and, as the opening bars of Beethoven's Fifth Symphony sounded tinnily, began to conduct:

Pom pom pom pom! Pom pom pom POM!

Stage fright vanished instantly. They went at the music with enthusiasm, violins and cello sawing back and forth, elbows digging into neighbours' ribs, Garry beating time with one hand, wiping his brow with the other. Padraic glanced furtively at Niall's French horn. All seemed well for the moment.

Garry began to relax as they swept further into the first movement. The audience were plainly enjoying themselves and had entered into the spirit of the thing.

As his confidence grew Garry began to enjoy himself too, allowing himself extravagant flourishes with his baton that produced spontaneous applause from the audience, Adrian included. Occasionally he had to gesture sharply at Brian, whose attention was prone to wander and, as the record was worn by age and use, he had to ignore the odd needle jump, but these seemed to increase rather than diminish the enjoyment of the audience. Niall, too, was not paying as much attention as he should, bending at one stage to put his ear to his instrument with a puzzled look, but the audience did not appear to notice.

The music reached its climax and came to an end. The listeners cheered and whistled; Garry bowed three times and gestured magnanimously at the musicians who stood and bowed as well. The concert was finished.

Niall put his ear to his instrument again. Padraic moved quickly away. Niall shook the French horn sharply. When he heard something tumble inside he said to Conor and

Brian: "There's something inside my bloody instrument!"

He turned the horn face upside down and shook it. Something small, brown and furry fell from it and sat for a moment, glaring at them with little glinting eyes before it shot across the floor towards the door. Between it and the door stood the audience, who looked at it in horror. Joyce and Jane screamed.

"It's a bloody mouse!" shouted Niall. "There was a mouse in my horn! A bloody m – hey, wait a minute! Where's Padraic? Where's that little bastard gone? I bet he did it. Where is he? I'll break his bloody neck!"

Padraic had hidden in the barn. He listened to the boom of the gale as rain drummed on the galvanized iron roof, and the calls of his brothers as they searched for him. When he emerged the family had returned to the drawing room and whiskey was flowing once more. He escaped with little more than a whack on his backside from his father, and a threat from Niall that was forgotten the next day. The mouse, he learned, had made a clean getaway.

The sea was warmer at Farracloe. The poet wandered barefoot, lighting cigarettes from his spectacles, looking at wildflowers, book in hand. The boys swam, played cricket on the beach; then, at their father's suggestion, competed to find wildflowers on the sand dunes that matched the illustrations. Even Padraic swam, not for long, but for long enough to say that he had.

In the early evening they rambled back in the car to Prospect, singing most of the way. Supper was waiting. Chinese chequers followed.

As the rest of the family went to bed the poet stood with Conor in the Paddock; faces upturned to the night sky. The poet's gesturing cigarette in the darkness drew lightning shapes that lingered on the retina. "Cassiopeia, the Lady in the Chair" he explained to his son. "And there – that one there, above the Pole Star. That's Draco." He took Conor's arm: "Look there, on the southwest horizon, yes, there. That's Virgo. Libra's to the west of it, right on the horizon. You can just see the two top stars. Look up to the north-west, far to the left of the Pole Star: that's Hercules. Isn't it clear! Orion sits down on the horizon at this time of year," pointing towards the dim glow of Eskerford, "so we can't see him." He paused. "Winter star," he said, and blew a stream of smoke, gazing up absently at the bears turning the earth on its spindle.

When Padraic climbed into bed and put his feet down the sheets he felt a warm furry body. Mutt! He leant down and stroked her. His cat moved up and lay on the cover beside him, purring in a soft wheeze.

He awoke when Ivan climbed into the other bed. He sat up, the distant beam from the lighthouse moving across the wall above him, then asked: "D'you know why Matt Lacey had to go away to get his hat straightened?"

Ivan said sleepily: "I think it means that he went a bit mad for a while. He went to something called an asylum where they cure people like that."

"Oh!" said Padraic, and went back to sleep.

Chapter Twenty-Five

Brian was out soon after dawn next morning with his rifle, walking stealthily along the headlands of the Wheat Field when he discovered the sparrowhawk's nest.

Rabbits had become scarcer as he and Garry hunted. They had to travel further to find them. Prospect's land was practically clear. That was good for the wheat, but the daily stalk took longer. His score was blank when he saw the hawk emerge from her nest with two of her fledglings.

The hawks nested in a tree that was part of a small clump of elm and ash. Brian crouched at a gap in the hedge beside a blackthorn and watched. The female was teaching her young to fly, swooping ahead of them, then circling back as they tumbled, calling to them, flying ahead of them again.

Brian watched for ten minutes then quietly moved on, keeping low until he was out of sight. He resumed his search. Three or four fields further on he saw a nest of rabbits in the far corner of the field and manoeuvred himself into a firing position. As the first rabbit tumbled he shot another quickly, then looked around. The remaining rabbits had vanished down their burrows. He moved on.

Half an hour later he swung back towards Prospect, six rabbits hanging from his belt. Not wishing to disturb the hawks, he avoided the Wheat Field and crossed into Prospect land through the Well Field.

When he reached the Hen-Run he found his mother

collecting the overnight lay. The jackdaw was on her shoulder, scolding angrily. He walked down to the farmyard with her and entered the byre where Conor and Niall milked, pestered by cats.

"Do you remember that sparrowhawk I saw killing the other day?" he asked them.

Conor looked up. "Yes. What about it?"

"I've just seen its nest," said Brian, easing the rifle from his shoulder. He was not quick enough. Hawthorn, copying Blossom, flicked her tail, streaking Brian's face with cowdung. He swore.

Conor took no notice. "Where was it?" he demanded. He had a passion for hawks. He watched them, sketched them, studied their flight, respected their nature.

Brian reached into the feed trough and pulled off a hank of hay. He wiped his face and said: "I saw the whole thing. She has two young. I watched them for quite a while. They never saw me."

Niall turned his head, careful not to disturb Phoebus. "Well, where is it?"

"It's in that clump of trees near the top of the Wheat Field," said Brian, preparing to leave. He still had to clean the rabbits before he began on his other chores.

"Thanks," said Conor. "I know exactly where you mean." He turned back to Hawthorn. Milk began to hiss into the bucket again.

Brian walked to the Dairy and laid his rabbits on the table. He skinned and cleaned them quickly, then carried them into the kitchen where he washed them under the tap. His mother had begun to cook breakfast and the smell of frying bacon reminded him that he was very hungry. The BBC Light Programme filled the kitchen.

Garry was already at the table, studying his charts. He was rubbing his hands. He looked up at Brian: "How many did you get?"

"Only six," said Brian. "They're getting very scarce."

"It's not surprising," said Garry, with a chuckle. "We've shot most of them."

"They're there if you go far enough," said Brian. "It just takes longer."

Their father appeared, looking pleased in spite of the fact that he had worked on a poem until four that morning. It had been light when he had gone to bed.

"Where are all those boys?" he demanded. "There's a lot of work to do today."

"Conor and Niall are still milking," said his wife. "Ivan and Padraic are not down yet, and I'm not going to wake them up for another half hour. They need their sleep. Garry, could you please move those maps? It's almost breakfast time."

"Come through to the dining room," the poet said to Brian, "and tell me what you think of this poem."

They walked through into the hall. Garry moved his charts and carried them up to his room. He looked in on his brothers. Both were fast asleep, Padraic with his arm around Mutt, who was awake and purring. He went downstairs again. He would begin work on the hot press after breakfast.

He heard the crunch of Benny's cartwheels on the gravel at the same time as he heard the clank and rattle of the milk pails as his brothers carried them down the farmyard to the Dairy. The milk would be poured into a wide cooler made of galvanized tin, scrubbed to a gleaming silver each day. When it had cooled the boys' mother would spoon the layer of cream from the top, pints of it, much of it churned into butter with the little hand-churn that held a gallon. Some of the skimmed milk would be set aside to turn into buttermilk to make bread, and to satisfy the thirst of Benny who liked a big mug of it on a hot day. None of the boys drank it.

The kitchen began to fill as breakfast was put on the table. Benny had already eaten. He sat at the end of the table, shaving a big black plug of tobacco, rubbing the results between his palms, filling his pipe before going out to the fields. He poured the cup of tea the boys' mother handed him into a saucer and blew on it to cool it before drinking. John arrived and sipped his tea, standing with his back to the Aga, looking out into the Paddock.

The poet called over to him above the noise: "How did you get on, John?"

John nodded shortly. "It's there, sure enough," he said. "But I don't know how far down. It's deep."

The poet nodded. He had been considering for some time switching the house's water supply from the Well Field to a new well in the Paddock. He and John had separately cut Y-shaped forks of hazel and walked across the Paddock, palms of hands uppermost, elbows almost touching their hips, each hand grasping a top of the Y-shaped sticks.

The poet had been able to divine as long as he could remember. Most of his sons could also do it. The fork would remain inert for many. These tended to be the people who scoffed at the practice, dismissing it as a superstition in this new, nuclear age. This group included many of his wife's family, city people who regarded strange country practices in the same way they regarded leprechauns.

All of John's family had the gift, his father, grandfather, and according to them, his great-grandfather and so on. To them divining was as straightforward as the fact that the moon controlled the tides.

When the boys lost an arrow in the briars at the edge of the Grove John found it for them by drawing a map, then swinging a ring on a string over the map to pinpoint the arrow. Most of the time it worked.

Benny, greasy cap looming above a cloud of blue tobacco smoke, said sombrely: "It'll be deep. That ground is full of marl. It's a holy terror to plough."

The poet was not convinced. They had established to his satisfaction that there was water there. Why should it be any deeper than the water in the Well Field, where the spring ran close to the surface and the ground was soft? He made his decision.

"We'll finish the work on the house, then you can dig a hole to explore the ground," he told John.

John nodded. "Fair enough," he said.

Conor and Niall had entered the kitchen during the conversation. Niall said: "I suppose we'll have to dig a bloody well next!"

Benny puffed another cloud of smoke. "Noill, you were born tired." He repeated: "Born tired," and chuckled with satisfaction.

Niall looked at the ploughman sourly. "It'll be us that does the bloody donkey work," he said.

"Stop that cursing!" said his mother severely.

Garry began to laugh. "You're an awful man for looking at the dark side of life," he said. Niall's ill humour disappeared instantly. "So will you be when you're teetotally charoosed," he said, with a sidelong glance at Benny, who chuckled again. It took an effort to be out of temper on such a sunny morning, even with the prospect of another two days of thinning turnips.

The household sat to breakfast. Halfway through Ivan appeared, looking sleepy. Sport came across the kitchen to greet him. Ivan petted his dog's head and sat, brightening when he saw the plates piled with rashers and eggs.

"Is Padraic awake yet?" his mother asked as she handed him his breakfast.

"No, but he was talking in his sleep," said Ivan. "He was

dreaming about Matt Lacey having his hat straightened."

"Begob-a-man, it needed straightening," said Benny darkly.

"Is that what Mary Anne thinks?" asked John mischievously.

Conversation around the table stopped as the family realized that this was a loaded question. The wireless seemed louder.

Benny blushed, if a man with decades of exposure in the open fields to all forms of weather could blush. He stopped puffing his pipe.

"Mary Anne?" said Ivan. "Who's Mary Anne? Mary Anne who?"

John continued to smile at Benny. "Mary Anne Broaders – perhaps?" asked Niall in a wheedling tone, taking John's cue instantly. John gave him a tiny nod.

"Are you courting Mary Anne Broaders, Benny?" asked Ivan ingenuously. "Are you?" He looked at Benny in wonderment. The woman did not appear to him to be very attractive, or young, or slim, or feminine. More to the point, she had a fearsome, sinister brother who wore a long black coat in winter and summer and who was said to have threatened to beat any man to death who looked at his sister sideways. The Broaders owned a sixty-acre farm, which made them people of substance. Mary Anne's brother rode to the local hunt. He may have been content to play forty-five – the popular card game of the Eskerford country people – with Benny, but he would scarcely bless his sister's wedding to a ploughman.

Benny recovered. "Go away with you, blast you!" he said to John and Niall. He turned to Ivan: "Don't be listenin' to them fellahs. They're after stirrin' up trouble." He rose from the table, still flustered.

"But she's Pat Broaders' sister," Ivan protested. "He'd

kill you! He's like something out of a gangster picture!"

"That's enough," said his mother severely. "Leave Benny alone!" She left the kitchen to call Padraic, thankful that he had not been present.

The field workers rose from the table and followed Benny out into the yard. The sun was already high. Martins and swallows wheeled overhead. Niall took John to one side. "Is he really courting Mary Anne?" he asked in a low voice.

John waited until Benny, who had been eyeing him grimly, had reached his horse and cart before replying: "He went to the pictures with her on Saturday night anyhow," he said finally.

"But didn't Pat see them?" persisted Niall.

"They probably arranged to meet somewhere along the New Road," shrugged John.

"Pat'll kill him," Niall prophesied.

"That's probably why it'll stop there," said John, as Benny, who had many attributes, was not a man to stand up to Pat Broaders, and had once said, in a statement the boys remembered: "I'd rather be a coward for an hour than dead for the rest of me life."

◆—◆

When Padraic came down to breakfast, Mutt in his arms, the kitchen was deserted except for his mother and Martha, who was washing up at the sink. "Where is everybody?" he asked, gazing at the empty table. The sounds of sawing came from overhead.

"They're all at work," said his mother. "Have your breakfast first, then I want you to run to McCann's. You can help in the field afterwards."

Padraic's face clouded at the thought of the wretched

turnip-thinning, but then, he reasoned as he ate his breakfast and drank a pint of milk, he could spin it out with a long visit to Nicky's.

His mother read his mind. "And you're to come straight back!" she admonished him. This time, she handed him a list.

Alphonsus flew in for his breakfast and stood on top of the dresser, tail quivering. Padraic slipped out of the kitchen, clutching his list, as the jackdaw was fed. He ran through the Grove, disturbing a female blackbird who set off her alarm instantly, through the path between the briars, over the Stile, and onto the road.

McCann's was empty. He rapped on the counter with a half-crown. Nicky appeared from the back, blue beret on head, still chewing, carrying a newspaper, slightly grumpy.

"Hello, Nicky!" said Padraic to his friend.

"Begob, you're like Sonny Sutton's greyhound." In a *hape o' form*, thought Padraic, but did not say it. "What is it?" Nicky asked.

"Dunno," said Padraic, "but here's a list," handing Nicky the piece of paper. He gazed admiringly at Nicky's stomach, then shifted his attention to the chocolate bars on the shelves, but it was only Thursday.

Nicky looked at the pencilled list for a few moments, then back to the boy. The shopkeeper began to hum: "And was you there Lacey sez she!"

"Oh! I know all about that," said Padraic importantly. "I know what you were getting at, I do. Matt Lacey had to go to an as-something to get his brain straight. It's not the hat, it's what's under it," he finished triumphantly.

"Begob! Is that so?"

"I think so, sez Martin Codd!" said Padraic, borrowing another of Nicky's favourite expressions.

Nicky turned; reading from the list, began to pick items

from the shelves, boring items like baking powder, salt, flour; not a sweet or a bar of chocolate among them. The sailor laid the items on the counter. He took a stub of pencil, licked the blunt lead; began to write numbers on a brown envelope, adding up several times.

He glanced slyly at the boy. "Have you seen Pat?"

Padraic was bewildered. "Pat who?"

"He's on the rampage, I heard tell," said Nicky cryptically.

"What's that?" asked Padraic. "What's a ram-page? Who's Pat?"

Nicky ignored the question. "I wouldn't like to be in yer man's boots when Pat's had a drop. That's two-and-ninepence."

Padraic handed him a half-crown and a threepenny piece. He grew worried about the delay, but hung there. "Pat who? Who are you talking about?"

Nicky leaned across the counter and said in a voice just above a whisper: "Tell yer man that Pat Broaders is looking for him!"

"Pat Broaders!" Padraic shivered. He pictured a thin man in a black overcoat and hat on a bike who nodded at others in a sinister way when he passed. "Who is he looking for?"

Nicky looked at him as if the answer should be obvious. "Shur doesn't he work for your father," he said.

Padraic knew he would be smacked if he waited any longer. He bolted out of the shop and ran back to Prospect.

He was still puzzling over Nicky's remarks when he ran into the kitchen.

"You took long enough," said his mother.

"Did you know that Pat Broaders is on the ram-page?" asked Padraic, seeking to divert her attention.

His mother stared at him in sudden alarm. "What did you say?"

Padraic was pleased that his words had caused such a stir, even though he did not know what they meant. "Nicky says that Pat Broaders is on the ram-page and to tell some man that he's looking for him. He says the man works for Daddy. That must be Benny or John. Why would he be looking for one of them?"

His mother looked pale. "What's the matter?" he asked her.

She sat down suddenly, struggling to regain her composure. She looked at him. "What else did Nicky say?" she asked.

"Something about Pat having a drink before going on a ram-page," he remembered. "What did he mean?"

She recovered quickly. "Never mind! Nicky shouldn't be talking nonsense to you like this. I'll talk with your father. You're not to mention this to anyone, do you hear? It'll only cause harm."

Padraic was a little frightened. "Does this mean he'll attack John or Benny?" he asked after a pause.

"No! No! Nothing like that," said his mother crossly. "Just don't say anything. There are some things you are too young to understand, and this is one of them. Say nothing. Your father will sort it out. Go and help your brothers."

◆—◆

Conor and Niall agreed as they half-sat in Benny's bouncing cart to the Flat Field that the antidote to thinning turnips was to fish the Edenbeg as soon as they finished work in the late afternoon.

"Besides," said Niall as he leapt lightly from the cart to open the gate into the Pond Field and a sombre Benny drove through the gap, "besides," he resumed as he climbed back on the cart, having closed the gate behind them, "we only have another two days of work on these turnips. Let's make some sandwiches at lunchtime, and load the gear onto the bikes. When we finish we leave straightaway."

Conor agreed. He had been contemplating spending the daylight hours left after work watching the sparrowhawk in her nest, but the cool pools of the Edenbeg were a bigger draw.

The Edenbeg was a small, hidden river that flowed into the estuary above Eskerford harbour. It meandered through a vale of relatively open farmland, past little copses of willow and alder and thickets of briars and whin bushes, until the ground began to drop sharply, when it entered a series of steep gorges, heavily wooded with towering beeches and elms. Here the little river descended through a series of green tunnels, forming short, deep pools as it cut, pools that only agile fishermen could reach. The gorges culminated in a sequence of small pools that flowed through a cathedral of tall trees. The slopes above the river were very steep, and the rock on one side had been quarried so that it presented an almost sheer face.

Part of Eskerford's drinking water came from there. Big iron pipes ran from a pumphouse sited above the gorge, along the bank over the pool, over the veined roots of the great trees, then sharply down through a jagged hole that had been dynamited in the living rock above the tail of the pool.

Fishing for brown trout ended at the jagged hole in the rocks. The falls below marked the top of the river's estuary. The stretch from the falls to the estuary of the Eskerford river was tidal and was preserved for sea trout fishing. Gabards, before the lorry superseded them, had been poled or sailed on this stretch, bringing grain up, flour down, between Edenbridge and Eskerford, avoiding the bridge toll.

The river was almost completely wild, with only one

house along its reaches, a lonely, whitewashed dwelling below an overhanging wood. The boys rarely saw other anglers on their visits, the solitude a magnet. Sometimes they saw the marks of the webbed feet of an otter – the *madra uisce* or water-dog – where it had entered a pool and where it had left it, generally above the bridge on the upper reach. They never saw the big mustelid itself, although they were convinced the holt was close to the bridge. In these slower, meandering reaches above the gorge, where the river was shallow, with clear, limpid pools, the flow was almost choked in places by olive-green weed that waved gently in the current; but clear channels ran through it, under overhanging bushes and willows. In these channels the boys frequently spotted the wild brown trout darting at a nymph or rising to an emerging dun or a spinner.

The trout were not big; nor was the river; but the fish were plentiful, and very game; hurtling out of the water when hooked, force out of proportion to their size, frequently breaking the boys' tackle. A very good fish was a pound and a half. The boys were delighted with anything over three-quarters of a pound.

They thought little of riding the three or four mile journey from Prospect to fish for two or three hours, cycling through the edge of the town, over the bridge and out into open country again, past the beautiful mansion of the popular Neaves, parking their bikes at one of the handsome, miniature stone bridges that spanned the river here and there, clambering down to the pools, jumping like gymnasts from one rock to another; climbing the steep bank to fish the next pool. The journey home was more of a challenge, as they were generally very tired by then, and much of it was uphill, but they cheerfully paid that price.

Adding to the magic was the never-failing flow of the sweetest water in the county from a tiny copper pipe that poked mysteriously from the sheer rock face above the lower pools. They did not know how it came there but they drank from it on every visit, silently grateful for the gift from Artemis to Arethusa, or from a quarryman long dead who had placed it for two brother anglers to slake their thirst on a hot day.

The cart reached the Flat Field and the three boys jumped onto the hard ground; looked at the drills left to thin, the evening a lifetime away, but the sun shone and the end of the work drew closer.

◆━◆

When Martha arrived from Eskerford the boys' mother ran up the stairs to talk to Garry, who was sawing busily. She told him of Padraic's conversation with Nicky.

Garry thought for a moment, then said: "We'd better tell Dad when he gets home." She nodded.

◆━◆

The poet's car came up the drive and halted on the gravel. His wife came to meet him. As Bruno rushed out to take the newspaper, she described the events since he had left for Eskerford that morning. He listened, questioned her, then walked through the hall with her, deep in thought.

He sat at the head of the kitchen table a few minutes later, brow furrowed, cigarette in hand, while his wife continued to talk. Garry joined them, then Brian, who had been sawing logs with his bushman saw for most of the morning.

Lunch was almost ready. They could hear Benny's mongrel Shot barking, the answering clamour of the Prospect dogs, and the sounds of Benny's cart coming down the farmyard. Soon the kitchen was full of noise, but before they sat the poet took Benny into the yard and talked to him for a few minutes. When they returned, Benny looked shaken.

‹◆›

By the end of the afternoon the field workers had made significant progress with the turnips. They estimated the job would be finished by the following midday, when Uncle Jim was expected. Niall said he never wanted to see another bloody turnip again. He suggested that this job might be replaced quickly by another.

Instead of returning by cart to Prospect, they returned on foot. Benny abruptly decided to leave the cart where it was, and his horse overnight in the Well Field. He would take the cross-country route, he told the boys, down the lane past Bayview, crossing the fields until he reached home. The boys looked at each other, but said nothing. They knew the reason, but thought it cruel to tease the ploughman. Instead they offered to carry the harness back to the farmyard and leave it in a shed overnight.

Benny set off, with an anxious glance around him as he reached the Stile and checked the road. He had only fifty yards to go before he turned off the lane past Bayview. He covered the distance faster than at his usual country pace.

‹◆›

Conor and Niall set off to the Edenbeg, Conor on his more modern bike with its Sturmey-Archer gears, Niall on his big clumsy machine, Sport running beside them, barking until they were halfway down the drive where the dog gave up and returned.

Ivan and Padraic hung upside down from the tallest

branches of the evergreens in the Grove, knees bent, legs hooked over the boughs, trailing their arms in the air, calling insults and dares to each other.

The dogs began to bark. The two boys dropped from branch to branch until they reached the ground, then ran to the edge and looked down the drive. A dark figure in a long overcoat and black hat was cycling past them up to the house, pursued by Sport and Colleen.

The boys ran to the drive in time to see the figure arrive at the open front door and dismount. Ivan stopped suddenly, gripped Padraic's shoulders and whispered: "It's Pat Broaders!"

"God!" said Padraic, mouth agape. "What does he want?"

"Quiet!" said Ivan. They watched as the tall figure pulled the doorbell and began to work the big brass knocker furiously. They saw their mother come into the front hall and confront him. "What is it you want?" she asked, voice betraying her nervousness.

"Where's that fellah Redmond?" demanded the man in a voice made to sharpen a scythe.

"What are you doing here?" their mother demanded. "What do you want with Benny?"

The man took a step forward into the hall. She drew back.

He looked directly at her. "I wants," he said in his gravelly rasp, "I wants to see him." He paused. "I wants," he said again, "I wants to bate the behokey out of him. I wants," he said yet again, "I wants to bate him so he never looks at another young wan again. Now," he said, coiling his long body like a snake about to strike, "now, where is he?"

"He's not here – and you've no right to be here," said the boys' mother, summoning her courage. "You've no right to barge into our house like this. Now get out!"

He looked at her. "Get out, is it!" he said, uncoiling himself. "And what right do you have – what high and mighty right do you have – to be shelterin' a lecherous fellah like that? A fellah after courtin' me sister! Where is he? I'm comin' in to get him!"

"You are not!" she blazed, angry now. "If you take a step into this house, if you don't get out immediately, I'll have you prosecuted. My husband will be home in a minute, and he'll get the Guards on you!"

He looked at her for a moment, then said: "I'll be back!" He walked out the front door, picked up his bike, threw his leg over the saddle, and looked back at the boys' mother. "Tell that fellah Redmond, tell that lecherous louse, if he ever talks to me sister – if he ever as much as looks at me sister – I'll bate him from here to Crossabeg!" Then he was gone, giving the two boys a vicious look as he passed.

The boys ran to their mother, who, though pale, stood resolute. When the dark figure disappeared down the turn of the drive, she sank onto the hall chair. "That terrible man," she sighed. "I don't know what I could have done. Has he really gone?"

The two boys hurriedly looked down the drive again. "Yes, he's definitely gone," said Ivan.

Conor and Niall had reached the other side of Eskerford, and were cycling hard. As they neared the bridge, they were joined by little groups of the townspeople on their bikes, making for the beach after work. The smells of salt water and estuary mud greeted them as they cycled past the tar barrels on the old bridge. When they were over the bridge each began to feel a sense of anticipation, the anticipation that only a fisherman who knows that conditions are right, that there will be fish in the pools, and who has the right equipment, can feel. They began to pedal harder.

—◆—

Garry and Brian had gone for a long ramble together, revisiting some of their old war-time walks. Garry wanted fresh air after his day's work in the bathroom, and Brian had readily accepted the offer of a stroll. They walked past the high stone walls of Cleary's farm, and carried on, up the road that led to The Mountain.

—◆—

When Conor and Niall reached the little stone bridge that separated the upper from the middle and lower reaches of the river, they parked their bikes in the hedge and removed gear and provisions. Each had brought a short spinning rod and a tin of small blue and gold devons. They would fish the upper reach together, then Conor would walk downstream to fish the lower pools. They would meet, as darkness fell, at the water pipe.

Conor stepped quietly across to the upstream parapet of the bridge and inched his head over. He saw what he expected: the marks of the semi-webbed feet of the otter on the sandy bank, but no otter. The boys looked upstream. A herd of shorthorn cattle stood in the river, cooling in the shallows. The sun was lower, casting longer shadows over the rough meadow, most of the pools in shade.

The two made their way down the path beside the bridge to the tail of the first pool. They assembled their rods, placed the reels on the cork butts and secured them in place; they stripped nylon from the little spinning reels and tied on their devons – Conor a gold one, Niall a blue.

Ducking low, they crept forward, holding the butts of the rods foremost. The small landing nets – Niall had made both from pieces of stiff fencing wire and bamboos removed surreptitiously from the clump that grew inside the great gates of Cleary's farm – snagged occasionally on the branches of the willows, but snagging objects on trees is part of fishing and the boys accepted this, patiently disentangling the nets as they went. When Conor, in the lead, put his head past the willow on the bank, he scanned the water in front, then upstream towards the neck of the short pool. The river was low because of the lack of rain, clear as gin. He could see there was not a trout in the tail, but the pool was so overgrown that he could not see further.

He motioned to Niall to move up alongside. Niall did so, swearing in a low tone as his net snagged again. They scanned the pool.

Conor had an almost extraordinary sense of where trout would be, whereas Niall's sense was not, as yet, so highly developed. Conor pointed to the top left-hand side of the pool, just below the neck, where the current flowed through a little dam of broken rushes and dead ferns.

"I bet there's a fish there," he whispered.

"Trout can't hear us talk, you know," complained Niall in a normal voice, and then he, too, lapsed into a whisper: "Why don't you have a go?"

Conor looked at him and grinned. "Why don't you?" he said.

"No," said Niall, with typical generosity. "It's your cast. Go ahead." He looked at the overhanging willows, then back up to the pool. "It's a difficult cast. If he's there, he'll be up near the neck."

They saw nothing rising, much to their relief. They had learned the hard way that a rising fish rarely takes a devon and had wasted many hours trying to disprove the rule. Unlike a dry-fly fisherman who will fish only for a rising fish, or a fish that he can see, those who spin with little artificial minnows on trout streams learn to move on when they see a rising trout.

Conor judged the spot where the devon must land. There was a strongish current of water flowing through the gap in the dam, skirting a bank of lily-pads. That might disguise the *plop*! of the dropping minnow. First he would have to manoeuvre himself into position to cast. That would be tricky.

"Tell me if you see a rise," he said and rose, crouched as low as he could, and stepped to his right, keeping back from the pool, manoeuvring himself to where he could gain an angle to cast diagonally across the neck, drawing the minnow close enough to where they thought the trout might be to entice the fish to chase it. His net snagged on a bunch of dock leaves. He unclipped it quickly from his belt, left it on the bank, and moved on again. He looked over his left shoulder, saw a high bank of nettles in the way, moved up the pool two or three feet and knelt on his right knee, careful not to cause a vibration.

He swung the little rod, bail-arm cocked, devon dangling on six inches of line below the top ring, and cast it sideways to prevent the bait catching in the willow at the top of the pool.

The minnow swept in a low arc up and across the pool and landed on the right hand side of the current. Damn, he thought, too far to the right. He had aimed at the centre of the current. He needed to be closer, and had been too anxious to avoid the willow.

Niall watched Conor swing the rod back again. The devon landed in the centre of the current. He clicked the bail-arm back instantly and began to reel.

The minnow had travelled three or four feet when a fish took it –*splash*! And then again –*splash*! It threw itself out of the water, showing the speckled colouring of a brown trout in perfect condition.

"Wuh-hoo! He's a beauty!" shouted Niall, as the fish fell back into the water and shot across the pool. Conor's rod bent and the fixed spool began to turn as the fish stripped line from the reel.

When the trout saw the bank approaching he turned immediately and streaked back up the pool, but the little rod held him as he ran for the neck. He turned again and shot back down towards Conor, who reeled as rapidly as he could, keeping tension on the line.

The fish had one more strong run, then began to tire. Niall had his net ready. Conor guided the fish in. It ran again when it saw the net enter the water, then Niall scooped it from the river, holding it victoriously while Conor began to breathe normally again.

They carried the fish to where they had left their gear. Niall, net in one hand, bent and removed his priest from his bag, turned the net over so the fish slid onto the grass and, dropping the net, grasped the fish in one hand and killed it with the priest in the other.

"That's a good fish!" said Niall. "A great bloody fish!" He found his weighing scales in his bag, slipped the hook through the trout's gill and called: "One pound and an ounce! Look at those spots! He's in perfect condition."

"I didn't put that first cast where I wanted," said Conor. "I meant to land it right in the current, but I swung it too far to the right. I was lucky!"

"It was a very difficult cast," said Niall.

"Well," said Conor after they had admired the fish, "let's see. Why don't we split now? There should be fish taking in most of the pools."

In a hurry, he picked up his gear, retrieved his net from the bank, and set off up the dirt path beside the bridge to his bike.

Niall also gathered his gear, and walked in a crouch to the next pool.

A cuckoo called from a copse.

The boy approached the pool slowly.

The cuckoo called again.

There was a bush slightly to the right of the tail of the pool, and Niall walked in a crouch to this, laid his rod, bag and net down behind it and looked carefully into the pool.

This was much longer than the first, and a little wider. Many of the pools in the Edenbeg were so narrow that a fisherman could almost step across them. It was oval-shaped and appeared to be deeper towards the tail. Above, the river bent sharply around to the right. The current hit the far bank as it negotiated the bend, to be deflected through a channel in the lily-pads, a channel overhung by willows.

He knew that fish sometimes lay in the deep end towards the tail because he had caught them there before only a few weeks back, but that had been early in the season. The warm weather had hastened the hatch of fly, but the trout were still very hungry. There was a strong possibility that there would be fish nymphing, or even taking the fly on the surface towards the neck.

Another call came: "Cuckoo!"

A meteor of blue and green shot past, startling him; a kingfisher. He resumed his study of the pool. Surely there was a sudden bulge on his left, towards the tail. Yes! He saw it again. There was at least one nymphing fish there, a trout close enough to cause a disturbance on the surface without breaking it. It was almost certainly taking the caddis after it hatched on the bottom, but before it reached the surface, shook off its casing, and took wing. Another! This one was further up, towards the deeper water in the middle. Surely there was a fish that would be interested in his devon.

He cast in a short arc from the side. The minnow flew across the pool and landed on the far side of the deep water. He reeled in steadily, drawing the minnow across and down the pool. Nothing took.

A voice called from the copse: "Cuckoo!"

The devon had just cleared the water and he was lifting it to cast when the fish bulged again. He shifted position a few feet and cast once more, drawing the minnow more squarely across the pool than before.

Again nothing, but the cuckoo called once more.

Niall was hot, and grew frustrated. "The fish are too busy nymphing," he grumbled. He cast again, and again, into the deep water, below it, and above it, and to each side of it, but the trout ignored his minnow. Frequent bulging below the surface showed that they continued to feed.

He looked gloomily at the pool, convinced that a trout would not take his devon. There was a good hatch of caddis on the water. "They're not even taking the dry fly," grumbled Niall. "They're gorging themselves on the blasted nymphs." He knew that he still had much to learn, and that anglers frequently learn the hard way, but it was a hard lesson for a boy, especially one who had just seen his older brother take a fish on only his second cast.

There was a little splash. Niall looked up the pool. There! Up towards the bend, where a fish should be, were the tell-tale rings of a risen fish. He could see a fly hatch above the neck of the pool, the flies dancing down through the neck, the fish plainly unable to resist. Again! The trout had come right out of the water, mouth open, showing the white of the inside of its jaws, sucking in the fly before landing back in the water, a perfect replica of the illustrations in his fishing books.

He could not resist. He moved in a crouch ten feet up the pool, careful to keep low. His landing net snagged. He freed it with only a muttered curse. When he was in position he cast the devon all the way into the top of the neck, waited a moment, and began to reel. The devon came home to the little rod without causing a movement in the water. He cast again; same result. He moved on, into the field to avoid spooking the trout, passing closer to the copse.

"Cuckoo!" called the voice.

The next pool had more shadow. Nothing moved other than a fly hatch at the tail. He cast towards the neck. Bang! There was a splash and the line tightened. The rod bent. The fish came vertically out of the water, flashing a golden brown in the evening sunlight, trying frantically to throw the hook which was firmly wedged in the scissors at the side of the jaw. Then it was back in the water, running for the weed on the far side of the pool. Niall kept the rod high, guided it away from the snags; continued to hold it high as the fish ran back and forth across the pool until it tired. Then he lifted the net, which he had been cursing only a few minutes before, and lowered it into the water. The trout promptly shot out into the pool again, but the hook held, and on the next run Niall grassed his fish successfully.

He looked across the field at the copse. "Cuckoo!" cackled Niall. The bird was silent.

The trout weighed nearly three-quarters of a pound and was in perfect condition; a wonderfully stocky fish, deep in body, powerful. Niall looked at it again and again before plucking tufts of grass from the bank nearby, then wrapped the fish carefully and stowed it in his creel.

As he stood there, the fish in the deep water below him bulged again. Niall's sense of triumph vanished for an instant. That bloody fish! He would have another cast at him before moving on.

He did, having moved carefully back down the bank. The fish ignored the devon.

"Cuckoo!" came from the copse. Niall swore and moved on.

He hooked a good trout in the next pool up, played him hard, and swung him in towards the net. The fish made another run and threw the hook.

The voice called from the copse once more.

He sat on the bank and scratched his head. His natural equilibrium returned. He had, he told himself, caught a bloody good fish; had fished hard for a difficult fish, had enticed it to take. The fact that he had lost it did not matter. That was simply fate, lumps in the stirabout. He moved on to the next pool, but not without a dark look at the copse, which was silent at last, and remained silent as Niall caught two more trout.

When he met Conor at the pipe in the rock, half an hour after the appointed time, it was dark. He reached it five minutes before Conor, who had caught five trout to Niall's three.

They pedalled home in the moonlight, first towards the lights of Eskerford, then out on the road to Prospect, cycling two abreast except when the occasional car went past, talking about fish lost – prime topic for any fisherman – and fish landed. When they arrived at Prospect they forgot about fishing. The house was in a high state of nervousness.

Garry and Brian had returned from their walk to find their mother looking alarmed but resolute. Ivan and Padraic told them the story of their visitor. John came in from the Well Field and stood in the kitchen, listening quietly. A few minutes later, the poet arrived home and the story was retold.

The boys' father was furious. "I'll get the Guards on him," he said. "We'll put him behind bars!"

John spoke for the first time. "No need," he said quietly.

Everyone looked at him. "What do you mean?" asked Garry, after a pause.

John spoke directly to the poet. "Can I have a word with you alone, Boss?" he asked.

"All right so," said the poet. "Let's go outside."

They walked out to the Paddock together. John began to speak in a low, persuasive voice. They could hear the poet object at first, but then, as John continued, his objections subsided.

When they returned to the kitchen, Garry asked: "Do you think he'll come back tonight, John?"

"He'll be back, all right," said John shortly.

"I've asked John to stay and eat with us," the poet told his wife.

Her face cleared. "All right, Pack. I'll get it ready – Conor and Niall won't be back until late. They're fishing."

Half an hour later they sat down to supper, quite happily at first, but as the evening went on and the sun sank below the Paddock tree line an unusual feeling of apprehension came over the table, particularly over the mother and the younger boys. Ivan could bear it no longer.

"When do you think he'll come, John?" he asked, breaking the silence.

"I'd say it won't be long now," said John. As he spoke, the dogs began to bark; rushed around the house to the drive.

The sinister figure did not appear. Instead, two tired fishermen walked in the kitchen door from the yard, proudly carrying their bag.

When the noise died and the story was retold once more the family cheered visibly, but the feeling of foreboding soon returned. The table was cleared. A half-hearted game of Chinese chequers began. Garry, psychic, raised his head in the middle of a move and said: "He's coming." They looked at him; waited. Several minutes passed before the dogs barked. Then a thunderous knocking began at the front door.

"It's him!" said the boys' mother, turning pale.

The poet rose. "It is. Now, all of you apart from John are to stay here," he ordered. John, too, stepped back from the table.

"Oh, Pack!" his wife said. "Let John handle this on his own."

"No," said the poet. "We'll handle this. John, come on."

The two went out into the hall towards the front door. The knocking began again, and the bell in the inner hall jangled on its pull. The dogs barked once more. They heard the poet say in a firm voice: "Now Pat! I want a talk with you, and so does John Roche here."

They heard the rasp and rumble of the voice of the visitor, but it faded quickly. The poet appeared to have taken Broaders out on the gravel, away from the house, John in tow.

"Damn it!" said Garry. "I want to hear this."

"So do I," said Conor and Niall together.

"We'll listen from the drawing room," suggested Garry.

"No, please," said his mother, looking more distraught. "Don't go near that man!"

"We'll be all right," said Conor. "But we'll have to be quiet."

The three boys walked through to the hall quietly, avoiding the loose floorboard near the foot of the stairs. As they entered the outer hall they heard voices. The poet appeared to be doing most of the talking, and the breeze brought a whiff of cigarette smoke into the hall.

They ducked into the drawing room, where one of the windows was propped open by a heavy book. Garry and Conor put their heads as close to the gap as they dared, while Niall chafed impatiently behind them. They heard only the odd word. That must be a good sign, thought Garry. If there was trouble coming, at least one of the three would have raised his voice.

They could see clearly, however, as the moon was high over the Front Field, lighting the three figures on the lawn to the right of the palm tree. The visitor no longer appeared as menacing as he had, Garry noted, while John had relaxed the boxer's hunch he adopted when he expected trouble. The poet continued to talk, gesturing as he did so, his cigarette end cutting a red arc in the night. His voice rose occasionally, but the tone was reasoned. The visitor rumbled a reply every now and then, nodding briefly once or twice.

"What the hell is going on?" asked Niall impatiently. "What are they saying? Can you hear?"

"No," whispered Garry. "But it seems to be going OK. Dad's doing most of the talking."

The meeting finished ten minutes later. John stepped back and began to walk across the gravel to the front door. The poet spoke a few final words, the visitor nodded and lifted his hand in salute, then walked across the gravel to his bike. The three boys shot back into the darkness of the drawing room, as the bike was propped outside the window. The poet stepped onto the gravel and watched the visitor mount. "That's grand, Pat," he said. "Don't do anything silly now."

"All right so," rumbled the visitor. "And tell the missus I meant no harm, that I was a bit shook." He rode down the drive, past the poplars, in the moonlight.

The boys met the poet in the hall. He did not seem surprised to find them there.

"What happened, Dad?" asked Garry eagerly.

"Everything's fine," said his father. "He caught Benny on his way home, and they had it out. Benny told him the sister was just a friend, and that there was no more to it than that. Benny still feels responsible for his sisters in any case, so he wouldn't get married. They'll be playing forty-five together for years yet."

"Why did he come here tonight then? "Niall demanded.

His father looked surprised. "Why, to say he was sorry, of course."

"So Benny will stay a bachelor," mused Conor.

His father looked at him. "Surely," he said. "For a while yet."

Chapter Twenty-Six

There was a further half-day of thinning turnips to come, but the mood at Prospect was light-hearted on the following morning. Benny arrived considerably more cheerful than when he had left; the household generally was relieved, and grew increasingly excited. Uncle Jim was expected some time in the afternoon, probably soon after one of his lorries.

Conor and Niall had milked the cows and turned them out. Niall had fed his pigs. Their mother had fed her hens and collected the eggs before skimming the milk and making breakfast. Garry and Brian had ranged a long way on the morning rabbit shoot, but brought only four home. Ivan had performed a few chores. Padraic had slept late as usual, as had the poet, who had worked until the small hours.

The lengthy spell of fine weather was breaking. The wind had risen and swung to the north-west, and the sky was beginning to darken with thunder clouds as Benny drove Conor, Niall and Ivan to the fields in the rattling cart. The wireless weatherman had told the breakfast table that thunderstorms approached, that a high was behind the front and that fine weather would resume in a day or so.

Benny was remarkably cheerful, frequently interrupting Conor's and Niall's discussion of their visit to the Edenbeg. Before they set off down the lane to the Pond Field gate, they heard the distant whistle of the Dublin train.

"They're talking about bringing in a Dizzler," shouted Benny, a minute later, above the rattle of the harness, the clop of the horse's shoes on hard ground, and the rumble of the ironshod wheels. He put his pipe back in his mouth; puffed.

The boys looked puzzled. "What the bloody hell's a Dizzler?" Niall demanded after a pause. They were passing the Orchard.

Benny looked surprised. "A Dizzler, a Dizzler!" he said, taking his pipe from his mouth. "The Dizzler train, begob-a-man, the new train, the new Dizzler!"

"Oh," said Conor, as he grasped the ploughman's meaning. "You mean the Diesel. The trains are switching from steam. That's what you're saying." Niall looked at him and made a face. Conor struggled to keep his own straight.

"That's hit! Shur isn't that what I said!" said Benny triumphantly, then yelled, "Ohmenarse!" as the cart hit a stone and bounced. Hysterical laughter came from the boys. Niall whispered in Ivan's ear: "Dizzler!" Ivan pushed him away while he laughed so hard his ribs hurt. Benny joined in for a different reason. The cart rocked and bounced, the boys jostling each other. Niall pretended to fall off the cart, ran behind, hands clutching the cart's tail, allowed himself to be dragged before leaning his stomach on the tail, falling forward into the cart, which rocked madly. Benny shouted at him; began to laugh again. Niall put his mouth close to Ivan's ear, stuck out his chin so that he looked like Bob Hope, and said once more: "Dizzler!" Ivan began to laugh again and pushed Niall so hard he half-jumped, half-fell, from the cart. This time he ran alongside until he vaulted onto the side, turning back to Ivan and making his Bob Hope face until Ivan's ribs ached.

Ivan jumped off when they reached the Pond Field gate and held it open as the cart passed. Niall stuck his chin out again and mouthed: "Dizzler!" as the cart drew level. Ivan doubled over once more. When he recovered he shut the gate, but Conor told Benny not to stop, to make Ivan run. Benny speeded up and Ivan tore after the cart like a sprinter, raised his hands and clasped the tail, but was not tall enough to swing his body up and over it as Niall had done. Conor reached and swung him up with a jerk of a powerful forearm. Ivan sprawled on the floor of the cart, hair and clothes covered in wisps of hay.

Benny struggled to look sorrowful and said: "Begob! I wisht I'd a-died when I was a yearlint!"

◆ ◆

Lunchtime approached. John was digging the foundations of the big greenhouse when he heard the Bedford lorry, heard it change into low gear as it ground up the drive, then rev its engine as it drove around the house to the back. Black clouds with yellowy-brown fringes piled in the sky, the light over the Paddock a yellowy grey. The wind gusted nervously, as if it could not decide what to do next, but the stocky young man sensed that it would begin to slacken soon, to be replaced by the heaviness that signalled thunder and heavy rain.

He watched as the lorry nosed its way around the house and into the yard. He waved a greeting, placed his spade beside his pick, shouted at Sport to stay away from the advancing lorry, and motioned the driver to follow him up the farmyard where the timber would be stored in one of the sheds until it was needed.

The heavily laden lorry ground slowly up the farmyard, scattering hens that had been allowed out of the run for the morning, until John waved it to a stop. The driver and his helper stepped out and looked about them. Padraic came running from the house, his mother walking more sedately behind.

"Prospect, is it?" asked the driver in pure Stoneybatter *(prospec'izzah?)*, with a look of cool contempt for the countryman who greeted him. The driver was a little fighting cock of a man, with a thin moustache. Like his mate, he wore the uniform of the building trade everywhere: a set of dark blue dungarees, known in the trade as *dungareens*. A half-smoked cigarette had been pinched out and placed behind his ear. He straightened when he saw the boys' mother approach with a welcoming smile and said: "You must be the boss's daughter. You're a dead ringer for him. I know your brother Jim very well, an' Dick, o'coorse." He added: "I'm Tommy, and this", flicking his thumb at his helper, "is Joe, though we calls him Joey."

"It's grand to see you both," said the boys' mother, with a look of genuine pleasure. "I hope you'll stay and eat with us. There's plenty of food. What was your journey like?"

"Only took us three hours," said Tommy. "It would have been shorter if we hadn't met so many bleedin' carts." He looked disapprovingly at John again. The carts were clearly his fault.

The boys' mother noted the look. She could imagine the conversation on the journey down, remembering how the people of her native city looked on country people as slow, not quite all there.

Tommy looked at Padraic, who stared at him. "Howr'ya, puddn'head?" the driver asked kindly, reaching into his pocket before shaking the boy's hand. Padraic had rarely shaken anyone's hand before. He found a silver sixpence had transferred itself in the process. He stared at it, holding his grubby hand out to his mother. "Look! Look at this," he said. "He just slid a sixpence into my hand!"

His mother said to Tommy: "You shouldn't have given him that. You'll spoil him, and he's spoiled already," but smiled as she said it, remembering how soft-hearted the city tradesmen could be.

Padraic said: "Can I go to McCann's now?"

"No," said his mother firmly. Then she turned back to the driver: "Tommy, would you like a cup of tea straight away?"

"We would, Missus," said the driver gratefully. "Then we'll make a start on unloadin' this lot before dinner." He gave John another contemptuous look as they followed her down the farmyard towards the house. John looked after them for a moment, then carried several armfuls of straw from one of the sheds and dropped them to one side. He climbed onto the back of the lorry and began to lift the timber, lowering it over the side, breaking its fall on the straw.

◆—◆

The rain arrived, slowly at first, then in torrents. When the poet turned into the gates the palm and poplars waved madly, the wind driving the rain across the Front Field.

He beamed when he saw the Dublin workmen. "You made great time!" he congratulated them as he entered the kitchen, where the lights were on, rain drumming on the glass roof of the extension. John stood by the Aga. They heard Benny's cart rattling down the farmyard and the sound of running feet as the field workers ran for the house. Brian sat in the big armchair in the corner, submerged in cats, reading.

A scrum of wet workers rushed into the kitchen, shouting about the weather; rushed through without stopping as they sought their bedrooms and dry clothes.

Benny removed his heavy, ragged topcoat, undid the binder twine that acted as a belt and took off his dripping cap.

The Dubliners looked at him. "Here's another one, Joey," said Tommy to his mate, with a knowing look, jerking his thumb at Benny.

Padraic said: "This is Benny."

"It had to be somethin' like that *(sump'nlikethah)*," said Tommy, winking at Joey, who winked back and muttered something to his friend about "another great *cultchie*" – the Dubliners' term for an unfortunate from the country. When he turned back to the table he saw that John watched him intently. He gave him a contemptuous look in return.

All of this went straight over Benny's head, which confirmed the city men's initial judgment, but the truth was that Benny was very hungry and wanted to sit and eat without these formalities.

As the boys reappeared, pulling dry sweaters over their heads and towelling their hair, the poet asked: "How are you getting on?"

"We're finished!" said Conor proudly.

"Until the next job!" added Niall darkly, eyeing his father, who did not return his look.

They sat to eat, the Dubliners opposite the two country men. Halfway through, Tommy looked up from his plate to see Benny lick egg from his knife and reach for his butter. He whispered in Joey's ear: "Don't eat that butther. The big bogtrotther's after lickin' his knife."

Joey stared at him, then at Benny's butterdish.

"Oh, my *Jaysus!*" he said, paling.

"What's the matter?" asked Tommy in alarm.

"I been eatin' it all along," said Joey, looking as if he was about to be sick. "The other cultchie pushed it across the table at me."

They both looked at John, who continued to stare at

them impassively. Then he gave them a slow, deliberate wink.

◆—◆

They recovered sufficiently to unload timber, tiles and other spoils from the site in Dublin, and to accept gratefully the poet's tip before setting off for the city again, but they departed with the air of men who had left a little of their pride behind.

The rain stopped as suddenly as it had begun, although the clouds still massed in the north-west, towards the mountains, and the wind was rising again, backing towards the north. There would be another deluge in an hour or so.

The tiles had been tipped into a pile opposite the site of the new greenhouse. Niall began to examine them under the slightly apprehensive eye of his father, who had called his workers together when lunch was cleared and laid out the detailed work plan for the next few weeks.

John, Garry, Conor and Ivan would work on the greenhouse, while Brian and Benny would do the summer farm work. Phase one, once the foundations had been dug, would consist of mixing cement and making the concrete blocks in the wooden moulds John had made. These would be used to build the wall, the lower part of the greenhouse.

Pat Fitz would begin on the following Monday, laying the concrete screed for the floor of the breakfast room, then lay the tiled floor, after which he would plaster the walls and build the surround for the big fireplace. That done, Pat would begin on the new sun room at the Grove end of the house. A french window would connect the breakfast room to the conservatory, another to the greenhouse. Niall and Padraic – here Niall groaned – would be Pat's assistants. The immediate job to begin, as it needed the longest lead time, would be to prepare the tiles. The other job that needed to be finished early – digging the foundations for the walls of the greenhouse – was well under way, and would be finished in a day or so.

As a plan, it was very sensible. His sons accepted it, more or less enthusiastically, though, of all the jobs, preparing the tiles would be the most tedious; "like thinning more bloody turnips," said Niall.

It would not be all work, the poet emphasized. On most afternoons he would take them to Farracloe. Work would stop at five o'clock, or perhaps six, in time for some of the boys to go fishing, or bird-watching, or to listen (with an eye on Garry and Brian) to a concert on the Third Programme. They would not work at weekends. He would take them each Sunday to Crook where they could swim, and spin for bass from the rocks. Of course, the particular stones (Crook was rich in fossils) for the fireplace would come from there. They would be individually selected by him, and his sons would only have to carry them up the short distance to the open ground where he would park the car.

This received a mixed reaction. Fishing from the rocks at Crook could be very productive, but as the short distance the poet referred to was the equivalent of climbing a low, but steep, cliff face they viewed this particular task with misgiving. The consolation was that the old car could not carry too great a weight and this would limit the number of stones that would need to be transported.

The four older boys visibly cheered when the poet reminded them of the prize when the work was finished: a voyage into the interior. There would be wonderful trout fishing; probably salmon fishing for those who wanted it; pitching a tent in a different place each day if they wished; exploring the river banks and adjacent countryside; campfires; cooking their own food; some of the best bird-watching in the country; all kinds of wild life, perhaps an otter. The picture the poet painted filled with colours and shapes.

Later, however, Niall grew gloomy as he contemplated his own particular task. All of the tiles had grout attached to them, and the grout was particularly hard. It would have to be chipped from each tile before the floor could be laid. Niall could foresee a week to a fortnight's work for three or four boys, on top of the farm chores, in the peak of the fishing season. He groaned a little, then brightened as he remembered that much of the summer would remain when they finished. As his cheerfulness returned, there was a giant clap of thunder almost directly overhead. Rain began to fall.

◆◆

Outdoor work would not be done that afternoon, but Garry had prepared for that. While John cleared the old tool-shed of everything stored there, and Benny washed and swept the byre, Garry led his brothers to the biggest attic, a vast room that had been refloored but was otherwise unused except as a playroom for wet days, and for storage. Copies of *The Bell* and the *Dublin Magazine* lay piled in a corner.

The big attic looked out over the Grove, its windows level with the tops of the evergreens. The opposite attic room gave excellent views of the countryside, including Eskerford racecourse in the distance. The views from both were of black clouds, zigzags of lightning and a steady downpour.

Garry had mocked up a scene from the Battle of Britain in one of these rooms. He had built from packing-cases, old tea chests, and cardboard boxes the cockpits and front fuselages of five or six fighter planes and bombers, painting Luftwaffe crosses on some, RAF roundels on others. He had drawn, in charcoal, other aeroplanes on the wall as a backdrop to the battle. The thunderstorm added an unforeseen sound effect.

His brothers sat in the cockpits and waited until he shouted, "SCRAMBLE!" then flew their fighters while he directed the dogfight, although Brian occasionally forgot the Messerschmitt on his tail. Conor and Niall had shot him down several times when Conor cocked his ear and said: "Sport's barking."

The youngest boys jumped from their cockpits and ran for the stairs. Niall took a short-cut by leaping the banisters on the attic stairs, missing the landing, alighting on the next flight. Ivan did the same, rugby-tackling Niall on the next landing. Padraic knew his short legs prevented him from taking the short-cut; jumped instead onto the banister rail and rode it down to the return, where he did the same again, but his brothers beat him to the front hall, Niall lifting his big knees in time to avoid another tackle. Their parents stood at the open front door, ignoring the chaos of shouting boys and barking dogs as they prepared to welcome the visitor from Dublin.

—◆—◆—

Uncle Jim was tall, six foot two or three; handsome; Clark Gable moustache; hair oiled and brushed back in the fashion of the time; immaculate suit; shoes with a high polish; big, clumsy feet.

He was a Dubliner to his fingertips: generous; sentimental, mawkishly so in his cups; his sister's favourite brother; social, liked the traditional Dublin pubs, the voices of Clanbrassil Street and the quays; loved children, and was an idol to his nephews. He cracked jokes on any subject, picking up a word or a line of conversation and inventing a quip on the spot. He believed, without question, that Dubliners were infinitely superior, a view he shared with every Dubliner.

He still lived with his parents; had not married. Girl-friends occasionally drifted into his life and drifted out again when they recognized his sense of duty to his parents. He worked in the family business, which his father had co-founded and which, with more than four hundred employees at its peak, was one of the largest in the city. He spent much of his time driving around Dublin, checking each job, and knew every street, avenue, or lane within a fifteen-minute drive of the Liffey, and most of the pubs. His nephews teased him when he had had too much whiskey, inducing their almost tone-deaf uncle to sing:

> *As down the glen one Easter morn*
> *To a city fair rode I,*
> *Where armed lines of proudly marching men*
> *In squadrons passed me by.*
> *No pipes did hum, no battle drum –*

Here Uncle Jim's voice would falter on the higher notes:

> *– did sound its loud tattoo.*

and sink to little more than a whisper:

> *But the Angelus bell o'er the Liffey swell*
> *Rang out in the foggy dew.*

He missed his sister greatly and had grieved when she moved to Eskerford. He had visited the family as often as he could through the War, through Niall and Ivan's births, and through Garry's illness; always a car full of presents when he arrived. In the War years he cheered his eldest nephews by taking them to the pictures, once asking the attendant as they left after a film about white hunters in Africa: "Which way to the kraal, Bwana?"

The rare holidays the poet and his wife took were often with Uncle Jim: to the poet's native West, to Gurteen, Shanballard, Killimordaly and Knockroe, to see the poet's favourite cousin, Maude, and other relatives; or to Cavan where Garry and Brian had been born; all country places where the Dublin wit found rich targets. The summer before, the three had driven into Killimordaly, near the birthplace of the poet's mother whose family name was Dilleen, on a blazing hot day, the two men in shirtsleeves in the front of the car, windows open, cigarette smoke drifting out to the clear air of the county Galway.

"Pack," said Jim, with a sidelong glance at the poet, "I bet they're all retarded here. Inbred. Soft in the head – particularly your family's relatives."

The poet took the ribbing easily. Jim was very fond of the poet's mother who was still extraordinarily healthy and vigorous, as was the poet's father. The old couple's declining years were spent mostly in prayer, but the poet's mother had been an elegant, organizing, Galway woman who took the waters at Harrogate in her middle years; the driving force in the poet's home; her husband a dandy – a masher in hand-made boots – a genial countryman who had crossed the fields with a fly rod to fish for salmon when he might have been about his business.

The Dubliner was a favoured visitor to the house in Baggot Street, where the poet's parents lived with his sister Mary and cousin Ellie, and where Jim was treated like a son; so the poet merely smiled, blew smoke out of the window, watching the familiar stone walls of his youth go by. He knew his mother's people well; was very fond of them, although he had been bored when he had come to stay here as a youth.

Jim raised the stakes. "I bet the first person we see in this one-horse village is a candidate for the asylum."

The first person they saw when they entered the village was clearly backward, a youth who stood by a pump and gaped at them. The poet drew up to him, leaned out and asked: "What's your name, *a mhic?*"

"Dilleen, sir," said the poor youth. "I told you!" shouted Uncle Jim.

━━◆━◆━━

Uncle Jim's sister hugged him while her husband shook his hand warmly. "You're very welcome, Jamesy," said the poet.

"Where are Ivan and Padraic?" Uncle Jim asked, pretending not to see them.

"Here!" they called, jumping.

"I have something special for both of you," said their uncle, "but you must promise not to take someone's eye out!"

"What is it?" they asked.

"Give me a minute to get everything from the car," he responded, winking at Garry.

"Have a cup of tea first," urged his sister. Her husband asked: "Would you like a little whiskey, Jamesy?"

"I might have both," he said, "but first I'll just bring everything in from the car. Did the lorry get here OK?"

"It did," said the poet, "and it had a great load. You're very good. We'll use every bit of it." He turned to his sons: "Give him a hand, you boys."

It had stopped raining, although more thunderclouds approached. They unloaded the parcels and boxes, excitement and curiosity rising.

Uncle Jim's case was left in the inner hall; everything else went to the kitchen. He gave his sister a bunch of flowers, a glass flower vase, and a box of Black Magic, her favourites; a bottle of de Kuypers gin to his brother-in-law; then a box or a wrapped parcel to each of the boys. Ivan and Padraic were given boxes that were identical, unusually long. When they ripped them open each discovered a bow and arrows, plus quiver.

Brian and Garry were each given records, Conor and Niall a set of German baits, saltwater spinners.

The boys' mother looked worried when she saw the bows and arrows. The arrows had blank tips, but the bows looked very powerful. She called above the noise: "You two be very careful with those! They could be very dangerous."

"We will," they promised, eyes gleaming.

◆ ◆

There was a very noisy table that evening until the poet took his brother-in-law, a bottle of whiskey, and a jug of well water into the dining room where the two talked long after everyone else had gone to bed. By then the storm had blown over, and the moon cast a silvery white light over the Grove and the Front Field.

Chapter Twenty-Seven

The fields sparkled in the early sunlight next morning as Conor and Niall made their way to the Well Field to bring in the cows to be milked. Jim the cock lifted his head to the sky as they passed the Hen-Run, issuing his morning call, finishing with a flourish. Hopeless Crower, the other cock, tried to do the same and failed, lowering his head as the hens eyed him with contempt. The air was cool and clear, with a tiny breeze. An ass brayed from Duggan's field.

The cattle called loudly, anxious to be milked, as they arrived at the gate. Hawthorn was first through. Niall looked up the field, past the pump. "There's that sparrowhawk," he said.

Conor swung around. "Where?" he asked.

Niall pointed. "To the right of Duggan's," he said. Conor looked further to the right and saw it hunting along the hedge. As he watched, it stooped. He lost sight of it for a moment, then it reappeared, turning in a slow arc towards the edge of the Wheat Field. A flock of hedge sparrows rose in alarm near the Rocks, flew down the inside of the Well Field, and vanished in the hedge.

"The wild life on this river trip should be tremendous," said Conor, watching the distant bird.

"Particularly the fishing," said Niall as they followed the cows to the byre, where a dozen Prospect cats waited.

Padraic, clutching bow and arrows, bounced into Uncle Jim's room to find him looking a little bleary-eyed. The boy watched his uncle as he shaved. "Everyone else is up," he pointed out.

Uncle Jim grunted as he concentrated on avoiding his moustache. "The cows are already milked," his nephew noted.

"So breakfast must be ready," concluded Uncle Jim, putting away his shaving brush and safety razor.

"Would you like to go fishing today?" asked Padraic.

"Why?"

"Because it's Saturday. We don't have to work," Padraic explained. His uncle seemed a little slow this morning. His father, too, had seemed slightly irritable.

"Are there any bass around?" asked Uncle Jim, who preferred his angling to be sedentary, in contrast to both of Padraic's grandfathers, keen fly fishermen.

"Lots," said Padraic. "I lost a monster. Niall caught the biggest."

"And you'd like me to take you there in the car?" asked Uncle Jim, wise to the schemes of children.

"You'd love it!" said Padraic, charmingly. "We'd have to dig the lugworms first, though."

"What in the name of Jaysus is that?" said Uncle Jim suddenly, looking out the window, down to the Paddock.

Padraic leant up to look out. "Oh! That! That's just Porky and Gert."

"But what are they doing?"

"Conor and Niall are having a race on them," Padraic explained. "The pigs love it. They think it's gas. But," he prophesied, "the boys won't be able to stay on for long, even though they hold them by the ears. There! I told you! Niall's off. Janeymack! D'you hear him yelling?"

The city man watched as Niall ran after Gert and

remounted, too late. Conor had reached the finishing line at the far edge of the Paddock, near the beech wood. He stepped off Porky and shouted at Niall, who urged Gert forward. Gert sat. Niall shouted something unsavoury. Gert rolled, throwing him off. The two pigs rooted in the grass for a moment, then scooted off together. Uncle Jim shook his head.

"Did you hear they're going on a holiday up the Bree in a boat?" asked Padraic.

"Who are?"

"The boys – the older ones, that is," said Padraic sorrowfully, then brightened. "We're going to have a trial on the river here. Ivan and I are going on that. We're going to camp for a night to try out the tent, and Garry is going to bring *Snipe* up the river. He'll take the mast out and we'll row her."

Jim offered to accompany the poet into Eskerford after breakfast, but not before he had agreed to take Padraic fishing with any of the other boys who wanted to join them, in late afternoon, when the tide would begin to make.

Jim and the poet drove companionably into Eskerford with Garry, who wanted to show off *Snipe* to his uncle, then take his boat out. There was little point in asking their guest to accompany him. Jim was nervous of the sea and it was a long way from a pub. He disliked physical exercise and sometimes went to eccentric lengths to avoid it. Garry had shared a bedroom with his uncle for a night at his grandparents' weekend retreat. His uncle had returned late, a little unsteady; had thrown his clothes on a chair, and collapsed into bed without turning off the overhead light. Garry woke later to see his uncle throwing shoes at the light. The third shoe hit and the bulb exploded. Uncle Jim grunted triumphantly, then began to snore. That story entered the family's lore, as did that of the goldfish.

One of the contracts Uncle Jim's firm had won was to build a large extension to a girls' school in the capital. The nuns' practice was to give the builders a present when each job was complete. Jim's brother Dick was given a barograph, something he had not realized he needed. Jim was given a bowl of goldfish. On his next visit to the convent, the reverend mother asked how the goldfish fared.

"Oh, those fellahs, Mother," said Jim, looking sorrowful, "I haven't had a wink of sleep since you gave them to me."

"Oh dear," said the reverend mother. "Oh dear. That's very surprising. I thought they were such peaceful things."

"These ones aren't," said Jim. "When these fellahs work up a temper, *they lash the water to a foam.*"

Garry and Brian had taken him to shoot rabbits at Ballydicken during the previous summer, putting the family's single-barrelled shotgun in his hands, escorting him to a field swarming with rabbits; stood behind him, helping him to point the gun, told him when to fire. He held the gun too loosely and almost fell when the butt recoiled against his shoulder. The field emptied of rabbits, white scuts bolting everywhere, except for a tiny one, too petrified to move. Uncle Jim ran to it, big feet splaying outwards, and grabbed the little rabbit by the ears. The rabbit kicked suddenly. Uncle Jim dropped it. The rabbit ran away. The day's bag was empty.

The poet turned the car opposite the railway station and followed the river as far as the bridge, then turned into the boat club. A light breeze from the south created a little chop in the estuary. Mermaids were setting off towards the harbour, the club full of weekend sailors discussing boats and sails and rigging and regattas.

Garry pointed out *Snipe* to his uncle. "There she is. No, not that one – the green one to the right. No, that's a Mermaid – the older boat, yes, that's her! Isn't she a beauty?"

Uncle Jim gazed across the short stretch of water at *Snipe*. The old boat appeared to be very small, frail. The last thing he wished to do was to sail around the harbour, but he did not want to hurt his favourite nephew. "She's a beauty all right," he nodded, picking his words carefully. "*Barnstormer* was much bigger, wasn't it, Pack?" he said, turning for help to the poet, who was looking up the harbour, jingling the change in his trouser pockets.

"Do you remember that regatta you won during the War with one of the Letts?" asked Uncle Jim.

"I do, surely. She was a great old boat," said the poet, remembering *Barnstormer* affectionately. "But God! She was hard work. It took about three trips from the shed at the Cot Safe to carry the sails and rigging down to her. The weight of it!"

Garry, who had done the carrying, said: "*Snipe*'s sails and rigging are as light as a feather. *Barnstormer* was a nightmare to rig. Those great canvas sails!"

He looked keenly at his uncle. "Would you like a sail in her? I'm going out in a minute. We'll just have a quick sail around the harbour."

"No," said Uncle Jim adroitly. "I'll go back into town with your father. I want to do a bit of shopping and have a stroll."

Garry entered the club to ask for a row out to his boat. The two older men drove back into the town, Uncle Jim gazing out the open window at the harbour. "Do any ships come in now, Pack?" he asked, opening a fresh packet of Gold Flake and offering one to the poet, who accepted.

"Hardly at all," said the poet, blowing smoke in a thin blue plume. "They keep the Cull Channel free by dredging it, but only the shallow draught ships make it through there, and they can only do that at spring tide, in daylight, when there's barely twelve feet of water. The silt keeps shifting, so they have to keep dredging. That costs a lot. The shoals outside the harbour keep shifting too. It's a hell of a job to get into the harbour. The big ships go to Uisceford and Rosspoint now. The harbour is dying."

Uncle Jim was enjoying his holiday, particularly since he had evaded the threat of being tossed around on the harbour. When they parked outside the Custom House he left the poet and wandered up to the Main Street. He walked past the Pikeman in the Bull Ring, looking in at Cosgrove's the grocers to say hello and to do some errands for his sister, then back to the little fishing tackle shop near Esker Abbey where he bought hooks and weights for the evening's fishing. He chatted for a while with George, the owner; strolled past the ruined abbey, then towards Shay Sinnott's hotel.

He entered the darkened bar. The Angelus had not yet rung, but there were already four of five people staring into their glasses. He sat on a high stool at the bar and ordered a small Power's with a glass of stout as a chaser. Shay Sinnott, wandering past, spotted him; joined him.

Uncle Jim knew this bar well. He had watched the poet and his sister play poker here in the evenings during the freezing winters of the War, games from which the poet, canny bluffer, generally emerged a winner.

They were still chatting when the poet arrived to collect him. Jim offered him a drink which the poet declined.

Apart from his trips to Dublin, he rarely drank during the day. After a few words more with the owner, they left, walking back up to the Main Street to collect the newspapers.

They passed the town's antiques shop on the way back to the car. Uncle Jim stopped. In the window was a vast oil painting of a naked man with bulging muscles. The man was plainly in agony, as well he might, since flames and smoke covered his enormous, corded legs, and his modesty too.

"What in the name o'Jaysus is that?" Uncle Jim asked for the second time that day. He turned to enter the shop. The poet followed him, slightly reluctantly, apprehensive.

The owner, a portly, bald man, greeted them importantly.

"That's a great painting you have in the window," said Uncle Jim. "What is it?"

"Oh, that!" said the owner. "That's *Paradise Lost* by Hennessy of School Street." The words came together: *Paradiselostbehennessy o'schoolstreet.*

"His balls must be roasted," said Uncle Jim, eyeing the figure in the painting. "No wonder it's paradise lost."

"Come away out of that!" said the poet crossly.

———◆—◆———

The poet had recovered by the time they collected Garry at the boat club and drove homewards past the convent. The open windows of the car kept the air and the cigarette smoke circulating as they neared Prospect. They overtook Willie Clane, slumped in his cart while his horse drew him home; Nicky Fortune, who sang as he rode his bike; and Padraic's witch in her pony-and-trap, the terrier yapping at the car as they passed.

When they turned into the drive at Prospect the car body

pinged as an arrow hit it. The poet swore. Another arrow greeted them from the nearest tree in the Grove as they drew up at the front.

◆━━◆

Lunch was finished. Ivan and Padraic had recovered from the smacks on their ears their father had given them. They lured Uncle Jim to McCann's, leading him through the narrow gap between the briars and through the Stile, where he had to bend almost double to climb through the hole in the hedge.

Nicky greeted them. "And was you there Lacey sez she!"

"Nicky's sailed all the way to New York," said Padraic.

"I know," said Uncle Jim drily.

"Several times," said Padraic.

"I know," said Uncle Jim again.

"Was you ever on Seventh Avenyah, Jim?" asked Nicky, resting his stomach on the counter.

"No," said Uncle Jim, fingering his moustache. "I was probably fighting the natives up at Tel-al-Khyber at the time."

All stared at him. "Is that a fact?" Nicky asked after a pause, clearly in doubt.

"Oh yes," said Uncle Jim, winking at Ivan. "Hardly a day went by without us killing a few dozen of those bloodthirsty savages. The rest of the time," he paused for effect, "the rest of the time, we went pig-sticking."

Nicky's jaw dropped, exposing his lower gums. "Is that so? Was you really out there?"

"I was out foreign for years," Uncle Jim told him blandly. "They called me Colonel Jim Sahib. I frightened the shite out of everyone on the frontier."

"Begob!"

"I've still got the medals," said Uncle Jim, fingering his moustache again.

Uncle Jim's only medal came from a few evenings parading for the Local Defence Force, or LDF, during the wartime Emergency, but Nicky did not know that.

"You never told me that," said Nicky to Padraic, who gaped at him. The shopkeeper turned back to Uncle Jim. "It must have been hot as hell in them parts?"

"Hot!" said Uncle Jim. "We used to fry eggs on our saddles for tiffin – that's a light luncheon," he explained. "Then we'd go back to the mess, drink a few gin slings, and beat the shit out of the punkah-wallahs."

Nicky's mouth fell open once more. "The whah?"

"The punkah-wallahs," said Uncle Jim. "They were the fellahs that had to keep the fans turning all night by pulling a bit of string tied to their toes. If they fell asleep, you took the flat of your sword and beat them on the arse until they yelled blue murder."

"Begob!"

There was a pause. Padraic seized the opportunity to remind Uncle Jim that this was a sweet shop.

"We're taking Uncle Jim fishing this evening," said Padraic to Nicky, who stared at the bloodthirsty colonel, picturing him in a solar topee, sabre dripping red.

"What're y'after?" asked Nicky, still digesting the conversation.

"Bass," said Padraic, "although last time we caught some eels as well. I hate eels!"

"Begob, I love 'em" said Nicky, recovering his poise and preparing to grandstand again. "Can't get enough of 'em. Kill 'em an' ate 'em, skin 'em and fry 'em, that's what I does."

"You *eat* them?" said Padraic incredulously. "You actually like eels to eat?"

"Sure," said Nicky. "They're great atein'."

"They're very good curried," Uncle Jim interposed.

"Would you like some, Nicky?" asked Padraic eagerly. "If we catch some, would you like them?"

Nicky was trapped. "Nothin' I'd like better," he said after a short hesitation.

Uncle bought the boys a bag of bullseyes and sixpence-worth of Cleeves Toffee. They left the shop, Nicky standing to attention, saluting the Terror of the North-west Frontier.

"See you at the next durbar," said Uncle Jim graciously.

He still chuckled as he drove them to the far side of the bridge at Eskerford. The tide was at the last of the ebb; gulls wheeling and screaming, swooping on the mudbanks.

The two boys jumped from the car and ran with their buckets and sprongs across the shell-and-sand beach. A black-backed gull rose from the point below them and flapped into the air. Uncle Jim lit a Gold Flake and gazed across the harbour, sprinkled with white and rusty red triangles. Every boat owner seemed to be sailing today.

They dug lugworms quickly. Uncle Jim looked at the big purple worms sliding over one another in the shell-and-sand mess in the bucket and wrinkled his nose. "They smell like a dead beggarman," he said, and quickly put them in the boot of the car.

He drove them up the river road. When they passed the tavern by the bridge at Carrig he asked: "Anyone know what that pub's like now?"

"They say it's a bad place," said Ivan cautiously. He was not sure what that meant, but repeated what others had said.

"We might have a look in on the way back," said Uncle Jim. "You'll be ready for a lemonade by then, won't you?"

"Yes, I suppose so," said Ivan doubtfully.

They drove past it to the spot where Niall and Padraic had fished. A salmon net was spread on the ground to dry. Two cot fishermen in flat caps and thigh boots sat on the rocky wall between it and the river, one smoking a big black pipe. A cot was pulled up on the edge of the water.

Uncle Jim parked beside the net and got out. The boys followed.

The man with the pipe turned to look at them, and said: "How's she cuttin'?"

"Fine," said Uncle Jim, politely nodding at each of them. "Is it all right if we fish here?"

"Go ahead," said the fisherman, sweeping his pipe at the river. "The tide is making now."

The boys quickly tackled up. They had borrowed Niall's rod for Uncle Jim, who shuddered slightly when the two boys baited the fat lugworms on the one-inch hooks. Ivan handed him the rod, everything prepared. Uncle Jim stepped to the rocky wall and hurled the bait and weight out into the river. The boys did the same. They wedged the rods in between the rocks and sat back.

Uncle Jim wandered over to the fishermen; took his Gold Flakes from his pocket. "Have a cig?" he offered. The pipesmoker refused, but his companion took one and nodded.

"Catching any salmon?" Uncle Jim asked casually.

There was a pause before the pipe-smoker answered: "Ahshur, it's just the odd one."

"Just the odd one," said his friend. "The odd one."

"Now don't forget," Padraic said to Ivan, "if you catch an eel, keep it for Nicky."

"I'm not completely sure that he wants them," said Ivan, watching his rod tip carefully.

"Of course he wants them," said Padraic, crossly. "Didn't you hear him say he wants them?"

"Your trouble is that you believe everything Nicky says," Ivan said. "I think he was just showing off to Uncle Jim."

Padraic was about to retort when both fishermen rose to their feet and gathered their net, folding it to shoot it easily, careful to keep the big cork floats and the stone weights from fouling the mesh. They carried it between them over the rocky wall and dropped it in the cot's stern. Then they sat by the shoreline and watched the river.

Ivan pointed across and up the river to where wooded parkland swept down to a quarry near the water's edge. He said to Uncle Jim: "That's where we're going to camp. Garry has permission from the owner to keep *Snipe* there, and the tent."

Uncle Jim nodded. "How many of you are going up the Bree?"

"All of us, except Padraic and I," said Ivan. "Kerry is coming down from Dublin." Kerry was a Dublin cousin, a frequent summer guest at Prospect. He was older than Conor, but generally teamed with Niall.

"You'd never fit that many of you in *Snipe*," Uncle Jim objected. "She's tiny."

"Oh no!" said Ivan. "Daddy has been given the loan of a huge herring-cot. She's twice the length of *Snipe*." The cot was twenty-six feet compared with *Snipe*'s seventeen, but young boys do not bother much with facts.

A three-pound bass took Uncle Jim's lugworm and swallowed it, jerking the rod madly. Uncle Jim picked up the rod and reeled, the two boys standing excitedly beside him, offering advice, frequently contradictory, until a smallish mass of green weed came to the surface. "You've lost him," Padraic shouted. "He's gone."

"He's still pulling," grunted Uncle Jim, reeling hard.

They looked again. Behind the weed appeared a flash of silver. Then the fish's body broke the water, its head obscured by the weed into which it had dived to escape.

They had landed the bass when Ivan caught an eel about a foot long, which Padraic insisted on keeping in an old creel they had brought, and into which they dumped seaweed to keep the eels fresh. Then Uncle Jim hooked another bass – at least, they thought it was a bass – and lost it. Padraic caught an eel which went into the basket, Ivan two small bass. Uncle Jim landed another three-pound bass, then three eels, while Ivan and Padraic caught another eel apiece.

The sun was lower when Uncle Jim looked at his watch. "I think we should pack it in," he said.

They threw the rest of the lugworms into the river, unshipped their rods and put everything into the car, placing the creel with its slimy cargo in the boot. The fishermen had long moved off downstream in their cot and were just in sight as they patrolled the river, evidently without seeing a salmon.

When they reached the bridge Uncle Jim turned into the space in front of the pub and parked beside a horse and cart. They went inside, Ivan still wondering whether his parents would approve.

They might not have done, but the inside of the pub appeared to be free of sin. It smelled of stout and stale tobacco smoke, and was quite dark after the river light, but apart from a grizzled middle-aged man – the owner of the horse and cart, as it turned out – with a flat cap and a few days of beard on his weather-beaten face, and the barman himself, who looked dim but innocent, the pub was empty. The weather-beaten man, nursing a glass of stout, nodded at them. A small window at the back looked over a neglected garden. Below that was the river.

Uncle Jim nodded to the barman. "A small Power's, please," he said. "Have one yourself? Boys, what would you like?"

"A Cidona, please," said Ivan.

"Lemonade, please," said Padraic, looking around. He had never been in a pub before.

"Fair enough," said Uncle Jim. The drinks arrived. He paid, then leant across the bar to the barman and asked, in a low voice: "Any Russian spies been in here recently?"

The man looked startled. "Whah?"

Uncle Jim looked at him gravely. "You look like a man who'd keep a secret." He motioned to the man to lean closer. He did so. Uncle Jim lowered his voice: "We've had a report that some spies have landed in the area, probably off a submarine, and that they're working their way inland." He paused. "You're sure you haven't seen anything?"

"I haven't," said the man nervously, looking at the face close to his. "'Tis very quiet around here. But what I meant to ask is, who are you, and what truck have you with Russians?"

Uncle Jim looked at him again. "Can you keep a secret?" he asked.

He had his man. The barman came around the corner of the bar, lifting the exit on its brass hinges, and said in a conspiratorial whisper: "I can, surely. Tell me what's goin' on."

Uncle Jim glanced around the bar. Ivan and Padraic watched him, mouths open. The man at the other end stared at the row of bottles behind the bar.

Uncle Jim hesitated, then said: "All right. I trust you. I'm a commandant in Army Intelligence in Dublin, and I'm using the cover of spending a few days with my nephews here and my sister's family to get on the track of the spies." He paused again, then said: "You're sure you haven't heard anyone in here speak Russian, have you, tovarich?"

The barman looked apprehensive. "Jezz, I have not. I

told you already, I have not. That's the truth – *dassdetroot* – and what was that you called me?"

"Just a bit of Russian," said Uncle Jim, airily, then tried to look serious once more. "Fair enough. But if you hear anyone speaking Russian in this bar, we want to know immediately. Is that fellah down there a local?"

"He is, surely," said the barman quickly. "Shur he's from just up the river. There's not a bit o'harm in him."

"All right," said Uncle Jim, who probably realized he had gone far enough. "We'll have our best undercover agents watching the place. You won't even know they're there. They're trained to be invisible. If you see or hear anything, switch your lights off and on three times as you close the place. My men will come immediately." He stepped down from the bar stool. "Let's go, boys." His nephews, still speechless, rose to follow him.

The barman came forward, flustered. "How do I get hold of you if I hear anniething?" he asked anxiously. "Will ye lave me a number to call, or whah?"

Uncle Jim looked down at him. "Of course not. Didn't I tell you we work in secret?" With that, they left.

The sun had sunk below the bluffs above the river when they drove away. They were about to turn up Carrick Hill when Uncle Jim said: "Did you see his face when I said we'd be watching the place? He nearly threw a seven."

When they reached the top of the hill, the engine labouring because he had forgotten to change gear, he chuckled again. "That place'll be very quiet for a while," he said.

McCann's shop was shut when they drove past. Padraic decided to bring the creel there next morning.

—◆—

Next day was Sunday. Padraic and his brothers sat and fidgeted in the Friary while the Franciscan priest said Mass. He sat or knelt between his mother and Uncle Jim, who appeared to be a sinner as he did not take Holy Communion. It seemed a crime to be cooped up in a chapel on a warm summer's day listening to the long mumble of Latin, the frequent coughing, the occasional interruption as one of the altar boys tinkled a bell; smelling the resinous scent of the incense; the family in a long row in the L-shaped friary, the altar sideways on to them. He struggled to ignore the even smaller boy on the seat in front, whose nose was running and appeared to have run for several days. The smaller boy turned frequently to stare at him, which annoyed Padraic so much that he made faces at him, causing the boy to stare even more persistently. The chapel was packed, many worshippers standing at the back.

He twisted in his seat and received a light slap on the knee from his mother. He sat up straight once more, gazing at the richly decorated roof and the marble pillars that supported it, then at the high stained-glass window of the Blessed Virgin, a goddess dressed in white and in a Mediterranean blue that was at odds with Eskerford's browns and greys; gentle face looking into the church, foot resting on the horns of a devil, surrounded by angels and little clouds. Padraic often gazed at that kindly face and sometimes prayed to it, particularly on Christmas mornings when the frost bound the ground to the hardness of iron, asking her to speed the ceremony so that he could return quickly to the magic of Prospect at Christmas. He did so again while the friar delivered his sermon. The pure face in the stained glass appeared to smile directly at him while the friar droned on. The friar finally finished, walked down the little set of spiral stairs and returned to the altar to resume Mass.

When he turned to the congregation and said: "*Ite, Missa est*," everyone blessed themselves, there was a collective sigh, a fresh outburst of coughing, and a great shuffling of feet as the Mass-goers stood. The family genuflected in turn as they stepped into the aisle and slowly made their way towards the door, which, as a gesture to the fine day, had been left open throughout.

By the big double-doors there was a holy water font; beside it a statue of St Francis of Assisi, the saint who had given the church a human face. The statue was frequently preferred to the holy water. Eskerford people believed that to touch the saint brought good luck, healing, and protection against illness, and the patina on the saint's bare big toe was evidence of this, as the fingers of the faithful had polished it until it shone.

Then they were outside in the bright sunlight. The people of the town stopped to talk before drifting to their homes, while the country people gathered beside the waiting ponies and traps, spring carts, bicycles and cars to greet friends and relations. The county had hurling fever and the talk among the men was of the prospects for the team which was strongly fancied to win the All-Ireland Final in the autumn. The younger boys, particularly Ivan and Padraic, were fast catching the fever.

◆ ◆

The poet sat in the sun near the Paddock while his family heard Mass, leaning over his typewriter that was perched on a kitchen chair. He was writing an article for *Ireland of the Welcomes*.

"We are lodged in a nook, I and the sun together, on top of the Three Rock Mountain, and I am in the comfortable situation of seeing what I am writing about," he typed, exercising a writer's license to rearrange facts to suit his purpose. A gentle breeze ruffled the trees in the Grove. He lit a cigarette, watching the smoke drift across the Paddock towards McCann's. He heard a snuffling sound behind him but ignored it, knowing it was Porky asking him to hose her with cold water. The pig disliked the heat.

He began to type again: "Almost the whole of County Eskerford, indeed, is mapped below me, in a colour scheme of green and brown that turns into all the shades of blue..."

He heard a grunt, then the pig confronted him, looking angry. He continued to type: "... on its way into the distances..."

The kitchen chair was tipped over and his typewriter flew into the air and landed on the grass while Porky, who had put her head under the kitchen chair and lifted it abruptly, watched him expectantly, head coyly to one side, a front foot wedged on his packet of cigarettes.

◆━◆

He had surrendered and was hosing the pig in the yard when the Mass-goers returned. Soon after, Benny appeared in his Sunday suit on his bike, followed by Mrs Fielding on hers. The teapot emptied and was refilled. The boys rushed upstairs to throw off their suits and smart shoes. Padraic went into the Dairy and picked up the creel.

He was puffing hard as he carried the creel to McCann's. He still panted when he entered the shop and rapped on the counter. He hoisted the basket and pushed it onto the counter, anticipation rising.

Annie emerged from the back. "I've brought you a present," said Padraic.

"Oh," said Annie. "What is it?"

"Open it and see," said Padraic, quivering.

Annie undid the old leather strap and lifted the lid of the creel. A smell of fish and dirty river water wafted. She lifted the weed and looked underneath. She screamed, dropping the lid shut. Padraic looked aghast.

Nicky came into the shop, puffing heavily. "What the divil! Whah? What's wrong?"

"I brought you your eels," shouted Padraic above Annie's sobs and screams. "I'm not sure she was expecting them."

Nicky lifted the lid, pulled back the weed, and looked. His mouth fell open, exposing his bottom gums. He looked at his wife, then at the face of the boy who was thoroughly confused. He recovered sufficiently to say: "I'm grateful to you. I'll skin 'em today." He picked up the basket, and said to his wife: "Come on, woman. Shur they're only eels. Goodbye now," he nodded hurriedly at Padraic, and he and Annie went through to the back, the woman still shaking. Padraic, mystified, turned to go, and could have sworn that the little man in the pipe-tobacco advertisement winked at him as he left.

Chapter Twenty-Eight

Work began in earnest at Prospect next morning. Uncle Jim left after breakfast for Dublin, but not before Pat Fitz arrived in his blue dungarees, a folding ruler protruding from the pocket on his knee, his small, sharp face wreathed in a smile. His tools were in an old canvas bag on the carrier of his bike, while the blade of a saw stuck out from a piece of sacking on the crossbar.

The entire family were out on the gravel at the front of the house to see off Uncle Jim when Pat rode up the drive. "How are you, Patcheen?" greeted the poet, while the dogs barked at the diminutive handyman.

"Oh! Snillalive. Snillalive," said Pat.

Uncle Jim kissed and hugged his sister, shook hands with everyone else and, climbing in his car, shouted "God Bless!" They waved him off as he ground through the gears. Once on the road he tooted the horn in farewell. Eskerford could be at peace again.

◆

They were well into the work by lunchtime. Conor and Ivan mixed cement steadily, shovelling it into the timber moulds that John had made, leaving each block to dry and harden. Niall and Padraic chipped grout off tiles. John had almost completed the foundations for the greenhouse wall.

Garry was hanging the doors on the hot press. Pat prepared to lay the screed on the floor of the new breakfast room.

It was hot work, but spirits were high. Work became almost fun as a result, and the older boys could see when their work would end and their holiday would begin.

Pat Fitz fizzed with energy, his little figure darting around the site to inspire and instruct, cracking jokes as he went. John, on the other hand, worked quietly and doggedly, his shoulders bulging as he swung his pick-axe. The brothers sang and swapped jokes.

Niall was right to expect that the job would be tedious. He frequently had to inspect, and in many cases redo, the tiles that Padraic was meant to restore. He had sharp words with his youngest brother, and by lunchtime he found that his words were having some effect. Productivity from the weaker side of the partnership began to improve, and so did the relationship between them. Although the work was slow, a respectable number of cleaned tiles began to accumulate, enough to receive an approving nod from Pat when he inspected them.

When the poet arrived at lunchtime he lit a cigarette and walked around with Pat, pleased when he saw the numbers of concrete blocks. Conor and Ivan stood in the sun, shovels in hands. The poet was not quite so pleased when he looked at the tiles, but Niall told him forcefully how slow the task was.

By then it was time to eat. Brian and Benny arrived from the fields and the extended family, full of high spirits, sat. They were halfway through lunch when the woman who Padraic thought of as a witch knocked at the kitchen door.

When she had visited them before, she had not knocked. She had banged the door with her stick and screeched for attention, but then she had always come to complain, about the boys disturbing her cattle, or a breach in the fence (her farm bordered one field of Prospect), or some other minor offence.

The kitchen fell silent apart from the dogs who rushed out to bark at the unwelcome visitor and her terrier. Again, she behaved strangely. Usually she lunged at the dogs with her stick. This time she stood relatively meekly.

The boys' mother went to the door. She did not like the woman and feared her ill temper, but was as courteous as ever.

Instead of haranguing the boys' mother, the woman took her aside and, over the barking of the dogs, asked awkwardly: "Could I see the Boss?"

"Of course you can," said the boys' mother, and called back into the kitchen: "Pack! Could you come out here?"

"I wonder what she wants," said Pat Fitz, who avoided the woman as often as he could.

She talked to the poet in a low voice for a few minutes, often halting to look, almost supplicatingly, at him. The poet asked a question from time to time, nodding at her replies. When she had finished, he spoke for a minute. She seemed to sag, as if a great weight had been lifted from her. Then she left, walking up the farmyard, the terrier snarling at the Prospect dogs who harassed the visitor until she had closed her gate into the Well Field.

The eaters were eager with curiosity when the poet returned to the table. "What did she want?" they chorused.

"She's had a summons from the Guards," he said, looking thoughtful.

"A summons!" said his wife in amazement. "What on earth has she been summonsed for?"

"Watering milk," the poet answered.

Everyone at the table stared at him.

"Begob-a-man!" said Benny. "Waterin' milk!"

"Is she going to court?" asked Garry.

The poet nodded. "Next sessions," he said.

"But whose milk?" his wife asked.

"The convent's," said the poet. "She has the contract to supply the nuns. They've laid the charges. She hasn't a hope. They got someone in to test it."

"Guilty as hell so," said little Pat Fitz.

"No doubt about it at all," responded the poet.

"Will she go to jail?" asked Ivan, wide-eyed, seeing her in chains in a damp cell. Padraic brightened.

"No, she wouldn't go to jail for that," said the poet, pushing his plate away. "She'll get a fine, and a criminal record, I suppose."

"But what did she expect you to do?" asked Garry.

"Oh, she knows Donagh is an old friend," said the poet, referring to the District Judge who was a frequent visitor to Prospect while the court was in session; a playwright of note, with a recent hit on Broadway. The judge was small, with black-rimmed spectacles and a hunched back, and drove an enormous black American car. His father, a signatory of the proclamation of the Republic, had been executed after the Easter Rising of 1916; Ledwidge's poem, familiar to every schoolchild, written for him:

> *He shall not hear the bittern cry*
> *In the wild sky, where he is lain.*
> *Nor voices of the sweeter birds*
> *Above the wailing of the rain.*

"And she wants you to ask Donagh to let her off?" the poet's wife asked.

"Oh, she knows he can't do that," said the poet, lighting a cigarette and patting Bruno's head. "I told her I'd have a word with him. She's not a bad old skin. I feel sorry for her."

All those around the table looked at him. "I feel sorry for her, too," said his wife, gathering the plates.

When the sessions came around the woman who had frightened the younger boys and most of the other neighbours was fined half a crown and let off with a caution; no criminal record. Afterwards, she appeared as grim as before, but she did not complain to the family again.

———◆———

They made good progress on the building work over the next few days as the fine weather continued. The wireless was taken from the kitchen on a long flex and the voices of the Test Match commentators echoed off the back wall of Prospect. Every second afternoon or so the poet took the entire family, packed like herrings, to the beach at Farracloe. The sea had grown warmer but still made the swimmers gasp when it reached their waists.

Sometimes they stayed at the beach until late. Their mother's closest friend and her husband owned a holiday house next to the beach, and the entire family occasionally stayed for supper. These friends had five daughters of roughly similar ages to the boys and, while Prospect was necessarily a male household, and the boys were self-conscious and awkward when they were forced to mix socially away from their own ground, they had overcome at least some of their awkwardness, largely because they treated the girls as they would treat other boys. They shared their jokes, and wrestled with them on the floor in a confusing maze of healthy brown arms and sandy legs, T-shirts and shorts.

It was noticed, however, that Niall constantly wrestled with the same daughter, who was more or less his counterpart in the other family, although he strongly –

sometimes violently – denied it when the subject was aired on the journey home on a clear summer night. He had reason to be sensitive. He still remembered when he had walked a girl to her home in Eskerford, stopped when they saw a house on fire, and sat on the opposite wall to watch the fire engine arrive. Niall reached to put an arm around her shoulder, leant back too far, and fell into the shrubbery. The girl had disappeared when he re-emerged, and he did not see her again except at a distance.

◆ ◆

Ivan and Padraic plagued Pat Fitz with questions during the breaks from the work. The little handyman was a fund of stories and had been a volunteer in the Civil War, which seemed in the immeasurably distant past to them.

"Did you ever shoot anyone, Pat?" Ivan asked, leaning on his shovel in the sun.

"Dunno," said Pat, shortly. Then he added: "Shot *at* them anyway." He refused to say more.

His favourite stories were of wrecks and ghosts, and he played to a packed house at Prospect. Eskerford people liked a story of a ghost that someone else had seen, or of a wreck, or, best of all, a combination of the two. As the coast appeared to be littered with sailing ships and steamers that had sunk or gone aground (seven ships had been wrecked on one day alone in the previous century) and as a ghost appeared to lurk around every graveyard, or in every abandoned house, stories of this type were plentiful.

In the breaks over lunch, and sometimes in the evenings when he stayed on for an hour or so, Pat told them of phantom ships seen by the people of the coast; ships at night in full sail, ghostly white in a storm, ignoring warning lights as they headed to their doom on the rocks; of the peculiar, sinister moan that wind and sea made against a great sandbar down the coast, a moan that heralded storm and death; of a fisherman who turned into a shark when he died and swam off the coast for seven years (here the poet nodded, as Irish mythology was full of stories of men changed into animals or fish by mischievous beings from the Other World). He spoke of cots that rowed in the quiet of the estuary at night, that could be heard, but not seen, even in bright moonlight; and of a brig that came ashore in perfect order except that not a single member of the crew remained on board.

He talked of how the shifting sands would swallow a wreck, and the younger boys shuddered at the tale of the ship that was swept ashore in a gale towards the end of the previous century, with the loss of all hands, and how the sands had soon buried her. More than fifty years later, just before the last War, the sands had opened after a storm and the wreck, like a grave opening, was exposed.

All the boys were fascinated by the mysteries of sea and river. Sometimes John, with his fund of stories about the river, joined in. Garry, who devoured books like Marin-Marie's *Wind Aloft, Wind Alow*, Childers' *The Riddle of the Sands*, and Slocum's *Sailing Alone Around the World* (he had built a model of the *Spray* during the winter and had given it to Niall) told of how Slocum, stricken with cramp, delirious, had awoken at night in a storm to discover a tall figure at the wheel, the pilot of Columbus' *Pinta* who had come on board while the skipper had been asleep to steer the *Spray* through to safety.

The poet, with his love of myth, joined in. Sitting at the head of the table, bow-tie hanging from an open collar, cigarette in hand, he spoke of how the Greeks believed that Alpheus, the river god, masculine symbol, was in every river and stream; how the Irish, in contrast, viewed rivers as feminine, universal sources of fertility, in the same way as the ancients associated the Great Goddess with springs and wells.

They moved on to *The Táin*; to Etáin – butterfly – and Midhir; the sons of Uisneach; Diarmuid and Gráinne and Finn; the cycles; myths and symbols; the reverence of the Gael for a poet.

The blind poet of the West was, of course, a central figure in the poet's own work, as was the blind harpist and composer who had written a planxty to one of his own people and who was the subject of one of the poet's verse plays. Then Yeats, Clarke, Æ – the last two close friends of the poet – Moore, Joyce, Pound, Tagore, and Yeats again were discussed and criticized around the kitchen table of Prospect. The poet and his wife had taken the mail-boat and train to London the year before and had seen Sam Beckett's *Waiting for Godot*, which had moved him greatly. He had discovered Powys' *Jobber Skald*, subsequently retitled *Weymouth Sands*, nearly twenty years before, and had hailed it as a masterpiece, so Powys' was a favourite topic.

They talked, in a free and unstructured way, of Ben Jonson, of G. R. Levy's *The Gate of Horn*, and of Graves' *The White Goddess* of many names: Demeter, Io, Ceres, Proserpine, Hecate, Paphian Venus, Diana, Isis, Dana, Astarte; the great earth mother, harvest goddess; of her universal presence; of sacred mountains and hills, Kilmishogue and Nephin and the Paps of Dana; of the *Song of Amergin*; of Hu and Lugh; of the language of symbolism; and of the poetic myth. They ranged into the Romantic poets; then back to Shakespeare – the poet's great love – then to the Classics: Propertius, Ovid, Horace, the Greek tragedians, and so on. For Ivan and Padraic, and probably Niall, the conversation at Prospect was not something to be endured for the sake of staying up when it was late, but something that was part of their lives. The boys accepted that there were worlds beyond that of the present, and beyond that again of the sermons and shallow homilies they could not avoid at school, beaten into them by the younger sons of strong farmers, brutish bigots who knew little beyond the world of Maynooth.

Not all of the priests and lay teachers at the college in Eskerford where Conor, Niall, and Ivan were pupils were bigoted and brutal, although many were. The boys accepted that they were subject to beatings by thick leather straps stiffened with pitch, by broken billiard cues, wickedly pliable Malacca canes, and the edge of a ruler on their knuckles, beatings given by pedants in shiny black soutanes or shabby suits, some of whom viewed giving pain as the norm; but they also liked and respected some of those in authority, particularly the teacher who gave them their lifelong interest in the Ancient Greeks, the wise priest whose spartan room gave the same prominence to the bust of Pallas Athene as it did to the plaster statue of Christ.

On the following Sunday morning they were to go to Crook. When the boys and their mother returned from early Mass they made mounds of sandwiches, filled with chopped egg-and-onion, corned beef, and sandwich spread, wrapping them in the greaseproof packaging that had protected the sliced bread. These went into cardboard boxes and baskets, along with flagons of Bulmer's cider (for the older boys) and cidona (for the younger), bottles of milk, and tins of tea and coffee; all placed in the car boot. There was a great deal of toing and froing, and shouts of "you've forgotten the rods/baits/reels," and so on. When the kitchen door was slammed it was found that someone had left the billy-kettle, or the big tin camping mugs, or something-or-other, in the kitchen, by which stage the poet had started the engine and had to switch it off again.

Eventually they set off, the car bouncing on its springs down the drive, eight people on board, Ivan on the bench seat in the front between his parents, three brothers on the back seat, two others perched on their knees. The car windows were open, and the later Mass-goers on their way into Eskerford by bike and trap and cart heard the sound of singing from the car:

Woke up one mawnin' on the Chisholm trail...

The younger boys were fascinated by Western songs and stories, which had inspired Garry to write one for them:

From Kansas down to Austin
On the prairie wide and free,
You won't find one fine hombre
'Bout half as tough as me.
I'm a-leathery and I'm a-thorny,
And mah temper's kinda thatchy,
And I wouldn't advise you rile me
'Coz mah trigger-finger's itchy.

Ivan and Padraic thought this to be a work of genius – they were very young, after all – and sang it loudly as the car ground through the gears, its speed reaching thirty miles an hour as they neared the crossroads before turning left down Mahony's Hill, cigarette smoke drifting from the driver's window into the slightly sultry summer air. Then Niall maintained the Western theme as he sang:

My sweetheart's the mule in the mines.

I drive her without reins or lines.
On the bumper I sit,
I chew and I spit
All over my sweetheart's behind.

This drew an immediate reprimand from his mother, hoots from his brothers, and a grin from the poet, who sat in his characteristic hunch over the wheel, as if by leaning forward he could make the car go faster.

At the bottom of Mahony's hill they turned right on to the New Road, the long, straight route across the county. They passed Pat Fitz's cottage, and by then the poet was singing too:

When boyhood's fire was in my blood
I read of ancient freemen;
Of Greece and Rome who bravely stood
Three hundred men and three men.

The long road stretched sometimes through a green tunnel of trees, sometimes through a more open landscape dotted with rock and bracken and mountain ash. They passed cottages and farmhouses with their characteristic county Eskerford gate piers (thick, round pillars with conical tops) whitewash glistening in the morning sun; past barns with red galvanized-iron roofs; crossroads where the local people gathered in little groups beside horses-and-carts, or standing holding their bicycles. All stopped to look curiously as the car approached. Many waved to it. Flags with the county colours draped gates and telephone poles to support the conquering hurling team.

After seventeen or eighteen miles the road bent abruptly as it met a bridge over the railway, and it was as the poet negotiated the sharp bend that they saw the Sikh.

He rode a bicycle from the opposite direction. He wore a high turban, embroidered red waistcoat, and baggy white trousers. He appeared to be in his early twenties, and he waved to them enthusiastically, white teeth shining below a black moustache.

Sikhs in their national dress – or in any other form of dress, for that matter – were not common in the Eskerford countryside. This one may have been a student, touring the country on his bike, but whatever he was, the boys had not seen one before.

At first, in the couple of seconds that it took the car and the bike to pass, they gaped. Then they shouted. Then – luckily the Sikh was well past by then – they laughed. "It's just as well Uncle Jim wasn't with us," said Conor.

They passed through the village which the poet had privately selected as the centre where Garry, when he had qualified and done a year or so as an assistant, would establish his practice. This was a prosperous farming area, and the nearest vet was some distance away. They passed the shop and bar, the General Providers, where the poet was quietly arranging for Garry to display his brass plate when the moment came, and stayed on the New Road.

Norman surnames predominated here. A garage they had passed belonged to a family who were probably not aware that they were related to one of the great landed aristocratic families in England, and who would have laughed in derision at the suggestion that their blood was as blue. Some of the fighters and robber adventurers who accompanied the Norman invaders were of the families that had been with Duke William when he landed at Hastings, over a century before they had turned their attentions to the other island. Names like Neville and Cadogan were common, as they were in Eskerford itself. The ruins of keeps and churches they had built, their castles with mottes and bailies, lay scattered around this weather-beaten countryside, sheltering cattle and sheep.

From here the New Road ran straight as an arrow for miles. The poet had decided not to turn left for Crook, but to carry on until they reached the estuary below Uisceford Harbour rather than take the more direct inland route.

Due south was the promontory of Crook, a long peninsula whose width narrowed to half a mile at one point, and which was very different from their own east coast. This south coast was very rocky, with small cliffs and high promontories. Wedged between these cliffs were small coves, often with sea caves hollowed into the living rock, and brief, sandy beaches. On either side of these beaches were rocky outcrops that jutted into the sea, even at low water, ideal places to cast from for a bass on the flooding tide.

As they drove south shale would give way to red sandstone, which, in turn, would give way to limestone. Crook Head itself, near where they would spend much of their day, was of limestone, much of it covered in fossils, and while the sea, over sixty million years, had eroded the softer stone around it, the limestone had resisted and a peninsula, defined by the poet as a piece of land that tried to run away, was the result.

They took the south-west fork at the next junction and soon saw the estuary of Uisceford Harbour in front of them. The poet stopped the car at the summit, switched off the engine to allow it to cool, and the family emerged to stretch their legs and enjoy the view.

The estuary broadened out sharply to their left as it prepared for the open sea. On the other side were the fields and farmhouses of the adjoining county. To their left, where a late morning sea mist hung in the air below a blue sky, the peninsula ran down to Crook Head with its ancient lighthouse. Upstream, to their right, the family could see the Spiderman light and the two other villages on the Eskerford side; above them the mingled waters of the three rivers. Around the corner were the approaches to Uisceford itself. The harbour was hidden from their view by a great bend in the river, but the ships making their way up to it were not, and the sound of the engines of one of them, a small coaster with a load of timber on its decks, came across the water to them, a deep thrumming sound, as it clung to the channel on the far side of the estuary.

They drove slowly down the hill into the village whose fort had once guarded the estuary and the entrance to Uisceford Harbour. Local historians had speculated that Napoleon had considered landing here, an argument that was strengthened when an Eskerford sailor had called on the deposed emperor at Longwood, and Napoleon had revealed to him that the guns at the fort were honeycombed, a fact unknown to the garrison at the time.

From this village the last Stuart king had fled by ship after his defeat by his Dutch son-in-law. Local legend had it that when he arrived here, exhausted from his flight, he had paid for his food with a gold coin. As he took ship for France, the widow who had fed him, but who had not known that she had just fed her king, glanced at the coin. The head on the face of the coin was that of the nobleman boarding the ship.

Here, too, a young revolutionary, martyred symbol of the Rising of the Moon, had been hanged and buried, betrayed by his cousin, as the ballad related, and rejected by his father:

> *As I was mounted on the scaffold high,*
> *My aged father was standing by;*
> *My aged father did me deny,*
> *And the name he gave me was the Croppy Boy.*

They sang the ballad in full as the car bounced down the narrow road that ran parallel to the estuary, the peninsula narrowing sharply until the road merged with that coming from the other side of the promontory. The combined road swung to the south-west, through the very centre of the peninsula, which had become narrower still. The view opened out on both sides. To the east the sea, a luminous blue-green, with shadows dancing on it where it passed over shallow ground, stretched to the horizon without interruption. Over their shoulder, to the north-east, was Bunnabeg Head, with its Martello tower and Iron Age fort, the waves breaking white against the rocks at its foot. To the west the estuary broadened further, and they could see pleasure boats heading in and out of the fishing port in the neighbouring county. Directly in front they could see the lantern of the squat lighthouse, one of the oldest in Europe and successor to the flame that a Welsh saint had lit as an act of Christianity in the fifth century and which his monks had kept burning for the next thousand years.

As they neared the T-junction they could see a grey, square mansion on their left, near the edge of a rocky headland. This was a nunnery, but once it had been the family seat of a rake of a landlord who drank and gambled and played for his soul with the devil who, disguised as a country gentleman, joined his table in the drawing room. One of the guests had seen the cloven hoof and the devil was seized – the boys pictured the table, green baize cloth and dice flying in all directions as he struggled – and locked in the attic in a windowless room with a strong oaken door. The devil had made a hole in the roof and escaped, and it was said that the hole was still there, that the devil returned each time the roof was repaired and thrust aside the slates, and would do so for ever until he was paid.

They trundled down to a village and there, on the edge

of the ancient churchyard, they stopped again. Below them was a tiny quay, with a small fishing boat moored to a rusting bollard. Nets lay drying on the quay wall. Gulls called and screamed overhead.

They moved on again and parked off the road, on a high bluff above the sea. The tide had turned an hour or so before and the flood was underway. Padraic, gazing across the immensity of water between where he stood and Bunnabeg Head, was cowed by the sight. The sheer breadth and power of the sea, even on a beautiful day such as this, frightened him a little, particularly when he speculated on how deep it might be. "Just think what it's like in a January storm, Poc," said Garry, smiling.

The shortest route to the cove where they would spend most of their day was down a steepish rock face. Three of the boys chose this route. The poet and his wife, with Padraic, who had been forbidden to join the more adventurous boys, and Garry and Brian who, as young men, should not be seen, as Conor put it, sliding down a cliff on their arses, walked down a twisting lane that meandered through a natural gap in the rocks to the cove.

The three boys climbed and slid down the rock face in a shower of dust and began to set up camp while they awaited the others. Niall and Ivan foraged for pieces of jetsam that would burn. Conor collected stones to build a fire circle. Niall and Ivan found broken boxes, bits of old lobster pots, and pieces of cork from fishing nets. Niall unpacked the frying pan and kettle from a basket and Ivan brought sausages and packets of sandwiches. The rest of the picnic would arrive with Garry and Brian. Conor lit the fire and smoke began to drift across the cove.

When the others arrived the boys' mother took charge of the cooking. Conor and Niall assembled their fishing gear.

"Can I go with them?" Padraic asked his mother.

"You go with Conor, and Ivan can go with Niall," she said, head bent over the frying pan and the sizzling sausages. "Conor! Make sure you keep an eye on him."

The boys' mother looked down the beach. The poet and his eldest son walked companionably along the edge of the waves, chatting. Brian had selected a comfortable rock a few yards behind her, in front of a sea cave, and was deep in his book. Apart from the family, the cove was deserted.

Conor, with Padraic at his heels, headed towards a rocky outpoint. Niall and Ivan had already set off for the other end of the cove.

The thunder of the sea grew as Conor and Padraic approached the outcrop. The rising tide was flooding the caves, the trapped air at the rear giving off a booming sound before the waves receded. Spray was everywhere as the tide rip met the rocks and retreated, to attack again in the eternal rhythm of the sea.

They climbed to the top of the outcrop. "Stay here!" shouted Conor. Padraic sat, bare feet sore from the rocks. Conor waited until he saw a silver flash, then cast his bait across the tide rip in front of the bass. They saw the splash as the bait hit a wave, and Conor began to reel.

The first bass took the hook with a jerk. It was a big fish, but it was well hooked in the scissors. Even so, it continually took line off the reel as it struggled to regain the open sea. Conor's short spinning rod bent and jerked as the bass fought tide and tension. Padraic was on his feet, excited, Conor shouting at him to keep still.

They saw the flash as the fish turned, using the force of the tide to fight the angler's hold, but the bass had tired and Conor was able to reel easily. He stepped down from the outcrop and brought the silver fish onto the beach. Conor killed it with his priest, then held it up in the sunlight.

His father and eldest brother had arrived from the other

end of the beach to watch. The poet shouted: "Well done!" to the angler as he hurried back to his fishing bag where he kept his scales. "It's seven pounds!" Conor shouted back. "A damn good fish!" said the poet.

They saw Ivan wave. Niall stood on the far outcrop, rod bent and jerking.

They caught six bass – four before lunch, and two after – between them, the smallest weighing four pounds, the largest, Conor's first, fishing for them as they saw them entering the cove in the clear water. They stopped for lunch near the smoking fire, having swum in the calmer waters in the centre of the cove. Garry, Brian, Ivan and Padraic swam again while Conor and Niall continued to fish. The boys' mother sat on a rock, doing her crossword while the breeze flapped the newspaper's edges. The poet sat on a nearby rock, bare feet in the sand, tin mug of tea beside him, cigarette in hand, reading.

The tide was beginning to ebb. Ivan and Padraic explored the rock pools, lifting the weed with their nets, watching tiny crabs scuttle across the bottom, netting tiny prawns and crabs they kept in buckets until it was time to leave.

The poet walked along the beach later in the afternoon, bending to examine stones at the edges of the outcrops. Every so often he picked a rock and placed it in a pile that had grown large when Conor and Niall decided that it was time to stop fishing.

"What do you think this is, boys?" the poet asked his middle sons, intercepting them.

Niall hefted his catch to a more comfortable position.

"A pile of old stones?" he suggested.

"Wrong," said the poet with a smile. "It's a fireplace."

They looked blankly at him for a moment. Then realization dawned. "Oh no!" said Niall. "We're not carting that bloody lot back to the car, are we?"

"It's for the breakfast room, isn't it?" Conor guessed.

"It is," said his father. "I want to set these into the big fireplace."

"And we've got to carry them up the cliff, I suppose?" asked Niall, rhetorically.

"It might be easier if you took them the long way round," the poet suggested.

Niall looked resigned. "What do we put them in?" he asked.

"I put a few old coal sacks in the boot," his father replied.

"I'm going to have a swim first," said Niall defiantly.

"Oh, surely," said his father. "Have a good long swim. I'll see if I can find some more in the meantime."

◆—◆

The sun was lower over the peninsula as the six boys struggled up the steep rocks. Occasionally, one would slip and a sack would fall open, scattering rocks past the others, forcing them to scramble back to the beach to retrieve them. The poet, who had ambled with his wife by the more circuitous but less challenging route, stood at the top, encouraging them. The boys' mother sat in the car, finishing her crossword.

The car rocked on its springs as the sacks were hefted into the boot. It sagged dangerously close to the ground when the third sack joined the others.

Garry knelt to look uneasily at the sagging springs. "She's very close to the ground, Dad," he said. "We may have to jettison some of the stones."

"Let's hope so," said Niall in an undertone.

The poet pondered. "I'd better drive it up to the main

road, just in case," he decided. "You boys can walk up and meet me there." He drove off, the car bouncing on the rutted lane, rear number plate barely clearing the surface. The boys followed, stopping at the summit of the hill to look at the view.

The sun, a red orb to the west, lit the mass of water in the bay between the boys and Bunnabeg Head. They watched the light change as it sank, then walked up to the main road where the car waited.

The back of the car hit the road once on the way home – a horrible scraping noise that set their teeth on edge – and the poet slowed, keeping his speed to twenty miles an hour until they were on the main road to Eskerford.

They sang and cracked puns all the way home in the setting sun, united and carefree. The stones were left in the car when they arrived at Prospect and the dogs rushed to greet them. They could wait for the morning. Conor and Niall gutted their catch. The family ate fried bass and new potatoes for supper. An hour of Chinese chequers followed, before all but the poet went to bed.

Chapter Twenty-Nine

Garry, with Conor and Niall, worked *Snipe* up the estuary; first under sail, then, when the fluky wind died, under oars, until they reached the grassy site where *Snipe* would spend the rest of the summer. They had permission from the landowner to beach her there and to pitch a tent.

It was a particularly suitable spot. The river made a long elbow below a disused sand quarry. In the crook of the elbow, beside a little freshwater stream that flowed from the spring in the wooded bluff above, they beached the boat. The three boys, grunting with the effort, pulled her up onto the hard ground and tied her fast to a sycamore tree.

They had passed one of Garry's favourite big houses on the right bank a little while back, and had seen its grounds running down to a long escallonia hedge, only the upper part of the house visible because of a grove of elms. On both sides of the house were scattered rhododendrons and azaleas.

The many snags in the estuary, particularly in the higher reaches, had worried Garry unduly, so much so that he had stationed Niall on the little foredeck to act as lookout. There Niall balanced on his knees, scanning the river ahead, waving either arm to port or starboard as Conor rowed and Garry steered.

They met two or three cots on the voyage upstream, one

of them with its net out in a buoyed semi-circle, anchored by a fisherman on the muddy shore. The fishermen gazed at *Snipe*, particularly at the figure in khaki shorts waving his arms like a semaphore on her deck, and greeted the brothers politely, while they continued to stare at Niall until they were past.

It was late evening and shadows were settling on the river when they secured *Snipe* to Garry's satisfaction, covering her with a heavy tarpaulin, relic of *Barnstormer*. Then they set off up the winding path, carrying *Snipe*'s mast, boom, and sails to the farm avenue where they would rendezvous with their father who would drive them back to Prospect.

◆—◆

For weeks the boys' mother had left the supper table earlier than usual. She had taken her basket and quietly walked towards the farmyard, returning twenty minutes or so later. The household was puzzled. The Hen-Run lay to the left of the top of the farmyard, opposite the byre, but she fed her hens in the morning.

One evening she invited those interested enough to go with her, to follow her, and to be very quiet. All went, walking quietly up the farmyard under a gibbous moon, the woman carrying a basket and a flashlight. She opened the gate to the Well Field and waited. When a few minutes had passed they saw what they thought was a smallish dog with a long, bushy tail emerge nervously from the shadows. Then their mother shone the light.

A young fox blinked at them timidly and took a step back, eyes glowing. Their mother threw it a piece of gristly meat from her basket. It looked hesitantly at it, then, hunger overcoming fear, ran forward and seized the meat in its jaws. It ran off into the darkness. As it did, the boys saw that it limped.

The following evening, some of them went with her again. This time, the little fox took the meat from her hand. The same recurred for a week or so. Then the fox failed to come, but returned a few nights later. It came infrequently for a few weeks after that, then stopped. They did not see it again.

◆–◆

The work at Prospect was on schedule. The wall that would support the rafters and struts of the greenhouse was built, as was the lower, inner retaining wall that would hold the earth for the vine and the tomato plants. The struts were being erected. Niall and Padraic had completed the dreaded tile cleaning, and Pat Fitz had laid the floor of the breakfast room. He was building the jamb for the door from the breakfast room into the greenhouse. The poet had received another cheque, this time for a repeat of one of his verse radio plays, and asked his family, only half-jokingly, whether they should name each new room after the play that had financed it. He decided that while his luck and the weather held he would build his sun room on the end of the breakfast room, on the side facing the Grove. Brian dug a new set of foundations while Garry spent a few days assisting Barty the vet. Conor and Ivan returned to their cement-mixing, their muscles bulging by now, while Niall, of his own volition, was building a stone wall along the front of the Paddock. Niall liked to work on his own, and summoned the others during the breaks to admire his wall. Phoebus lay on top of it, dozing in the sun.

Padraic had been given what he regarded as another filthy job. The struts and rafters of the greenhouse were rough and dirty when they arrived on the builder's lorry from Dublin, and the poet had decided that they should be washed and sanded before they were erected by Pat Fitz and John. It was unskilled work. Padraic was chosen.

He was given a heavy wire brush and a metal bucket of soapy water after breakfast, while the others watched and waited for him to complain. When he obliged, the poet uttered a few sharp words and Padraic hurriedly set about scrubbing the first rafter. Soon his arm and elbow hurt. When he had scrubbed hard for ten minutes, he looked at the rafter. It seemed as dirty as ever. He scrubbed again, showering everything around him, including himself, with dirty water from the brush. "Nothing's happening!" he shouted to anyone who would listen. "Get on with your job," they chorused in return, while Pat Fitz gave him a wicked smile.

He persisted for a further half-hour, growing more disheartened as he saw how little progress he had made. He grew more discouraged as he surveyed the line – the infinite line – of rafters that still awaited his attention. "Someone else will have to help me!" he shouted. "Get on with it!" they shouted in return.

He stood in the hot sun, looking hopelessly at the rafter he was cleaning. The bottom part looked a little different from the others, but it had taken him half an hour to accomplish that much. At this rate he would still be scrubbing at Christmas.

He ignored the calls from his brothers as he walked into the kitchen where his mother was baking bread. "What are you doing here?" she asked him sharply.

"Need anything from McCann's?" he asked hopefully.

"No, I do not," she said, in a tone that discouraged argument. "You were given a job to do. Go and do it."

"But I can't!" he protested. "It's too difficult. And it's so boring. Anyway," he said, playing the best card he had,

"I'm not strong enough."

She softened a little. "Well, do the best job you can, and we'll see what your father says when he comes home."

That was all he could expect, so he scrubbed without enthusiasm until lunchtime when they heard the poet's car approaching.

The poet was eager to see the work. He spoke a few words to Pat Fitz, then to Conor; nodded to Niall, who had a trowel in his hand and stood proudly by his wall, then came straight to Padraic and his rafters.

His face fell as he picked up the rafter that Padraic had decided was finished. "Is this all you've done?" he asked. Padraic began to explain how tough the dirt was, how the few remaining nails in the rafter had cut his fingers, how weak the wire brush was, how hot the sun was, how he was not strong enough, and so on, until the poet's brow grew darker.

"I've a good mind not to take you to the beach for a week," he said at last. "You should be ashamed of yourself. Look at the work your brothers have done. Everyone's working hard except you! Have you no shame?"

Padraic had none whatsoever, but he resorted to his usual excuse. "It's not my fault! I can't do any better than that. I can't!"

His father looked across the yard. "Here, Conor! You and Ivan will have to drop everything and prepare these rafters. Pat and John will be needing them soon." He looked at Padraic. "*He* can riddle the gravel."

———◆━

The poet relented and included Padraic in the party to the beach where Conor and Niall threw Ivan, then Padraic, in the sea in retaliation for some jeer or insult. Niall was making his way to bed that night when a pillow hit him on the ear. He swung around to see Ivan jump down the short, steep stairs to the landing and run. Niall yelled, picked up the pillow and ran upstairs to Ivan and Padraic's room. The door was closed. He threw himself against it. It yielded a little, then was pushed closed again. Voices argued inside. The defence was clearly split, tactics not agreed. He was about to barge it again when Conor appeared. "What the hell's happening?" he asked. Niall grinned: "Ivan ambushed me with a pillow. I'm going to skin him alive." He threw himself at the door again, met no resistance, flew into the room, off balance, tripped and fell, and a well-aimed water-bomb hit him on the forehead and drenched him.

Conor ran into the room to see Ivan scuttle under his bed. From the corner of his eye he saw a white object approach but was too late to duck the pillow that Padraic had thrown. He picked it up quickly, but Padraic had quickly crawled under his own bed. Niall grabbed a towel, wiped his face dry, and was too slow to trip Ivan as his younger brother sprinted to the bedroom door.

"Come out!" Conor ordered Padraic. "Won't!" said a muffled voice. Conor was about to go in after him when Ivan reappeared, threw a water-bomb at Conor and missed. It exploded against the wall. Conor hurried to the open door and heard Ivan running up to the attic. He turned to say something to Niall. Padraic raced past them both, shrieking, and ran up the attic stairs.

Niall grinned again. "They must have planned this," he said. "I saw them making water-bombs earlier." Water-bombs were made by folding sheets of paper into a sphere, basic origami, with a hole into which the boys poured water from a tap or a jug shortly before they were thrown.

Padraic's voice came from the darkness of the attic: "Fatty!" Then, greatly daring: "Farty!", since he inclined to lavatorial humour, unlike his brothers. Ivan, more subtle, joined in: "Coalman! Hey, Coalman!" a play on Niall's second name, Colman, which Niall hated.

The older two took a pillow each, ran up the attic stairs, fell over the boxes of books placed there to ambush them, and swore. More water-bombs rained down, then shoes, and pieces of the broken statue of St Francis. The dogs barked from the kitchen, excited by the hubbub upstairs. Conor and Niall heard the youngest two arguing again, then silence. They advanced up the stairs, cautiously now, reached the return, and prepared to charge. A shout came from above as Ivan leaped the banisters of the attic stairs, then vaulted onto the flight below, behind Conor and Niall. Another shout came as Padraic did the same. Conor and Niall, cleverly outflanked, turned immediately and ran after the youngest two, but the youngest two had a clear lead and were bounding down the stairs, three steps at a time, sure-footed as cats. They were in the front hall, about to make it through the front door, when an angry voice called from the dining room doorway: "What the hell is happening?" The poet stood there, plainly irritated at the interruption. Ivan flew by him. Padraic bounced off the poet's stomach and ran on. Conor and Niall hesitated, then stopped. "What are you boys doing?" their father demanded.

"We're going to flay those two," said Niall.

"You are not," his father replied sternly, and went to the front doorway. "Ivan and Padraic! Come back here at once." They came and stood before him. "Go to bed!" said the poet. "And if I hear another sound, I'll beat you."

They obeyed and went to their rooms. The house settled.

Later, all in bed and asleep, Conor was woken by a barn owl. Niall snored gently in the next bed. "Niall! Niall! Wake up!"

Niall sat up straight. He had dreamt that he was jumping from one rock to another on the Edenbeg and that he had slipped. Phoebus clung to him; why, he could not imagine, since who would take a cat fishing? When he sat up in bed, there was Phoebus clinging to him, sure enough, but why wasn't he, Niall, sinking in the sunlit pool into which he had just fallen?

Instead, Conor was hissing at him. "Wake up, for God's sake! Wake up! Don't make so much noise or it'll be gone."

Niall gazed about him in the darkness. "What? What'll be gone? I nearly drowned."

"Don't be stupid," said Conor in a low voice. "You were dreaming."

Niall, sitting up, saw bright moonlight through the open window. "Why the hell are you waking me up?" he demanded. "It's not time for milking yet."

Conor was pulling on his trousers and stepping into his shoes at the same time. "There's a barn owl in the Paddock. Or there *was*," he added darkly. "It's probably gone after all the racket you've made."

Niall climbed out of his bed, lifting Phoebus gently from his shoulders, not out of consideration for his cat, but from fear that Phoebus would sink his claws into his shoulder to prevent himself falling, as cats do. He was reaching for his clothes when they heard the barn own call again. *Skerreek*!

Barn owls were rare in their part of the world, their rarity an attraction in itself. "By God! There is a barn owl there," said Niall.

Conor was ahead of him. "The best place to see it will be from the bathroom," he whispered. "I think he's in the ash tree in the Paddock."

They padded down to the landing, looked through the window, then climbed up the corresponding flight of stairs into the bathroom. The grandfather clock struck three.

They opened the windows gently and looked across at the ash. The night air brought the smells of the farmyard, mingled with honeysuckle and dewy grass. They stared at the tree for several moments, trying to distinguish the bird before it called again.

"There it is!" said Conor. "He's right on top of the tree, just a little to the left of the top. See him?"

Niall's eyes adjusted. He could see most of the owl quite clearly, particularly the whiteness of its disc and facial feathers. "Let's go and wake the others," he suggested.

"That was the noise we heard in the attic chimney, the one that's blocked off," said Conor suddenly. "That snoring sound, you remember? He must live there."

They went to wake the others, Niall to Ivan and Padraic's room, Conor to Garry and Brian's.

Niall shook Ivan. "Ivan! Wake up! There's a barn owl in the Paddock."

There was a stirring from the other bed. "What is it?" asked Padraic. "What's happening?"

"Quiet!" hissed Niall. "Go back to sleep! Ivan! Are you awake? Come and see the barn owl."

"I want to see it," said Padraic, hopping out of bed.

"Well, keep quiet then!" hissed Niall.

Ivan, who had not said a word, crept out of bed and followed Niall. Padraic followed them both. When they reached the stairs they met Garry and Brian.

All six boys gathered in the bathroom to stare at the bird. Just then the owl called again: *Skerreek!* the omen that women in child-birth dreaded. As they watched, the bird lifted off the tree, unfolded its wings, and flew slowly, without a sound, across the Paddock, dipped and swooped several times, and was gone.

Conor shivered in the night air. For a moment he imagined the departing owl as the spirit of Prospect, or of his father, two things that to him were indivisible.

◆—◆

Ivan and Padraic were walking past the barn next morning when a bucket of water was dashed in their faces. They heard a cackle from the barn window and looked up, faces dripping, to see only a big yellow cat sitting on the sill of the window opening, watching them as it cleaned its whiskers.

◆—◆

As they worked the next day at the back of Prospect, there was a stronger sense of excitement than usual. One of the poet's verse plays, his latest, would be broadcast on Radió Éireann that evening. The artist would drive over in the late afternoon. Michael and Maisie, close friends of theirs and of the artist, would come to hear the play.

The boys found it a solemn moment when they heard the announcer speaking through the ether, reading the name of the play, then the poet's name. They found it difficult to believe that this name belonged to their father, the man of the West with the big head of white hair and rounded glasses, who sat, cigarette in hand, at the head of the long kitchen table. The voice of the announcer seemed unreal; Boydell's music, commissioned and written for the play, to belong somewhere else.

They found it equally hard to believe that the words spoken by the actors had been written in this house, produced by the tapping and clacking of the old Remington typewriter, that the sheets of words reproduced on the smudged carbon copies, loosely bound into a document with the title and author's name typed on the light blue cover, were being repeated out of the night – at this moment, this living moment – from the wireless on the shelf over the fridge.

They found it stranger still when one of the plays was broadcast on the BBC Third Programme. It seemed impossible that the man with the perfect Oxford accent was reading *their* father's name, reading it from the centre of the world's biggest city, capital of the British Empire; stranger again to imagine listeners in East Germany, dark side of the Iron Curtain, tuning in to the translated versions. How could they understand the poet's modern interpretation of the Ultonian Cycle? Could these listeners, in turn, visualize the poet, on a winter's night at Prospect, when the vixen barked in the Well Field and the wind surged through the Grove; could they imagine him, cigarette smouldering in the ashtray at his elbow, pounding the keys of his typewriter as his eyes stared beyond the words; did they guess how passionately he felt about radio as the perfect medium for a play in verse, that he believed that Shakespeare would have seized on it with delight?

Everything halted at Prospect when his play came on the air. An hour before, the boys had been warned that they must be silent, an instruction needed only in the case of the younger boys who would begin to fidget as the play began to pass their comprehension. The housework would be finished or postponed. Supper would be long finished, milking too; the cows shooed into their field for the night if it was summer; into the byre in winter.

In summer, the light in the kitchen remained off during the performance, possibly to help the listeners' concentration. As the sun sank behind the trees at the head of the Paddock, the pink light that came into the kitchen caught the faces of the listeners as they sat, ears cocked to one side, around the table, perched on the arm of a chair, or sitting on the floor with their backs to the Aga, one with a huge yellow cat on his shoulders. Then the sky would darken further, and the figures would become silhouettes, shadows.

Occasionally the poet, bow-tie undone, would grunt during the performance or exclaim at the end of an act: "They did that well," or "that man can't act. Listen to him! Why can't he say his lines as they're written?" He had a low opinion of the intelligence of actors, as a rule, with the exception of his friend Liam Redmond.

When the play finished the poet and the artist began an immediate dialogue in which the others, usually Brian, gradually joined. The lights were switched on, wireless switched off; there was a great scraping of chairs on the kitchen flagstones and the poet, wife and friends and older boys went to the dining room, where a late supper of sandwiches, cold meat and potato salad had been placed on the big dining table, with a drinks tray. They talked into the small hours, the boys' mother on the left side of the fireplace with Maisie, their father and the artist in discussion on the other. Michael, with shining face and a glass of whiskey, talked to the boys. Ivan and Padraic were in bed by then, the sweep of the Fascar beam lighting the wall above their beds.

Chapter Thirty

The glass for the greenhouse and the sun room had not been delivered. Garry seized the opportunity.

They would take the big khaki army surplus tent that the poet had borrowed for their holiday and pitch it close to where *Snipe* lay. They would spend two nights there; would slip down on the ebb almost to Eskerford and return on the flood, fishing as they went.

Garry led his brothers into the shed to show them the secret weapons that he and Brian had made.

Brian had cut a series of ash branches to which he had spliced lengths of bullwire, hammering the wire into sharp barbed points. They would use these to harpoon flounders in the shallow waters of the estuary.

The second weapon puzzled them. It seemed to be the hub and spokes of an old cartwheel, mounted on a triangular base, the wheel suspended on a wooden spindle. On the end of each spoke Garry had hammered two six-inch nails, to give a Y-shape. Around the perimeter was a hundred yards of nylon fishing line running between the nails on each spoke. A round wooden handle – meant for a cupboard door – was screwed to the outer rim.

The boys gazed at it for a minute, then grasped its purpose.

"It's a bloody great fishing reel!" said Niall.

"Got it in one, boy," said Garry, pleased.

"What are we going to do with it?" Conor asked, gazing at it doubtfully.

Garry rubbed his hands briskly together. "It'll go on the deck of *Snipe*," he said. "You unwind the line, with a German bait or a rubber eel at the end, cast it by hand, then reel in." He sensed the doubt. "D'you not think it'll work?"

Niall began to laugh. "Can you imagine catching a bass on a bloody cartwheel?" he said when he could catch his breath. "They'll be talking about this for years!" He began to splutter. Soon Garry began to shake, too, and the brothers clutched each other helplessly as the infection spread. "A cartwheel!" shouted Niall, tears streaming as his ribs began to hurt. "We're going fishing with a cartwheel! What will they write in *Stream & Field*? What will they say in the Flyfishers' Club? What'll they say," – he shook again – "what'll they say when we tell 'em we've caught fish on a cartwheel!" He leant on Ivan's shoulder, unable to go on. Garry looked a little abashed, less confident.

"Let's try it, anyway," said Conor, anxious not to hurt his eldest brother's feelings.

"Oh, let's," Niall wheezed. "I wouldn't miss this for anything."

◆━◆

They loaded it into the car boot, with the tent, dozens of tent pegs, a mallet, a shovel, a metal bucket, the harpoons, a new Primus stove, the groundsheets, a paraffin lamp, worn blankets – including a dark brown linen one, nap worn away, made by their grandmother for the poet to take to boarding school – old cork boat fenders as pillows; cardboard boxes packed with bacon, eggs, bread, butter, milk, baked beans, tinned salmon, and Heinz sandwich spread.

The poet drove them to the river, then left. They carried

everything down to the riverbank in one journey. It took them an hour to pitch the tent, which was not surprising as they had not done it before. Garry and Conor shouted instructions from the outside, answered by muffled complaints from Niall, who stood inside holding one of the two tent poles, clearly not enjoying the stuffy heat. Brian remained aloof from the arguments, waiting with the mallet to bash tent pegs into the ground. Ivan and Padraic ran to the water's edge, watching the cot fishermen work the flooding tide, then back to the campsite. It would be the first time they had slept out of doors.

The older boys eventually discovered the secret of erecting the tent. Brian began to bang in the pegs, stretching the guy-ropes as tightly as possible. Conor gathered wood and lit a fire. Much of the wood was green. Garry poured the blue methylated spirits into the Primus, then pumped a little lever on the side. The stove began to hiss, and Garry lit it. Within minutes a pan of bacon and eggs began to sizzle. Clouds of woodsmoke billowed from Conor's fire, drifting upriver towards the setting sun which had turned the river upstream into an orangy-yellow mirror. Then the breeze shifted southerly and pan and Primus stove were shrouded in smoke.

"You built that fire in the wrong place, Conor," said Garry, a little tetchy after the warm work of erecting the tent.

"Can't you see the wind has changed?" Conor retorted.

"Shut up, the pair of you," Niall intervened. "Just move the Primus."

They did, and peace descended as they waited for the food to cook. Niall, in the meantime, was sitting on a tree-stump making sandwiches. "We forgot the bloody salt," he said, and buttered more bread, watching with satisfaction the mound of sandwiches grow.

They ate enormous amounts of food around the fire, although the breeze was fickle and they frequently had to change positions. Garry brewed coffee in an old tin coffee pot, dropping in ground eggshells, a recipe he had discovered in a cowboy book.

"Ah," said Garry, sipping the bitter brew, pretending he found it perfect. "This is the life."

For once, none of the brothers disagreed although Ivan spotted Niall quietly pouring his coffee on the ground behind him. Conor had taken the family binoculars from Prospect and sat watching a heron wading in the mud past the reeds on the far riverbank, the bird cautiously lifting one leg before planting it in the mud, long, pointed beak aimed at the shallows below, feathered peak at the back of a long neck, blue-grey plumage, short tail, and long yellowy legs partly immersed in the water; a bird that was said to eat the same eel several times, and to drop its first young from the nest as a sacrifice to its creator.

They were very tired by then and agreed to Garry's suggestion that they make an early start in the morning and leave the business of rigging the giant reel to *Snipe*. It grew chilly as the sun sank. They piled more brushwood on the fire, moving closer to it. They sang for a while, enjoying the sounds of their voices travelling across the water, then Garry told them stories from Slocum, then of the *Marie Celeste*, then of the Flying Dutchman. Brian told ghost stories, one of his enthusiasms. These frightened the younger boys, but only a little. Above them, the stars were very bright, the Milky Way a swathe of silvery white.

They doused the fire and burrowed into the tent, piling the blankets over them while Garry turned off the oil-lamp. As they drifted off to sleep, with the sound of the tide ebbing fast a few yards away, they heard Niall cackle: "I've always wanted to catch a fish on a cartwheel." Garry muttered sleepily: "Just you wait."

One by one, they fell asleep. Hours later, Ivan awoke. He listened, wondering drowsily what had roused him. Then he heard a stealthy thump of oars in their rowlocks, as though a cot was creeping close to the riverbank. The sounds receded, and he drifted off to sleep again.

Garry was first up, hammering busily on *Snipe*'s little foredeck while Conor and Niall cooked breakfast. Brian wandered on the riverbank. Ivan and Padraic slept until the smell of cooking bacon reached them, then joined their brothers after a wash that would not have passed at Prospect. Niall was making another pile of sandwiches for lunch.

It was a beautiful morning, with a light downstream breeze. Below them, the river entered the wide gorge, the banks on both sides rising sharply into steep bluffs, heavily wooded with ash, sycamore and oak in full summer leaf.

Upstream, on the far bank, they heard a southbound train approaching, clouds of stream rising as it came out of the cutting and approached the tunnel. It whistled, the sound cutting across the water.

There were no cots out, but they could see nets hung to dry at the station on the left bank below them.

Garry was anxious to capture the ebb tide to take them down to the estuary mouth. They breakfasted quickly and loaded the harpoons and the rest of the fishing gear into *Snipe*. The giant reel, secured to the foredeck, ruined *Snipe*'s neat lines, but they felt a quickening of anticipation as they speculated whether it would work. They would not know until late afternoon since they would not fish for bass until the tide was making.

They pushed *Snipe* into the water. The younger boys and

Garry crowded in. Conor and Brian, barefoot, with trousers rolled up to their knees, pushed her into deeper water, then clambered over the transom. Brian and Conor took the oars and rowed her across to the centre of the river, the current bearing them downstream.

They rounded a slow bend, the bridge over the gorge below them, the ivied Norman castle of the Roches on the great rock above on the left. Garry swung the rudder to port to aim *Snipe*'s prow at the gap between the two centre arches.

Snipe ran safely through while Garry held his breath. The river opened out into a great, wide pool immediately below the bridge, and the countryside on both banks flattened. They were entering the lower estuary and the approaches to Eskerford. Once this had been a busy waterway, with gabards and sailing cots ferrying cargo between Inish Gortaídh and Eskerford Harbour, but the coming of the motor lorry and the railway had killed the traffic, ending centuries of river traditions and customs.

They ran past the estuary of the Edenbeg, the boys leaning on their oars, letting the ebb drift the boat, Garry putting the rudder over to starboard to take them towards the shallows of the left bank. When he judged they were close enough he called: "OK, boys, back water!" The rowers dug in their oars and the way came off *Snipe*. Garry peered over the stern, searching the bottom for flounders and dabs, then decided they needed to drop down further.

They could see the houses on the outskirts of Eskerford and the point where the countryside ended and the town began. Garry once more ordered the rowers to back water. "We'll drift for a bit here," he said. "Niall, shift over to the port side – slowly – and watch for fish. Take one of the harpoons."

Niall, who had stepped on Brian's toes as he crossed,

took the harpoon, brandished it aloft and cried: "Where's that bloody great white whale? The curse of the seven snotty orphans on him! I'm going to get him!"

Garry called: "Don't upset the boat! Ivan, move over to starboard! We need to keep her balanced."

Niall leant over the side and peered into the water. He could see the bottom clearly, the sunlit patches of mud and shell-sand, strands of weed waving in the current, and the occasional small green crab darting along the bottom away from the shadow of the boat. "No fish here," he reported. Garry let her drift further, the water continuing to shallow. Niall saw a small flounder on the bottom, a shape slightly darker than the mud. "Hold it!" he shouted, and plunged the harpoon towards the fish. He missed cleanly. The fish shot into the depths under the boat. "Blast!" he said.

"Don't forget to allow for the refraction of the water," advised his skipper.

"To hell with the refraction of the water," Niall cried, hitching his shorts, peering into the water again. "Padraic, would you ever get the hell out of my way?" His youngest brother, who had been leaning over the side, received a warning glance from the skipper and hastily moved back onto the thwart. The boat continued to drift.

Conor spotted two flounders on the bottom fifty yards further down. They were almost invisible against the mud, but the sun was still high and lit the bottom. He shouted, but by this time Niall had also seen them. Garry put the rudder over and steered *Snipe* into deeper water, deliberately avoiding the fish. "What the hell are you doing?" demanded Niall. "We've just found them."

Garry focused on the bank nearest to where Conor had seen the fish, establishing a marker. He ignored Niall and ordered the oarsmen: "OK, row gently now. I'm going to do a complete circle, then anchor above them. Ivan, stand by to anchor!"

The boat swung around to stem the ebb. They rowed upstream for twenty or thirty yards. Garry put the helm over again and *Snipe* headed towards the bank. The skipper looked for his marker – a gap in the reedbed – and when he saw it about twenty yards downstream, he shouted to Ivan to let the anchor go. There was a splash, the anchor chain shot off the foredeck, paid out, and *Snipe* jerked to a halt, swinging sharply to face upstream.

"Good!" said Garry. "She's holding. Ivan, you'll find a length of rope in the forepeak. Tie it to the anchor chain. When you're happy it'll hold, you can loose the chain. We're going to lower ourselves down to the fish."

Ivan did so, and reported all ready. Garry said: "OK, pay out the rope gently. Conor, let us know when you can see the fish." Ivan paid out the rope slowly, but it was the skipper who saw two or three flounders in the shallows on this run down. "Stop!" he shouted to Ivan. "Hold her there. Niall, get ready. Conor, you take a harpoon as well. OK, we're about to drift onto them. Ivan, let out another few yards."

Conor and Niall saw the flounders to the side of the boat. They appeared to be asleep, resting on the bottom. "Look at this!" said Niall, arm and harpoon upraised. "There's a big bastard there." He thrust the harpoon into the shallow water, whooped, wrenched it out again with a biggish fish wriggling madly on the metal spike, then lowered the harpoon and shook the fish onto the duckboards, where it flapped against Padraic's bare feet. Garry leant forward and flipped the fish into a bucket. They heard a shout from Conor: "Got it!" and another flounder landed abruptly on the duckboards. Niall waved to Garry to move the boat downstream again. "Let out another few yards, Ivan!" Garry commanded, and Ivan paid out the rope, holding it over his shoulder while he turned to watch the harpoonists.

They drifted on, and four or five more flounders came aboard amid shouts and laughter. "I haven't had so much fun since Ma caught her tits in the mangle," said Niall, who had been reading too many cheap Westerns.

"OK," said Garry, when the hubbub died. "Let Ivan and Padraic have a go. Conor, take the rope from Ivan." Conor did so, letting the boat down the river slowly. There was a noticeable drop in the force of the current. The ebb was almost finished.

Ivan and Padraic stood poised over the side, looking anxiously at the strands of weed and the muddy bottom. "There they are!" Garry called. Ivan struck, wrenching out the biggest. Soon after, Padraic hurled the harpoon into a fish directly beneath him, and held up the harpoon. Two fish wriggled on the spike, one on top of the other. Brian took the harpoon from Ivan and speared another couple of fish.

Garry looked around him. It was slack water, and mudbanks were exposed all the way down to the harbour. There was an almost eerie quiet. The breeze had died, and it was hot in the open boat. Conor paid out more rope, but the bottom was bare of fish.

"OK," said Garry. "I think we've had enough. Let's put those harpoons into the forepeak. Shove the corks back on the points, or they'll stick in someone's backside. We'll run the boat ashore on that little point there, and have a quick lunch. We want to catch the flood."

Conor pulled on the rope and the boat moved upstream to directly above the anchor. He tugged on the chain, but the anchor stayed where it was. He tugged harder. The anchor came out of the ooze abruptly, mud and bubbles rising to the surface. Conor fell backwards, hitting his shoulder on the nails of the reel. He recovered, rubbing his shoulder and swearing quietly, then laid the anchor in the forepeak. Brian and Niall took the oars and rowed them downstream for a hundred yards to the point, where *Snipe* grounded gently. They stepped out onto the muddy bottom and tugged and pushed *Snipe* out of the water.

Conor quickly made a fire of brushwood from the little glade nearby, then boiled the billycan for tea and coffee. Ivan and Padraic explored the muddy banks and inlets. Niall unwrapped the sandwiches he had made that morning, then called them to eat. The sandwiches disappeared within minutes.

Conor studied the harbour through the binoculars. The quays were out of sight, hidden by a bend in the estuary. He could see three or four sailing boats in the harbour, becalmed. Beyond them a haze obscured the southern shoreline. Further round to his left was the tall stack of the engine house where the water was pumped to drain the north sloblands.

The previous summer he and Niall had caught seventy-two rudd in three hours in the tank under the engine house. They had been cycling back from fishing the Edenbeg, down a track they had seen but not explored before, had seen the reservoir into which the fresh water had drained before it was pumped out into the harbour, and had decided to fish it. They had taken fish – inedible, coarse fish – on practically every cast, and had brought one home to place in a water tank at Prospect, cycling frantically to keep it alive until they got there. The rudd had entered the tank alive, but had died within a day. They had fished the reservoir again several times, taking Ivan with them once; returning the fish.

Conor was studying the heronry on the opposite bank when Garry and Brian returned from a walk along the bank. "OK," said Garry, "the tide's beginning to turn. Let's clear up here, and we can start back up the river."

They stirred from that peculiar lassitude which affects fishermen who have eaten to the full after a long morning on a river. They washed and stowed the utensils, then pushed *Snipe* back into the river, climbing aboard in turn. Niall and Conor took the oars, Ivan the helm, while Garry busied himself on the foredeck, preparing for the experiment. "Just steer her out towards the middle of the river," Garry ordered, "then keep her head pointed straight upriver." Ivan did as he was told, ignoring advice from Padraic, while the two middle brothers leant into the boat, pulling the oars through the water with long strokes until the water began to hiss against *Snipe*'s prow. The tide was making fast.

They rowed her back upstream, past the castle and through the arches of the bridge, then paused when they were within easy hailing distance of their campsite. Garry had attached a rubber sand eel to the line, which he handed aft to Ivan at the tiller. "Drop that into the water when I say so," he said. Ivan nodded. Garry gently turned the cartwheel, stripping off lengths of nylon. "OK, let her go," he ordered. Ivan dropped the sand eel in the water. "Now pay out the line, bit by bit, as we go," said Garry. Ivan did so, taking the line from Garry and letting the bait pull it from his hand as the tide and the boat's momentum took hold. When they were trolling about forty yards of line Garry stopped and checked the boat's position. "Steer gradually for the other bank," he said, gesturing towards the railway tunnel. "Make a big circle." He looked at the oarsmen. "Ease off a bit, would you?" he said. "Let that bait come round."

In spite of the ribaldry, the boys were intensely interested in what might happen next. The boat moved in a wide circle in the centre of the river, towing the bait in the brownish water. When it had completed a full circle, Garry decided to see how the reel would perform. "I'm going to start winding in now," he announced. He did, and the line shot off the nails and wound itself around the spoke. "Blast it!" said Garry. "It'll only work if the boat is travelling in a straight line. Ivan," he called, "midships the rudder." Ivan put the rudder straight, and Garry began to wind again. The others watched, keyed with anticipation. This time the line stayed on for three or four winds, then slipped off again, Garry moving quickly to disentangle it while Ivan rapidly pulled in the bait by hand to prevent it fouling the bottom.

They tried again, keeping the boat as straight as the oarsmen and Ivan could hold her, but a tiny shift in course lifted the line from its spokes and another tangle resulted. Garry decided, after several attempts and much ridicule, to cruise for a while while the bait trolled aft.

They were totally unprepared when the cartwheel abruptly began to rotate madly under a frantic pull from the bait. It spun wildly out of control and the line went everywhere. "Keep clear!" shouted Garry as the nails missed his arm by inches and the wheel whizzed. There was a crash as the wheel seized completely, the line flew into a crazy tangle around the spokes and the spindle itself, then snapped at the point nearest the tangle. One of the supports of the wheel split, the wheel collapsed on the foredeck, and the brothers sat in shock.

"What the hell happened?" asked Garry in the silence as the boat drifted, the oarsmen staring at the splintered wreckage.

"We must have caught the bottom," Conor suggested.

"Caught the bottom!" Niall said. "That was a fish!"

"D'you think so?" asked Garry, who seemed the most affected. "D'you really think so?"

"No. That was the bottom we caught, or a piece of

waterlogged timber," said Conor, with authority.

"I tell you that was a whopping great fish!" said Niall doggedly, staring at the water where they had parted with the bait. "Probably a salmon. Or maybe a monster bass."

"A salmon would never take in salt water," said Conor.

"Sometimes they do," said Niall. "They've been known to."

"Very rarely," said Conor. "It's a thousand to one against."

"Maybe," said Niall, "but that was a fish. The bottom doesn't pull like that. And a salmon takes a lot more violently than a bass."

"Let's go back to camp," suggested Brian, who appeared to be the only crewman detached enough to think coolly. "We can sort out this mess there."

Garry recovered and took command again. "OK, Ivan, steer for the camp."

———◆◆———

Their spirits rose again at the prospect of fish for supper. Niall cleaned and gutted the flounders while Garry and Conor removed the wreckage from *Snipe*. Garry, in an inspired moment, decided that the broken cartwheel would make an excellent cooking fire. Brian smashed it into short pieces, muttering as he did so.

The flounders were inedible. "Mud!" Niall exclaimed as he took his first mouthful. "They're full of mud!" The others pushed their plates away, except for Conor who took his to the river's edge and hurled the contents into the water. He returned to hear Garry say: "Now we know why the locals don't eat them."

They were debating whether to cook a stew or have sandwiches when Conor, who had been washing the plates, cocked an ear. "Listen!" he commanded.

They heard the sound of a familiar car engine, gears grinding. It seemed to come from the avenue above. "It's them!" exclaimed Garry.

They heard the car stop, then two doors slammed. A few minutes later the poet and his wife appeared, waved to them, then started down the hill towards the camp. Their sons climbed up by the stream side to meet them.

Both parents carried bags of groceries and bottles of cider and lemonade. "It was very quiet at Prospect," their mother explained, sitting next to Brian on a fallen tree. The poet lit a cigarette and listened to the account of the day's events.

They stayed until long after it grew dark, eating cold pie from Prospect, sitting around the fire while the boys sang and told stories, watching the cot fishermen lay their nets out to dry on the station above the bridge. Then they went back up the hill to the car, accompanied by three or four of their sons. "I'll be back about eleven in the morning," said the poet before driving away. The boys watched the car sway down the long avenue, headlights catching the trunks of the beech trees.

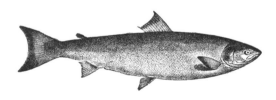

Chapter Thirty-One

The next two weeks were a whirlwind of activity at Prospect. The greenhouse was almost complete, helped by the speed at which the boys had learned to cut large panes of glass, lift them carefully onto the puttied rafters, hold them there in their frames, tap in a tingle, pinch the lead fasteners over the bottom of each pane, and lay a neat line of putty along the sides. Pat Fitz had moved on to the sun room, the walls of which were almost complete. The structure itself would be finished within a week. The poet had found a piece of Victorian ironwork to give the roof an eccentric flourish.

Niall's wall was finished, to the disappointment of Porky and Gert who had been allowed out of the sty to follow him as he worked, to root in the Paddock. Phoebus, too, had spent most of his days asleep on the wall, hunting at night.

They went to Crook several times, fished for bass, picnicked and swam, hauled more loads of rock up the cliff; went to the beach three or four times a week, generally in late afternoon, occasionally staying to eat in the friends' holiday house. Sometimes Conor and Niall cycled to the Edenbeg in the evenings, sometimes to another little river which flowed past a great house that had been burned down in the Troubles. Its ruined walls still showed the marks of the fire that had ended its era as a Big House. One Sunday the entire family went there. It was too hot to fish, so they lazed outside the old house, watching the cattle wandering freely through what had been the great reception rooms, flicking their tails at the warble flies they hated. The more energetic boys climbed the nearby hill, close to the birthplace of the dashing admiral, Churchill's favourite, who said he had won Jutland. This was sleepy, backwater country; hardly a soul to be met.

The poet spent a few hours a day at his office, and worked late almost every night. There was talk of one of the great London publishing houses publishing a book of his poems, a prospect he seemed to view with indifference.

Most of the talk over the kitchen table concerned the approaching expedition up the rivers. Garry listed inventories of tents, gear, and food and produced endless charts he had drawn, estimating the distance they would row each day, studying the Ordnance Survey maps to decide where they would camp, communicating his fever of anticipation so effectively to the older boys that they, too, thought of little else.

The equipment for the expedition was piled up in the attic: the brown tent, innumerable guy-ropes and pegs, poles, ground sheets, tins of bully-beef, dozens of tins of baked beans, cooking utensils, and so on. The boys' mother added extra blankets, wet weather clothes and more tins and bottles of provisions each day until the poet, inspecting it one evening, called a halt and told her firmly that the boat would not hold it all.

—◆—◆—

Ivan and Padraic became unerringly accurate with their bows and arrows. The poet, as angry as they had ever seen him, confiscated the weapons for bad behaviour.

The first offence involved the Eskerford grocer's

messenger boy who rode the standard delivery bicycle with its big basket at the front of the handlebars. He was an unpopular lout, rude to everyone he met. The boys disliked him because he sneered at them when he rode up the drive at Prospect.

The two boys ambushed him one day, halfway up the drive, Ivan, the deadlier of the two, shooting him in the bum with an arrow before the two ran for the shelter of the treetops. The messenger boy – actually a young man in his early twenties – shrieked, "Oah, me arse!", fell off his bike, danced on the drive with rage and shook his fist at them, swore he would break their feckin' necks, just wait until he got his hands on them, and so on, then complained rudely to their mother. She reprimanded them, but not as strongly as she might have done because even she shared the general dislike of the grocer's boy, whom the boys had nicknamed Oah Noah after his standard reply when asked to deliver anything.

The two boys stayed at the tops of the evergreens until Oah Noah had finished complaining and remounted his bike. "Oah Noah!" shouted Ivan, sending a token arrow after him. "Eejit!" called Padraic as Oah Noah disappeared down the drive. "Feck off, ya lousers!" screeched the messenger boy.

The ambush of the baker's van was far more serious. It was driven by Sonny Sutton, greyhound fanatic, genial soul, the louvred panels of the horse-drawn vehicle releasing the smells of Larkins' fresh bread when he halted at the front door. He would have dismissed the ambush as a boyish prank, but the boys' mother was talking to him when the arrows arrived in a hail from the Grove. They had gone too far, and she reported them to their father.

The poet chased them up the stairs with an ash plant, slashing angrily at their backsides as they shot under their beds. They huddled as close as they could to the bedroom wall, bawling for mercy while he knelt to swipe at them. He was very stout and found it difficult to bend, and so he grew angrier. He took the weapons and hid them in the barn. They would be confiscated for a week. When he drove away after lunch they re-emerged and found the bows and arrows within minutes. They were careful for a day or two not to attract notice, although they lay low when they shot at Nicky Fortune from the Stile and he threatened to tell. A week later they returned the weapons to the barn. The poet, true to his word, dug them out and handed them back, unaware that they had lain there for only an hour.

◆—◆

The back of Prospect looked less like a building site. The work was mostly indoors. John, with Niall, was finishing the fireplace. There was a surplus of stones, as Niall had forecast. Both greenhouse and sun room were weatherproof, but the family from habit continued to eat in the kitchen or, on special occasions, in the dining room.

Garry cut a table-tennis top of plywood and mounted it on trestles in the new breakfast room. He made four serviceable bats, also from plywood. The new breakfast room was used for indoor sport.

The boys' father showed his ability to surprise his family. He joined in the table tennis with enthusiasm, cutting and spinning the ball with guile and cunning, revealing instant reactions that amazed his sons, generally losing only to Ivan whose speed and deadly serve were almost impossible to match. Once, when asked in a newspaper interview to describe what he did, the poet replied that he was a poet and armchair farmer, a description his family agreed with completely. This was the first time they glimpsed his past as an athlete.

The tiled floor and the lack of carpets or curtains to absorb sound combined to make the breakfast room as noisy as a madhouse. Shouts of players, screams of frustration as a shot missed, yells of exultation when it did not, and cries of supporters made the new room the noisiest in the house; a place to be avoided by those, like Brian, of a peaceful disposition.

When the space in the greenhouse between the outer and the low inner retaining walls had been filled with soil, the tomato plants went in and Ivan and Padraic were placed on daily watering duties. A hole had been left in the outer wall for a vine to be planted outside, then trained back through the hole to the inside of the greenhouse. When Brian planted the vine the poet appointed himself on watering duty and peed on the root every night before he went to bed, left hand on hip, gazing at the blaze of stars above him. It was a week before this self-appointed ritual was noticed by Niall, who predicted the early death of the vine. Failing that, he said, he would never eat a grape from it.

"Why d'you have to pee there?" Niall demanded of his father, who shook with guilty mirth. "You've got the whole of the bloody Paddock – the whole bloody place, come to that – so why do you pee on the vine?"

"Because it's good for it," replied the poet, and began to shake again.

It was about this time that the poet turned his attention to his next project: the gates of Prospect and the piers on which they hung. The existing gates were shabby, rusting things which were not even very old. The piers, however, were probably early nineteenth century, or earlier, but they were too close together. Lorries had great difficulty driving through them and frequently had to back and fill several times before entering the drive, sometimes scraping a pier. The threshing machine that came once a year rumbled through very slowly with nothing to spare and the new combine harvesters replacing the traditional combination of reaper-and-binder and threshing machines would not have a chance.

There was nothing else for it, concluded the poet: one pier must be removed and rebuilt to match. It should be done soon while he had his full team of workers in place. Why not, he thought, go further, and have new gates made while he was about it?

Garry, because of his fascination with old country houses, was asked to design a pair that would reflect the age and style of the house. The designs were discussed over the kitchen table, and when the selection was made by a rough system of voting – where the poet retained the casting vote, as it were – the design was taken to a blacksmith, a man known to Pat Fitz. He gave his best price and began work within a day or two. The gates that resulted were passable, but they would not have graced a stately home.

That left the problem of removing the pier. Should it be demolished with sledge hammers and crowbars, or blown with dynamite? Explosives were difficult to obtain for security reasons – although the country was almost boringly peaceful – but the poet could use his official post to overcome the problem. Hammering the pier to small pieces would take longer. John claimed to be experienced with dynamite, a statement that swung the poet in favour of a big bang.

He bought the dynamite and hid it in one of the outhouses, terrified that his youngest sons would discover it. He was determined to finish the job quickly for the same reason. He would need to keep the road clear but only for around fifty yards either way, according to John, because the force of the explosion would not be great. It would be as well, however, said John, if the neighbours were warned.

The poet knew how to do that. He sent Padraic to McCann's, with instructions to tell Nicky that on such-and-such a day, at such-and-such a time in the afternoon, one of the piers of the front gates at Prospect would be blown. "Tell him to tell everyone who comes into the shop, and tell anyone else you see as well."

Padraic, swollen with importance, whizzed over the Stile, saw Matt Lacey cycling into Eskerford and shouted the news at him. Then he ran into McCann's where he spent a few seconds telling Nicky the news and the next half hour listening to the shopkeeper's views on this-and-that. On his way home he saw Mrs Fortune in her donkey-and-cart and told her, too. That, he thought, ought to do it.

Th pier was so tough that it took John three days to bang a hole in it large enough to hold the dynamite, detonator, and fuse.

Everyone received their orders over the lunch table at Prospect. Pat Fitz would stand with a red flag below McCann's and halt Eskerford-bound traffic. Benny would stand fifty yards below the gates and halt the traffic going the other way. John would light the fuse and go immediately to the front lawn. The others would watch from there.

Everything was in place twenty minutes before explosion time. Benny, pipe in mouth, waving his red flag, halted the odd cyclist or cart on the Eskerford side. Pat Fitz did the same on the other. A buzz grew as the locals, Nicky Kelly prominent among them, waited.

The poet lent Garry's watch to John, having synchronized it with his own. "Be sure to light the fuse at five minutes to three," the poet told John, who nodded and put the watch in his pocket. They checked the dynamite, which sat comfortably in its last home, and the detonator, firmly attached.

"Everyone back to the house," ordered the poet. They stood on the lawn beneath the palm and waited, the poet holding his watch, glancing at it every few moments.

John shouted that the fuse was lit, then ran to the lawn, breathing heavily. Minutes passed. Conor yelled: "There's someone in the Front Field!"

An old man in a serge suit, flat cap and a stick walked casually along the headland at the bottom of the Front Field, head bobbing above the waving wheat, plainly making for the gates of Prospect and the road.

They shouted and waved and gesticulated, but he went on, oblivious. John ran into the Front Field, keeping low, and waved at him. The man saw him and stopped, confused. The dynamite blew.

The pier was obliterated. They failed to find a piece afterwards larger than a cricket ball. The explosion would have destroyed a bridge.

The man was unhurt, shaken but unscathed. He called to John: "Did you feel that big wind just now? It nearly blew me over."

"Did you not hear the explosion?" John asked, sweating with relief.

"What?" asked the man, cupping his ear.

"Did you not hear the dynamite blow?" roared John.

"I heard nawthin'" said the man, reading John's lips. "I've been deaf as a post these twenty year."

◆—◆

Shoppers in the main street of Eskerford heard the bang. So did the surrounding countryside. The little crowd on the road bolted as the shock wave reached them. A small, still-smoking hole in the ground showed where the pier had been.

"It was like a bum," explained Benny later on the gravel at Prospect, still holding his red flag. "Teetotally like a bum. I never heard a bum like it, begob-a-man."

"Deadly," agreed Pat Fitz. "Deadly. Snill, it saved us a job. It saved us a job, b'y. After all that, it saved us a job. Boss," he said, sharp little face full of mischief as he turned to the shaken poet, "Boss, did you see Nicky run up the road when she blew? He left Annie snill standing there. He ran so fast he'd a bate Christie Ring!"

Chapter Thirty-Two

The hay was ready to be brought in, thanks to the
wonderful weather. Benny drove his horses to the Pond
Field, pulling a strange cradle of chains. John and the four
youngest followed. The ploughman went to the haycock at
the furthest end of the field, backed the horses up to it,
wrapped the cradle around the haycock, kneeling on the
ground to manoeuvre the chains around and under the
cock itself. Then he took several coils of rope, shook them
loose and tied them around the cock as reinforcement.

He led the horses slowly forward when he was satisfied
that it would hold. The strain came on. The chains and
rope straightened. Very slowly at first, the haycock began to
move. Benny walked abreast of the horses' heads, keeping
the pace to a slow walk. The haycock left twists of hay in
its wake, the product of friction between it and the field.
Ivan and Padraic played with these, throwing them in the
air and watching the light breeze scatter them.

They dragged the cock across the field, chains jangling,
into the lane towards the farmyard. Benny halted the horses
when they reached the door of the barn, and removed rope
and chains. Conor climbed to the top of the haycock with
a pitchfork and began to toss the hay to the ground beside
the door of the barn where Benny stood. The ploughman
pitched the hay into the barn where the three younger boys
waited.

Their job was to pick up the hay, carry it to the far corner of the barn and trample it. This seemed easy at first, but as the layers built their legs tired as they had to lift them further each time they sank into the soft hay. Yet it was exhilarating. They could throw themselves flat on it and bounce like gymnasts without risk of injury. And they did, in spite of Benny's shouts about time-wasting, you're-no-use-to-me, I'll-tell-your-father and so on.

The lane to the farmyard was littered by lunchtime with the wispy snakes of hay as the horses pulled haycock after haycock to the barn.

They lunched on two dozen fried eggs, three dozen boiled potatoes, two big rice puddings and more than a gallon of milk. Benny took his plug of tobacco from his waistcoat pocket and began to slice it in fine layers with his penknife. He rubbed the layers in his cupped hands, a man pleased with life, filled his big pipe slowly and lit it. When it went to his satisfaction he placed the windshield over the top. Clouds of blue smoke lofted to the kitchen ceiling. Outside, the Paddock was bathed in sunshine.

The work began again. The cool breeze helped, but in the barn it was very hot. When the time came to halt even Benny was weary.

He was not too weary to make a last inspection of the Pond Field. He rattled down the lane and through the gate. As he entered the field he saw a naked man run from behind a haycock at the far end of the field and jump over the bank into the next field.

Benny took his pipe from his mouth. "Begob-a-man" he said.

Chapter Thirty-Three

A few evenings later John told the boys the story of the Hedge. Garry had persuaded him to bring his fiddle to the drawing room and had brought from his room some scores of Schubert. John could read music as easily as he could read print. Benny had not benefitted from the National school system that would make the country among the best educated in the world, but John had. His family believed in education.

On that evening John played, first a few airs of his own, jigs, reels and so on, then, hesitantly, the Schubert that Garry placed before him.

The boys' mother had expelled them from the kitchen to allow her to work in peace. Their father worked at his desk in the dining room.

The drawing room was little used, since the family rarely entertained formally. It was a big, square room, full of oak furniture and tall bookcases. On one wall hung a painting – a mystical representation of Deirdre, or Etáin, or Emer floating on a cloud shaped like a swan – by George Russell, Æ, a gift from the romantic who had been the poet's mentor in the early days of his literary career. The wall beside it bore heavy patches of damp. The walls of Prospect, for all their thickness, wept liberally, particularly on this side of the house. Conor and Niall had wallpapered this room only a few months before. In a matter of weeks the damp worked its way through again.

It was a pleasant, formal room, in spite of that; much of the furniture bought at auctions of country houses. By the fireplace hung a frayed silk bell-pull that still rang one of the bronze bells in the inner hall. The room smelled pleasantly of mildewed books, damp, and of the flowers that their mother placed daily in summer in the three reception rooms and the front hall.

John put down his fiddle on the ottoman sofa beside him and said: "There was some quare goings-on on the river this year."

The boys sat up. They were very aware that John, who lived near a village up the river, knew much of the inner life there. He was the quiet man who would be told the whispered secrets of the men who worked the river at night.

These night fishermen – he did not call them poachers – said John, operated from a stretch on the bank of the river called the Hedge, below Killinin Bridge, several miles upriver from where Niall and Padraic had fished. It was a dark, wild place even in daylight. Escallonia and rhododendron bushes swept down to the river, whose thick reed beds hid the men's cots. That part of the river gave the fishermen cover on even the brightest of moonlit nights and sheltered them if the nights were cold. Here they hauled up their cots while they waited for the tide to bring the salmon up to them. They had a crude shelter there of old sacking hung on a loose wooden structure. Under this they built a small fire to boil a kettle or fry breakfast.

As John spoke, the boys watched him closely, not daring to interrupt; wondering whether John occasionally took part in these midnight adventures, so well did he appear to know of them.

The land on the opposite bank from the Hedge – beautiful, rolling parkland dotted with chestnuts and copper beeches – was part of an estate owned by a Miss Wilkinson, an old lady who had inherited the estate many years before. She came from a family that traced its lineage back to the secretary of war to the Stuart kings, and she had been a beauty in her day.

The house was a splendid Irish manor, almost square, with a balustrade on top and decorated stone finials on each corner. It was wonderfully sited, its back to the river, with lawns, rose gardens and an avenue at the front. A great set of stone steps led up to the front door. To the side of the house were the stables and outhouses. The house was of four storeys, not counting the attics. Tall chimneys showed above the balustrade.

On the night in question, said John, the fishermen had assembled an hour before midnight, when the tide had been flooding for two hours. A young moon gave a little light on a cloudless night. The river seemed unusually quiet but that, said John quickly, may have been said with hindsight.

The fishermen talked in low, rumbling voices, listening to the murmur of the river, smoking pipes and cigarettes as they waited for the tide to bring up the salmon.

Suddenly, one of them shouted: "Look at the Big House beyant! Look at it – it's on fire!"

They looked and saw flames sweeping the roof of Miss Wilkinson's house, spreading rapidly to lick the sides of the chimneys.

The fishermen argued among themselves over what to do next. They did not see the old lady or her servants run from the house, although the flames lit the grounds. Nor could they hear shouts or cries for help, and sound carried easily over water. Perhaps the old lady was asleep, one suggested with a knowing look, and was about to burn in her bed.

They rushed to the cots and pushed them into the river, splashing in their thigh boots until the cots were afloat, climbing in with the expert vaults that boatmen use. They rowed hard, gazing at the inferno on the other side of the river, and the flotilla of cots soon approached the far bank. When they grounded on the gravel below the house they looked up. The fire had gone out, and the house was in darkness again.

They halted and looked again. They could see the house in the faint moonlight. It appeared untouched. They listened, but heard only the lonesome call of a night bird in the woods and the rustle of the river as the tide lapped the shore.

They argued briefly but without decision, since all had seen the flames and none could see them now. They grew afraid. The riverbank rang with stories of the pooka, of ghosts and spirits. Some of them cast frequent glances at the dark river, fearing that some sinister thing might emerge from it.

Eventually they made up their minds. They huddled together and climbed the bank; walked across the parkland until they reached the gravelled grounds. The dogs in the house barked.

A light came on in a bedroom upstairs when they reached the back door. The fishermen's leader knocked, the dogs barked madly, and a light came on in the scullery hall. A querulous voice called: "Who is it? Who's there?"

"Only the fishermen from the other side, Mam," said the leader. "Only the cot fishermen, Mam. Shur we come to save you."

The door opened and an old lady in a worn dressing-gown looked at them. "Save me! Are you mad, boys? Save me from what?"

"From the fire," said the leader, feeling foolish. "Shur your house was on fire only a minute ago. We saw it as clear as day. Flames was leppin' everywhere."

Miss Wilkinson stepped quickly past them, her three spaniels following, walked onto the lawn and looked up at her house. "What fire?" she asked with a trace of a Roedean accent. "I can't see any fire. Have you all been drinking?"

In truth, admitted John, some of them had, but not all, and those that had had drunk only a nip or two. They were certainly not drunk, and thought it was a little unfair of the old lady to accuse them.

They explained as well as they could, stumbling over their words as they did so, then backed away, mumbling apologies, returning to the river and their cots. For once, the traditional silence they employed on the river was abandoned and they argued all the way across. They still argued an hour later. There was little fishing done that night, said John.

Padraic interrupted: "You mean there wasn't a fire at all?"

"Wait until I finish," said John, not unkindly.

Miss Wilkinson died a few days later, he said, found in her bed where she had gone for an afternoon nap. She had gone peacefully, the doctor had said.

She was buried in the local Church of Ireland cemetery, and her dogs, who howled for days, found her grave and tried to dig up her body. Her relatives put them down.

There was a strange silence when John finished the story. It was broken by a shout from the boys' mother in the kitchen. When they raced to her side they found her clinging to the towel-rail on the Aga, staring at the conservatory windows.

"What's wrong? What did you see? What was it?" they shouted.

"There was a face at the window," said their mother, shakily. "A man. He ran off when I looked at him."

Her husband came in and listened.

Early the next morning they heard him start the car and drive towards Eskerford. He turned at the outskirts of the town and drove up Boycotts Lane. He stopped at a cottage, knocked on the door and entered. He left half an hour later and drove to the Garda barracks in Eskerford, where he spent a further half-hour or so. Then he drove back to Prospect, explained something to his wife, and ate breakfast.

Two hours later, an ambulance and an escorting Garda car drove up Boycotts Lane and stopped at the same cottage. They left with a man – a shambling, awkward-looking, youngish man – who stepped into the ambulance without a struggle.

◆───◆

"He was harmless really," Niall explained to Padraic when the story of the madman emerged. "He never harmed anyone. He just frightened people."

"He frightened me, be the hokey," said Benny. "He frightened me, begob-a-man. He was teetotally nekked. Nekked as a jay. Not a stitch on him, atall, not a stitch, begob-a-man." It was lunchtime, and the big table was crowded and noisy. He licked his knife clean of egg and stuck it in his butter, pushing Greedy away with his boot. "Begob! Keep that balldoon cat away, cain't ye?"

Chapter Thirty-Four

The house seethed with excitement the evening before the older boys set off on the expedition. Kerry had arrived on the Dublin train earlier in the day, and he and Niall soon set off with their rods for the Carrick, Kerry brandishing a fly rod given him by Uncle Leo, one of the older brothers of the boys' mother. They had tramped overland, by the Tortoise Rock, and the night was pitch black when they returned. Kerry's fly came loose from the rod butt and floated in the night breeze as they crossed the Well Field at midnight. When they reached the corner of the Orchard, the reel began to scream.

A bat had seized the fly, or flown into it by accident, had hooked itself, panicked, and flew around them in circles, but they did not know that. What they did know was that an invisible hand was stripping line off the little fly reel and that the rod was jerking violently. The accounts differed after that. Niall said that Kerry threw the rod on the ground and ran, screaming, towards Prospect. Kerry said he only did so after Niall took off, leaving him to fend for himself against the fiend alone. They arrived at the kitchen door of Prospect in a dead heat, and told their stories.

Garry and Conor, taking an electric torch, led a little expedition to the Well Field. They found the rod on the ground and the bat flying madly about in circles. They pulled in the line, and Garry, winding a handkerchief around his hand to protect against bites, gently disengaged the hook from the little animal; examined it quickly, and released it into the night.

"Pipistrelle," he said.

"What?" said Niall.

"Pipistrelle," said Garry. "It was a pipistrelle."

"Oh!" said Niall, nudging Kerry, "I thought it was a bat."

Chapter Thirty-Five

The big herring cot lay against the harbour wall at Ballykeep, rocking gently in the estuary swell. A thunderstorm had raged most of the night and rain had come in torrents, to clear by breakfast. It was a sunny morning then, though slightly humid. The forecast was for showers from the West, dying out gradually, with a high following in from the Atlantic.

Garry stood in the stern, at the foot of the slimy metal ladder set in the harbour wall. A procession of boys ferried equipment from the coal lorry, parked at the other end of the wall, and handed them down to him. Conor stowed the cargo, at Garry's orders, filling the forward area first with the tent and tins of bully-beef.

The borrowed lorry, complete with driver, coal-stained face all good humour at the unexpected change in his schedule, had collected them soon after dawn at Prospect and taken them, in roaring high spirits, to the quays at Eskerford where the cot lay. The poet, with Garry, Brian, and Conor had called at the cot-owner's house on the previous day, collected the twelve-foot oars and the spurs, then driven to the little haven near Farcur. The three brothers freed the cot from the mooring, splashing and straining, undid the rusting chains that had held her there through winter storms and spring gales for years, and pushed her into the making tide. Brian and Conor took an oar each and rowed her down the harbour, hugging the shore to avoid the tide that swept past them up to the estuary.

The skipper looked anxious as he steered. The weight of the crew had clearly exposed a serious weakness; water bubbled in from the lower gunwale near the stern. He was glad that they had only a few hundred yards left to row and decided they would do the repairs on the slipway at Ballykeep. The brothers tied the cot to the ring-bolt on the wooden quay near the poet's office, then climbed the steel ladder to the quay where the poet awaited them, spectacles shining in the morning sun as he looked down at the cot with intense interest.

The harbour crane, generally used to lift cargo from a coaster, plucked the cot from the water next morning, the boys watching closely as it swung the vessel to hover above the back of the coal lorry, then lowered it gently onto the sacking. Garry stood to one side of the bed of the lorry, Brian to the other, guiding the cot's flat bottom to rest. Garry roped the cot to the lorry's sides, proud of his yachtsman's knots.

The five boys climbed onto the back of the lorry and sat in the cot, holding on to the timbers as the driver started the engine and ground up past Boycotts Lane, then past the convent and right at the Gaelic stadium towards Prospect. They cracked jokes and punned relentlessly, the driver's face turning to grin through the dirty window at the rear of the cab, catching their high spirits.

They attracted a great deal of attention as they cleared the town, waving to passers-by and greeting people they knew. They presented a strange spectacle: a lorry loaded with a tarry old herring cot and five waving youths, several of them clearly over-excited and smeared with coal dust.

They stopped at Prospect to load tent, gear, and food, the

boys' mother fussing as she checked lists, hurrying from kitchen to lorry and back again. When they left she was calm, laughing at the sight of her sons and her nephew sitting in the cot.

They presented an even stranger spectacle when, in holiday mood, they raised the mast and hoisted the old canvas sail, its flapping drowned by the engine noise. They waved to Nicky and Annie Kelly who stood in front of the shop as they passed, and to Richie Cleary on his tractor at the crossroads, before they turned left down Mahony's Hill and right on to the New Road, opposite McQuillan's great house.

It was cool on the back of the lorry, and sometimes a little wet as a summer rain shower passed, but their excitement did not diminish. It rose further as the lorry began the steep descent into Ballykeep. They had lowered the sail and mast when the Uisceford Estuary and the Spiderman light had come into sight. The lorry turned its flat face into the village, then reversed towards the slipway. The boys jumped off. Garry signalled to the driver to stop, and the cot was carefully manhandled off the lorry to the ground.

The arrival of the cot created a minor sensation in the village. The locals came from the boatyard, from the pub-fishmonger-grocer, from the salmon yawls in the harbour, and from the thin air that spectators always appear from in an Irish village when anything out of the ordinary appears without warning. The people of Ballykeep – a dozen at least – walked slowly around the cot, peered underneath at the flat bottom, commented on the lack of decking and the need for a keel. That wouldn't do here, they said without saying it, and wasn't it a strange thing, like, to have the ends the same, like, as if 'twas a canoe?

Garry lit a fire and placed his pitchpot on its tripod when the lorry left and the spectators dispersed. As it began to bubble and smoke he took a flat piece of lead and shaped it with his sheath knife, measuring it against the hole near the stern. He had inspected the gap in the gunwale where the cot had leaked so profusely while his brothers and cousin had been waving at passers-by on the journey, and was satisfied that he knew its extent. When the pitch was hot he pressed the lead piece that boatmen called a *tingle* over the leak and held it in place while Brian covered it in boiling pitch.

When the pitch hardened they covered the whole in several layers of tar. Garry looked closely at it and was satisfied. It would not do at sea, but they were not going to sea.

It was past noon when they launched the cot, pushing and pulling her into the water with the help of the salmon men. Once in the water, Garry and Conor worked her in the green, translucent water to the seaward end of the slip at the harbour wall, where they tied her, fore and aft, to ring-bolts. They finished the caulking of the upper gunwales with oakum and putty, the cot rolling slightly on the tide, an hour or so before low water. The combination of pitch and tar smells and the rolling of the cot made Garry and Conor seasick, ashamed to admit it even to each other, but definitely seasick. Both were glad when the caulking was completed, relieved to step onto the harbour wall and breathe the clear estuary air.

Garry was completing his final inspection when they heard the poet's car descending the hill. His father had brought two dozen eggs from the hens at Prospect, a gallon of fresh milk and a mountain of soda bread the boys' mother had baked that morning. The poet lit a cigarette as he inspected the cot, told Niall and Kerry to bring the food from the car, and said to his eldest: "You're all set now, Gar."

◀▶◆

With the time of departure close, and perhaps because they had talked of little else for much of the summer, the boys felt strangely apprehensive, Garry particularly so, since he was responsible for the safety of a vessel which would contain three brothers and his cousin, and which was about to venture into the currents of the inland waterways where he was bound to encounter obstacles and snags that would require rapid decisions.

Garry was not a gambler and he had tried to overcome his apprehensiveness by planning each stage of the route, estimating the distance they would travel each day and the rise and fall of the tide. The sea stretched its tongue twice a day as far inland as Killmoling, thirty miles from the mouth of the estuary at Crook, and his plan was to take the cot beyond that, into the fresh water where they would navigate past weirs and through locks.

Soon, however, he began to relax, as his brothers' high spirits, jokes from Conor, droll comments from Niall, puns from Brian, and quiet encouragement from his father affected him. He became positive again.

The cot was fully loaded. The tide began to flood. Brian and Conor took an oar each, Niall stood with the bow painter in hand, Garry checked that the way was clear out into the fairway, the poet called goodbye, and they were off into the tide.

◆◆

The rest of the family at Prospect had to rely on individual accounts from each of the five boys to follow the events of the next few weeks. The family were reunited only once during that time when the poet drove his wife, Ivan and Padraic to the riverbank camp.

To begin with, Conor said, the voyage went smoothly. He and Brian settled into a steady rhythm at the oars, and the big cot, once she gathered momentum, proved surprisingly easy to row. She made little water; the repairs had clearly worked. Brian, Conor noted, was very particular about his oar handling, feathering carefully after each stroke, re-inserting the sweep into the water at the correct angle as if he were back in a university eight.

The river was empty of vessels above Ballykeep as far as the eye could see. There were salmon yawls below them, taking station down to Crook Head, nets trailing.

Above them there was nothing visible, not even a skiff, or a steamer stemming the tide from Uisceford or Rosspoint. They saw only a big, vacant estuary, as if they sat on the dividing line between sea and river, and as if the river slept.

They made surprisingly good time up to Creek Point, where the estuary forked and the Saor bent to the west to Uisceford. From there on they were in the estuary of two rivers rather than three.

Garry held his bearing-compass on his knee, grasping the tiller and jotting bearings on his charts as if he navigated the South Seas. He kept the cot on a steady course, hugging the dark brown water close to the eastern bank, looking up occasionally at the wooded green bluffs to starboard.

He relaxed visibly and grinned as Niall shouted from the bow thwart: "Ahoy there, skipper! Avast behind!"

"Where?" grunted Brian, who was as slim and fit as the rest of them.

"Yours!" said Niall, and cackled madly.

To starboard but out of sight were the ruins of a great abbey, a monastery built by a Montmorency for the Augustinian monks eight hundred years before. They passed under the great railway bridge that linked the two counties, gazing up at its red spans as they went, and entered a big bend in the estuary. A Welsh ship was coming down from Rosspoint, throwing a heavy bow wave. Garry put the helm over to point the bow at the wash. They had a scare when the ship appeared to be heading straight for them as if the lookout was asleep, but she passed with room to spare, the boys gazing in awe at the great iron sides, flaked with rust, towering above them. Even a small coaster will look daunting from a cot, and the wash made the herring cot dance like a crazed ballerina, pots and pans and tin mugs banging as the vessel rocked.

It rained twice, once heavily, but they were well prepared and quickly donned sou'westers and raincoats, covering the forepeak with a tarpaulin. Then it cleared and the sun came out again, and stayed out. After that, Conor said, they hurtled along. Garry called out that the tide appeared to be three knots or so, and that they were making faster progress than he had planned. And how! said Conor afterwards. Garry had planned to travel six miles before camping. In the event, said Conor, they travelled twenty-three miles, heavily underestimating the rise and fall of the tide, so much more volatile than their own river.

They did not see a single person from the cot. The high, wooded bluffs above them, thick with oak, beech and ash, seemed to slumber in the hot afternoon sun. These bluffs swept steeply down to the river, leaving little between them and the water except exposed mud when the tide was out.

The only signs of habitation were the salmon weirs, nets suspended above on great poles. They looked at the first of these fish traps in wonder, reminded of old mezzotints of similar nets on the rivers of Cochin China, sights that belonged to exotic, distant places.

They followed the river around a great bend to the east, and reached the outskirts of Rosspoint, and it was still only early evening. The town was on a hill over the river, with handsome old stone warehouses and three church spires. Its harbour had rivalled Uisceford's for centuries. These two had once been Ireland's busiest ports, and although Rosspoint was recovering at the expense of Eskerford and its shallowing harbour, it was not what it had been.

Three Bullet Gate, where Cromwell fired his warning shots that frightened the garrison into surrendering, lay out of sight. Garry pointed out the castellated house of the shipowner, proprietor of one of the great English football clubs who had named the club's ground after the lane behind his mansion at Rosspoint. They passed under the point where the rebels had lost the decisive battle of the Rising of the Moon, where defeat had followed an apparent victory as the pikemen had prematurely celebrated in a frenzy of drunkenness, and the forces of the Crown had counter-attacked, the turning point of the rebellion.

There was little river traffic here. They saw the occasional lighter ferrying its cargo across the estuary. Two smallish coasters were berthed at the stone quay.

They heard a call from the quay. "Garry! Brian! Hey! Boys!" They turned to see the artist hurrying towards them. "Tony!" they shouted in unison. "Back water, boys!" ordered Garry and the cot halted on the strong tide, the oarsmen working her in towards the quay.

The artist had finished a tedious day at the bank and had left for a walk on the quays. "God, boys! You've done well. What time did you leave?"

"We've flown up on the tide," replied Garry, taking a boat-hook in case they went too close to the palings. "It's much stronger than I thought, and it'll last several hours yet."

"Where will you be by the weekend?" asked the artist.

"Probably around Killmoling," Garry guessed.

"I'll pop up there in the car and have a look around for you. Leave a message with the lock-keeper if you can."

"We will," Garry promised. "We'd better get going again, Tony, and use the tide."

"Good luck, boys," said the artist. "I'd love to be going with you. It's wonderful country up there, full of history. And haven't you got the weather!"

◆

Brian told his youngest brothers later how they had felt they had crossed an unseen boundary when they had rowed above Rosspoint. This was a very different Ireland from the flat coastal plain of south Eskerford, with its beaches and shallow bays on one coast, its rocks and rips on the other, the sea always near. In many ways, he said, this part of the country, with its rolling country and rich history, was the old Ireland, a beautiful, sleepy, inland backwater, a land that had changed remarkably little over the centuries.

The big brown river was full of mystery, with its beeches and sallies that dipped their branches in the water. Little creeks, lines of willows concealing their entrances, provided ideal cover for those who did not wish to be seen. Further up, towards the confluence with the Owenore, the countryside opened and the land appeared to fall below river level. The landscape was very different, more wooded, and it appeared to sleep in the soft evening light. They could see for miles: farming valleys with miniature whitewashed houses and tiny red roofs of barns in the distance, dozing under a sky streaked with vermillion.

The Owenore came in from the west. They rowed past it, keeping east and north on the Bree. There was a farm above the confluence, and the smell of pigs drifted on the breeze.

They had decided to make the most of the tide, to have

supper when they had chosen their camp and pitched the tent. When the tide was almost spent they saw a grassy levee in front of a disused limekiln. A creek lay to the side. Clumps of willows ran into the river. Below them were four or five canoes, with lines of stakes between them. The only sign of the owners was a flattening of the high grasses above the willows.

They rowed the cot in gently to the bank, on the lookout for underwater snags. Niall leaped ashore and made the painter fast to a big willow. Brian landed next, wielding his axe, which rang within minutes from the wood above them. It was probably on that first evening that they realized that whatever they might lack on this trip it would not be wood. When Brian reappeared, half an hour later, he dragged what appeared to be half a tree behind him and, like a good historian, reminded them that he followed in the footsteps of the Kaiser, who had died a woodcutter. He began to cut the tree into small logs.

They pitched camp efficiently, experts after the rehearsal on the home river. The tent went up without a hitch. Conor lit a fire. Woodsmoke drifted across the levee, past the limekiln and into the willows. Niall dug for worms, assembled his rod, baited his hook and caught eel after eel which Garry cut surgically into small morsels with his scalpel and fried in the hissing pan. Conor baited his own rod and added more eels to the pan. When Brian took over the cooking Garry checked the cot, loosening the bow painter and attaching a second to the stern. The tide would drop sharply. He did not want the vessel to be suspended in midair from the levee when it did.

Kerry was to catch several more bats during the holiday. They seemed, Garry told him, tongue-in-cheek, to be very attracted to him, perhaps because of his height, or his big feet, or possibly because they preferred Dublin jackeens, but that evening Kerry also caught the ugliest fish – the ugliest creature of any kind – that the boys had seen.

It took the worm as an eel would, and fought the rod in much the same fashion, but broke surface a little earlier. The others lined the riverbank alongside the angler and wondered whether he had hooked a ferox trout, a cannibal, as the head looked very large. Kerry brought the fish to the bank and landed it. Niall hit it on the back of the head with his priest and they looked at it closely.

It seemed prehistoric; big, angular, bony head, eyes protruding from a ridge below the top; each scale very distinct from the other, its mouth lined with a row of spiky teeth. The boys recoiled. "It's a cœlacanth," said Garry. "I'm sure it's some kind of cœlacanth, but they're supposed to be extinct." Kerry, disgusted and disappointed, hurled the fish into the river where the ebb tide whirled it away. "We should have kept it," said Garry. "God knows what it was." The others were secretly glad to see it go.

Their first riverbank supper, said Conor afterwards, was delicious. Fresh eel and new potatoes from Prospect, boiled with a little salt, made a wonderful combination whatever scruples Padraic might have had.

The feeling of isolation, of being utterly alone in this beautiful river country struck them most when they had eaten and begun to relax, said Brian. The country around Prospect was peaceful, but the house was never far away, and the twin spires of Eskerford and the horizon beyond them were generally visible, or if they were not, Brian said, you knew they were there, and at night the light of the Fascar gave a constant reminder of this. This was very different: pastoral, not littoral, he said, and then seeing the expression of puzzlement on the youngest boys' faces when he told them this, he added: country, not the coastal land we're used to.

They had passed under Ormonde Bridge a mile or so downstream, its eccentric shape the design of an engineer who had created great iron tanks to be filled with water until their weight counter-balanced a section to allow ships through; the name of the bridge a clear sign, said Brian, that they were in the country of the Butlers, the family that had held the chief butlership of Ireland under the Crown, a position that predated even that of the Steward of Scotland, whose title altered later to the royal family name of Stuart. His brothers and cousin respected his knowledge of the history of the land, but it was hard to connect the violence of those times with the peace of this goodly river.

They sat around the fire at dusk and Niall played his mouth organ. They heard the calls of the night birds over the swish and swirl of the river, the croaking of frogs, and a fight in a heronry close by. A fox barked, then was silent.

The swifts had been visible in great numbers, long sooty wings shooting them to great heights, then down to a few inches above the river, instant changes of course, braking, wheeling, seizing flies in mid-air and leaving rings on the water as they picked spent insects from the current, chasing each other, screaming: *"Smee-ee, smee-ee;"* hunting until it was too dark to see.

The boys doused the fire. The sky was pierced with stars in the clear air. It was turning chilly, and a mist hung a few feet over the river. The air had cooled to a temperature below that of the water. As they settled down in their blankets inside the tent Garry murmured sleepily: "I wonder what they're doing at Prospect now." An equally sleepy reply came from Niall's side of the tent: "I know what *he's* doing. He's peeing on the bloody vine."

"If that vine had any self-respect, if it had any moral fibre whatsoever," said Brian out of the darkness, "it would be planning its revenge. D'you know what they'll call it when that happens?"

"What?" someone asked.

"The *Grapes of Wrath*," said Brian.

"If you make any more jokes like that I'll throw you in the river tomorrow," promised Niall.

The poet, had he been there, would have told them that you do not know a country except by sleeping nights in it. A house, he would muse, is too much insulation in summertime: the grasses do not talk to you, or the reeds, or the trees. You do not hear a badger snuffle or an otter plunge, or a salmon hit the water like the flat of an oar. He would have added that to lie warm in a blanket on the ground is a strange way to meet the dawn, to waken and find it in bed with you.

His sons were not given the opportunity to sleep through and meet the dawn in peace. On that first night they began to realize why the summer river appeared to sleep during the day. It was because it awoke at night.

The first signal of this came when they had been asleep for an hour. Garry was the first to wake. "What was that?" he whispered.

"What is it?" Brian asked. "What did you hear?"

The others awoke, one by one, and listened. The river sounds came clearly into the tent. A distant farm dog barked.

Then someone spoke in a low voice, only a few yards from the tent: "Janey, Pat, there's somethin' here that never was here before." The last word had three syllables: *be-fo-wer*.

Garry rose quickly, stepped over Kerry's legs, opened the tent flap and looked out. Four shadowy figures skirted the tent, one of whom appeared to have tripped on a guy-rope. He watched as they walked towards the moorings of the canoes, two of them carrying dark bundles, the others bearing what appeared to be pairs of paddles. They halted, and Garry guessed they had seen the cot. He was right. The men deposited their loads in the canoes and sauntered quietly over to the old craft, walking around it, peering underneath, running their hands along stem and stern posts as if they had never seen a herring cot before. Perhaps they had not, thought Garry.

When they turned, they saw him. Each gave him a friendly wave, and one called: "That's a great lump of a boat you have."

"Isn't it?" Garry returned. The others joined him, standing in their pyjamas as they watched the men unmoor two of the canoes. The fishermen blessed themselves, then disappeared into the darkness of the river a few minutes later, paddling quietly, a murmur of low voices drifting across the water.

The boys climbed under their warm blankets. They heard more voices, more clinks of chains being loosed, more soft thumps as the night fishermen took their places in their canoes, and more muted paddle splashes. Conor said: "Janey, Pat, there's somethin' here that never was here before," and they laughed. Then one by one they slept until they met the dawn.

◆—◆

The night fishermen returned soon after sunrise with part of the flood still to run. The only signs of them that remained when the boys emerged from the tent were bootmarks in the mud and fresh partings in the high grass. The river was bathed in sunlight, the air fresh with a light breeze.

Conor went to fill kettle and bucket from the little rivulet that ran down the hill and saw a song-thrush knocking a snail against a big stone. He watched it as it broke the snail's shell and ate the contents. Then it flew unhurriedly into the woods to find another. A little pile of broken shells lay scattered by the stone.

He saw a set of otter prints on the riverbank nearby, the half-webbing of the marks bringing instant identification. He waited, wondering if the animal was still nearby, perhaps even in the rising water. He rose and scouted further up the bank and found the prints of the returning otter, then the remains of a frog the otter had evidently skinned. He followed the prints across the soft mud as far as he could, but they faded when the mud turned to grass.

The cot was still out of the water, its size dwarfing the neighbouring canoes. They breakfasted off thick rashers of bacon and fried eggs, the open air giving them an appallingly keen hunger, before launching the cot. Garry hoped to move further upriver before the ebb.

When the cot was free of the browny-black ooze and she began to rock gently in the current they rolled their trousers above their knees and removed shoes and socks. The water was surprisingly cold.

Brian wandered along the riverbank, studying the plant life. Niall rolled his eyes at the sight and said to Conor: "He wishes he'd brought Abdul." Conor grinned.

They set off soon after they had struck camp, Niall said. The weather was sunny and warm, the humidity gone. The tide carried them up, and when they rounded a bend in the river they saw the bulk of Slievelaigheann, the summit of the range visible in the distance from Prospect on a fine day. In the blueish haze they could see clearly the fields running up its foothills and the line where the fields stopped, and whin, rock, and stunted mountain ash took over.

River and banks were deserted; not a soul to be seen, though they passed several weirs with monstrous stake-nets suspended above them, seemingly unattended.

Rowing was relatively easy at first, though not as easy as on the evening before when they had had the full flow of the tide to carry them up. Soon, however, the tide began to ebb, barely noticeably at first, but then at a pace that astonished them, until the rowers struggled to keep the cot moving at more than a crawl. The brown river appeared to race past them.

A wooded bluff to port towered above them, descending precipitously to the water's edge, almost a sheer cliff face of living rock with bushes and ferns in earthen niches. At its summit, commanding the river from several hundred feet above, was a Norman castle, once home to the Roches, backwoods barons who had preyed on the river trade. The top of the castle was barely visible to them above the tall trees below it. Near it was a stone watchtower. The river's course described a great horseshoe bend opposite the cliff face, around a low, grassy flat on the left bank, so low that they guessed it would flood at spring tide. The cliff face upriver ended abruptly, to be followed by a low, flattish piece of ground with a stream running through it into the river.

"Look at that," said Garry, eyeing the spot, "that's a perfect place to camp." The others, perhaps cowed a little by the tide's force, agreed.

They pulled like maniacs to cross, rowing almost due upstream to avoid being swept down, sweeps bending and cracking, spurs rattling against the gunwales, meeting the full force of the tide as they reached the middle; anxious moments until they were out of the full force of the Bree's current and, with a collective sigh of relief, they reached the calmer water near the right bank and rested on their oars, Brian and Kerry displaying palms blistered and bloody.

"We won't try that again," said Garry, angry with himself at not having anticipated the steep rise and fall of the Bree. "We'll use the tide from now on." The oarsmen, puffed and sweating, nodded and began to row again, more slowly.

Niall chortled from the bow: "On deck there! On deck! Land on the port bow!" The others grinned, eager to reach the land a few yards away.

<hr />

They called this camp The Ruar after the tiny village that was marked on the map to the west of the river.

The riverbank appeared devoid of humans, but they had begun to learn how deceptive that impression could be. Around twenty canoes lay in neat rows in the mud, each protected by a line of stakes. The wood above was wildly overgrown, beech and oak intermingled. Within half an hour, Brian's hatchet was ringing again.

The camp gave them a wonderful view of the river. The cot fitted neatly beside the creek and floated except at low water. They pitched the tent on the grassy bank, unpacked, put everything in its place, and set off to explore. They climbed through the wood, up and up, a very steep climb, until they reached the castle, and when they saw the view they understood why it had been sited there. It commanded a view of river and country for miles.

They rowed the cot on the flooding tide to Killmoling, planning to explore river and village before returning to camp on the ebb. Niall and Kerry took the oars and they rounded the great bend on the flood, the rowing easy.

Soon they were in a gorge, at the end of the mountain range. In front of them, on the left bank, was the ancient village of Killmoling, named after the miller saint, a man of Gaelic royal blood, who had arrived in what was foolishly called the Dark Ages. Now a more modern milling family, neighbours of their maternal grandparents at their weekend retreat in the county Kildare, still produced flour at this, one of their many mills, which the boys could see clearly as they lay on their oars to look at the village. Seven or eight houses, a big shed with a rusting red roof and a pub completed the village. Here salt water turned to fresh, or nearly so, as a tidal cut ran past the sea lock and up to a weir, the tidal limit. Directly behind and in line with the village rose Brendan Hill, farmland at its feet, bald head rising above the mill.

They ran aground on the Scar, a ledge of rock below the village, and had to heave the cot off, slipping and swearing as they pushed her into deep water, Brian using his great strength to lift the stern while the others pulled.

They moored in the cut and went ashore to explore. The village had plainly seen busier times. Several houses were abandoned. They walked upstream, along the path by the cut, admiring the grey, elegant house that had been built for the lock-keeper, but which lay empty.

There was a considerable flow over the weir. The rain they had met on the way up clearly had been much heavier in the catchment areas above. They saw a salmon jump, silver body flashing in the sun as it threw itself up the weir. It was followed by another, and they realized they were watching a run fresh from the sea thirty miles below. Even Garry, who placed fishing a long way below boating, was impressed. There were two anglers on the bank by the weir. The boys heard their shouts clearly as the fish showed.

They dropped downriver on the ebb, anchoring below the Scar, and fished for trout, catching half a dozen in an hour, trout in beautiful condition, speckled and golden in the evening sun. They ate them for supper when they returned to The Ruar.

The ebb still flowed as dusk descended on the river, the sun sinking behind the battlements of the castle high above them, throwing a pink light on the water and the opposite bank, the camp almost in darkness. The river appeared to smoke as the air temperature cooled, giving off a mist that hung on the surface.

They were sitting on groundsheets and oilskins around a blazing fire fuelled by Brian's logs when the night fishermen arrived.

They came in fours, carrying nets and paddles, walking down the little track that ran beside the bank. They came to the fire, were given mugs of tea, and long before the ebb had ceased they were a larger group, more than twenty of them, talking in the soft accent of the county, telling the boys stories of fishing, of characters of the river; stories of the wildlife and of strange events; told in a matter-of-fact way that fascinated the boys, in the tones of men who waited to begin their daily work.

They left the camp fire, four at a time, unshackled their canoes, stepped into them when they had splashed in their black thigh boots to a depth where the canoes would bear them, paddling out until they reached their stations. Two canoes would move in parallel, then both would halt, a paddler in each, holding ground, the snap net stretched between a crewman in each, the weighted bottom sunk in the water.

The boys could hear the murmured voices from the river long after they had sought their blankets, and the occasional thump as another salmon met its end. They awoke to hear the canoes reaching the shore, the clink of the shackles, and the padding of boots on the grassy bank as the fishermen returned, some of them calling a greeting as they passed.

They stayed at The Ruar for a few more days, fishing for trout in the mornings and evenings, seeing no one but the night fishermen except when they shopped at the pub and shop at Killmoling, or when Brian tramped into the little village of The Ruar to shop, slaking his thirst at the ornate village pump.

Brian trapped Niall several days in a row. He had watched Niall eat, at a single sitting, eleven rounds of bully-beef sandwiches. He caught him completely unaware on the first occasion, waiting until Niall took a mighty bite and began to chew, before saying: "You know, Niall, I'm very worried about you."

Niall, mouth full, could only raise his eyebrows and mumble: "Ugh?"

"Yes," said Brian. "Very worried."

"Ugh?"

"I don't think you're eating enough."

It was time to move up, beyond the tide, up the upper Bree navigational system. On a glorious morning, two hours of the flood remaining, they struck camp and rowed up once more to Killmoling in time to shop for bread and milk before the tide forced the river to back up and the water pressure to equalize in the lock.

They grew nervous when they brought the cot up the cut towards the great gates, Niall said. They waited for high water, anxiously holding the cot against the weeping green wall below the gates. The big wooden doors opened and they entered the lock. The downriver gates closed behind them, the upriver ones opened and the water in the lock rose. When it settled they pushed on the slippery sides with the boat hook and oars and were through into the fresh water.

They rowed steadily up the boatstream, a dense wood on their right. Soon they were opposite the weir where they saw the anglers waiting for another run of salmon.

The upper river was even more beautiful in many ways, though tamer, with none of the force that had shocked them on the way up. They glimpsed Slievelaigheann in a blue haze. Brendan Hill, which they had first viewed from Rosspoint, watched over them for much of their voyage, the hill named after the navigator saint who had built a house in the foothills and then left, to discover America in a vessel smaller than theirs.

◆—◆

Prospect was strangely quiet but very busy. The chores were shared among fewer people, and Ivan and Padraic were given tasks that were usually performed by their brothers. John and Pat Fitz were painting the greenhouse and the sun room. Benny, with Ivan's help, had taken over the milking.

There were only four cows to be milked. Blossom would not calve until the following spring. The two great pigs looked forlorn until the boys' mother began to take them for walks in the fields, where they followed her like faithful dogs, gazing up at her, puzzled or impatient, when she stopped. The orchard trees were heavy with ripening apples, and the pigs followed her there with particular alacrity, their round, pink bodies wobbling with excitement as they rooted among the windfalls. They were scolded by

Alphonsus who resented the attention they were given.

Phoebus looked lost for the first few days after the boys' departure, spending much of his waking hours sitting on Niall's bed, clearly expecting him to reappear at any moment. The great yellow cat was seldom seen after that, except for odd glimpses of him in the fields.

—◆—

Garry was determined to climb Brendan Hill, probably because the poet was fascinated with pagan sacred places and had told the boys of the importance of the hill and of the mystery of the miller saint who succeeded Brendan a few centuries later. They would climb it together, Garry told his brothers as they rowed the herring cot steadily up to the next lock and the hill grew larger.

Niall lifted his oar from the water and said: "Sez who?"

"Sez I," said the captain, grinning.

"On one condition," Niall grunted, as he lowered the blade into the water and pulled against it.

"What's that?" asked Garry.

"I want to fish tonight," said Niall. "And so do Conor and Kerry. I think we should find a good trout stretch and camp there for a few days. We've got plenty of time, and I don't want to row all day."

"You've hardly rowed at all, you clot!" said Garry, good-humouredly. "But our plan was always to spend a few days in each place. You tell me when you find the likeliest place and we'll pitch camp."

This was agreed, and goodwill continued to prevail in the herring cot. It would have been difficult to find much to argue about, as the river wound gently around through beautiful though flatter country until they were pointed due north, and the next lock appeared. They moored before the cut and clambered ashore to look at the eel weir, then the weir itself, half-expecting to see another run of salmon swim through. The keeper took his short key and emptied the lock. Garry, Brian, and Kerry went back on board to man the cot as the basin flooded while Conor and Niall remained on the lock quay. As the lock filled, the crews' heads rising to level with Conor and Niall's feet, they saw several trout rising on the edge of the fast water below the weir.

"Hey!" said Niall. "Did you see that last one! A lulu!"

They reboarded the cot and Niall said: "There are fish here. Let's stop on this next stretch."

"What kind of fish?" asked Brian, idly parting his hair.

Conor looked at him, and said: "Shark."

"That's very interesting," said Brian, clearly elsewhere.

"I knew he wasn't listening," muttered Conor to Niall, as Garry and Kerry grinned.

They found another limekiln levee, this time in more open country, and moored the cot smoothly. There was flat ground to pitch the tent, with a gently sloping hill behind it, but no stream nearby, though that mattered little as they were in fresh water. They had a late lunch of more bully-beef-and-onion sandwiches. Smoke from their fire drifted out into the river.

"The wind's changing," said Garry. " I think we may have a bit of weather coming in. Look at the clouds behind Brendan." They looked at the sky behind the summit. "I wonder if we're OK here," added Garry, worried. "We're a bit exposed."

"Exposed to what?" demanded Niall. "Everything is waterproof. We're not at sea, you know. We can hardly be wrecked by a storm!"

Garry's nerves called a clear message, but he yielded. The three fishermen in the party rigged their gear. They set off,

Conor and Niall walking upstream along the muddy bank, Kerry down to a pool below.

They chose their pools and cast their devons, sending the baits looping out into the clear water, but caught nothing. They moved up further, drew another blank; then further up, again without a take. They fished for an hour or more, saw nothing, and caught nothing. Disappointed, they walked slowly back to the camp together, where Garry roamed restlessly, looking at the sky which was beginning to darken as the clouds obscured the sun.

They sat for a while, then heard a *plop* from upriver. They looked and saw another trout rise. "Quick!" said Conor. Grabbing their rods, they ran to the bank, Niall fishing upstream from Conor, who caught a trout on his second cast. Niall hooked another as Conor brought his to the net. Within half an hour they had three trout on the bank, the largest over a pound. Then all went quiet.

The two boys' blood was up, as was Kerry's, who had returned, fishless, as Conor was landing his second trout. "Let's take the boat out," Niall suggested. "There could be a hell of an evening rise. We can cover it better from the boat. What do you say, Garry?"

Garry looked doubtful, but they climbed into the cot, leaving Brian. Garry took an oar and sculled the cot out into the river, upstream, then let it drift slowly down, giving an occasional flick with his oar to keep station. They fished from both sides of the cot without result until it began to grow dark. It was windless, and Garry seemed to have forgotten his concerns about the weather.

They had almost given up when they saw a trout rise only a few yards off the bow, over a hundred yards below the camp; then another, and another. They cast furiously at every rise, but the fish spurned the baits. The boys grew frustrated. Niall put up his fly rod, cursing in the darkness as he tried to thread the line through the rings, tying a fly to the leader in the light of the matches that Garry struck for him. Trout continued to rise all around them, slashing at something unseen, a frenzy of feeding fish. Swifts darted past, picking flies from the surface.

Niall finally rigged his fly rod. He cast immediately, splashing the line on the surface in his anxiety to cover the fish; but the fish would not take. He changed his pattern, bitterly regretting that he had brought only wet flies from the camp. The fish continued to boil unheeded, cruising with backs exposed in the half-light, sometimes so close to the boat that the fishermen could see the white of their mouths. Then they stopped, as if someone had flicked a switch. The fishermen sat in the cot, fishless, in almost total darkness.

There was silence, except for the lap of the river against the cot, then Niall shouted at the unseen fish: "The curses of the seven snotty orphans on you. Shitehawks! Bastards!"

Garry began to laugh. "That'll larn 'em," he said. The others began to laugh too, until Garry realized that they had drifted several hundred yards below the camp. "Quick, Kerry!" he ordered. "Grab the other oar, and we'll row her back up."

They were halfway towards the camp when they heard a voice from the riverbank. "Who's that?"

"It's OK, Brian," called Garry. "It's us. We're on our way back."

"I thought you were pishogues," hailed the voice. "Or kelpies. Or, at the very least, the pooka. You have disappointed me greatly. I shall make my solitary way back to camp."

"Well, throw some more sticks on the fire," called Garry, "so we can see what we're doing when we land."

They had eaten supper and were drifting off to sleep when the rain came, a light patter on the tent roof.

"There's your rain, Garry," said Kerry.

"Let's hope we don't leak," Garry muttered. "Whatever you do, don't anyone touch the canvas, or it'll come in."

They lay in their blankets as the sound grew to a steady drumming. Garry at length lit the oil-lamp to inspect the roof of the tent. "Not a leak so far," he said with satisfaction, and drifted off to sleep.

He woke suddenly to hear Brian muttering: "Jesus Christ! Jesus Christ! Ohjeesuschrist!"

A muffled yell came from the other side of the tent. "My bed's soaking! There's water everywhere! I'm wet through!"

"So am I," said Brian. "Everything's under water." Similar calls came from Conor and Kerry. Garry, feeling the ground around him found what felt like a small river running between he and Brian. He lit the lamp in the confusion and they looked around them. The roof appeared intact, or it was until Kerry, hopping about in his pyjamas, put his head against the canvas. He was deluged immediately and a pool of water that had gathered on the tent roof dropped on his blankets. "Clot!" shouted Garry. "I told you not to touch the canvas!"

"That's not where it first came in," said Brian, relatively calm. "It must be flowing below the groundsheet."

Garry rushed outside holding the lamp, leaving the others in darkness. The rain teemed as he ran to the back of the tent, almost tripping over a guy-rope.

He found the source. A great pool of water pressed against the back of the tent, some of which had flowed under the groundsheet.

Garry reacted quickly. "Let's clear the tent out, and get all the stuff under the trees," he said when he entered the tent, wet through. "We'll stretch the groundsheet between branches and use it to shelter us until it stops. Find some dry clothes and rainclothes. Quick!"

They did so, in a misery of wet and cold, using the spare painter which Garry cut into four lengths, to suspend the ground sheet between the branches of the alders. They piled blankets and clothes underneath. Brian ventured out and after a few minutes searching found a dry spot under a rock and returned with a bundle of twigs. "Let's see if we can build a fire," he said. Garry emptied the Primus of methylated spirits over the twigs and put a match to the little pile. It burst into flame, flickered and almost went out, but one of the twigs caught and within minutes they had a small but respectable fire. They fed it as best they could, taking it in turns to brave the rainstorm and forage in the woods above them. They kept the fire going although the wood smoked mightily, and sometimes they felt they had to choose between choking to death or standing in the rain. It was another two hours before the rain stopped, and soon after that the sun rose.

<hr/>

They had to admit it was a beautiful dawn, although the scene it presented looked pitiable. The early morning light, lovely but callous, showed five figures huddled around a smoking fire, a few yards uphill from a big brown tent still inches deep in water. The remains of the evening campfire, the clean cooking utensils that had been stacked tidily beside it, the bread and bacon laid out neatly for the next morning's breakfast, had all been washed into several miserable piles. The site was a desolate place to behold as the sun lit the top of Brendan Hill.

Yet it had stopped raining, and the terrible night was

over. The sky was a clear blue. With the bounce of youth and a terrible desire for an early, hot breakfast, they began to reorganize the camp. The tent was struck and left to dry on a bed of rocks. They lit a bonfire, piled logs on it, then stretched a spare painter from the sallies beside it. They hung blankets, clothes and anything else that needed drying from that line. The groundsheet, which may have saved them from pneumonia or a nasty chill, was left where it was.

They set about salvaging breakfast while everything dried. The bacon was clearly ruined. Many of the eggs from Prospect had been broken, but not all. They had eaten the trout the night before, but the bully-beef was undamaged. It had survived the War, after all. It was that morning that Niall, ever the improviser, invented his version of the bully-beef fritter: take a piece of bully-beef, mix it with chopped onion and the yolk of an egg, and fry it in a hot pan over a heavily smoking, open fire. It was better, said Brian afterwards, than starving to death, but only just.

They did not argue as to who was to blame for the night-time disaster. Perhaps Garry did not remind them that he had warned them of the approaching weather because he felt at fault over the choice of the campsite. Perhaps each felt that everyone had done all he could when the alarm went. Perhaps they even guessed the truth: that no tent could withstand a deluge so great. Perhaps it was the beautiful morning, and the serenity of the hill above them, or the fact that they were full of hot food, even if it was a little indigestible and greasy, but as the sun rose and warmed their backs, the camp rang with laughter and bad puns, and those that wished to went fishing.

They caught five trout before lunch, which cheered them further. Garry and Brian walked up the hill, found a boreen, and followed it until they reached a road. By midmorning they were walking back, laden with groceries from the pub and shop at Killmoling. By lunchtime, as they ate the trout, the camp was almost back to normal.

They climbed Brendan the next day, after they had moved up river through another lock to a campsite they were satisfied would not flood, and where they would spend the next few days.

The view from the top of Brendan was spectacular on a particularly clear day after rain. They saw the river winding through the valley below; the villages and farms; and great tracts of the surrounding landscape. Opposite them, to the east, were the Bluestairs, reaching up to the summit of Slievelaigheann to the north-east. Almost directly below them, to the south-west, lay the beautiful, heavily wooded valley of the Owenore, a dark, enchanted river, one of the two sisters to their own Bree. Further to the north-west lay another two hills, while to the north itself was an enormous swathe of green valleys and farmland, stretching out into a purple haze, the southern midlands of Ireland.

◆━◆

The Muse favoured the poet, as he had finished one poem and begun on another. He worked late and sometimes slept late, since his western blood had never been infected by the Protestant work ethic, probably because there were few Protestants with a work ethic west of the Shannon. He had a work ethic of his own which was at times far more demanding than any other. He ignored the nonsense of the nursery rhyme, often working at his desk, bow-tie dangling from collar, until the grandfather clock in the hall banged three times and he climbed the stairs to join his sleeping wife in the two-poster bed. Even then he would sometimes not sleep for a time, enjoying the voices of the trees in the

Grove and the whispered answers of the poplars. He was not at peace, as a poet is rarely at peace, but he had the ability to be still and to allow the world to come to him.

He had written a radio verse play from his bed during the previous winter when he had caught a cold. Bored after a day, still coughing and sneezing, he had brought his typewriter, paper and carbon upstairs, and had begun to type, head and shoulders propped against a stack of pillows like a sultan. He stayed in bed even when he recovered, continuing to work as snow covered the little farm until the play was finished a fortnight later. It was one of his best.

In this summer he rolled into Eskerford late and parked his old bus carelessly on the quays, while Horgan did what was necessary to keep the authorities happy at the Custom House in Dublin.

He clearly missed the stimulation of conversations with his older boys, as did his wife and the youngest two. He took the three of them to the cinema in Eskerford beside the walls of Esker Abbey, to see the latest Errol Flynn or John Wayne, and the manageress nodded them through without charge.

One morning he took the two boys halfway across the county, to a cottage down a lane in the back of beyond, where the maker of the finest hurling sticks in Ireland lived, and where the boys gazed in awe at the rows of hurls carved from the grove of ash trees that surrounded the dwelling. Their father wandered through the sacred grove as the hurley-maker showed them how he selected each piece to work from, and how the grain of the wood must curl around to make a strong boss. The county was aflame with enthusiasm for its hurling team which was headed for the All-Ireland final, and the boys shared it, so the poet bought them each new hurls.

Conor, Niall and Kerry explored every pool, run and

stream a mile either side of the camp, and at some of these met other trout fishermen. One gave them a selection of dry flies – mostly big sedges – and showed them how to fish them upstream, without drag. They still found the fish highly discriminatory and choosy and it was hard to recognize at first when the fly dragged, but fishermen must learn by doing. After frustration and failure with the dry fly they began to get the hang of it. Between spinning and fly-fishing they kept the camp so well supplied with trout that even the bully-beef provided a welcome alternative.

On one of these evenings Niall fished out of sight of the others. He watched his fly closely as it danced on the water in the dusk when a wave abreast of him in the river startled him. He saw a row of bubbles coming towards him. He remembered Brian's remarks about river goblins and spirits and drew back, stripping his line in great handfuls as he retreated.

A wet, furry head with big eyes emerged only a few feet away, looked at him calmly, then submerged again, leaving a surge in the water as it swung its rudder and turned out into the river. It was Niall's first otter.

Garry and Brian tramped the country together. They walked upriver to Monksgrange, where the white-cowled monks from the shires of chalkstream and henge in England had built a great monastery. The monastery's founder had ruled that the monks would speak only English. They had had a difficult time as a result from the wild Gaelic Irish, who thought it fair to plunder the monastery and its lands, and did so with enthusiasm, as they believed the land was theirs.

The two oldest boys looked at the ruins of the monastery and strolled along the quays, then examined the lock they would take the herring cot through in a day or so. They made a telephone call from the town to the Custom House in Eskerford, and Garry spoke to the poet, telling him where they were, and where they would meet. He found it hard to imagine the poet in his office, the view of Eskerford Harbour filling his window.

They were back in the town two days later, this time in force. They struck camp in the morning, and rowed through a series of rain showers and sunny spells to the lock at Tighnahinse. They floated up and out into Monksgrange, which was only a village, as Brian remarked, as it was a tenth of the size of Eskerford, and Eskerford could not be called a city. They moored at the old stone quay and restocked with food at the grocery shop. An hour later they were on their way again, passing under an elegant bridge. This would be the final leg on the upstream journey on this river. They would need to turn back at Buiris if they were to spend time on the Owenore, and they had decided unanimously to stick to this plan.

If the lower river was handsome, the stretch between Monksgrange and Buiris was even more so. This was a wonderful, heavily wooded valley, almost empty of people. They saw old demesne walls, overgrown with ivy, with frequent gaps where the stones had fallen over the years; Famine walls that had been built to relieve the great hunger of the 1840s; ruined houses and empty cottages; weeds and wild flowers intermingling above the riverbanks; and everywhere an impression of wildness, where nature appeared to rule without interference.

They had a more difficult passage up to Buiris than they expected. The river had dropped. The heavy herring cot occasionally grounded her bottom on the bars of silt that the river deposited between the locks. Most of the time she came free with a twist of an oar. At other times some of the crew had to roll up their trousers, drop into the river, and push her off.

They were very glad to halt at a bend in the river below the lock at Buiris. There they pitched camp, the fishermen looking greedily at the wide pool below the lock.

The pool was as long as it was wide, and was very shallow in some places, with pale gravel patches and olive-green weed showing in the early evening sunlight. Between the shallows ran several distinct channels through which the salmon probably ran on their way up to the weir. The edges of the pool were overhung by willows, branches nodding in the current. The tail disappeared into a narrow, dark stretch of water, cut off from the evening sun by a thick wood of beech and alder.

They ate quickly, anxious to begin. "There must be fish there," said Niall, munching a sandwich and swigging coffee from a tin mug. "And there are at least four fishermen on the weir. They must be after salmon." Conor studied them through the binoculars. The fishermen sat on the rock-lined banks below the fast water. They appeared to be worm-fishing, as every so often one would reel up, open a tin beside him and rebait before casting into the fast water. He guessed that the bottom was gravel. If it were not, the fishermen would have used floats to keep their worms clear of rocks or other snags.

They decided to begin by spinning. If a rise began they could switch to fly.

Conor, Niall and Kerry, rods in hands, left the camp as soon as they could. Garry and Brian washed up, and Brian quickly settled in a comfortable place with a book.

Garry felt restless. He rarely fished, but he knew how to put a worm on a hook. Rather than read a book or saunter along the riverbank, he decided to fish.

He checked for a spare rod and found Conor's that he used for bass. He took the spade from the camp and wandered until he found a patch of soft ground. He dug enough earthworms to fill his tin, went back to the camp, found a fixed-spool reel and secured it to the butt, tied swivel, weight and hook on, then baited the hook with the worms. Brian was happy where he was, so Garry set off alone.

He did not want to disturb the fishermen on the weir, so chose a grassy bank where the river bent around to the left before entering the big pool. He cast his bait squarely across the river, feeling the line stop running as the weight sank to the gravel bottom.

Many fishermen frown on worm-fishing, and generally they are right, since it can be a little too efficient, particularly in a pool where the fish are packed in their lies, reddening as they wait for a rise in the water level to restart their upstream migration. They will also tell you, correctly, that there is nothing in fishing to compare with the sensation when the salmon first takes a fly, but for those who like to feel the pulse of a river as they fish, who wish to feel the current and the very life of running water, ledgering a worm on the gravelly bottom of a river is the most sensitive.

He could feel the weight bumping along the bottom as the current swung it in an arc, and the vibration of the stream against the line as he held the nylon between thumb and forefinger. When the weight swung out of the current into dead water and halted, he reeled in, adjusted the weight because it did not bounce along the bottom as much as he liked, checked his bait, moved down a few yards, and cast again.

It was on the third cast that he knew he would catch a fish. He did not know whether it would be a trout or a salmon. He simply knew, in a moment of intuition, from some additional sense, that the line would tighten before it swept out of the current.

When the line did tighten, he thought: God, I must be psychic! He stood, semi-paralysed, as he felt two hard pulls, one quickly following the other. He waited, not because he should have done, but because his conviction had become reality and the conscious part of his brain was still puzzled. As it happened, he had done exactly the right thing. A salmon frequently nibbles a worm to begin with, and the experienced fisherman will generally count to ten before lifting the rod sharply and starting to reel.

The rod was well bent by the time he did so, and then it began to jerk and buck. The line began to move across the current. Out in the pool a big salmon threw itself from the water, the sunlight catching the silver on its flanks. It was a second or two before Garry realized that the fish that jumped was the fish at the end of his line, and by that time the salmon was halfway across the pool and the rod was bent like a bow. Tension, he thought, it's too tight! He'll break me! Shaking, he turned the butterfly nut to the left. The fixed spool whizzed. Too loose, he realized, and turned it back part of the way. That was better. The rod was still bent, but not like a horseshoe.

He heard a shout from one of the anglers on the weir. So did Niall, who was working his way upstream towards the camp, casting as he went. Mystified, Niall looked upriver and saw one of the fishermen on the weir waving at something on the bank. When he looked more closely he saw his oldest brother, apparently motionless, right shoulder hunched.

He saw a big salmon jump in the centre of the pool. Another shout came from the weir. One of them must have caught a fish, he thought, but why were they gesturing towards Garry, and why was Garry suddenly walking, running even, down the bank towards him?

It was when he saw the fish jump again further down the

pool, then saw Garry clutching a rod that was bending and jerking, that he grasped the truth and sent a mighty hail down the pool to Conor and Kerry: "HEY! GARRY'S CAUGHT A SALMON!"

The others heard him even if they could not distinguish the words. Without waiting to discover whether they had, Niall quickly placed his rod upright against a willow branch and ran. When he arrived beside his brother, he whooped: "Mother of God! How the hell did you do that?"

"Oh," said Garry, nonchalantly, trying not to pant, "I thought it was time to teach my brothers how to catch a real fish." Niall stared at him, speechless. The fish jumped again. Niall shouted: "Lower the rod when he does that or he'll land on the line and break it!" Garry obeyed, and began to reel. The fish had changed its course. It shot towards him.

The others arrived, breathless, as the fish jumped again and ran. "Hold him in the pool!" panted Conor. "If he gets down below the wood, you won't be able to follow him!" Garry, outwardly calm, tightened the tension.

"My God!" said Niall, remembering. "We don't have a net big enough. You'll have to beach him."

"What d'you mean?" grunted Garry. Was the fish tiring? The muscles in his arms were burning.

"You'll have to walk him up the gravel," said Niall. He had never caught a salmon, but he had read every article in *Stream & Field*, hoping one day to use the knowledge he had acquired. "Walk back when you're sure he's tired out. Don't jerk anything. Just keep everything taut!"

Five minutes later Garry lifted the fish's head out from the water. It made another run, and another, but each time the runs grew shorter. Garry, guided by Niall, backed up onto the grass behind him, and the salmon, its great tail flapping, began to slide up the gravel. When it reached dry ground, Niall lay on it.

Later, when asked why he had done so, he shrugged, as if to imply: why take a chance? In any case, Conor had seized a stone and hit the salmon on the back of its neck. Then he lifted it and gave it to Garry, who seemed dazed and held it for only a few moments before passing it to Niall, who cradled it in his arms, and said: "Janey, Pat, there's something here that never was here before."

The only weighing scales they had was limited to a fish of five pounds, gauged for a mere trout. The salmon was clearly a great deal heavier than that, but by how much? One guessed the fish weighed ten pounds, another twenty.

Kerry solved the question by volunteering to go to the weir and borrow a set of scales from one of the anglers, who fished on in the descending night, probably encouraged. He returned ten minutes later and they weighed it, striking a match to see the result. The fish weighed fifteen pounds.

They returned triumphantly to camp, Garry holding the salmon. Brian looked at it in the lamplight and said: "It'll make a nice change from bully-beef."

$$\blacktriangleright\!\!\blacktriangleleft$$

They had eaten it by the time they struck camp at Buiris, sick of salmon when they left, as Conor had caught a four pound grilse the next morning. They also felt slightly sick of trout. The river at Buiris was rich in beautifully speckled fat trout that took a fly or a devon like tigers. As for bully-beef, whether in sandwiches, or stews, or fried in fritters, even hungry youths can eat too much of anything. It had improved their abilities to improvise, but each of them was secretly looking forward to the first meal back at Prospect.

The river was dropping quite quickly, a concern to Garry.

It was six inches below the height it had been on the journey north. If it continued to drop at this rate the downstream run would be very difficult, if not impossible. The herring cot had been wonderfully faithful, he thought, but it was a pity it drew so much water.

They felt torn when they left, but all were eager to see the Owenore. It began to rain when they edged the cot out into the current, with little squalls from the west creating waves on the surface as they dug in their oars, but it was intermittent, not enough to raise the river level; probably not even enough to stop it dropping, Garry thought as he held the cot's course near the east bank where the boatstream was marked on his chart. They would have a faster run, but he would have to be careful about where to let the oarsmen rip. There were many more hazards on a river at low levels.

They grounded on a sandbank, but briefly, soon after they had passed through the next lock. A mile or so further down, just when Garry was beginning to breathe more easily, they hit a rock, the flat bottom scraping horribly as they passed over another beside it. When the cot emerged into clearer water Kerry shouted: "We've lost something!" A rectangular piece of wood floated alongside. Garry swung the tiller, leaned over and scooped it up with one hand. It was the skeg, the wooden piece that protected the cot's rudder. He ordered the oarsmen to slow the stroke.

It was exposed and cold in the cot and they donned their waterproofs. This was a very different river to that of a few days before, less friendly, almost threatening. The countryside seemed greyer, lacking a welcome. The crew felt it and the boat grew quiet, the oarsmen looking grim as they focused on their stroke, waiting for a warning call from the bows. Perhaps, Garry thought morosely, he had taken too great a risk when he had navigated them so far upriver. They must reach Killmoling, where they would meet the tide, the blessed, blessed tide that would carry them down to the Owenore, and up it, too, without this constant fear of ripping the bottom from the cot, or of capsizing in a hidden rapid.

He slowed the stroke further, and it was as well that he did. They passed through the next lock where the lock-keeper advised them to be careful "in such a deep craft, a feckin' great seaboat, you should have more sense," then hit a series of snags, one of them probably a waterlogged tree trunk, and ground to a halt on a sandbar.

Brian and Kerry stepped out and pushed, grunting in the cold water. She shifted, but they were hardly back in the vessel before Kerry shouted and they looked ahead to see a snag, with white water surging over it. "Back water!" shouted Garry, and they did so, bringing the cot to a standstill. "Keep moving astern!" he shouted again, his voice cracking with worry. The cot began to inch upstream and Garry brought her into the side. He leaped ashore with the after painter and held her there.

They were safe for the moment. "Throw me the anchor, Kerry," he ordered. Garry hurriedly buried the hook firmly in the ground above the bank. Conor had jumped ashore to help and stood, holding the after painter that Garry had thrown him. Brian had seized a tent peg from the sack in the forepeak and banged it into the ground with his mallet. They tied the after painter to this, then had time to think.

Garry decided to reconnoitre. He and Kerry would scout the water below to see if there was an obvious channel through the rocks and snags. One consolation was that the weather was changing, the wind shifting around to the south-west. It was more of a breeze than a wind, and there were patches of blue sky to the south. It was warmer. He did not trust the weather to hold for long, but instinct told him that if he could bring them through the next mile of water they would be past the worst hazards.

The change in the weather and the absence of immediate danger changed the mood of the crew. "Bring me a dark Circassian maiden," said Brian as Garry and Kerry set off. "Watch for crocodiles, bwana," advised Niall.

They saw a clear path through the rocks and snags as far as the next bend, helped by the drop in the wind. Garry grew convinced that they had been through the worst. Near the bend they saw an elderly man driving his cattle across a field. "Quick, Kerry!" he said. "Head over to him and ask him if there are any rapids below us."

Kerry jogged across the field and came up to the farmer. "Hello!" he shouted. "Are there any rapids around here?"

The man cupped his hand to his right ear. "Hah?" he said.

Kerry raised his voice to a bellow. "ARE THERE ANY RAPIDS AROUND HERE?"

The man looked at him as if he were retarded. "No. Not wan. Not a single wan."

"OH! GOOD!" shouted Kerry in relief. The man lived here, and must know.

"No," said the man reflectively, scratching his stubble. "Not a single wan. As a matter o'fact," he said, ruminatively, "I haven't seen a rabbit around here for years."

"Oh! God!" said Kerry. He shouted: "HOW FAR TO THE NEXT LOCK?"

He had to shout it again before it was clear that the old man understood. "'Tis a mile. Not more. No, not more."

Kerry jogged back to Garry.

"What did he say?"

Kerry began to laugh.

Garry, unconscious why he did so, began to laugh too.

Kerry spluttered something about rabbits and broke down, ribs aching. Garry began to shake, Kerry clutching his arm, both unable to speak. Finally, he delivered the punch line and they fell about again.

◆—◆

They set off with a definite spring in their step. After they had walked for some time, Garry grew puzzled. "Did he say a mile, and no more?" he asked. "He did," Kerry replied. "We've walked more than a mile," said Garry, "because I've kept count of our steps, and the lock should be visible. We can see another half a mile downriver."

When they had walked nearer two miles than one they came around a bend to see the lock below them. Later, when he told his father about this, the poet told him the man almost certainly meant an Irish mile, rather than a statute one. Many of the country people clung to the old measurements.

◆—◆

The poet was having trouble with a ballad singer in the drawing room. He had tracked the man down in his search for material for his radio programme. The singer was a sailor home from a voyage, an affable man in his fifties who seemed determined to spread his custom across all of the pubs in the Main Street before returning to sea. Someone had told the poet that the man had a wonderful voice and knew more local ballads and sea shanties than any other singer in Eskerford.

He solemnly promised the poet to be at his home near the Cot Safe on the following day, where the poet would collect him and drive him to Prospect. The tape recorder was set up in the drawing room.

He had evidently drowned his promise, as the poet found only the singer's wife at the house on the next day. She told the poet that the man was in the nearest bar. The poet gritted his teeth, walked to the pub and found the singer swaying gently, one hand on a table for support, eyes crossing as he tried to focus on his glass, voice quavering as he sang of a distant voyage. The poet put him in his car and drove to Prospect, hoping that he would sober quickly.

It was a vain hope. Ivan and Padraic entered the drawing room to find their father looking exceptionally cross, his teeth gritted as he tried to persuade the singer to concentrate. The poet grew more exasperated when the man stood, then collapsed on the ottoman.

"In the name of Jaysus, Lar, will you sit still!" he said, laying the microphone on a side-table and switching off the machine. Lar blinked and burst into a popular favourite:

> *There was a wild colonial b'y,*
> *Jack Duggan was his name...*

"That's enough of that!" the poet muttered. "Here, you boys give me a hand. Let's get him into the car. I'm taking him home." Lar's chance of national fame had gone.

Chapter Thirty-Six

The cot was moored to the bank at the junction with the Owenore, waiting for the tide. They had made it through the upper stretch with scarcely a bump.

They had halted above the lock at Killmoling to wait for the flood. At Brian's suggestion they had hoisted the cot's old canvas mainsail and, as an afterthought, raised both sweeps to the vertical and placed the camp tablecloth over them, sailing down to the Owenore at an astonishing six knots, confident that there would be no one to see them who would laugh at their outrageous rig.

It was good to be back in salt water, Garry thought. They had seen a seal that morning below the weir at Killmoling that had probably chased a shoal of salmon up the tideway. It had popped its head out of the water and one of the fishermen had left quickly and returned with a rifle, shooting at it several times, missing. "It's probably come all the way from Crook Head this morning," said Conor.

Garry lay in the sun, Brian sitting quietly by him, and watched a duck flight past. The night before had brought a tremendous thunderstorm, with lightning flickering everywhere and crashes of thunder. The lightning had lit landscape and river as if it were noon, and they had gazed from the door of the tent as it had flickered across the top of Brendan Hill. Then they had slept, the tent dry, the air fresh and cool.

Friendly old Brendan Hill looked down at them from the north. It would be a couple of hours before the tide would turn. The skipper dozed in the sun.

——◆———

When their chores were finished the two youngest boys hit a hurling ball back and forth over the high roof of Prospect, one of them standing in the Front Field, the other in the Paddock, excited by the county's prospects for the All-Ireland Final. Each shouted his imitation of Micheál Ó'Hehir's commentary, the radio voice familiar to listeners in both islands during the Grand National, the voice that held all Ireland on hurling Sunday afternoons:

He bends. He lifts. He strikes...
It's a GOAL!

Occasionally one of them sent the leather ball smacking against the chimneybreast at the Grove end, scattering the jackdaws. There was a great deal of time spent in looking for lost balls in the thick grasses at front and rear, but looking for lost balls in grass or nettles was a common occupation at Prospect. They had grown skilled at finding them.

Their father slightly dampened their hurling ardour, but only slightly, when he told them that the Eskerford full-forward, one of the hurling hero brothers from Anneschurch, in the foothills of Slievelaigheann, needed the ball in his hand and both feet planted on the ground to score, that the Eskerford men were mere air hurlers, players who shunned the natural ground game, deadly enough on their day if they had the ball in their hand, but lacking the artistry and elegance of Galway or, with a nod to the artist,

Kilkenny. The boys took this in and felt slightly divided in their loyalties, but they redoubled their faith in the brothers from Anneschurch when it became clear that the opposition would not be Galway or Kilkenny, but the common enemies of Cork and Christy Ring.

When they wanted a change they climbed the trees in the Grove, racing each other. They fell often but suffered nothing more than bruises, since the floor of the Grove was covered in pine needles and their limbs seemed made of rubber. Sometimes they played cowboys-and-Indians, stalking each other through the trees, nettles and briars with bows and arrows. They knew every inch of the Grove: every briar, bush, tree or ditch, the wooden bridges over the ditches, and the paths. They were adept at ambushing visitors, appearing at the drive end of the Grove one moment, at the other the next; circling swiftly past the jungle of briars behind the Grove before their absence was noticed, surprise their chief tactic.

They fell in trouble again when they organized the boys from the cottages above Prospect to join their games and the poet and his wife returned from Eskerford to find one of these boys roped to the trunk of a tree, surrounded by a fire, while the other boys danced and whooped around him. It was perfectly safe, but the parents were horrified, since they could see little but the boy's head above a ring of flame and a great deal of smoke from twigs and leaves, and they did not know that the boy had volunteered to be the Indians' victim. The ashplant came out again and the boys went to bed early with their bottoms stinging.

Generally it was peaceful. The poet took them to the beach on most afternoons, and they played table tennis or Chinese chequers on most evenings. One evening they went to Fossetts' Circus, which the poet enjoyed even more than his sons. Circuses had fascinated him since he was a small boy, and the magic held him still. He took them to watch the mail-boat put to sea on another evening, then brought them to Charlie Dukelow's, the jolliest pub in the county.

Padraic visited McCann's as frequently as possible, hearing Nicky's yarns again and again, responding to the familiar greeting: "And was you there Lacey sez she," with the equally familiar: "I think so, sez Martin Codd."

They were very bored one evening when the poet and his wife had felt forced to attend a reception in the town, and were coming to blows over the ownership of a hurling or cricket ball when they saw a figure loom from the sunset. They welcomed the artist, who had called as he was passing. He stayed with them for two hours, telling story after story, and they were each richer by a shilling when he left.

One day their mother returned from shopping with extra boxes of groceries and fussed for hours into the evening, baking bread and making Battenberg and chocolate cakes. The following morning, a Sunday, they would leave immediately after the poet had picked them up from Mass and set off for the next county to visit the camp on the river.

◆—◆

The camp was near The White House, a deserted dwelling in a cleft between two bluffs. It lay on the west bank of the Owenore, below Inisteach, the most beautiful village in Ireland.

The White House had been a minor dwelling on the Tadgh estate, dwarfed by the family seat, a great ruined house above the village, relic of landlordly grandeur. Upriver from the White House, between the camp and Inisteach, was the Big Net.

They heard of it in snatches of conversation with the night fishermen who came from nowhere at dusk. One moment the bank along the woods was deserted, quiet except for the rustle of animals and the calls of the night birds. When they next looked down the riverbank they saw a procession of figures, grey in the failing light, walking towards them. Some had bundles they recognized as snap nets, others paddles and bags.

The fishermen greeted them courteously, as the fishermen on the Bree had, and stopped to talk and drink tea at the campfire. Over the next few nights they learned more of the Owenore than many who lived within hailing distance of the river.

They discovered quickly that the cotsmen had a strong sense of history, or their own version of it. The boys heard how the Owenore fishermen, incensed by the landlords who built murderously efficient weirs and stake-nets, had gathered more than a century before in a convoy of two hundred cots and swept down to the estuary mouth – as far as Ballykeep itself, in their frail canoes – destroying the scotch weirs that employed only a few people but took up to two hundred salmon each tide. Ten years later, the law relented and most of the weirs were outlawed – or abated, as the official verb had it – but one of the landlords, having lost his weir at the White House, replaced it with a great draft net further upriver, near the top of the tidal water. The Big Net entered the folklore of the Owenore.

They rowed the cot up the next day to see it, passing several islands in the middle of the river, islands wild and overgrown with timber and bushes, wild flowers a splash of colour above the water's edge.

When they reached Gowlaun, the last of the islands before the river turned a bend to show the ten arches of the bridge at Inisteach, they kept to starboard, passing through the narrow channel between the island and the riverbank. Their view was confined because of the growth on the bank until they passed the island and turned into the deeper water to port, where the river opened and they passed a small, square stone hut on the left bank. It had a galvanized iron roof and a wooden bench at its front.

Beyond it were two strange wooden towers on the bank, one very tall, with a tar barrel that had been cut in two and placed on a platform halfway up the tower, the other tower further up the bank, half the height of the first. The towers, said Conor, resembled the watchtowers from a prisoner-of-war film. A boat was beached below the first.

Four men in flat caps sat smoking by the stone house, lounging on the seat in front of a windowless opening with a shutter on each side. They sat up and stared at the great black cot that appeared without warning between the island and the bushes on the bank below them.

The cot passed only a few feet from them, the waiting netsmen seeing five boys who stared at them, some of them open-mouthed, two of them forgetting their stroke as they turned to look. They heard the skipper at the helm remind his crew sharply that the cot would ground if they did not row her out into the current, then call a nervous greeting to the netsmen.

A monstrous net lay stretched to dry in the field by the hut, seemingly a hundred yards wide.

———◆—◆———

Upriver from the Big Net was a jetty made of heavy cut stones, the boat slip of Inisteach. The boys moored the cot to it and climbed ashore.

Below them was a gate into the field where the Big Net lay. Nearby was a canal cut that ended abruptly, the only attempt that had been made to create the first lock on the Owenore. On the opposite bank the ground rose steeply, a towering bluff of beech and mature woods, part of the same estate where they camped. A walk ran along its edge.

Garry and Brian, leaving the others to guard the cot, walked up the path from the boat slip to the road, stopping to look from the bridge that led into Inisteach. Below this, in the fast water, were three narrow, cut stone piers through which the current ran like a sluice. Wooden boards were placed on top. This was a working salmon weir, with iron spikes set at an angle into the side of each pier to prevent the salmon escaping downstream.

◆ ◆

The three crew members left behind at the boat slip idly watched the river when through the gate below them emerged one of those who hauled the Big Net. He stopped to talk, an elderly, friendly man, removing his cap and scratching his grey poll, standing at the edge of the jetty and looking curiously down at the cot. When he had answered the first barrage of questions, principally from Conor, he took his pipe from his mouth and suggested they come and see for themselves, to ax away, ax away, ax all the questions they had, and fair play to ye, b'ys.

They would, they said, as they could spend only a couple of hours there because of the tide, but if he did not object they would wait for Garry and Brian who should be with them any minute now – yes, there they were, trekking along the path from the bridge to the boat slip, arms full of groceries in brown paper bags – and would it be all right if they all came?

◆ ◆

The oldest two had crossed the bridge and turned left at the pub. They sought a shop and found one overlooking the village green.

They bought their bread, bacon, milk, butter and eggs from a friendly woman at the shop, a woman who plied them with questions: where had they come from at all, was that so, well, well, well, 'twas a long way in a boat, and was the *tint* dry, and how many were they, weren't they great to set out on a holiday like they had, had they been up to see the ruins of the Big House above, yes, just up that hill there, and here's a few toffees for the younger ones.

It was burnt down in the Troubles, she said, lowering her voice; destroyed, some said, because of the Big Net, revenge like, because the fishermen had hated it for so many years.

◆ ◆

The tide was almost full when all five boys walked through the gate into the field. They saw one of the men at the top of the first watchtower, leaning forward like a heron, waving at the others to hurry, shouting that he could see a run of fish coming into the pool. One of the men was already in the boat while another loaded the Big Net into the stern; a mountain of net, roll after roll. A third stood on the gravel, knee-deep in water, in thigh boots, holding a rope attached to the Big Net.

The boys noticed something they had missed on the way up: a hatch cover, propped open by a stick, in the field near one of the towers. They stopped, Brian kneeling to put his head inside. It was a tank lined with concrete. There appeared to be more than a dozen salmon on its floor.

The man on the watchtower was clearly the boss and called to his men to hurry, to get the *nit* across the river, row hard now Michael, the fish were well up the pool, get the *nit* shot now, hurry, okay boys, all right, they were there, steady now, wait, wait, wait until I tell ye.

The boys watched them from the strand, seeing the man in the stern throwing armfuls of net into the river, a line of corks stretched aft, the man at the oars pulling to bring the clinker-built boat – a boat, not a cot – up, then across the pool, swinging to bring the vessel inside two stanchions standing in the water near the opposite bank. As the boss in the tower shouted instructions the oarsman slowed his stroke, keeping the boat stationary on the brimming tide, the man at the stern kneeling at the transom, arms full of hemp, ready to shoot when the call came.

The man on the tower, hat pulled low over his forehead, peered into the pool, arm raised as he prepared to signal. "They're still runnin' in," he called. "A fair few of them, too." As he spoke, a silvery object jumped below the top line of corks, then another, much larger, in the middle of the pool. "Did you see that?" yelled Niall, almost pushing Conor over as he scrambled for a closer view. "Why the hell is the boat waiting?"

"I think they'll bring the net around in a full circle when the fish have stopped running into the pool," Garry guessed, rubbing his hands in excitement.

"There must be quite an art to it," said Brian. "That net's enormous. Just look how much of the river it covers, and they haven't shot the whole thing."

The man at the oars called: "Are they all in now, Packy?"

Packy hesitated, staring into the river. Then he said: "You might as well draw her in now, Michael. I can't see any more comin' in, except mebbe the odd straggler."

Michael leant forward and pulled, the boat moving down, then across the pool towards the strand, a line of corks following as the remainder of the Big Net was shot, the corks forming a nearly perfect circle as the boat ground on the gravel and the men pulled her bows onto the bank.

Two or three more salmon splashed inside the circle of corks, a circle that seemed to cover almost the entire pool apart from a narrow pass on the opposite bank beneath the overhanging beech trees, on the inside of the stanchions. Later, the men told the boys that the stanchions marked the legal outer limit for the Big Net, and that the narrow pass by the opposite bank was called the Queen's Share.

———◆—◆———

They watched as the four men took the ropes on either side of the Big Net and slowly drew them in. The trapped salmon jumped and splashed as the circle of corks dwindled. The strand was dotted with silver when the last of the net came ashore. The men lifted each fish and killed it, running a length of twine through the gills until they had as many as they could carry, weighing each salmon before placing it in the cool of the concrete tank. There they would keep until the ass-and-cart took them to the fish dealer at Rosspoint. There were twenty-eight fish to go from this haul, the head man announced as he wrote with a stub of pencil in an exercise book. The netsmen told the boys later that their best single haul had been sixty-seven fish; that on some days they did not shoot the net, and that their largest salmon had weighed forty-seven pounds.

———◆—◆———

The netsmen showed them the watchtowers and the stone shed they called the Lookout; told them how they shot the Big Net when they saw the pool beginning to fill with salmon, cutting off the fishes' escape at the top; completing the circle when the last of the run passed

Gowlaun Island, keeping the trap open until the run finished.

They climbed the ladder of the tallest watchtower to look down into the pool and could not see a single fish. The head man told them that the half-barrel on the first platform sheltered them from the keen winds of spring, as the season opened on February 1, St Brigid's Day. It ran until August 15, the day the snap net men ate their traditional feast of salmon. They kept a fire in the Lookout on cold days, but in warm weather they sat on the seat at the front wall of the Lookout, shutters open, enjoying the sun.

The netsmen spoke as if they were on friendly terms with the cotsmen. They held snap net licenses in their own right. As fishing with a net in tidal waters was prohibited from Friday night to Monday morning each week during the season, the boys wondered when the men of the Big Net took to their own cots. They had enough discretion not to ask, but they began to wonder whether the head man himself was not, in his spare time, the most skilled poacher on the river.

◆—

They had eaten a stew for supper when the snap net men appeared at the camp near the abandoned White House. On this, and on successive nights, they asked many questions and heard many answers.

They heard that an official inquiry had been held more than forty years before, at which the landlord had testified that the Big Net took eight hundred salmon in a single season, some of more than forty pounds. "Eight hundred!" scoffed one of the netsmen at the campfire. "Bedamn with eight hundred! They'd take twice as much as that in a bad year."

Fishing with nets on the inland fisheries – those that the

tide did not reach – had been banned by law only recently as the runs of salmon declined. Ninety years or so before, the courts had outlawed night fishing above the tidal limit at Inisteach. Five years later, the same courts had declared that the inland fisheries belonged to those who owned the banks, a ruling similar in character to the enclosure acts in Britain. The common rights of most of the cotsmen to fish above the bridge of Inisteach were removed, yet the Big Net, which was believed to take more fish than all the cotsmen combined, remained, because it was in tidal waters. It was commercial, unsporting, but legal. Towards the end of the previous century the Big Net's efficiency, driven by the landlord's agent, a retired major who zealously pursued the poachers at every opportunity, increased. The runs of fish on this, one of the finest fisheries in the two islands, where thirty-five pound salmon had been common, declined steadily, but the Big Net continued to draw fish from the river.

The local fishermen responded to this assault on their rights to fish the inland waterways in a simple fashion. They continued to fish. Towards the end of the previous century, the law, which had allowed riparian owners to prosecute privately, was tightened to allow police and bailiffs to charge the fishermen with a criminal act, but the fishermen, some of them masked, continued to flout the Queen's justice, and the justice of the Free State that followed. Tronnicking or stroke-hauling might be unfair, they told the boys at their camp, but the Big Net was murder.

◆◆

Conor and Niall caught two good sea trout below the weir at Inisteach next morning. All had lazed in the sunshine for much of the day, watching a big cot with a crew of two coming up on the last of the tide, under engine, then moor until the ebb exposed big sandbars near the bank.

While they waited for the ebb the sandcot men sang in clear voices that carried across the water to the camp, each man joining in the chorus, then singing alternate verses:

> *"Arrah, mother," sez she,*
> *"sure I know what'll aise me;*
> *an' all me dis-aises most certainly kill.*
> *Give over your doctors and medical tratement;*
> *I'd rather wan squayze from the bould*
>   *Thady Quill."*

The cot then unmoored, ground on a sandbar and the crew stepped out, lifted planks and wheelbarrows from the cot and began to shovel sand steadily into the cot in a race with time before the tide covered the sandbar again.

They were to see this repeated several times, reminded of a Van Gogh drawing of Arles: sun on the river, big sandcot perched on the end of the bar, two men in caps and shirtsleeves loading the cot before taking the sand downriver to Rosspoint where it would be sold as the purest of river sand, free of earth, washed each day by the tide.

◆◆

Garry, relatively fresh from his experience of rebuilding *Snipe*, examined with great interest the Owenore cots or canoes, so much lighter and more fragile than those on their home river, thoroughbreds against cart-horses. The snap net men told him they were made to be pulled from the water quickly with a minimum of effort. The cots were double-ended like the older of the Eskerford cots; narrower, to give speed and manoeuvrability; many of them painted blue on the upper scodges, as the upper and lower planks were called in Ossory Irish; red on the lower; white on the inside to improve visibility at night; colours the boatbuilder's marque. They were built without a plan except that in the boatbuilder's eye, each cot unique. They looked more like racing canoes than cots, trimmer and more elegant than the Eskerford breed, but cots they were, with the obligatory flat bottoms.

Paddles and nets were equally simple. Paddles, short and long, were made from ash and hazel; handles of hazel; blades or boshes, like hurling sticks, from ash, as was the little gripping bar at the top of the handle, the *croisín*, little cross, a term possibly given because the fishermen were either religious or superstitious, or both, and kept the parish priest's kitchen supplied with salmon and *gilleen*, as they called grilse, throughout the season. In return he blessed their nets, a union of God and salmon.

The snap nets were nine yards wide, thirteen deep, simple purse nets with two strings, one attached to the bottom of the net, the other to the top, held by each netsman who sat on a riser seat facing aft. When the net jerked as a salmon swam into it in the darkness one of the netsmen would call: "Draw your hand!" and the purse would enclose the fish as the four ends of the string were pulled tight between the two cots.

The snap net men fished at night during the week because the darkness concealed their nets from the salmon. That was legal. Many of them fished at night at weekends because the darkness concealed them from the bailiffs. That was illegal. Their warning system, their river telegraph, consisted of a low whistle when they saw the bailiff from Inisteach cut his engine and drift down river when the tide had turned. Sometimes the warning was the unearthly night sound a poacher made blowing into the neck of a bottle. The boys suspected that there existed an unspoken understanding between bailiff and poachers: if the fishermen did not overdo it and boast in the pub of their catches, the bailiff would opt for a quiet life and give a subtle warning of his approach, feeling a kinship with the poachers who struggled to feed their families.

Their suspicion hardened when they learned that one bailiff's brother worked for the same fish dealer in Rosspoint that bought the poachers' salmon, although, to be fair, it would have been hard for dealer or bailiff to determine which fish brought down to Rosspoint by ass-and-cart were taken illegally.

Salmon frequently halted at the bridge of Inisteach on their upward migration. On the night of the boys' return from seeing the Big Net a cotsman told them of an over-zealous Civic Guard at Inisteach, recently posted, who had correctly suspected that the poachers' relatives were dropping stones from the bridge to drive the fish downriver to where the cots were working, illegally, as it was Saturday night.

The poachers' ally was a small, elderly man who stood, pockets filled with stones, smoking his pipe as he looked over the bridge wall into the stream below. He stiffened as he saw the Guard, a giant, approach.

"Grand evenin'," he said as the Guard stood beside him.

"'Tis," said the Guard in a West Cork accent. "'Tis. You wouldn't be thinkin' of droppin' an ould stone or two off the bridge, would ye, to scare a salmon, like, would ye? Would ye now?"

"Would I? Would I?" said the Inisteach man, wondering what to do next. "Would I? Why would I? Of course I would not. I came down to have a smoke."

They stood in silence, watching a run of salmon moving into the pool below the bridge, the Guard suspicious, the local man agonizing.

"Look at the fish!" said the man suddenly, leaning over the wall and opening his mouth at the same time. "Jezz, me pipe is gone on me!" It splashed in the water, said the cotsman at the campfire, and the salmon fled downstream.

◆━◆

The returning cotsmen spoke of anything but of how many salmon they had taken, cleansing the *smaichtín*, or wooden priest, over the side before they stepped ashore, although when they poached they discarded the *smaichtín* in favour of a piece of lead. It was quieter.

On their second night on the Owenore, one of the poachers showed them the largest perch they had seen.

The canoes were out in force after dark, upriver and down, each pair adhering rigidly to its own drift, ten or a dozen pairs, the snap nets strung between them, an occasional call of "*Draw your hand*!" as a salmon swam into a net.

The men had spent an hour or so with the boys, immensely friendly, calling to the others not to *stob*, or steal their places, drinking tea from tin mugs at the campfire before setting off into the river, always one eye out for a bailiff if it was a weekend, the atmosphere a little fraught until they returned. When one of the canoes returned, the men came once again to the campfire, gratefully accepted a mug of tea, and summoned the boys to look in their canoe. A perch as big as a salmon lay in the bottom.

◆━◆

The poet found the camp easily enough, after a minor mishap when he drove down the wrong lane. Ivan and Padraic stood on the back seat looking over their parents' heads, hoping to see the site first, but they parked the car on the edge of the lane where the camp was still not in view, and walked the rest of the way down the dusty boreen until the river, then the camp, came in sight.

The tent lay in the middle of a clearing. Away from it, towards the river, was a stone circle with a blazing fire at its centre. A blackened tin kettle hung from a tripod. At the edge of the camp a clothes-line was strung between two alders, bending under the weight of the boys' laundry. They had been very busy since they had walked back from Mass, and the camp was immaculate, ready for inspection.

The poet and his wife drank tea that tasted of woodsmoke while the older boys unpacked the car and carried the boxes of food down to the camp. The poet lit a cigarette as he surveyed the camp and the river, then the heavily wooded bluff above them, and said to Garry: "You chose this well."

"We learned the hard way," Garry said, and told him of the night the tent had flooded. As the boys' mother helped prepare lunch and Ivan and Padraic ran hither and thither around the site, the poet listened to the details of the holiday, nodding at each juncture of the story.

They ate stew for lunch, with bottled beer and cider for the older members of the family, lemonade for the younger. Tinned pears followed as dessert. Then Garry and Conor took the youngest two out in the cot, giving each of them a hand line to troll with. They caught nothing but listened with excitement as Garry vowed that he would buy a cabin cruiser and take them on holiday soon after he qualified. "It'll have proper bunks," said Garry, eyes gleaming at the prospect of owning a Rippingille stove and a caribou sleeping bag, "and cabins, and an engine. What do you say to that, Poc?"

———◆◆———

The poet said to Garry before they left in the late afternoon: "Can you be home by Wednesday?"

"I'd say so," said Garry. "I'll ring the Custom House to confirm. I'd like to take the boat downriver. The boys are keen to try the fishing further down."

"I'll pick you up at Ballykeep," said the poet. "You can leave the gear in the boathouse there and we'll pick it up later. I'll need you all for the harvest."

———◆◆———

This would be the final part of their holiday before setting out for home. They rowed down to a lower reach. They saw no one; the river was almost inaccessible unless by boat. They passed muddy creeks overhung by willows whose branches trailed in the muddy water. The sunlight struggled to peer through the trees.

The dusk was an eerie mixture of light and shadow as they made their way back to camp. They rounded a bend and passed a skiff with a furtive-looking man rowing, a man with a face like a rat: greasy hat, thin face, short scraggly beard, several missing teeth. He lay on his oars as they passed and asked, in a rough Border voice: "Did yiz see a boat out tonight?"

"No," said Garry and Conor simultaneously.

"What are yiz at?" asked the man nastily, looking them over.

"We're just fishing." said Garry, uneasily.

"I hope yer not after the salmon," said the man. "Have

yiz got a net in that boat?"

"No," said Garry hotly. "We're not poachers, if that's what you mean. We're just after trout."

"Is that your camp above at the White House?" asked the man.

"It is," said Garry. "But who are you?"

Without replying, the man pulled hard on his oars and the skiff shot upstream. Within minutes he was around the next bend and out of sight.

"What did you make of that?" Garry asked the others.

"He's not a local, and he's after poachers," surmised Brian. "He's a water bailiff."

"God!" said Garry. "I wouldn't want to be him. Did you hear what we heard in the shop – that they caught a bailiff last week and held his head under water until he swore not to bother them again? Last year in the marshes at Owensbridge one of them shot a .22 over a bailiff's head. They forced him to lie with his face in the mud until they removed the net."

It was growing dark, and they had some distance to row. They set off, silent, rowing hard. They could see quite well as the moon had emerged from behind a cloud, the willows catching flashes of silver.

They slowed a little when they rounded the next bend. They were passing a creek when two canoes shot out from the overhanging willow that covered the entrance and swung alongside them.

The suddenness of it shocked them. One moment they were rowing peacefully. The next they were threatened by cots full of dark, menacing figures.

"What are yiz at?" demanded a figure in the bows of the canoe.

"We're just fishing for trout," said Garry, as calmly as he could. "We're camped below Inisteach."

"Did y'see anyone on the river tonight?" demanded the voice.

"No," said Garry, heart thumping at the lie. "We've only been up above for a couple of hours."

There was a silence, then the dark figures began to mutter among themselves. Occasionally a shaft of moonlight lit a rough face. Otherwise the figures were in darkness or shadow.

Then the voice spoke again, this time in a kinder tone. "I hope we didn't give ye a fright. We was lookin' to meet a fellah. That's all. Goodnight, anyway."

"OK," said Garry, very relieved. "Let's go, boys."

They did not need to be urged. The herring cot gathered way as the oarsmen tugged hard, catching crabs in their haste. They rounded the next bend within a few moments.

"God! Garry!" said Kerry, quavering a little. "You took a chance, saying we hadn't seen that bailiff!"

"I know," said Garry. "But they might have drowned him if they'd caught him! I didn't want that on my conscience."

They reached the camp, moored the cot and restocked the fire which had dwindled to embers. Garry brewed a pot of coffee. They were drinking it from their tin mugs when they heard shouting from upstream. As it came closer, they could hear a shrill voice shouting: "Help!" followed by angry yells from further up.

"What the hell's going on?" Niall demanded of no one in particular.

Brian looked at Garry and said: "I think they've found the bailiff." Garry nodded grimly. "I think so too."

They went to the riverbank and waited. The yelling grew louder. This stretch was well lit by the moon, more open, and they could see clearly.

The bailiff came in sight first. He was rowing madly,

glancing frequently over his shoulder, shouting in panic as he pulled his skiff downriver. He shot past the White House camp in the moonlight and disappeared into the darkness around a bend.

Then came the poachers in their canoes, four cots, the crews thrusting purposefully with their paddles. Their heads were down, arms working in a steady rhythm, paddles throwing spray that seemed yellowy-white. They were silent, with deadly intent, except for a strange cry from someone in the second canoe, a sound that chilled those in the camp, as it sounded like a great cry of vengeance, an echo of the Ireland of earlier times. Then the poachers, too, disappeared around the bend.

They heard a shout or two again from the bailiff, then the strange, baying call once more, but the sounds grew fainter as they listened. The moon had ducked behind a cloud and the night was suddenly black, apart from the wavering glow from the fire. It grew very chilly, yet they stood there still, heads to one side. They heard only the chuckle and slap of the river, and the night breeze in the sallies.

They gathered by the fire, throwing more wood on it to make the blaze as cheerful as possible, wondering whether they had seen humans or spirits. They slept poorly, waking frequently, with the sounds of the yells of panic and the vengeful call that promised retribution and death still fresh in their ears.

◆━

They rowed back to the village the next day, as soon as the tide favoured, to buy bread, milk, and eggs. When Garry emerged from a chat with the friendly woman at the shop he told them all he had heard about the events of the previous night. It had not been a simple case of a bailiff chasing poachers, he said. The bailiff was deeply unpopular in the village; not because he was a Cavan man who chased poachers, but because he had abandoned a local girl who was carrying his child and who had fled in shame to England. The girl came from a family of poachers.

They were out on the ebb, with Brendan looming over them once more, passing the Big Net and the narrows between Gowlaun Island and the bank before Garry finished the story. The rumour in the town, he told them, was that the bailiff had set up an elaborate ambush in co-operation with the Guards, and that the Guards had later decided that common justice would be better served if they stayed in barracks that night. The bailiff, according to the rumours, was probably in Uisceford by then, taking ship for a distant place.

◆◆

They struck camp for the last time soon afterwards. A friendly sandcot gave them a tow down to Rosspoint, and they relaxed and joked as the *thud-thud* of the diesel drew them south. They met the Bree flowing in from the left, then the three steeples and the quays of Rosspoint appeared and the sandcot cast them off, the crew giving the boys a wave as they did so. Brian and Conor took the oars and rowed them down into the estuary. They moored and ate their sandwiches, then Niall and Kerry took over. Several hours and a change of oarsmen later, they passed under the Bree bridge; then the Saor joined them and they could smell the sea and see the promontory of Crook reach out into the ocean. The Norman bailey at Ballykeep seemed to nod a welcome as they brought the herring cot on the final part of its voyage to its berth against the harbour wall, where a familiar round figure sat, smoking, with a beaming smile.

———◆◆———

They arrived at Prospect in the early evening. The dogs ran to the car, Sport barking madly. When the fuss subsided, Niall went to see his pigs, and the two great animals trundled up the farmyard behind him, nuzzling him as he called for his cat. A yellow animal shot from the open window of the barn and landed on Niall's shoulders, scrabbling at his collar to keep its balance. Conor was already at the gate to the Well Field, the cows trotting towards him.

Pat Fitz had finished painting the sun room that morning. The greenhouse smelled of ripening tomatoes, and the vine, to Niall's surprise, was flourishing.

The boys' mother told them that her jackdaw rarely appeared, that he had finally been accepted by the cackling brood in the Prospect chimneys. She said he called to her from time to time, and a week before he had landed on her shoulders as she strolled up to the Hen-Run, had chuckled something in her ear, and flown away.

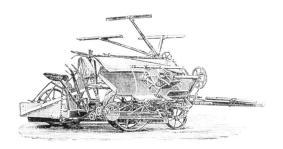

Chapter Thirty-Seven

Benny was cutting the wheat with his reaper-and-binder, and the boys gathered the sheaves. The weather had continued kind. When the sheaves had been stooked, then stacked, the harvest would be taken to the Old Fort, beyond the byre of Prospect, to be ricked, then threshed in late autumn long after the boys had returned to school or university.

◆ ◆

Local custom would bring their neighbours to help when threshing time came. When the tractor would pull the great machine through the widened piers, Nicky Fortune, Pat Broaders and Matt Lacy would follow, wheeling their bikes up the drive. When the work was finished the men would be fed and bottles of frothing Guinness handed to them by the excited boys; Benny in his element as the Prospect foreman, declaiming loudly on this and that, John and Pat Fitz grinning as he enjoyed his finest hour.

◆ ◆

A few days after the wheat was stooked, the poet opened his post. When he reached the third letter down he read it and smiled. "Look at that, Don," he said to his wife, "it's from Traynors." She wiped her hands on her apron before taking the letter from the Eskerford grain merchants who gave their best guess for the value of the Prospect harvest. "That's very good, Pack," she said quietly. "It is," he said. "That's Garry's fees covered for his final year."

◆ ◆

The evenings were growing noticeably shorter. The swifts had flown from Prospect; the swallows would soon follow. Noisy games of table tennis prevented the family from thinking too much of what lay ahead when the summer holidays would end. The boys would refuse to accept it until the night before, and Conor and Niall had already decided to visit the Edenbeg on most days. Upstairs, Garry wound the gramophone, sat in his armchair and re-read Slocum while Sibelius' *Swan of Tuonela* played in the background. Brian sought the privacy of the ottoman in the drawing room and was deep in a book. The boys' mother ironed an unending succession of shirts in the kitchen.

The poet stood on the thin strip of lawn under the palm tree, smoking a cigarette and looking at the horizon. He welcomed the slight chill in the air as the forerunner of autumn. He loved the changing seasons, particularly when autumn changed to winter. That was his season. He had been born in January, and believed that everyone's favourite time of year was the month of their birth. The winter landscape was his favourite, when the trees were skeletal, the ground was like stone, and Orion hung high in the cold night sky.

The Fascar lighthouse swept sea and coast. He watched the beam rotate across the faithful evergreen sentinels in the Grove, then walked across the gravel, through the open front door, and to his desk.

THE END

Epilogue

The family remained at Prospect for a further eight or nine years. As the boys moved to jobs or university in Dublin, the poet and his wife grew lonely for them and moved to the city.

The first book of Padraic Fallon's poems was published by Dolmen Press in 1974, a month before his death. He and his wife Don spent part of each year in Cornwall between 1967 and 1972, close to Conor, who had moved there after he married the artist Nancy Wynne-Jones in 1966. When Conor and Nancy moved to Kinsale, Co. Cork, in 1972, the poet and his wife moved with them to live nearby. He died while visiting Ivan in Kent. More of his works were published subsequently, and a monument stands to him in his home town of Athenry. Don lived until 1985, devoting much of her time to her twenty-two grandchildren. They rest in the churchyard above the sea in Kinsale. A room in the local hospital is dedicated to her.

Garry became a successful vet, then a marine artist. He stayed in the county, and bought a farm overlooking the sea and the islands of the south coast. He owned a succession of boats and yachts, and was planning to buy the next when he died while on holiday with Ivan in South Africa in January 1996.

Brian became Literary Editor of *The Irish Times*, then the paper's Art Critic until he retired. He was a board member of the Irish Museum of Modern Art. He lectures on Irish art and has written a series of books on painting and painters. His biggest work to date is *The Age of Innocence*, a history of Irish culture from 1930 to 1960. He was awarded the Royal Hibernian Academy Gold Medal in 2002.

Conor was first painter, then sculptor, creating works in steel and bronze that form part of many public and private collections of Irish art. He became honorary secretary of the Royal Hibernian Academy, a member of Aosdána, and is a board member of the National Gallery of Ireland.

Niall became a journalist, then a business executive on *The Irish Times* before leaving to write full-time. He was a dedicated trout fisherman, and wrote *Fly-fishing for Irish Trout*, regarded as a classic work of its kind, as well as *The Armada in Ireland*. He also collected and edited *The Irish Game Anglers Anthology*. He died within a fortnight of Garry.

Ivan is chief executive of the UK arm of an Irish-based newspaper group, and a director of its parent company. He wrote a series of successful books on business figures while a financial journalist and City Editor, before he moved to run a newspaper group in South Africa where he lived during the transition to majority rule.

Padraic is chairman of an international financial publishing company in London, and a board member of an Irish bank and of a UK newspaper group.

The artist Tony O'Malley lived until 2003, returning from St Ives to live in Co. Kilkenny to become one of the most successful Irish painters. He lived long enough to read the first draft of this book.

The family kept in touch for some years with friends and neighbours in the town and county, but gradually lost contact.

Prospect stands, as does the Grove, but the local landscape changed utterly as the town expanded. Prospect's fields are covered with houses.

The family geography

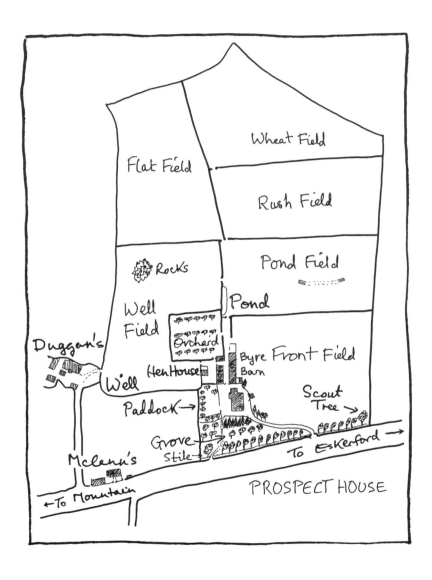

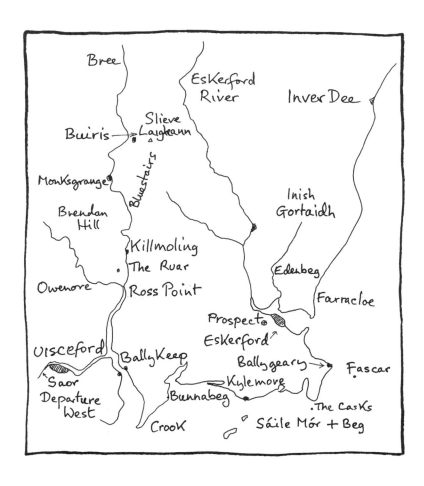

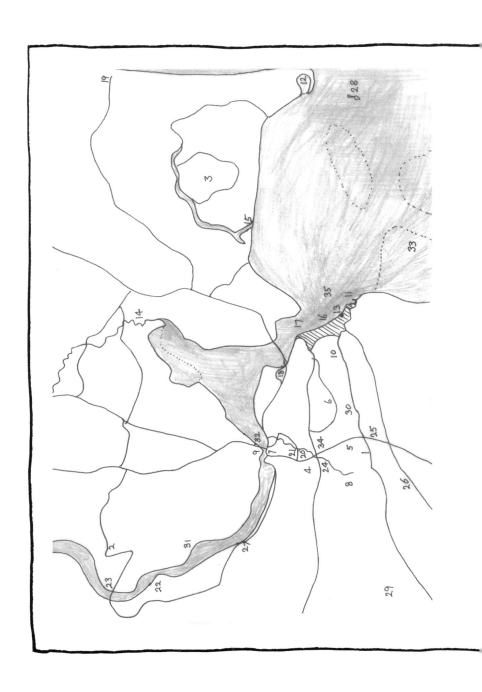

KEY

1 Ball Alley
2 Ballydicken
3 Beag Érin
4 Belmont
5 The Birdless Woods
6 Boycotts
7 The Bridge Inn
8 Carrick River
9 Carrig
10 The College
11 Cot Safe
12 The Crow
13 Customs House
14 Edenbeg, The
15 Engine House
16 Eskerford
17 Eskerford River

18 Farcur
19 Farracloe
20 Graveyard
21 Haunted House
22 The Hedge
23 Killinin Bridge
24 Malone's Forge
25 Mahony's Hill
26 The New Road
27 Niall's Bass Place
28 The Old Battery
29 The Pinnacle
30 Prospect House
31 Quarry
32 Roche's Castle
33 The Slimes
34 Tortoise Rock
35 The White Boy